The Life to Come

ALSO BY MICHELLE DE KRETSER

The Rose Grower

The Hamilton Case

The Lost Dog

Questions of Travel

Springtime

The Life to Come

Michelle
de Kretser

Catapult New York

This is a work of fiction. All of the characters, organizations, and events portrayed in this novel are either products of the author's imagination or used fictitiously.

First published in Australia in 2017 by Allen & Unwin
First published in the United States in 2018 by Catapult (catapult.co)

ISBN: 978-1-936787-82-1

Catapult titles are distributed to the trade by Publishers Group West
Phone: 866-400-5351

Library of Congress Control Number: 2017950927

Printed in the United States of America

10 9 8 7 6 5 4 3 2 1

For Chris

and in memory of faithful Oliver

CLOV

Do you believe in the life to come?

HAMM

Mine was always that.

SAMUEL BECKETT, *Endgame*

I

THE FICTIVE SELF

THE HOUSE BY THE RIVER belonged to an old man whose relationship to George Meshaw was complicated but easily covered by "cousin." He had lived there alone, with a painting that was probably a Bonnard. Now he was in a nursing home, following a stroke, and George's mother had taken charge of the painting. It was her idea that George should live in the house until it was clear whether or not their cousin was coming home. She had flown up to Sydney for the day, and George met her for a late lunch. George's mother wore a dark Melbourne dress and asked the waiter for "really cold water," between remarking on the humidity and the jacarandas—you would never guess that she had lived in Sydney for the first thirty-one years of her life. She bent her head over her handbag, and George found himself looking at a scene from childhood. His mother was on the phone, with the orange wall in the living room behind her. As he watched her, she bent forward from the waist, still holding the receiver. Her hair stood out around her head: George saw a dark-centered golden flower. He couldn't have been more than six but he understood that his mother was trying to block out the noise around her—he folded like that, too, protecting a book or a toy when "Dinner!" was called—and that this was difficult because the room was full of the loud jazz his father liked to play.

Over the years, George's mother's hair had been various colors and lengths, and now it was a soft yellow sunburst again, still with that central dark star. She produced a supermarket receipt from her bag and read from the back of it: "Hair Apparent. Do or Dye."

"The Head Gardener," replied George. "Moody Hair."

They were in the habit of noting down the names of hairdressing salons for each other. His mother said, "Also, I saw this in an airport shop: 'Stainless steel is immune to rust, discoloration, and corrosion. This makes it ideal for men's jewelry.'"

George and his mother had the same high laugh—*hee hee hee*—and otherwise didn't resemble each other at all. The Bonnard was beside her, done up in cardboard and propped on a chair. When George asked what it was like, his mother said, "A naked woman and wallpaper. He needed an excuse to paint light."

The house by the river was spacious and built of bricks covered in white render. It was late spring when George moved in, but the rooms on the ground floor were cold and dark. There were mortuary-white tiles on the floor, and the lights were fluorescent tubes that looked as if they would be fatal to insects. They had to be switched on even in the middle of the day. George remembered that his mother had described the house as "Mediterranean." Ridiculous secondhand visions—a turreted pink villa with terraced gardens, a bowl of red fish at a window—had opened at once in his mind.

He had been back in Sydney for four years and still swam gratefully in its impersonal ease. In Melbourne, where George had lived since he was six, he had wanted to write about modernism in Australian fiction for his Ph.D. After some difficulty, a professor who would admit to having once read an Australian novel was found. At their first meeting, she handed George a reading list made up of French and German philosophers. When George settled down to read these texts, he discovered something astonishing: the meaning of each word was clear and the meaning of sentences baffled. Insignificant yet crucial words such as "however" and "which"—words whose meaning was surely beyond dispute—had been deployed in ways that made no sense. It was as unnerving as if George had seen a sunset in his east-facing window, and for a while it was as mesmeric as any disturbance to the order of things. When despair threatened, he transferred his scholarship to a university in Sydney. There, George read novels and books about novels and was wildly happy. He taught a couple of tutorials to supplement his scholarship. Recently, with his thesis more or less out of the way, he had begun to write a novel at night.

A loggia with archways ran along the upper floor on the river side of the house. That was where George ate his meals and sometimes came to sit very early, as the park detached itself from the night. Koels called, and currawongs—the birds who had whistled over his childhood. Fifteen minutes by train from the center of the city, he lived among trees, birdsong, Greeks. The Greeks, arriving forty years earlier, had seen paradise: cheap real estate, sunlight for their stunted children. Fresh from civil war and starvation, they were too ignorant to grasp what every Australian knew: this was the wrong side of Sydney. Where was the beach?

There were mornings when George left the house at sunrise, crossed the river, and turned in to a road that ran beside the quarried-out side of a hill. The sandstone was sheer and largely obscured by greenery: giant gum trees fanned against the rock, and native figs, vines, scrub. Brick bungalows cowered at the base of the cliff and skulked on the ridge above—it seemed an affront for which they would all be punished. In the moist, gray summer dawns, George felt that he was walking into a book he had read long ago. The grainy light was a presage. Something was coming—rain, for certain, and a catastrophe.

Opposite the quarry, on the river side of the street, driveways ran down to secretive yards. They belonged to houses that faced the river, with lawns sloping to the water. A sign warned that the path here was known to flood. But bulky sandstone foundations and verandas strewn with wicker furniture soothed—these houses were merely domestic, nothing like the foreboding on which they turned their backs.

After Pippa moved in, George often came home from his walk to the smell of coffee. They would drink it and eat Vegemite toast on the loggia, and then George would go to bed. Pippa, too, kept irregular hours. Saving to go overseas, she was juggling waitressing with part-time work in a sports store, and George could never be sure of finding her at home. That was fine; the idea was that they would live independently—at least so it had been settled in George's mind. In her second year at university, Pippa had been in his tutorial "The Fictive Self": a Pass student whose effortful work George had pitied enough to bump up to a Credit at the last moment. Not long ago, he had run into her near the Reserve Desk at the library. Her hair lay in flat, uneven pieces as if something had been chewing it. As the year drew to a close, a lot of students looked like that: stripey and savage. She had only one essay left to write, "in my whole life, ever," said Pippa. A peculiar thing happened: she held out a piece of paper, and George feared he would see a note that began, *Help! I am being held prisoner . . .*

It was an invitation to a party. Pippa shared a house in Coogee with a tall, ravishing girl called Katrina. When George arrived, Katrina was standing by the drinks table on the side veranda, talking about her cervix. He placed his six-pack in a plastic tub of ice, and Pippa told him a few people's names. George had left

Marrickville on a warm day, but by the time he crossed the city, a southerly had got up. Every door and window in Pippa's house stood open. The dim corridor and all the rooms were full of cold air. In his T-shirt and loose cotton trousers, George moved from one group of people he didn't know to another, trying to get out of the draft. The girls didn't seem to notice it. They were Sydney girls, with short skirts and long, bare arms. Recently, George had gone to an opening at a gallery in the company of a visiting lecturer from Berlin. The artist was fashionable, and the gallery's three rooms were packed. Over dinner, the German woman expressed mild astonishment at the number of sex workers who had attended the opening. "Is this typical in Australia?" she asked. George had to explain that she had misunderstood the significance of shouty makeup, tiny, shiny dresses, and jewels so large they looked fake. Eastern suburbs caste marks, they identified the arty, bookish daughters of property developers and CEOs. George was still adjusting to them himself, after Melbourne, where the brainy girls wore stiff, dark clothes like the inmates of nineteenth-century institutions, with here and there an exhibitionist in gray. Pippa had stick limbs, that chewed fringe, a sharp little face. She would have made an excellent orphan: black sacking was all that was needed, and heavy, laced shoes. But she came out of the house in scarlet stilettos and leopard-print satin, and found George on the back patio. He had taken refuge there, in the lee of the kitchen door.

Ashamed to mention cold to this waif, George conjured a headache. Pippa offered Tiger Balm and the use of her room. The windows there were open: Katrina could be heard describing a minor surgical procedure on her ovaries. But when George shut the door and lay down, he was out of the wind at last. A long painting, purple and blue swirls, hung on the wall facing Pippa's bed—George closed his eyes at once. Long ago, his mother had been a painter. A few survivors from that era—severe, geometric abstractions—could be seen in her flat in Melbourne, but for a long time now her involvement with art had been confined to the upmarket school where she taught.

George fell asleep. When he woke, Pippa was there on the end of the bed, unbuckling her sandals. She flexed her toes, then sat sideways and swung her feet up. They were small, chunky feet, George noticed, and her toenails were painted blue. Katrina passed down the corridor, saying something about her menstrual cycle. George wondered what she was majoring in. Gender Studies? Performance Art? Obstetrics?

"Communications," said Pippa. She was drinking bubbly; it was the late 1990s, so people still called it champagne. The soft white plastic cup dimpled under her fingers, and Pippa remarked that she was stuck. The house would shortly be reclaimed by Katrina's aunt, who was returning from Singapore. Another house had been found for the girls—Katrina's family had several at their disposal—but it wasn't available before the beginning of March. Katrina was moving home for the summer, but there were reasons why that wasn't an option for Pippa. George told a lie about the purple painting and learned that it was the work of Pippa's boyfriend, Vince. "He's back at his folks' place in Mudgee, to save money so we can go traveling next year." She spoke of "Asia," of "Europe," collapsing civilizations in the sweeping Australian way.

In Marrickville, over Vegemite toast one morning, Pippa asked whether the barking wasn't getting to George. He hadn't noticed it but now heard the high, repetitive protest that went on and on. "He's lonely, poor love," said Pippa. "And bored. Stuck in a yard by himself with nothing to do for hours."

"Greeks," said George. "They don't like animals indoors. It's a Mediterranean thing. The Arab influence."

Pippa said that in Mudgee they were exactly the same. "And no one in Vince's family's ever been outside New South Wales. No way do they know any Arabs, either."

A few days later, she told George that the dog's name was Bruce. He belonged to "a hippie dipstick" called Rhiannon, who was renting on the cheaper, landward side of the street. Pippa had grown up in a country town and still talked easily to strangers. Bruce was a kelpie cross, George learned. "Twelve months old. Rhiannon got him from the RSPCA. She drives him to an off-leash park when she's got time, but she works in some mall up in Chatswood, so she's got this huge commute. And then Tuesday night's the ashram, Friday night's the pub. She's not a bad person, she just hasn't got a clue. You should see her yard: she's bought Bruce all these toys, like a dog's a child."

Pippa had offered to walk Bruce when Rhiannon was busy. "He's a working dog, he needs exercise. Guess what she said? 'Dogs should run free. It's demeaning for an animal to walk on a leash. It does really confusing things to their auras.'"

It was good of Pippa to have tried to help, said George.

"I just feel so sorry for that poor dog."

She said the same thing a few evenings later. Bruce was barking again. George heard him all the time now. It was difficult not to hold Pippa responsible. "I love animals," she went on.

"That must be why you eat so many of them," said George. He didn't intend unkindness but was opposed to illogic. Pippa's fondness for broad, blurry statements twitched his nerves. "I love India," she once announced, after watching a documentary on TV. She had never been there. George, who had, most certainly did not love India. He could also see that these declarations weren't really about animals or India but about Pippa: what they proclaimed was her largeness of heart.

She was saying that she had considered being a vegetarian. "But the thing with personal food restrictions is they make eating with other people really difficult. They destroy conviviality." She brought out "conviviality" in the way people had once said "England" or "Communist": as if it settled all discussion. George detected a borrowing: Pippa had come across the word somewhere and been impressed.

George looked on cooking as time stolen from books. When he invited Pippa to move in for the summer he hadn't thought about arrangements for food. He would have been content to go on as usual, defrosting a pizza or grilling a chop. But the day after she moved in, Pippa said, "I'm going through a Thai phase. You can't cook Thai food for one." The cold, white, murderous kitchen filled with the scent of coriander and lemongrass pounded to a paste. George kept the fridge stocked with riesling and beer. Pippa stir-fried fish with spring onions and purple basil. She served a salad that combined ginger and pork.

With nothing said, they had divided the house between them. There were three empty bedrooms on the upper floor, but Pippa installed herself in a room off the hall. She liked to lie reading on a divan that stood under an aluminum-framed window. There was nothing else in what must have been the old man's living room; he had dotted cumbersome furniture throughout the house. Any one of his rooms would have done as the set of a European play—the forbidding, minimalist kind.

Paperback novels accumulated around the divan. George looked them over one day when Pippa was out. Most were secondhand, and all had been published in the past twenty years. Pippa read nothing older, nothing in translation, and very little that didn't concern women's lives. Her knowledge of history was cloudy. Referring to a biography of Joan of Arc that she planned to read, she placed its heroine in the Napoleonic Wars. George's own novel sang inside him. He was taking apart everything he knew and putting it back together differently in ruled A4 notebooks. He used a laptop for his thesis, but his novel had woken an instinct that mingled superstition and veneration, and he was writing the first draft by hand.

Summer intensified. George and Pippa ate mangoes for dessert. Their flesh was the same color as the wall behind George's mother on that long-ago day with the phone. The memory of that scene kept following George around. It said so much about his parents: for a start, the invasive way his father played records full blast so that he could hear them no matter where he was in the house. And why hadn't his mother turned down the volume before answering the phone? Think first! George wanted to shout. She often remarked that women of her generation had been deceived. He knew that this meant "I was deceived." It was her way of alluding to his father's girlfriends. She had left when she could no longer ignore them; the latest one had turned up on Christmas morning with a present for George. But the reason George and his mother ended up in Melbourne was a man she had met at a party. He lasted two years, just long enough for her divorce to come through, then scampered home to his wife.

Pippa produced a dish of bananas prepared with turmeric and cream. That was the evening two boys came to the door in search of the old man. They looked like teenage real estate agents, with ties and short, waxed hair, but suggested melodrama because they arrived during a storm. Lightning turned the sky biblical behind them. For a blazing, vertiginous instant, the iron veranda post was a cross. The boys shouted at each other in Vietnamese, over the downpour, and everyone shouted in English. At last, George wrote down the address of the nursing home, and the boys plunged back into the rain.

It rained for three days. George went on with his novel at night. The river rose, ran across the road, and stopped the cars. Long after the sun came back, and the traffic resumed, the path beside the river stayed treacherous with mud. George slept naked in the swampy afternoons; there was air-conditioning in the rooms upstairs. Pippa wore shorts and a lime-green bikini top; she was pretty much flat-chested. She rubbed ice cubes on her wrists and went barefoot on the tiles. George noticed her feet again. They were nuggety and rectangular, like a young child's feet—even the sparkly turquoise nail polish belonged to a child. He wondered if Pippa bothered with right and left shoes.

George's father taught computer science at a technical college on the North Shore. Two or three times a year, he met up with his son over a drink in the city; what followed was a conversation between strangers. George had left his new number on his father's answering machine, but it was his mother who called. She was in Lausanne, where an expert had declared that the Bonnard was a fake. "A good fake, mind you," said George's mother. He could hear her breathing in Switzerland. "I guess I'll be hanging on to the day job for a while."

The phone often rang. George took down messages from Pippa's friends. The friends dropped in. They stayed for meals. George and Pippa moved a table out to the strip of concrete that passed for a yard. They strung fairy lights over the back door, and set the table with blue-and-white plates; Pippa had found a cupboard full of old china. "I love pretty plates," she said, giving them a wipe with a tea towel. She asked if George was sure he wouldn't change his mind about dinner. George said again that he really needed to work.

One night, he stretched his arms, cracked his spine, left his desk. Standing on the loggia, he identified Katrina: her voice floated up, describing the mole between her breasts. He had retained a distinct mental image of her breasts, George discovered. As a change from Thai, Pippa was serving prawns with lemon juice, brown bread and butter. George had seen her tip the prawn heads into the bin—they would stink like anything for the rest of the week.

He was returning from his walk one morning when *eggs for breakfast* passed from an idea into a need. He went up to the shop on Illawarra Road. The eggs had just hit the pan when Pippa came into the kitchen; there were tiny grains of sleep in the corners of her eyes. George watched her arrange the remaining eggs in a green majolica dish. She picked up the empty carton. "These are cage," she said. "You should get free-range."

George replied that free-range chickens, too, were killed.

"But there's no unnecessary suffering."

George picked up a metal spatula. He almost said, Ah! So that's OK, then. He said nothing: he had remembered, just in time, that he was talking to someone whose idea of ethics was a dinner party. Besides, his eggs had started to brown.

In February, a heat wave struck. The air-conditioning gave out. At night, after Pippa came home from the dinner shift, George would light mosquito coils and a lantern. They sat on the loggia drinking mojitos; Katrina and her boyfriend had left a present of a bottle of rum. George asked one or two questions about Katrina.

There was room for a character like her—a minor figure—in his novel.

Pippa said, "That's a relationship where the names say it all." George looked at her. Her eyes were bright with dislike. "The Kat and the Matt," said Pippa. There was mint and sugar on her breath.

On one of the mojito nights, the inevitable happened: Pippa grew confessional. She wanted to be a writer, she told George. When she got back from overseas, she intended to enroll in a creative writing course. George thought back to her essays: a stew of passionate opinion, mangled argument, atrocities of usage and grammar; that Credit had been the purest largesse on his part. He remembered her hanging back one day, as the other students were dispersing, to say, "I love English."

"In that case, I suggest you learn to write it," answered George.

Pippa was talking about her travels now: they were to provide her with raw material, experiences. George, whose novel was set in Heidelberg, where he had spent a day at the age of nineteen, said that literature and the world were two different things. Pippa grappled with this, slitting her eyes. She said, "You mean, look in thy heart and write?" George meant nothing of the kind: girls like Pippa understood "heart" as a license to gush. But coming from her, the quotation so astonished him that he merely grunted. He divided what was left of the cocktail between them, and ran his finger around the rim of the jug.

They were eating strawberries; Pippa had brought a big, soft bag of them home from work. Passing along the loggia the next morning, George saw a cut-glass bowl of miniature Father Christmases. Overnight, each berry had grown a moldy white beard.

Day and night, bushfires burned in the mountains. Sitting out on the loggia, George and Pippa could smell the smoke. But there was no longer the high, intolerable sound of barking: Pippa had persuaded Rhiannon to give her a key. Bruce tore up and down the yard, chasing the ball Pippa threw for him; he slept, content and exhausted, for hours. Sometimes she sneaked the dog out and took him for a walk along the river. She invited George to go with them, but he explained that he was allergic to pets. He was conscious of a fresh danger: Rhiannon's landlord wanted his house back, and she was having difficulty finding a rental place that would let her keep a dog. It looked as if she might have to return Bruce to the pound. The way Pippa relayed all this, George got the distinct impression that she was putting out feelers. So when she said, "I thought it was cats people were allergic to?" he answered firmly, "Dogs, too." There was no point raising anyone's hopes.

Autumn came, and George's father died. A classic end, a cliché, really: lobbing a ball into a net one minute, a massive coronary the next. He was between girlfriends, as it turned out, so it fell to George to pack up his flat.

The flat was only a couple of streets away from the Meshaws' old house. George hadn't been in that part of Paddington for twenty-three years. The last time he saw his father, they had eaten big, juicy kangaroo steaks—George remembered the blood slobbering out across their plates. Running lightly up the stairs, he dreaded entering the flat. But it was as impersonal as a showroom. His father had never been a hoarder; even the piano seat held only a cardboard wallet filled with dull documents. One of them was a birth certificate. George knew and always forgot that Meshaw wasn't his father's real name. Syllables had been trimmed, vowels altered, consonants suppressed to create something that could fit into Australian mouths. His father was a product of the old world, and his vices, like his virtues, had been old-fashioned: wine, women, music, an unshakable faith in the rational mind.

The last item in the wallet was a yellow envelope. George hesitated, afraid of embarrassment, of pornography—there had been a packet of condoms beside the bed—but at last he looked inside. The envelope held twenty or so Polaroids. They were photographs of George's mother, angled, arty shots, many of them out of focus—one showed only a blurry fan of fingers. George crouched, moved his hand, spread the images over the floor. The instant before he examined the last one, he already knew what he would see: his mother, bending forward from the waist, a wavy cord trailing to the phone. Everything in the photo was exactly as George had remembered—the orange wall, his mother's bright, dark-centered hair—although the image had taken on a brownish yellow tinge. What memory had blanked from the scene was his father's presence: he must have been there, in that room full of jazz, aiming the camera at his wife. The pieces in the puzzle of George's parents shifted, acquired new angles. All the Polaroids showed that yellow discoloration; the chemicals were breaking down from exposure to light. George pictured his father handling the photos, laying them out like data along the lid of the piano. He studied the images again: unstable proofs of tenderness, the only photos in the flat.

That evening, he called his mother. She hadn't come up for the funeral, merely saying, "I'm sorry for your loss." George told her about finding the Polaroids. What he was really saying was, Do you understand now? Admit you were wrong to leave him! He started to describe the photo with the phone and the orange wall.

His mother cut him short, saying that she remembered the picture. "The one where you can see my roots have grown out? It's so typical of your father to have kept that. I never liked it—I didn't like you poking that camera at me ever."

"Wait," said George. "*I* took that picture?"

"All of them. Don't you remember?" She said, "An idiot girl gave you a Polaroid camera. It became your favorite thing. You loved watching the colors change as the image developed. When you ran out of film a second time, your father told you the camera was broken. He knew that seeing you with it upset me."

With the change of season, it was cool at night. George stood on the loggia, inspecting the loose shapes of trees. There was only ugly furniture around him and big, tiled, silent rooms. Pippa was living in Stanmore, in a house with Katrina. Bruce was barking—he had been barking for hours; Rhiannon must have talked her way into staying on, after all. George had just finished the first draft of his novel. It was called *Necessary Suffering.* At least for now; that was one of the things George wanted to think about. But first he had to put together the puzzle of his parents. Sometimes the reason his father saved the Polaroids was George's mother and sometimes it was George—sometimes even the idiot girl was involved. George's brain wouldn't stop showing him the photo with the telephone. He saw his mother folded in two with her back to the wall. Something like a smudge kept dancing on the edge of his mind. To study it calmly, George turned it into a sentence written out in black on the white frame of the Polaroid: "Maybe she was trying to get away from me."

The sun rose over the misty park: an autumn sun, a flat red disk that had strayed from a Japanese print. Later that day, George closed the door of his father's flat for the last time and went for a walk. It was a bright afternoon, but the street where the Meshaws had lived was black with shadows. Tall plane trees arched over it; the leaves remained thick overhead but were starting to change color and fall. George saw what he had known, what he had forgotten: the row of houses, with their wooden balconies, looked into the face of a sandstone escarpment. He came to a gate where he had stood on a summer morning: looking back at the house where he had always lived, looking out at the waiting taxi. The escarpment and the trees kept the sun from the street. What was coming was a life in which his father was a stranger. George looked from his father, barefoot on the veranda, to his mother, sitting in the taxi with her face turned away. Who was the cat and who was the mat? George's father said, "If you stop crying, you can keep anything that falls out of my pockets." Then he stood on his hands.

II

THE ASHFIELD TAMIL

CASSIE SPOTTED THE SPICE MART because she was on the lookout for a South Asian grocery. At the launch of their university's Centre for Australian Literature, Ash had expressed his disappointment with a Sri Lankan restaurant where he had recently dined. The dhal had proved particularly unsatisfying, said Ash. It was thin and sour, nothing like the comforting curried lentils, velvety with coconut milk, that he had eaten as a child.

Ash—as Ashoka preferred to be known—mentioned the dhal because he had noticed that women were moved by references to that aspect of his past. When they learned that he had lived in Sri Lanka as a child, they pictured him in a tropical garden where fruit fell to the hand, too innocent to divine the vicious historical turn that would soon cast him on the grudging benevolence of the West. This satisfying nonsense simplified everything, clearing factual clutter to reveal the way forward. Now whatever needed to happen next could happen.

It had been explained to Ash that the government funded the Centre for Australian Literature after a ministerial survey of humanities graduates found that 86 percent of English majors had never read an Australian book. Asked to name a contemporary Australian novelist, responses were more or less equally divided between "that *Oscar and Louise* guy" and Stephen King. Most declined to "Name a novel by Patrick White," although one student recalled *Riders on the Storm*. These results were welcome: they could be blamed on the ousted Labor government.

Predictably, the national broadcaster—a viper's nest of socialists, tree huggers, and ugly, barren females—had seized on the survey, exhuming one of its bleeding-heart ideologues to moan about funding cuts to education. The flagrant bias of the national broadcaster was a gift to the government's spin doctors, but the survey struck an unexpected chord with the right-wing press. "Aussie Heritage Lost to Multiculturalism" (broadsheet) was backed up by "Our Classroom Shame" (tabloid). At this warning shot from its chief ally, the government acted decisively, and the Centre for Australian Literature opened after just five years.

At the launch, Cassie watched the men whose speeches followed one another. She was in the first year of her doctoral candidature. Leanne, her supervisor, was the inaugural director of the Centre, but Cassie saw that Leanne was of no account. The Aboriginal elder whose customary welcome had opened the ceremony was equally beside the point. These two were required by protocol but only got in the way, like a debutante's white gloves. The men on the podium had smooth or corrugated faces, they tolerated the symbolism of women and Aboriginal people, and they were in charge. Their various speeches came down to one: "Do not imagine we wouldn't crush you if we chose." Cassie had been brought up to believe that the world these men inhabited—the rage and spite and cruelty that were its grim, medieval furnishings—had been swept away. Now and then, the realization that it had not swam blackly before her like a frightening malfunction of vision.

While she listened, Cassie went on eating, having edged her way to the buffet as soon as the speeches began. She was a bony girl who was always hungry. As a child, she had craved white bread, and thin slices of dried sausage spread with mustard, and dark plum jam in which you could stand a spoon. All these things, which Cassie was fed by her grandmother, were banned at home. At home there was nourishing sugarless cake, and soybean casseroles in which tomato skins floated. From the mud-brick house in a valley up north, where two kelpies had succumbed to snakebite, Cassie fled during the holidays to Sydney and her grandmother's flat: to plate-glass windows and Schubert, to creamy veal and embroidered tablecloths, to a toilet with no spiders and no scary notice about blockages taped to the wall. Oh, the wonderful, modern pleasure of a toilet that flushed!

The minister for education said, "I like to begin every day, the pressures of public office permitting, by dipping into one of our world-class Australian writers." He misquoted a line of Henry Lawson and beamed. The mistake was spotted only by the Lawson specialist, an alcoholic, who by that stage of the evening was incapable of speech. Education being a trivial portfolio, the minister, a golden boy, had also been entrusted with immigration. "Young people are the wealth of our nation," he announced. He had forgotten, momentarily, that he was in an institution that catered to lazy, feral degenerates, for his own children had come into his mind: a trio of cherubs.

All the bottles within sight were empty. The Lawson specialist began to drain the contents of abandoned glasses, believing he was the only person present who remembered that the minister had once left children seeking asylum to drown off the Australian coast. As often happened, the Lawson specialist was quite wrong. The minister himself recalled the incident perfectly: the children were foreigners and Muslims, and the pressure of public office had not permitted their rescue. "As Shakespeare reminds us," improvised the minister, "the child is father to the man." Shakespeare, while unfortunately not Australian literature, was universal and, like the minister, beyond reproach.

Cassie's mouth was full when a man she didn't know asked if the pastry she was eating contained meat. A girl came out of nowhere to confide, "I often think about going veggo. But I just really love a good steak!" Smiling, she shook all her curls at the dilemma, extravagant in a rose-colored dress. She turned her rosy shoulder in such a way that she was addressing only the man and said, "And bacon!"

"Yes, it's the kind of thing that must have once taken up many a conversational hour in Rome," he replied. "You know: the injustice of slavery versus the inconvenience of life without slaves."

The girl's enthusiastic body went still. Then she went away.

"Hi," said Ash. "I'm Ash."

Cassie was a little shocked. But she saw a knight: brutal in a just cause.

A bunch of people ended up at a Lebanese restaurant later that evening. Cassie found herself sitting next to Ash. They asked each other questions that had nothing to do with what they really wanted to know, while their bodies conducted a separate, unambiguous conversation. Ash learned that Cassie was writing a thesis on Australian expatriate novelists. He was at the dinner because he knew Leanne from a library committee, he explained. It had rained earlier, and drops clung to the cars parked outside the window by which they sat—Cassie thought of fish with rivers still slipping off their fins.

Menus were brought. By means of urgent gestures, the Lawson specialist indicated that he needed a drink.

Someone asked, "Shall we share?"

Ash said that he was a vegetarian. "But the rest of you, please go ahead. I'll order for myself."

"Why don't we all get vegetarian?" said Leanne, glancing around. "I can't remember the last time I ate meat anyway."

Her research assistant said helpfully, "When Baniti took us to that halal restaurant in Auburn last week. We had camel."

"Well, obviously I didn't want to be culturally insensitive," said Leanne.

Ash told a story of getting lost between his apartment and the university. It was a ten-minute walk, but he had found himself on the Princes Highway. It had been plain to Ash from day one that the natives adored an idiot Pom. "I've no idea how it happened, but I wound up on a bus heading to Kogarah," he concluded. He gave the suburb three syllables, *ko-ga-ra*, transforming it into an Italian resort.

"*Kog*-rah! *Kog*-rah!" the Australians shouted, and split their sides.

Ash told Cassie softly, appealing to her alone, "When you're still finding your way around, you make mistakes."

At the Spice Mart, which stood across the road from Ashfield Station, rice was heaped on the floor in stitched cloth bags as well as in giant plastic packs. The man behind the counter was as elongated and flat as if he had passed under a roller. Wrapped in the dusty smell of lentils, he was anomalous among the spices and Bollywood DVDs, having clad his two dimensions in a bureaucrat's pressed trousers and pin-striped shirt.

When she discovered that he came from Sri Lanka, Cassie inquired after his "ethnic group." It was an excuse to speak about Ash. "My partner has Sinhalese ancestry," she explained, "although he identifies as British." She realized that she had almost said "husband" when even "partner" was a stretch for someone she had known barely a month. The shopkeeper continued to examine her through the heavy glasses that turned his eyes into aspic set with beetles. He was a Jaffna Tamil, he said. "But here no one knows who we are. What to do?"

Cassie was familiar with this kind of thing. Her grandmother had grown up in Vienna, and laments about Australian ignorance circulated readily with the torte.

The shopkeeper asked if she had seen an Indian grocery. "That side, on Liverpool Road?"

"No."

"I have been here three years. They came last month. You didn't see them?"

Iron-spined, he came out from behind his counter to show her the chutneys and pickles, and was revealed as a darkly varnished plank. On his advice, Cassie came away with onion sambol and a little curry-leaf plant in a pot. Ash was pleased with the sambol, which he said went tremendously well with grilled cheese. Cassie told him about the Ashfield Tamil, concluding, "He used to be a postmaster in Sri Lanka." As soon as he had said that, his clothes had made sense: Cassie saw that he was dressed for the past.

"Tamils do very well for themselves," said Ash. "They're hard-working, intelligent people. Terrifically good at maths." He knew no Tamils but was repeating the kind of thing his father said. The only other person who had offered Cassie fixed pictures of this or that race was her grandmother. When Cassie's grandmother was young, her politics had landed her in a camp. She emerged from it at the end of the war despising everyone she had once loved: the poor, the oppressed, Communists, Jews. The other prisoners had spat at her and threatened her and taught her to steal. She had gone into the camp trusting in goodness and come out knowing there was none. By the time Cassie knew her, she lived in Cremorne with a view of Sydney Harbour and hated Australians. Her daughter had betrayed her by marrying one. The flaxen grandchild—a throwback to her girlhood—was forgiven. As time went on, the harbor became a casual blue insult hurled at the grandmother's life. To thwart it, the curtains in her flat were kept shut. In aquarium-like gloom, the grandchild listened to ravishing lieder and a voice that said Italians were liars, Slavs were animals, and Gypsies spread disease. Between the girl's visits, the grandmother lived for dumplings and strudel, for childhood recovered spoon by spoon. Merciful childhood turned her arteries to concrete and killed her before the blond sprite grew tall enough to say, "You are a bitter, crazy old woman, Oma, and your hair has fallen out."

Ash's mother was Scottish; he had been born in London, and educated at universities in England and the States. For five years in the 1970s, well before the civil war, the Fernandos had lived in Sri Lanka. Ash went to an international school in Colombo where the little girls wore pale pink or pale green or pale blue dresses. "International" meant an Egyptian boy, four Taiwanese sisters, and Ash. Everyone else was white. The only language Ash had ever spoken fluently was English, although he had enough French to deploy, in a respectable accent, various phrases made essential by Derrida and Foucault.

When Ash was born, the British had been gone twenty years from the subcontinent. Empire was a concept, deplorable of course, but nothing to do with Ash. He was a political scientist, and had written incisively, and at times intelligently, on the "global subaltern" in his book *Mobility and Modernity in a Transnational Age.* Ash's father was a GP, his mother a gynecologist. Their professional disparity engendered a tension that must have informed Ash's childhood, although he had not been aware of it. Yet it might have been at the root of the mild rebellion that turned him from medicine, which was so plainly his destiny, to politics. As soon as Ash left school his parents divorced, and he realized that all three of them had been waiting for this to happen. His parents remained friends, living only streets away from each other in Swiss Cottage with new partners and stepchildren. Ash acquired a half sister. Christmas, by tradition a grave festivity at which the three Fernandos had opened expensive gifts and peacefully dismantled a goose, developed into a riotous affair with reindeer antlers and aunts. A preposterous ceremony known as Kris Kringle played its part in Ash's decision to apply for the lectureship in Sydney that he saw advertised on a sleety November day.

Women—but not only women—were drawn to Ash, to his politeness and his eyes. His eyes suggested, obscurely, that he had suffered. In Sydney, an emeritus professor offered him the use, rent-free and for as long as he liked, of a pied-à-terre in Newtown. It consisted of a big, high-ceilinged room on the top floor of a subdivided Victorian mansion. A bathroom opened off the hall, and a short stair led to a room at the top of a tower. It contained a hard chair, and a table that served as a desk. On clear days, the view reached to a distant, glinty line that was Botany Bay. It was the long stair down to the street that had defeated the professor's knee. For most of his life, he had been a radical with a kingly beard. Now, having retired to the Hunter Valley, he was writing a monumental work that examined everything by which he had lived and judged it a sham. His wife had stopped speaking to him. Introduced to Ash, he saw a foreigner newly arrived in Australia: that meant someone who needed help. He lied, "My heart," hitting himself on the chest to explain about the stairs. He wouldn't confess to arthritis, which made an old man of him. That night, resting between savage paragraphs, the professor began to cry. He was remembering what Ash had said: "In every way that matters your heart is entirely sound."

Everyone Ash knew in Sydney lived in houses in which rooms opened off a long passage. These corridors were unfailingly dark and cold—why didn't Australians heat their houses? There would be, at best, a dodgy, unflued gas heater in a living room. Sydney remained for Ash a city of cold bedrooms, cold bathrooms. Oh, but how he loved it! For a long time after leaving Sri Lanka, he had remembered leafy lanes held in a sea-blue rind. He went back when he was twenty-four. Colombo was full of soldiers and dust. Ash went away again quickly and didn't return. In Sydney he recovered lost mornings of steamy gray warmth. The city was regulated and hygienic—occidental—yet voluptuously receptive to chaos and filth. It knew the elemental, antique drama of the sea. Whether or not Ash could see it, the sea was there with its deaths and its ships. Whenever a storm stirred the Pacific, every hill in Sydney was an asphalted wave. The city smelled briny and fumy. It was a smell that made Ash feel something like homesick but without sadness. In those first weeks, when he was at his most porous, past and present fused. The understanding cries of crows—*Ah! Ohh! Aahh!*—rang out from his childhood. A botched arpeggio overheard on a humid afternoon revived the Czerny exercises played by nine-year-old Ash. He recognized things he couldn't name: trees that ruined concrete with their toes, reckless floral perfumes. Even the fruit bats rotting on power lines were dreamy visitants from the past.

Sydney was a summer city as London was a winter one. Its dusty golden light set a nimbus around bodies moving unhindered in floaty clothes. When dark jackets and heavy scarves appeared in the streets, the city looked hangdog and shifty. That yolky light was one of the things Ash had missed without knowing it. His e-mails to friends around the world said, "I spent too many years in places where the light was blue."

Cassie was oaty porridge: pale, reassuring, wholesome. Ash thrilled to her satisfying breasts, her orderly teeth. Her eyes, widely spaced, gave her the remote look of someone listening to distant music. She wore empire-waisted velvet dresses, with sleeves gathered at the wrist, which had belonged to her mother. Cassie was taller than her mother, and the jewel-colored dresses barely skimmed her knees. Evoking a vanished age, they intensified her faraway air. Her reading glasses had large frames that made her look like a girl playing at being a grandmother; when she took them off, there were a few seconds when she seemed dopey and pitiless. All her effects were like that, uncalculated, incidental, and her artlessness was part of her power. Sometimes she turned up in jeans topped with a vintage blouse, pin-tucked and demure, in a lilac-y sort of blue. Tiny fabric loops fastened two nacre buttons at the back. At the sight of Cassie's shoulder blades, faintly shining through the blouse, Ash wanted nothing more than to undo those buttons.

There were fragile, potent, slightly witchy things on Cassie's windowsill: a bird's skull, lavender sea urchin cases, a view of the Prater painted on glass. There was also a photo of her parents: solid, dark strangers. They proved what Ash had known all along: Cassie was a changeling, magical. That was the kind of foolishness she called up in Ash. He would have been embarrassed for any friend who indulged in it.

Cassie had the Sydney imperviousness to cold. Her velvet

dresses—emerald, sapphire, topaz—were unlined. When an icy gale blew from the west, she slipped a weightless coat over her dress, or a lambs' wool cardigan. She seemed to own neither scarf nor gloves. Her concession to winter was socks inside her boots. Previously, Ash had thought of Australians—if he thought of them at all—as no-nonsense, practical people: Canadians with tans. Now he realized that he had overlooked what history had required of them: they were visionaries, adept at denial. Australians had seen pastures where there was red dust, geraniums where there were trees as old as time, no one where there were five hundred nations—they dealt with winter as a tank deals with a blade of grass.

In bed, arching beneath Ash, Cassie bit the side of his palm. There was salt in her, he decided. That made him think of his mother: her salty Scottish eyes. His mother had e-mailed Ash on the day he left: "Australians are hardworking and very successful. They are suspicious of their success and resent it. They are winners who prefer to see themselves as victims. Their national hero, Ned Kelly, was a violent criminal—they take this as proof of their egalitarianism. They worship money, of course. Anyway, enjoy yourself."

Cassie always wore two rings, a garnet and a square-cut emerald in old-fashioned claw settings, which had belonged to her grandmother. Her friend Pippa had told her, casually, "You'll be murdered for those one day." People often remarked that Pippa and Cassie were like sisters. That was quite true in the sense that each girl kept track of, rejected, and coveted whatever belonged to the other.

In the winter break, not long after Ash met Cassie, a colleague invited him to his family's sheep station in western New South

Wales. "It's the real Australia out there," said Lachlan, as if Sydney were a collective hallucination. The real Australia was called Yukkendrearie, or so Lachlan said—it wasn't so very different from the name on the map. Ash and Lachlan crossed mountains blue with menace. A distant viaduct had the look of all out-of-place objects, sinister and forlorn. Then the mountains were behind them, and there were the carpet rucks of threadbare hills. All this was disappointingly familiar: sheep, hills making waves.

Ash asked, "Will we see real Australians?" It was a joke, but not wholly. He was keen to encounter the outlandish, to be enlarged or overwhelmed.

"Bound to. Strong, silent types. Famous for self-reliance and endurance. Hardworking and practical. Stoic."

"So the real Australian is a Victorian Englishman?"

"All archetypes are fossils."

Ash didn't say, Shame to have a borrowed one, though.

Lachlan sent a text message whenever they stopped to stretch their legs. His partner of eleven years had recently left him and wasn't returning his calls. Zipping up his jeans beside an empty highway, Ash saw a row of canaries in a windbreak. But it was only an arrangement of light.

In the afternoon, the scenery drained away. What was left was flatness and sky. There was no end to either, and a peculiar light. All that space might have been restful but scraped Ash's nerves instead. Like reality TV, it was both harrowing and dull. How did Sydneysiders trim their children's fingernails or buy stuff from the Apple store or sign up for Fun Runs with this enormity breathing down their necks? Ash wondered what word might apply to what they were moving through: certainly not "landscape." It was a presence that spoke of absence; it brought to mind the desolation left by a plundering army—which wasn't, after all, very far from the mark. Half a cow lay near a fence, its head twisted away from the ivory basket of its ribs. It was only a stray splinter from the coffin of pastoral romance—that had perished here long ago. Ash had pictured himself striding up a hill in a borrowed Akubra hat. What lay around was less disconcerting than the magnitude of his mistake.

"See that signpost?" said Lachlan as they flashed past. "Bony Track. Half a dozen Aborigines were tied up and shot there in the 1830s. Plenty of those colorful local names all over the country. We've a Butcher's Creek ourselves. Stone dry."

"What happened there?"

"My forebears were much too canny to keep a record."

In a far paddock, a broken feather was stuck into the ground: some weirdo had neglected to cut down a tree. The Subaru rushed at the dead, discarded distance. A hawk appeared, strung up in the white air.

Lachlan said, "Not much farther now, couple of hundred k. We'll be there in time for tea."

He said, "Dinner, I mean."

He said, "Since Dad died, Mum likes to have tea on the table as soon as it gets dark."

"It's dark at five," said Ash.

"Yes."

An e-mail had not been sent or had not been read or had failed to arrive. The fragrance of dead lamb enveloped them as they drew up before the sprawling timber house. But food was irrelevant—on getting out of the car, Ash discovered that he was ill. A light-eyed dog stood a little way off and barked at him. The wind came and slapped everyone. Ash spent the three days of his visit in bed.

Plastic ring binders filled a fireless fireplace in his room. A massive wardrobe, sturdy and somewhat scarred, loomed against one wall. Ash looked inside, hoping for something useful, like extra blankets, but found only a wire coat hanger and an emery board. He spread his coat over his bed and climbed in. Pressed-metal walls tightened around his dreams.

His door opened. It was hinged in such a way that from his bed Ash couldn't see who was standing there. After a while, a child with a dirty face edged around. The farm was run by Lachlan's sister, Bob. Presumably the child belonged to her. A hard brown arm connected the door to the child. The arm was paler on the inside, like the limbs of the yellow-eyed creature he had seen on arrival. Ash concluded that it was Bob's child who had barked at him—it made perfect sense.

A second door gave on to a side veranda shared with Lachlan's room. The wind shouted at the English elms, and Lachlan shouted at his phone: "You can have the Eames recliner." "No, I never said Glen could come and get it." "Well, what I mean is, we'll say it's yours." "That's right, it'll stay in our lounge room. But now you'll be the one who sits in it." "Well, if I say Glen can have it, will you come back?" "What do you mean that's bloody typical?" "No, you can leave the Thermomix out of it." "No, Glen can't have it either." "That's right, one or the other." "What do you mean, typically binary?"

Sometimes Ash woke to hear Lachlan's keyboard. Lachlan had a major research grant and was writing two books at once. Meanwhile, Ash shivered unproductively. He wore a cashmere sweater, a Christmas present from his mother, over his pajamas. He struggled into his coat and scarf, and tottered along a passage that struck icy through his slippers. There was the sound of splashing behind the bathroom door and someone—Bob?—bawled, "Afternoon delight! Afternoon delight! Ah-ah . . ."

On the last day of Ash's stay, his mother brought him a piece of toast as he lay in bed. She said, "Are you sure you couldn't manage a boiled egg? Or a beer?" She wasn't Ash's mother, of course, but Lachlan's: they had the same voice, *echt* Aberdeen. Margaret's straight, short hair, the delectable pewter of pencil shading, was parted on one side like a child's and fastened with a child's flowered clip. She picked up Ash's coat and hung it in the wardrobe. Ash felt shivery again and decided to risk a cup of coffee. Lachlan brought it to him in a mug that said "Farmers Do It in the Dirt"—it was excellent coffee, frothy and strong.

Lachlan said, "Feel up to a tour? Shame to have to leave without seeing the old place." He was wearing only a woolen vest over his red RB Sellars shirt, so Ash was too abashed to retrieve his coat from the wardrobe. He lifted his scarf from the hook on the door, and Lachlan peered at him, saying in an incredulous way, "Not feeling cold, are you?" as if Ash had taken it into his head to challenge an unassailable proposition in logic.

Ash trailed his host in and out of big rooms with empty fireplaces. They were like rich people's rooms anywhere, only colder. Lachlan said things like "1869" and "the Twenties" and "1976"; Ash gathered that the original homestead had been added to or remodeled at these dates. He was shown the former telephone room—larger than his study in the tower—and a room that had once contained the family silver. There was also a ballroom with stained-glass windows built to impress a duke, who sent a last-minute telegram in his place.

They crossed the ballroom, emerged onto yet another veranda, and went back into the house by a different entrance. Ash remarked on the number of doors.

"Fifteen external ones," said Lachlan. "I counted them once. Handy for Bob's boyfriends—always an escape hatch somewhere. I'd look out my window and see the latest bloke running away."

"Does your bedroom door open in such a way that you can't see who's standing there?"

"They all do in the old part of the house. Very practical, the ancestors: you can give the maid her instructions without having to look at her."

A wonderful surprise waited in the kitchen: it was warm. Margaret sat by the Aga, peeling potatoes onto a sheet of newspaper. "We're having mash for our tea," she told Ash. "With Thai green curry."

Ash offered to peel potatoes—it would be a reason to linger in the warmth. When his offer was refused, he said firmly that he felt too weak to continue and sat at the table anyway.

"Have you shown your friend the gun slits?"

"His name's Ash, Mum."

"I know that." Margaret turned to Ash. "My children think my mind's going because of my old woman."

Ash looked polite. Lachlan said, "Mum!"

"When I wake up these days, there's an old Aboriginal woman waiting," explained Margaret. "She gave me a scare the first time, but I look out for her now."

"It's called hypnopompic hallucination," said Lachlan. "A kind of dream that carries over into waking."

"That's what you say. But I spotted my old lady outside the bank last week when Bob took me into town. She was wearing a blue tracksuit." Margaret added the last pale potato to the bowl and dipped her fingers in the earthy water, saying, "Well? Are you going to show him the gun slits?" She told Ash, "They're in the old cold-storage room. It's Bob's office now. You should take a look before it gets dark."

"I'm not sure I'm up to that," said Ash. The phrase "cold storage" had filled him with dread.

"They're just slits in the walls," said Lachlan. "For shooting at marauders. In case there were escaped convicts about. Or blackfellas."

Ash said, "I thought Butcher's Creek had taken care of one of those problems."

"Oh, you know about that? Well, you see, a shepherd was found speared," said Margaret. "So whole families were slaughtered at the creek in retaliation."

"You know there's no actual historical record of a massacre, Mum."

"My husband's grandfather was alive when I first came here," said Margaret to Ash. "He told me all about it. It was spoken about openly when he was a boy. Mind you, I always thought there was Aboriginal blood in my husband's family. You've only to look at Lachlan."

Ash looked at Lachlan: milk and ginger, sanitary blue eyes.

Standing behind his mother, Lachlan tapped the side of his head. He opened the fridge and peered inside, saying, "Is it too early for a beer? Do you want one, Ash?"

"I think that's what my old woman comes to tell me. You can say she's a dream. But another word for a dream that recurs is 'truth.'"

"Bob still hard at it?" asked Lachlan, pulling the ring off a can. He told Ash, "There's a downward spiral of genetic selection on most family farms. The smart kid goes away, the dumb one stays home and manages the property. Luckily, it happened the other way around with us."

Margaret said, "This kitchen was the front room in the original homestead. If you go over to that window and look out, you'll see Bob's office. Of course, the gun slits are on the other side."

Ash felt obliged to comply. A low building with a hipped roof stood across the yard. The old glass in the kitchen window was faintly rippled. The child who had appeared at Ash's door strolled across this cockeyed view. Ash saw Margaret at ten: the straight hair chopped off at the tips of the ears, the triangular face. The eyes were different: not the grandmother's hooded blue but a shallow, creaturely yellow. They looked directly at Ash. The child was holding something—an apple? an iced bun? a cricket ball?—that Ash couldn't quite identify. It displayed a semicircular white scar. Ash thought that he had never seen anything as unnerving as the conjunction of that mauled missile and the small brown hand.

After dinner, Lachlan came to Ash's bedroom to take away his tray. He said, "I can remember when it became fashionable to have a convict in the family tree. All the amateur genealogists hoped to find one. Now you get people who dream up an Aboriginal ancestor. Is it progress? Or another kind of stealing to persuade ourselves we're legit?"

They were driving back through the not-landscape when Ash saw the wardrobe from his room. It stood in a paddock, upright and empirical and empty: a survivor. What was horrible was that *the wardrobe was the Ashfield Tamil.* No one else knew this, only Ash, and he was not allowed to tell. He woke to a delirious magpie and a distant shout: "Man up, Stevie!" That would be Bob, calling encouragement to her daughter or her dog.

The first thing Ash had bought in Sydney was a heater. Three or four times a week, Cassie and Ash would have dinner in a restaurant before going back to Ash's warm flat. There was a smell there—also detectable on the stairs—that was very strong in the built-in cupboards: a musty smell, but pleasant, like old apples and loam. Ash and Cassie would drink vodka in bed, tell jokes, show off a little to each other. These hours were dedicated to the business of bodies but strayed easily into myth. The flat became their castle, the city was transformed into a forest, the preserve of bears; a stranger arrived with urgent messages from the emperor and was turned away at the gate. At different moments of their affair, each of them felt it: the sense of timelessness and fate that underwrites old tales.

In the morning, Cassie liked to climb the stair to the tower. She claimed it was for the view, trying to conceal her fascination with the room: the books, the journals, the printouts, the piles of student essays. The framed Constructivist prints on the wall were of no interest, as they belonged to the old professor. On Ash's desk, an upturned lid held paper clips and a staple remover. Cassie swiveled slowly on an ergonomic chair. There was something here that held the key to Ash—something more intimate and revealing than the mouth guard he wore to keep from grinding his teeth in his sleep. She carried a book stuck with markers downstairs. "Why are some of the Post-its yellow and others orange?" she asked.

"I ran out of yellow ones," said Ash, just out of the shower.

At that moment Cassie came close to seeing that he was only an instrument in her quest, which was really for a system and an answer. How was she to live? The riddle was crucial and therefore hard to unlock. She believed that Ash had it under control—this had to do with the white split of his grin.

Spring came like a wind in sudden warm gusts. Underneath the air remained cool. "The bottom of the air is fresh," said Ash, remembering a phrase acquired on a school trip to France. How pleasing to find life fitting itself so smoothly to words! On a hot October Sunday, he brunched beside the ocean—its pomp and flash!—and risked a swim at Coogee; the sunny Pacific, too, harbored cold depths.

With the improvement in the weather came evenings when Ash walked up the hill to Cassie's place in Glebe. But drafts and chilly lino weren't all that he had to contend with there. Cassie rented two second-story rooms at the back of a Victorian house. One of them was really a wide balcony that had been enclosed to make a sunroom. That was where Cassie and Ash ate, on mismatched chairs at a table by a row of clear-paned louvres that sliced up the view. The sunroom was Cassie's study: her laptop was always open on the table, beside a pile of books. When Cassie served a meal, she never bothered to clear the table, but simply pushed the paraphernalia of work to one side. The resulting juxtaposition of food and books worked on Ash like a stray lash floating in an eye. One day Cassie had left a hefty volume propped spine-up like a tent. Ash hadn't treated a book like that since the age of seven. Coming upon it, his father had shouted, "You will break its spine!" as if Ash were torturing a kitten. His father's anger was always connected to the idea of *waste*. It could be traced to an austere past when a light shining in an empty room was a bill mounting up, books were for the lucky, and no one left anything on their plate. His father would often remark that when he was a boy, whatever food there was in the house was kept locked up—once it was half a packet of biscuits.

Cassie usually made pasta and a salad for dinner, but one evening she produced a feast. A recessed space at the top of the interior staircase had been fitted out as a kitchen that Cassie shared with the other tenant. She went to and fro between this dingy nook and the sunroom, returning twice with a laden tray. She laughed at Ash's amazement—she had been cooking for days, she said. Surely, thought Ash, it would have been a simple matter to clear the table first? Vegetable curries, a bowl of dhal, an array of pickles and glutinous chutneys encroached on the streamlined laptop, the right-angled books—they threatened *knowledge* with stickiness and slop.

Ash wouldn't allow himself to remark on this; he believed in the separation of powers. He had intense, almost violent feelings about Cassie's body, which he entered every few days. But he wouldn't ask her to tidy her table, or make a move to clear it himself—he would not be masculinist or proprietorial. And it had to be said that the change from pasta to lentils and vegetables was a relief. It was obvious that Cassie could eat whatever she wanted without affecting the hollows under her hip bones, but Ash had begun to count calories of late. When he had first seen his baby sister, Ash had fleetingly wondered how many more siblings there would be. His stepmother was still in her thirties and had hips like a Soviet peasant—a Soviet peasant was what she had been born, after all. Ash saw his inheritance dwindle with the appearance of each new little Fernando: he envisaged a procession of them, all with serene, Madonna faces and backsides like sideboards. The baby couldn't possibly have guessed what was on Ash's mind but began to scream anyway. She was twelve now, and Ash's inalienable paternal inheritance had finally come down to him intact: the makings of a potbelly.

When his plate was empty, Ash said, "Wow! That was absolutely delicious!"

"Have more—there's heaps."

About to help himself, Ash recoiled before the aptitude of dhal to splash. The bowl that held the curried lentils was a shallow one; already, the table around it was flecked. Ash's hand hovered, brown as a hawk. Then he chose fried eggplant as a safer bet.

"Don't you like the dhal?" asked Cassie. She slid the dish forward, to Ash's alarm. "I followed the recipe exactly. But obviously leaving out the Maldive fish."

Ash assured her that the dhal was terrific. "Everything is. But I absolutely couldn't eat another thing."

Cassie helped herself to wine. Her expression as she drank was particularly aloof. He had disappointed her, Ash saw. But why? Their conversation seemed inoffensive yet at cross-purposes, like her clashing chairs. Cassie had told him the story of her childhood, describing the rain forest and the way it rained. She had been traveling in South America when her parents sold their mudbrick house and the acres in which it stood, and moved to a coastal town. Cassie didn't say, The minute my back was turned; but Ash understood that betrayal was involved. She had become a visitor in a museum, said Cassie, by which she meant that the near past had turned mythical and remote. Its glassed-off exhibits made up a kingdom that she had imagined would last forever. The name of her museum was Time, but she was still young enough to believe that everything that happened to her was unique. "Exhibit A," she said, showing Ash a framed photograph of a lush valley bridged with a rainbow. It was nothing like Yukkendrearie. But now, sitting among the ruins of their banquet, Watch out! said Ash to Ash. This pliable girl was a product of the real Australia. There was the heedless way she treated books. No striding up hills in a hat, Ash warned himself. Cassie, too, might prove unimaginable. She might turn out to be nothing like porridge, not even porridge with salt.

Cassie arranged to meet Pippa at a bookshop. She found her in the Australian section, a mazy arrangement in a poorly lit area near the back. Pippa emerged, hissing, "They have exactly one copy of my novel. I turned it face out."

In the place that had the best coffee that side of Parramatta Road, Pippa asked, "So how'd you go the other night? Did you make the pumpkin curry in the end?" Pippa was an amazing cook. She put on dinners for twelve that involved lemons she had preserved. It was Pippa who had recommended the Charmaine Solomon cookbook that Cassie had consulted to prepare her feast.

"I couldn't go veggo for anyone," went on Pippa. Her sharp little face turned pensive. "But I guess you got used to all those chickpeas growing up."

Pippa and Cassie had met at high school up north. Cassie was one of the few people in Sydney who knew that Pippa had once been called Narelle. Pippa had filed the application to change her name on her eighteenth birthday. She said, "No one called Narelle's ever going to win the Booker." Even before that, even when Pippa and Cassie shut themselves into their bedrooms and sobbed because River Phoenix was dead, Pippa had known that she was going to be a writer. The clarity Pippa brought to her objectives was one of the things Cassie envied about her. Cassie was twenty-nine, and the future, as she saw it, remained uncontrollable and vague. She was afraid of being twenty-nine. It was much worse than thirty, the ax hovering before it fell.

She said, "I don't think Ash liked the dhal."

"Too salty, maybe? Or not salty enough? Lentils can be tricky," said Pippa. The offhand way she spoke told Cassie that Pippa didn't care for the sound of Ash. As if to confirm it, Pippa asked, "So when do I get to meet the great man?"

"It's early days still," said Cassie. It was three months. Cassie and Ash only saw each other alone, never with other people; Cassie told herself that what they wanted from each other didn't involve other people. To counter Pippa's expression, Cassie told her about something that had happened the previous week. Ash and Cassie were heading to the city on a bus. They had risen for their stop when a woman shouted, "Speak English, you fucken boat jumpers!" This was directed at two African men, an old one and a younger one, talking quietly to each other. Ash and Cassie got off the bus, and Cassie said, "How awful. I should have said something. I'm so sorry."

Ash replied, "Oh, that woman was probably afraid that anyone speaking a foreign language was insulting her."

He was capable of that, of surprising grace. It struck Cassie as such generosity of spirit that it couldn't fail to impress. However, all Pippa said was, "'Boat jumpers' is pretty good." She took a notebook from her bag and wrote down the phrase. Reading upside down, Cassie saw: "the possibility of being bold, confident, and fun." Pippa had underlined this twice. She put her notebook away and said, "Why don't you guys come to dinner on Friday?"

"Ash is at a conference in Canberra this week," said Cassie. "How's Matt?"

"Good. Hey, listen: George. You know he's back in Melbourne, right? The latest is his mother's bought him a warehouse apartment in Fitzroy."

"That's nice." Cassie wondered if she would have a baby with Ash. She tried to picture the baby's face—it was beautiful, she knew. If a thirty-five-year-old man didn't have children, did that mean he didn't want them or that he would be eager to become a father without delay?

"Obviously, I didn't hear that from George," went on Pippa. "You know how guarded he is. He calls it 'private.' But one of my Melbourne mates told me."

Cassie stirred herself to ask, "How's the difficult second novel going?"

Soon after Pippa and Cassie moved to Sydney and their respective universities, Pippa had become involved with a guy called Vince. When they broke up, Vince would stand outside her house, crying. Pippa called this "stalking"—why couldn't Vince see that it was over and move on? Dumping Vince was another thing Pippa had known all along that she would do. Cassie wondered what it took to be loved so grandly, so operatically. She helped Pippa load Vince's paintings into her car; Pippa said she was returning them so that Vince could sell them or reuse the canvases. To fling Vince's work in his face seemed an ingenious cruelty to Cassie. But when she protested, Pippa said, "The alternative is the paintings go out in the rubbish—or do you want them?" Cassie had to admit that she didn't. Pippa pulled down her bedroom blind and said, "Vince can cry on demand. It doesn't mean anything, it's his party trick." In that same calm, reasoning tone, she had once told Cassie, "Vince is a brilliant kisser." Cassie peeped around the edge of the blind and saw Vince in the street, his hair and the trees streaming—the rain, at least, was not any kind of trick. Pippa was quite plain, with no figure to speak of and a mouth crowded with teeth, but Cassie couldn't persuade herself that any boyfriend of her own would wait in a downpour, without an umbrella, hoping for a glimpse of her. Against her will, it became a standard by which she measured men. Ash wouldn't do it, she thought, stirring her coffee while Pippa talked about her book. At once she thought of things Ash did do and was shot through with delight. She was almost unnaturally happy that year and she was a girl with a great capacity for joy. When Cassie read of war and suffering and children without enough to eat, she knew that she had no right to happiness and would try to reject the sensation. But it welled up again, natural and persistent, at the sight of clouds chasing each other, or the first wave of scented mock-orange in the street. When that happened, time receded and the world shrank to a rainbow-hung valley that Cassie could frame and keep close. The kelpies vanished and the snakes, and the death-dealing spiders in the toilet. Ash became another version of Cassie's gentle parents: an older, wiser person whom she scrutinized and loved.

•

The Ashfield Tamil said, "Those Indians are selling frozen paneer cheap. But you can be assured that everything I stock is highly fresh." He was following Cassie around the shop because she could never find what she wanted. This was partly because the shelves were stocked according to an elusive logic—why were the dried chilies beside the tinned ghee rather than with the chili powder?—and partly because Cassie rarely had a specific purchase in mind. When preparing for her Sri Lankan feast, she had shopped according to a list of ingredients copied from Charmaine Solomon, and was still plentifully provided with things like turmeric and cinnamon sticks. On subsequent visits, she allowed herself to be guided by the Ashfield Tamil. "Sandalwood soap?" he would suggest. "Desiccated coconut?" His gray hair, flattened with something like oil, was combed back from his forehead in a style Cassie associated with young men setting off to fight for the Spanish Republic; it brought old, lost causes to mind.

In the far corner of the shop, a door led to the storeroom. A length of reddish cloth banded with gold that might have been sari fabric hung in front of the door. The shopkeeper noticed Cassie looking at it. "My wife made the curtain," he said. "A door without a curtain is like a person without clothes." His oiled hair gave off an odor as he stood beside Cassie in the narrow aisle between the shelves. That top note was followed by the smell of his scalp. Cassie was unable to decide whether these scents were unpleasant or exotic.

"My curry-leaf plant died," she said. "Do you think I overwatered it?"

"What to do?"

Relaying this to Ash, Cassie mimicked the gesture that accompanied the Ashfield Tamil's stock phrase—the wrist twisted sharply, "like a spin bowler." She also said, "His shoes don't go with the rest of him. They're the kind with Velcro fastenings."

"They're cheaper," said Ash. He was too polite to add, Obviously.

The shopkeeper wasn't a refugee, Cassie told Ash. Two of his children had migrated to Sydney, and he had followed with his wife. "So it was quite easy for you to come here?" Cassie had asked, pleased. She clung to an idea of Australia as a place where kindness prevailed over expediency. It had rarely been true in her lifetime, but was one more creed that had emerged from the rainbow valley, like the belief that the human race would tire of shopping. The Ashfield Tamil repeated, "Easy," in a neutral tone as if hearing the word for the first time. Cassie remembered something her Viennese grandmother used to say: "The worst thing is, we are required to be grateful."

Cassie always came back from the Spice Mart with another segment of the shopkeeper's "story"—that was what she called it when talking to Ash. The Ashfield Tamil had three sons. The middle one was still in Sri Lanka, although his parents pleaded with him to leave. He was a teacher in a seaside town; in Australia, he would have to drive a taxi or clean hotels like his brothers. "What to do?" asked his father, and Cassie echoed him, twisting her wrist. Whenever she mentioned the Tamil, Ash remembered his dream of the wardrobe. Cassie's interest in the man mystified him. To Ash, people were not figures in a story but subjects in history. He was familiar with the historical sequence that had brought a Tamil civil servant from Sri Lanka to the counter of a shop in the west of Sydney.

When he said something along these lines, Cassie, postmodernly tutored, replied pertly, "Isn't history just a set of competing stories?"

"Not really," said Ash.

If someone had informed Ash that Cassie thought of him in conjunction with the shopkeeper, he would have been merely incredulous. No brain, however feverish, would ever place Ash in a paddock, not even disguised as furniture and in a dream. Yet the connection persisted in Cassie's mind, not just because the two men were the only Sri Lankans she knew, but because she secretly believed that they had entered her life to alter its course. Her relations with each had an atmosphere of inevitability. She was aware that these fateful beings were partly her own invention, but that didn't diminish their power.

As if he had peered into her thoughts, Ash told her, "Your Ashfield friend dreams of improvement—all immigrants do. You and I, on the other hand, would like to be more fully what we are. The fulfillment of the will is an old aim, the fulfillment of the heart a modern one." The purpose of this lesson was to point out an unbridgeable gulf, as deep as history, with the Tamil on one side and Cassie and Ash on the other.

Cassie said, "I'm so happy I was born." Ash feared that she had heard only "You and I" and "the fulfillment of the heart." She lay naked on top of her cold bed. It was past midnight, but Ash was not to join her yet. She said, "I want you inside me, but I want to imagine it first." That was just silly. Ash felt himself vaguely stirred by the shell-pink luster between her parted legs, but what remained uppermost in his mind was the meeting he had to attend at nine the next morning. Cassie was an overgrown child whose emptiest make-believe had been labeled "creativity" by her parents. In Ash's view, that indulgence was directly responsible for Cassie's grubby habit of bringing home scraps of paper that had been written on and discarded in the street. They were stored in a tin whose germy contents she had spread before Ash like treasure. He read, "Tickets.

Facial. Jackie—card. Teabags, cheese, stock cubes, matches." The list had been trodden on and bore the muddy imprint of a heel. Cassie believed that handwriting was disappearing, and that her gleanings would one day have the status of precious artifacts. She asked Ash, "Have you ever seen your little sister's writing?" Her chin lifted slightly when she scored a point. Ash was reminded again of his mother. His future didn't contain Cassie, he was sure of that.

Another thing that grated was her habit of referring to the shopkeeper as "the Ashfield Tamil." Surely the man had a name! Then Ash thought, benevolently, She can't pronounce it. He remembered his mother's tongue twisting around Tamil names. Jeyarajasingham. Saravanamuttu. It would be something like that.

Ash didn't know that on her first visit to the shop, Cassie had said, "My name's Cassie." The Ashfield Tamil received this as impartially as if she had said, "The chief export of New South Wales is coal" or "There are ten mammals, four birds, and thirteen fish on the list of critically endangered Australian animals." As time went on, it was too late to ask his name—it would have embarrassed them both. By then he was greeting Cassie warmly, saying, "Welcome! Welcome!" even though she typically bought only a few inexpensive items. One day, when there was no more of Ash's favorite mango chutney on the shelf, the Ashfield Tamil produced two jars set aside especially for Cassie, bringing them out from under his counter with a triumphant flourish.

"A very good brand," he said. "MD is Marketing Department. Government guaranteed."

When Cassie reported this to Ash, he said he found it strange that a Tamil would have faith in anything guaranteed by the Sri Lankan government. "Other than torture and extermination, that is."

The shopkeeper confided his anxieties about his rivals to Cassie. The Indians had chosen their location with cunning. There were more pedestrians on the main street, and the Indian shop was also readily visible to drivers stuck in the sluggish river of traffic on Liverpool Road. Once, when Cassie had let three weeks pass before returning to him, the Ashfield Tamil asked, "Have you been going there?" The Indians sold packaged curries, he told her. "Highly convenient for young people." Cassie took this to mean that he had forgiven her, although no disloyalty had occurred. He was as easily alarmed as a bird. When she stumbled over one of the giant packs of rice on the floor, he cried, "Please be careful! What will happen if you fall and break your leg? You will sue me!" Cassie didn't take his fears about being ousted by the Indians seriously. Curiosity had taken her to their shop: a pastel-walled, air-conditioned box, where a girl whose plait was thicker than her wrist played with her phone and ignored Cassie. In fact, there was nothing she could have done for a customer, as the stock was brightly lit, rationally arranged, and clearly labeled. One shelf held an assortment of incense, but the shop smelled of nothing. Cassie, inclined by nature to hopefulness, felt confident that these antiseptic premises could pose no threat to the Ashfield Tamil's chaotic, atmospheric cave.

One morning, there was an elaborate geometric pattern on the pavement at the entrance to the Spice Mart. It had been somewhat scuffed by feet. The Ashfield Tamil told Cassie that it was a kolam, drawn in rice flour by his wife. "She didn't lift her hand once," he said proudly, as Cassie surveyed the intricate design. A kolam brought prosperity and protected against evil spirits. "It also provides food for ants."

"But it's being destroyed," protested Cassie, watching a woman wheel a shopping cart over the drawing.

"That is the way. My wife will make another one." But Cassie never saw a kolam outside the shop again.

Cassie claimed that she could read auras. Ash stood against a white wall like a prisoner about to be shot. His aura was orange tinged with red, said Cassie. He was confident, creative, and sexually passionate. Ash smiled. She could also see flickers of gray, she went on. They signified guardedness. "A fear of loss."

Her upbringing had left its mark in other ways. First thing every morning, before eating or drinking, Cassie swilled cold-pressed sesame oil around her mouth for twenty minutes. She said, "It's an ancient ayurvedic practice that draws toxins from the body." Ash, child of doctors, believed in antibiotics, vaccinations, flossing. Oil-pulling was a harmless eccentricity, like the olive-leaf extract Cassie gravely spooned into him at the first sign of a sore throat. She spoke mistily and reverently of self-sufficiency and sustainable living—what that amounted to, as far as Ash could see, was no heating and a row of potted, yellowing herbs.

Whenever they left her flat after dinner, to see a film or go for a walk, Cassie would leave the light on in the sunroom. "You've forgotten to turn off the light," Ash's father said one evening in Ash's voice.

Cassie said, "I know I should," but left the light on anyway. When they had walked some way from the house, she placed her palm on Ash's spine, urging him to turn around. The house stood near the crest of a hill. Ash saw a long, golden rectangle suspended in the darkness. Cassie said that she liked to see it waiting there for her. "It reminds me of a ship."

It clanged with idiocy, even to her ears. It was also only the least part of the truth. Her landlords, elderly Romanians, lived in terror of assassins, informers, vampires, and that shadowy, tentacular, punishing entity, the state. Fifty years earlier, a baby had died of hunger, so now no one was granted access to the ground floor of her parents' house—they might steal all the food. The Romanians' tenants had to come and go by means of an external wooden staircase that Cassie called Cockroach Mansions, accessed from the rear of the house. The garden there, once a formal square, had got away from the old people: it was shrubby, bird-haunted, wild. Cassie feared it at night and was ashamed of her fear. When she first moved to Sydney, she had seen the security bars on windows and laughed at the cages in which city people lived. Then a girl she knew was raped by an intruder. Cassie no longer dreamed about it, but she turned her rings so that the stones faced inward and switched on the sunroom light when going out after dark. Why not say all this to Ash as they walked down the hill? She realized that she wanted to appear enameled, unassailable. She held his arm tightly. They had no past, so she was obliged to look to the future. There she had just come face-to-face with an Ash who could harm her—it was as if a steel curtain had descended to divide them.

Pippa's e-mail said: "Matt and I are going to Bali for eight days. I've finished my first draft: reward! Would you like my car while we're away?" Cassie scrolled down to the PS, which was where Pippa always buried what she really wanted to say. She read: "Whenever George is asked to name an Australian writer he admires, he says, 'Christina Stead' or 'Patrick White.' The safely great, the safely dead. Where is his support for his fellow writers? I heard him on Radio National the other day. The interviewer called his novel a masterpiece."

The car was an ancient white Peugeot, liable to stall on hills. There was no air-conditioning, so Cassie drove with the windows down. She steered the heavy machine carefully around curves, proud of her thin, strong arms, picturing herself at the helm of a boat if a sea-scented northeasterly was in.

One afternoon, she was driving through Annandale with Ash when he asked her to pull over. It was a sticky, overcast day, the kind of weather that turned him contemplative, and he hadn't been saying much. He climbed out and stood with his back to the car. Along that part of Johnston Street the houses were perched high, above a long retaining wall. Ash looked at the big sandstone blocks in the wall, which was inset with an iron gate behind which steps led to the house above. His lips felt wrinkled. He waved vaguely at his surroundings as Cassie came around the car to join him. The shadow of old events lay across him. How was he to explain that the humidity, the massive, grimy stones, and the trees in the gardens overhead had caused time to run backwards? For the rest of his days, Ash would believe that he now said, "I thought I was in a place I visited long ago, a place I dream about." In fact, he remained silent. Cassie saw that he needed something, so she gave him her hand. It felt as dry and papery as real life to Ash.

At Cassie's monthly meeting with her supervisor, Leanne explained that Cassie's discussion of Shirley Hazzard's fiction was unsatisfactory. While remaining perfectly still, Leanne could make her face go bigger and her eyes shrink. Since taking up her role as director of the Centre, she had seemed brusquely unimpressed by Cassie's work. Cassie assumed, humbly, that this was because Leanne now had more glamorous and sweeping responsibilities to Australian literature than the supervision of her thesis. "Admiration is a problematic starting point for analysis," went on Leanne. "I have to say how surprised I am that you haven't grasped that by now." The thing about Leanne was that she had a low, scented voice, excellent for conveying disappointment. It pointed out that one of Hazzard's stories sinned in implying that a former colony's efforts to modernize might entail painful consequences for its citizens—Cassie had failed to take the writer to task for this.

From the edge of her chair, Cassie said, "But what if she was right?" The jacaranda across the quad was in flower. A group of tourists could be seen through the window, photographing one another in front of the tree, giggling and adopting rock-star poses. Cassie, too, found a kind of freedom in the luminous purple blur. She said, "I mean, life in developing countries might have been as awful after independence as before—just differently awful." What was in her mind was something Ash had told her: that Sri Lanka, in the 1970s, was given over to national socialism. "Small 'n,' small 's,'" said Ash. "But not too far a stretch."

Leanne said, "I expect you to interrogate the colonialist point of view, Cassie, not take it over." She began to go through Cassie's bibliography, finding fault. But her face had returned to its normal dimensions, for it was gratifying to have identified an ethical slippage. The previous summer, when Leanne still seemed to have time for Cassie, she had confided that she intended to take up rowing—she even invited Cassie to join her. Nothing came of the invitation, but Cassie noticed that something had sharpened her supervisor's cheekbones. Leanne's hair, freshly hennaed, chimed with her statement lipstick—any one of these things by itself could have made Cassie feel small and inept. Her supervisor's old, kind voice asked, "Is everything all right? It's easy to get caught up in things that carry you out of your depth." Cassie took this to mean that she was being informed she wasn't cut out for academic life. Leanne was staring across the desk very intently, and Cassie looked away with a slight frown. Leanne sighed. "You're still very young," she observed. It was the worst thing she could have said.

Cassie came away with a list of reference works about post-colonialism. In the corridor, the Lawson specialist was just coming out of his room. He asked Cassie what she was working on. When she told him, he said, "Hazzard's no good. Sentimental, women's magazine fiction. You're wasting your time." Cassie's bright face among all the closed, dark doors was a reminder of the last graduate student he had attracted, several years ago, a porcelain virago who attacked "the symbolic masculinity of the bush ethos" with cold brilliance. What the Lawson specialist really couldn't forgive was that in order to refute her arguments he had been obliged to dip into, and occasionally even read, Luce Irigaray.

Cassie went on her way, round-shouldered as if she were protecting her chest. In the quad, she sat on a wall and looked up into the jacaranda. She saw that the short upper lip of each blossom was bent back to display an opaque white tongue. Light striking there was deflected outward, creating the tree's radiant effect. The jacaranda was itself, but so vibrantly itself that it seemed charged with hidden meaning—it could have been a sentence composed by Hazzard. Cassie took out her notebook and wrote:

The Problem with Shirley Hazzard

1. She is a woman.
2. She is a great artist.
3. She is fearless.
4. She has stayed away instead of coming home to be punished for 1–3.

When she reported her conversation with Leanne to Ash, he replied that he wasn't surprised. "Every Friday afternoon, Leanne shuts herself into her office and reads *Who*. Cover to cover, every week without fail. She's a perfect example of a type in the humanities, caught between theory and trash. Of course Shirley Hazzard's beyond her." Hazzard was the one Australian novelist Ash had read (under the impression that she was American).

"How do you know what Leanne reads?" asked Cassie, thrilled.

"A library meeting got shifted to Friday lunchtime at short notice. Leanne sent apologies. I bumped into her later on, and she confessed why she hadn't turned up." Ash went on, "The problem with Leanne is that she's invented a story about Asians and wants to stick us in it."

Cassie was about to tell him that Leanne had objected to Hazzard's depiction of a North African country, not an Asian one. Then it struck her that it was the first time she had heard Ash refer to Asians as "us."

He said, "You mustn't repeat what I've told you, obviously."

She wondered which disclosure had alarmed him.

It was summer, a season that lasted from the beginning of November to the end of March. Light fell in yellow sheets. The true Sydney weather set in, damp and hot. Cassie's velvet dresses had given way to denim miniskirts and limp floral shifts. She told Ash, "Summer Hill's a size-twelve suburb. All the women there have two kids, and the secondhand shops are full of the clothes they can't fit into anymore. That's where I come in." The shifts, and the sleeveless cotton tops that showed her bra straps, were easier to remove than the lilac blouse but made her seem ordinary. Ash spent

November marking essays in his tower. A student quoted Marx: "Men make their own history, but they do not make it as they please; they do not make it under self-selected circumstances, but under circumstances existing already, given and transmitted from the past." It was an observation that had long exercised Ash. It was self-evidently true. But did it matter?

Pollution veiled the city in brownish gauze and obscured Ash's view of Botany Bay. But if he craned his neck he could see a jacaranda flowering in a park. By the middle of the month the tree was exactly poised between fullness and decay. Ash saw a pillar that ran between a carpet and a cloud, both the color of Cassie's blouse. There were jacarandas in his street as well; Ash's shoes slipped on petals after a storm. One day he saw a wondrous thing: a car made out of flowers. Drawing closer, he realized that fallen blooms had covered an old Holden set on blocks under a tree. Ash had received an interesting e-mail that morning. At the conference in Canberra, he had met an Iranian-Canadian anthropologist. She had skin like an apricot. Now she had wangled him an invitation to a symposium in the States. Ash was thinking about that.

Cassie was thinking about Christmas. She was sure there would be invitations for Ash: to Yukkendrearie and the Hunter Valley and an assortment of celebrations in Sydney. Cassie hoped that he would go north with her to her parents. Pippa, to whom she confided this wish, said, "Parents *and* Christmas—sounds like the full catastrophe." Pippa's aura was invariably the muddy green that signified professional resentment and low self-esteem. She had met Ash at last, at a harbor bar one evening. Ash and Cassie got there first, and Ash ordered champagne: the real deal, French. Pippa arrived alone, perfume-first. Her hair, newly styled, was combed over her forehead. "It's a pixie cut," said Pippa, touching it in answer to Cassie's compliment. Ash kissed her on both cheeks.

Cassie knew that Pippa would remember this display of middle-class pretension; an evil teacher in her first novel had been in the habit of campaigning for animal rights and kissing everyone she met. The Moët, too, would be a black mark.

Pippa said, "Matt says hi and he's so sorry. He got his dates mixed up—he has a school concert on tonight." For Ash's benefit, she explained that Matt was a music teacher. Pippa was wearing dangly earrings, and an intensely pink dress with straps that crossed at the back. Whenever Pippa got dolled up, Cassie was reminded of weddings in their country town: the frocks, hairstyles, and makeup that aspired to the social pages of provincial newspapers and whispered of tightly banked-down fear.

Ash informed Pippa that he intended to buy her novel and read it over Christmas. "Oh, please don't feel you have to," said Pippa. "You'll probably hate it."

"Why do you say that?"

"Well, you know. It's a small book about a family. No one could call it a masterpiece."

Ash was flummoxed by this, Cassie could tell. He had spent the best part of a year in Australia but still couldn't read the signs that shouted, *Reassure me, please!* He said, "Tell me what I should read to really get a handle on Australian fiction."

"Patrick White," Cassie heard. "Christina Stead." At the next table, backpackers were shouting with laughter and drinking beer. Cassie turned her head to look at the view. The view, like champagne, amplified every emotion that was offered to it. When Cassie turned back to the others, she saw that Pippa looked superb. Her neck and arms glowed. Ash mirrored her resplendence: his teeth gleamed, and his shirt. Pippa was telling him that she always kept a notebook to hand in which she recorded observations and snatches of conversation. "It's a way of keeping my writing honest."

"Do you know Cassie's theory that handwriting is dying out?"

"The world is one amazement after another to Cassie," said Pippa with airy treachery. "You know she was homeschooled until the age of twelve, right?"

That night, Cassie told Ash, "You've never asked me for suggestions about books to read."

"Darling Cassie," said Ash. He had recently begun to address her that way, she noticed, not just saying "Darling," which might have suggested affection, but "Darling Cassie," as if soothing a cantankerous child. She also noticed that the reflection from the bedside lamp hung in the window in a disturbing sort of way. It occurred to her that she had ended up drinking quite a lot of champagne. "Darling Cassie," Ash went on, "did you hear me trying to talk to your friend about the elections? She said she couldn't bring herself to vote for the Greens because the guy handing out their How to Vote cards looked like her father. Every conversation led back to her. A narcissist, like all artists."

When Cassie called Pippa to find out what she thought of Ash, Pippa said, "If I found him in my bed I wouldn't sleep in the bath." It was a formula taken over from a young Frenchwoman who had taught at the girls' school for a year, and still carried a corrosive charge of teenage contempt. Cassie could remember lying on her bedroom floor with Pippa's head in her lap while they agreed that they didn't have the same taste in men. By this they meant that Pippa was in thrall to the surly, pretty countenances of Duran Duran, while Cassie had discovered the Cure.

Cassie told Pippa, "You made quite an impression on Ash. He calls you an artist." Early on in their relations, Cassie had hit on the strategy of dousing the envy that flickered up in her around Pippa with a stream of compliments. Even when the compliments were more or less fabrications, it worked. There remained the stark fact that Pippa was an artist and Cassie was a student. "Student" brought to mind something squidgy and malformed like a snail without a shell. Cassie took her phone into her bedroom and studied herself in the mirror as she asked Pippa's advice about Christmas. Was long, straight hair timeless and classic or just boring? She was still undecided that evening when Pippa e-mailed her. Cassie never opened an e-mail from her friend without believing that it would contain magical remedies. This dated from their first year of high school when Pippa had mysteriously known the answer to everything: which bands it was safe to like, whether a French braid was tragic or cute. She had advised Cassie not to believe all the awful things she heard on the news. Then she told her different awful things.

"Yesterday I went over my first draft," wrote Pippa. "Today I shredded the printout and deleted the files from my hard drive. I'll have to start again from scratch but I feel like someone's scraped me out with a spoon. I wish I could be a successful writer, because then I wouldn't have to want to be a successful writer." The PS said: "Matt always says he loves my writing but what does he know about books? You are so lucky to have an intellectual you can discuss your work with. Your parents will love Ash."

Cassie thought about the boyfriends her parents had loved: the high school basketball star, the drummer, the student vet, the Chilean, the IT guy. Her parents hadn't met the pastry chef (married) or the architect (married, coke addict), but no doubt they would have loved them, too. There remained the question of whether Ash would love her parents. At some point on Christmas Day, Cassie's father would bring up the subject of her "Nazi grandmother." He would play his Doobie Brothers CD after lunch. Cassie's mother would pluck absentmindedly at the hair in her armpit. She would brew ostentatious quantities of red clover tea, and if that didn't get Ash's attention, she would talk about her night sweats at the breakfast table. A willow-hooped dreamcatcher would sway on its hook in defiance of Cassie's lecture on cultural appropriation. And it was quite possible that the topic of ley lines would arise. What was certain was that before the day ended, her parents would sing harmonies on "Desperado." Worst of all, they would hear Ash's crystalline English vowels but see only his eyes; they would make up a story about the blameless, wounded children of unfortunate nations and stick him in it. Having concocted a victim, they would set out to rescue him; they had attempted it with the Chilean, sending him brochures about migrant services and tins of rocky, health-giving biscuits long after he and Cassie had split up. Cassie saw that she had been crazy to consider exposing these ridiculous, cherished innocents to Ash's excellent manners. He would explain them to her afterward. He would say, "Darling Cassie, your parents exemplify a generation. They set out to make love and they ended up making money." Then she realized that Ash didn't know about the killing made from the sale of the rainbow valley to a health resort. The sentence passed on her parents was her own. Love had survived her judgment and it would survive his. Her natural buoyancy reasserted itself. She would cook a perfect dhal for Ash—she had practiced on friends and grown confident—and he would agree to spend Christmas with her parents.

Meanwhile, there were to be no secrets between them, so the next time she saw Ash, Cassie told him about the embarrassing fortune that would one day be hers. "Of course, I would have preferred Mum and Dad not to sell. But they believed they were doing the right thing by me. They don't care about money for themselves." Ash received this in silence. He had never met anyone who didn't care about money—even the most unworldly found it useful for paying the rent. On the other hand, there was nothing to say that the parents were not as naïve as the daughter. Ash had seen Cassie's face when champagne fizzed in her glass or the first frangipani flowers appeared: it denied the existence of evil, the possibility of despair. Ash was conscious of a secret wish, so shameful he could hardly examine it even in private: that something would happen to wipe that expression from Cassie's face for all time.

Cassie told the Ashfield Tamil, "I'm planning a special meal." It was Friday morning. The Spice Mart should have opened at ten but was still shut when Cassie got off the train at half-past. She wandered up to Liverpool Road and went into a restaurant where she drank green tea. The restaurant had a smell Cassie remembered and disliked from a stopover in Hong Kong: it made her think of noodles cooked in dirty water. Stiff red ducks were strung across the window. She left after fifteen endless minutes, thinking, If he's not there now, I'm going to the Indians.

The Ashfield Tamil switched on a light that was dimmer than the glowing day. He told Cassie that his journey to work involved a bus and two changes of train. The second train had stopped for forty-two minutes between stations—a rumor ran through the carriage of a body on the track. "What to do?" he concluded. He asked Cassie how long she had been waiting. Before she could answer, a couple laden with shopping came in, the woman in a blue sari. A conversation began in what Cassie supposed was Tamil: a language as rounded and floaty as bubbles. The Ashfield Tamil tapped his chrome-plated watch. Cassie had a vision of him behind a desk, reprimanding a clerk who had spent too long at lunch. The clerk looked down and shuffled his sandals. The postmaster's mouth was a thin, violet line that said, "Forty-two minutes." His aura stood out clearly: its lemony hue announced that he was struggling to maintain control of the situation. The couple left without buying anything, and the Ashfield Tamil told Cassie, "They couldn't wait. They went to the Indians."

"They came here to tell you that?"

"They come every week," he said, as if that explained anything.

Cassie was after fresh green chilies, pandan leaves, and raw cashew nuts. She also wanted palm sugar and cardamom pods. She trailed after the shopkeeper as he located these items for her, one by one. When he reached up to a shelf for the sugar, his sleeve slipped down, exposing the white tufts on his wrist. Cassie was still annoyed about the delay, and the sight increased her irritation—that narrow, womanish wrist looked like a bid for sympathy. The Indians' prices were cheaper, she reminded herself.

The Ashfield Tamil stooped and retrieved a small packet that seemed to have slipped between shelves. "*Muthu samba* rice," he said.

"I've still got heaps of basmati, thanks."

"This is Sri Lankan rice. Very special."

She inspected the white grains. The plastic packaging was slightly greasy to the touch, and some of the lettering had worn off.

"The last packet," he said. "For your husband."

"He's my partner, actually."

"What to do?"

On Saturday evening, there was a storm. When Ash was climbing Cockroach Mansions, the first plump drops arrived; he held out his palm to receive them. The whole of Glebe was gardenia-scented. Cassie appeared in the doorway, her toenails painted silver. She had darkened her eyelashes as well, and looked starey and judgmental. Ash said, "Warm rain!" and kissed her—how he adored this weather!

The lease drawn up by the Romanians forbade their tenants to remove so much as a dead twig from the garden, but Cassie had risen before dawn to steal gardenias from the laden shrubs. They gleamed in tumblers on the table, along the windowsill. Amazingly, the table, set for two, held only flowers, candles, and a bowl of pistachios. Cassie poured water from a jug, made of milky green glass and hand-painted with pink roses, in which ice cubes tapped.

Ash opened the wine he had brought. They clinked glasses as the room darkened and the wind grew huge. Cassie moved along the louvers, closing them as lightning began its epileptic jig. Thunder and the racket of rain on corrugated iron made conversation difficult. Standing at the window, Cassie and Ash drank wine and ate pistachios. Lightning produced one weirdly lit, arty still after another: the tinsel roof of the shed, the tattered banners of a banana palm. The gale was blowing the rain sideways and breaking it up into millions of tiny droplets, so that a horizontal stream, furious yet fine as mist, flowed past the tops of trees. Ash slipped an encircling arm around Cassie. Part of her face and the candle flames were reflected in the glass—they looked like pieces of heaven. Farther along, a branch was hitting against a pane. The scent of gardenias neither increased nor faded but merely drenched.

Cassie raised her voice over the din: "Anyone could be out there, watching."

Ash said that he thought it unlikely.

"If I left you," shouted Cassie, "would you stand in the rain without an umbrella hoping to see me?"

"Are you saying your old boyfriend is out there?" Ash tried to remember what Cassie had told him about her previous partner; surely she had painted a picture of a smart-arse who laughed at his own jokes, rather than the portrait of a lunatic?

"It was a hypothetical question." She wanted to say: I would like to believe you were capable of it, that's all.

Ash gestured at the apocalypse. "Darling Cassie—it would be suicidal."

She said, "It's OK, I know you wouldn't do it."

It was the moment of bafflement that arrived in all Ash's dealings with women: a crystal filled up with smoke. He moved away from the windows as lightning returned to produce more shivery photographs. Now it was difficult not to imagine how the room would appear to someone looking in. The Ashfield Tamil was outside in the downpour, peering up at a beautiful girl who questioned him about his life as if it mattered—Ash was sure of it, for thirty seconds.

Cassie asked him—cheerfully, as if their last exchange hadn't taken place—if he was ready to eat. Left alone, Ash refilled their glasses and gulped the contents of his. Cassie reappeared with a tray of dishes, went away, and returned with more. She said, "Everything's still warm but won't be for much longer. Start helping yourself while I get the rice."

Ash set out all the dishes and placed the tray against a wall. He surveyed the banquet, wondering why, from time to time, Cassie lavished so much labor on a meal. Then his mind slid to a period during his own graduate student days in New England when he had smoked spliff after spliff while watching a videoed television drama set in a legal practice in Amsterdam. When the last tape ended, Ash watched the whole series again and then a third time. He was particularly taken with an episode in which one of the barristers defended a man accused of having sexual congress with a hen. The lawyer argued successfully that his client loved the bird, was gentle with it, and that no cruelty had occurred. Why should a man not desire a fowl? That struck Ash as both tender and profound. Weeks passed pleasantly. In the dead of night, he would wake in terror: the mountain of undone work weighed on his chest and it was difficult to breathe. But the next day, nothing was as pressing as the next episode and the next spliff. He concluded that Cassie's cooking was another kind of displacement scheme elaborated to avoid working on her thesis. For much the same reason, she had recently attended a two-day St. John's Ambulance first-aid course. She had said, "I might be able to save a life." Ash, who knew that there was more to saving a life than preventing someone from choking on a fishbone, could have predicted Cassie's fantasy. It was the kind of dream girls with clear, remote eyes could offer themselves because nothing ever happened to test it.

Cassie returned with a two-handled pan that she stood on a cork mat. She said, "It's special *muthu samba* rice from Sri Lanka," and lifted the lid. A stench that had been born in a sewer rose like a fog. Vanquished, the gardenias retreated. Ash had the presence of mind to hold a napkin to his nose. Cassie, a stricken statue, remained there clutching the lid. "It's special," she repeated. "From the Ashfield Tamil." Her face wore its blind, uncaring look.

Ash took the lid from Cassie's lifeless fingers and replaced it on the pot. He opened windows. The gale had died down to a stiff breeze. Cold air filled the room, spreading rather than dispatching the reek. One of the candles succumbed to the draft.

"Does *muthu samba* rice always smell like that?" asked Cassie. She sat down—abruptly, as if an invisible intruder had whacked her behind the knees.

"How on earth would I know?" Ash added, "I doubt it."

"Could it have been off? Can rice go off? I thought it just went weevilly." Cassie was turning her rings. She closed her hands so that the jewels dug into her folded fingers.

Ash joined her at the table. They faced each other across a spread of cooling food. The spare chairs looked on like witnesses. Cassie should have made a move: to take the saucepan away, to make a fresh, odorless bowl of rice. She did neither of those things, but after a while began helping herself to curries—she couldn't help it, she was hungry. She scooped food into her mouth with her eyes lowered over her plate. The tepid dhal was particularly delicious. Ash looked on in wonder. His face said, What is wrong with you Australians? You eat curries without rice, a barbarism. You fear being attacked by people you've killed. You stole their land for animals that you slaughter in their millions, when you don't leave them to die by the side of the road. Your shamefaced paddocks— But Ash couldn't go on, because another part of him wanted to uncurl in giggles. The candles and flowers, the stink! A dinner party gone wrong: the first-world definition of tragedy.

Across the table, Cassie's white forehead was as defenseless as a rib. Controlling a smile, Ash looked away. Her books caught his eye: lined up on shelves, stacked on the floor. There were so many books, safe in a room where gardenias flared and the roof held through a storm. He thought soberly, She has no idea how lucky she is. It wasn't an accusation but a recognition: Cassie was alone on her side of the gulf. On the other side, Ash stood shoulder to shoulder with the Ashfield Tamil, lashed by rain, transfixed by an enchanted girl whose notion of loss was a real estate deal that had made her a minor heiress.

Cassie looked up without lifting her head, checking out Ash through her blackened lashes; there was a tiny smear of yellow at the corner of her mouth. Ash knew that he would undress her before the evening ended. He would spend moments savoring the sight of her: the scene loomed plain as pornography, the girl's pearly flesh, the man's clothed, formal limbs. Ideally, she would be wearing a red bead necklace to set off her nakedness—there had been a Spanish girl who liked to do just that. Cassie's hair was falling over her face. Ash scratched his neck. He began to help himself to food, not realizing that he was doing it. He saw the rest of his life: the books that would make his name, the solid comforts. He thought, I will die alone.

In retrospect, Cassie would look on the evening as a watershed, although nothing seemed to change at the time. She went on seeing Ash. It was accepted between them, without discussion, that they would be spending Christmas apart. On Cassie's last evening in Sydney, Ash gave her an expensive French perfume that smelled like a rainy garden. Cassie gave him a copy of Pippa's novel. If Ash received any Christmas invitations, he hadn't accepted them. He said that he intended to spend the next two weeks writing a conference paper undisturbed.

Cassie looked out at the Pacific from her parents' terrace in the north, and tears came into her eyes: she had seen Ash working alone in his tower in the hot, empty city. The old professor's white walls were heartless. All Ash had for consolation was Australian literature. Cassie hunted down her mother's copy of Pippa's novel and skimmed it: ". . . kisses me good night . . . my honest forehead . . . I notice . . . Caesar salad with free-range eggs . . . I answer . . . I am . . . beautiful, glazed organic carrots . . . my father . . . I notice . . . my honest toes . . . I whisper . . . my beautiful brother . . . I see . . . I notice . . . moon rises like sadness . . . my honest . . . organic strawberries with balsamic . . ." Cassie's tears flowed down her arms. What were they really for? Having asked the question, she was frightened of the answer. Her suffering was so intense, it never occurred to her that Ash might not share it. The possibility that he was indifferent to her absence couldn't enter her mind—there was nowhere for it to go.

For the rest of her visit it went on like that: Cassie would be floating on her back, or lying in a hammock with a book, and she would start to cry. The tears dried as suddenly as they started—if anyone tried to talk to Cassie about them, for instance. A cousin with young children came to stay. Cassie's tears dripped onto the baby's bald head. The infant of rare, startling beauty she would have had with Ash appeared to her that night: he was a stout child running away across a yellow field. She checked her phone five or six times an hour. But the day before she returned to Sydney, she lost the phone on a beach. She had been back in the city for about a week when Ash e-mailed to say that he had been texting her. He asked if she would like to have dinner. Cassie discovered that her excessive tears had been preemptive: it was as plain as a plate that she didn't want to see Ash again. She replied to him the next day, saying that she planned to do a lot of work over the summer. She sent him her love.

One evening some months later, Cassie ran into Ash in King Street; she was wearing a velvet dress the color of rubies, so it must have been after the season turned. The scene came back to her long afterward, when years had passed. So much had changed since that encounter with Ash that Cassie could no longer remember what they had said to each other or whether she had gone back to his place for the night—it was quite possible, it was a period of idle buccaneering when she counted off men like someone climbing a ladder and keeping a tally of rungs. Ash had come into her thoughts now, as she was driving away from a medical center, because her car radio was telling her that the Australian government would be returning yet another group of Sri Lankan Tamil refugees to their executioners. Cassie felt profoundly ashamed, but not sad: sadness had been impossible from the moment her doctor confirmed what Cassie already knew. She had texted her husband, but he was in a meeting all morning. She wanted to call her parents, but it didn't seem fair to talk to them first. She was gripped by a longing for the smell of the house in which she had grown up: sandalwood, mildew, bergamot, rooms in which log fires had burned the previous night.

The news gave way to indie pop, and Cassie's mind drifted, as of old, from Ash to the Ashfield Tamil. After the *muthu samba* dinner, she had never returned to the Spice Mart; she bought curries in cardboard boxes at the supermarket now. But presently, arriving at an intersection, she gave in to a whim.

It was a roasting summer day, blue booming overhead. Cassie parked under a tree in a side street, and made her way on foot along Liverpool Road. She passed the Indian shop: a girl still sat at the counter, playing with her phone. Cassie went on, past a Thai massage parlor and a Korean butcher, past restaurants proposing pho. She asked herself what story she could offer the Ashfield Tamil to explain her disappearance. She saw him tapping his watch: "Nine years," he said sternly. She wondered if he would recognize her when she walked in.

The Spice Mart sign remained in place, but the shop behind it was empty. A "For Lease" notice was stuck to the window. Cassie put her hands on either side of her face and peered through the plate glass: a sheet of plastic packaging and a copy of the local newspaper lay on the floor. Without its curtain, the door to the storeroom looked naked. Cassie thought she could detect traces of a geometric pattern on the concrete, but that might have been only dust.

There was a travel agency on one side of the shop, and on the other a stair that led to a kickboxing gym. Cassie went into the travel agency, where a woman was speaking Vietnamese on the phone. The young man at the other desk said that the Spice Mart had closed at the end of December—he didn't know what had become of the owner. His colleague finished her phone call and looked across at Cassie. "I think he's gone to Seven Hills," she said. "Or maybe Blacktown? Somewhere out west. Cheaper rents."

Cassie said, "I used to be his customer. A long time ago."

The woman nodded. There was nothing else to say. The phone on her colleague's desk began to ring. She smiled at Cassie and asked, "When are you due?" Startled, Cassie glanced down at her stomach. The travel agent said, "You're not showing yet. But I can usually tell."

In the street, Cassie realized, I'll never know what became of his middle son. A flower of nausea opened and rose within her without warning. She leaned against a tiled wall until it passed. Her phone rang—it was her husband. Cassie answered the call, thinking, I must tell Ash.

As it happened, a snowstorm over New Jersey brought power outages, and Ash didn't read Cassie's e-mail until late the next day. She wrote: "The kolam kept his business safe all these years." Ash came to the end of her message and smiled: she was still telling him a story about the Ashfield Tamil. Ash and Cassie had kept in touch, e-mailing each other now and then, and there was Facebook, of course. Ash knew that Cassie had given up on Australian literature and now worked as a fund-raiser for a conservation group. He knew that her husband wrote speeches for a politician, and that she had cropped her hair—a mistake, judging from the photos on

Facebook. He wondered if she still collected scraps of grimy writing and whether she had saved anyone's life. He said her name aloud: it conjured the ugly stones on her fingers. He pictured her asleep on her continent of gum trees and flies. Why had she stayed there—why did any of them stay? The calm violence with which Cassie had cut herself free of him still had the power to stupefy Ash. Months afterward, she had come up to him somewhere in one of her bedraggled velvet dresses and flung her arms around his neck. Her eyes were chemical stars. It was plain to Ash that Cassie had always belonged with the Ashfield Tamil on the far side of the gulf: camouflaged, wrenched out of place and thrust into outlandish scenarios, those two would always be identifiably themselves. It had nothing to do with the will or the heart but with a talent for existence. Ash realized that he knew nothing about Cassie that mattered—did she still paint her toenails silver? He opened the folder called "Sydney" on his laptop. He was after a photo of Cassie, but the images were identified only by number. Ash found himself looking at a woman in a stripey T-shirt on the deck of a ferry; her blown hair was a red flag. It took him a minute to recall her name: Leanne. He reread Cassie's e-mail: he was watching his fingers fumble at a lilac-blue loop. He remembered the cold breath of the houses. Cockroach Mansions returned, and an old car bridal with fallen flowers, and an afternoon when time streamed in reverse.

Ash hit Reply. He wrote with no corrections and without a pause.

"In August 1977, when I was nine, my father was working in a town in the North Central province of Sri Lanka. He had accepted a temporary appointment at the hospital there. My mother and I stayed in Colombo, where I came down with measles. When I was out of quarantine, I was sent north to convalesce, away from

Colombo's noise and pollution; my mother was to join me in a week or so. My father met me at the station, and we caught a taxi to his house, which was not far from the hospital. As the car passed the hospital compound, I noticed a boy who sat on a patch of grass just outside the gate, selling lottery tickets nailed to a stick. He was wearing only a pair of shorts, and I saw that his legs were twisted below the knee.

"The town, which had once been the capital of Sri Lanka, was famous for its ancient monuments. My father took me to see them at the first opportunity: colossal temples and palaces, and stone reservoirs of green water that were the remains of an ingenious system of irrigation. I grew bored pretty soon. The old city is spread out, and the day was overcast and moist. Despite the deep shade cast by the giant trees that stand along the roads and among the ruins, I felt thirsty and hot. Unused to having sole responsibility for me, my father had neglected to pack the thermos of iced, filtered water that accompanied my mother on our outings. I refused to drink king-coconut water, and there was no question of my consuming one of the unhygienic, violently colored sherbets sold in the street. My father gave in to my whining and we turned back. I could tell he was disappointed by my lack of enthusiasm for the history that lay around us, but all he said was that I was right not to overdo things while I was still convalescing.

"I was happier in my father's cool bungalow. In those days there was no TV in Sri Lanka, and I would spend the morning reading in a planter's chair with a tall glass of sugared lime juice at hand. I'd brought my favorite comics with me, and they were supplemented by an old storybook I found in the bungalow, a tale of derring-do called *The Captain's Revenge*. I've forgotten most of it, but I know that the Captain was slim and plucky and always carried a dagger—sometimes between his teeth. When I grew tired of reading, I would go in search of the cook. He had a really majestic silver mustache, and he told me a ghost story about a water carrier who appeared at dusk and made his way with his cart to a spot near an outbuilding where a well had once stood. There was also a tale about a white dog that brought misfortune to whoever saw it. My parents were rationalists, and my father would certainly have put an end to the cook's stories if they had come to his notice. But he would no doubt have been pleased to learn that the ruins we had visited together had made quite an impression on me. Although we'd spent no more than an hour among them, they had begun to invade my dreams. Night after night brought stupendous domes, flights of steps, tall stone figures, ancient trees whose massive branches formed archways through which I had to pass. That sounds alarming. In fact, I would wake from those dreams, in which I wandered among the ruins on grassy paths, filled with a tremendous sense of well-being.

"One morning, lolling about in my chair, I became aware of a commotion in the street. I went outside and down to the gate and looked down the street. People and vehicles were rushing through the junction with the main road. There was an odd smell—then I saw smoke rising from the direction of the shops. The cook appeared on the veranda and called me inside. He said there was 'trouble with Tamil people.' The phone started to ring, and I ran past the cook to answer it, sure that it would be my mother, who put a trunk call through to us every day. It was my father. He told me that there had been 'an incident at the station.' An 'incident': I was struck by the word, at once portentous and vague. My father said there was nothing to be concerned about, and that I was to stay indoors and do as the cook said. Then he asked to speak to the cook.

"My father didn't come home for lunch that day. I pestered the cook for information, and at last he told me that when the Jaffna train pulled into the station that morning, a mob had boarded it and assaulted the Tamil passengers. The violence spread and escalated, and soon Tamil shops were being looted and Tamils attacked in their homes. Casualties were still streaming into the hospital, and my father expected to be there all day. The cook related these facts dispassionately and assured me that, being Sinhalese, we had nothing to fear.

"'Why do people want to kill Tamils?' I asked. 'What have they done?'

"The cook considered this, smoothing his mustache. Eventually, 'They are not like us,' he said, and went away.

"I felt intense excitement as I ate my rice and curries in solitary splendor in the dining room. The events unfolding outside had the unreality and glamour of the books I read. They would bring the test of courage I had always longed for—the Captain and Batman collaborated in the scenarios my imagination supplied. At the head of a daredevil band, I issued brutal orders: 'Spare no one!' 'Holy smoke—stand back, you dogs!'

"In fact, time dragged, heavy and slow. I must have taken the siesta that had become routine when I was ill. The smell of smoke intensified as the day wore on. My sense of eager anticipation had vanished, and I felt aggrieved by my father's prolonged absence. Self-pity, which lies close under the surface in children, took over. My mother's failure to call exacerbated my sense of neglect. When I complained to the cook, he lifted the receiver and held it out to me: there was only silence, and I understood that the line was down. This often happened in Sri Lanka, so it seemed unimportant and increased my sense of injustice: my mother should have found a way around the problem. It was an endless day, characterized by grievances and tedium.

"That night, I was woken by a bustle. There were voices: a

woman's, a strange man's. My father came into my room. When he saw that I was awake, he sat on my bed. 'One of my colleagues and her husband have come to stay for a few days,' he said.

"'Why?' I asked.

"'Their house was set on fire.' He took off his glasses and rubbed his eyes. They were red with exhaustion. He said, 'A lot of the medical staff, Sinhalese and Tamil, left in a rush. But Dr. Rajanathan is very brave. She insisted on staying and helping me. We've kept a skeleton service going.'

"I laughed. I saw bony figures bending over patients, tending their injuries. My father smiled. He told me that early the next day, I was to take the train to Colombo in the care of one of his Sinhalese clerical assistants. He touched my hand briefly and said, 'Go to sleep now, son.'

"It was a time in my life when I was fascinated by the idea of *character.* I would scrutinize people I had heard described as 'thoughtless' or 'stubborn' or 'generous,' trying to discover those traits in their faces. I woke early the next day, eager to study brave Dr. Rajanathan, but she had already returned to the hospital. Her husband must have joined us for breakfast—I can't remember him at all.

"On the way to the station, our taxi passed a truck full of soldiers traveling slowly toward the center of town: the army had been called out. I saw roofless buildings and others that were only charred remains. Broken glass twinkled beside the road. Very few people were about. Even the boy with the twisted legs had deserted his post at the hospital gate. I pointed this out to my father, who looked half-asleep. He was unshaven and smelled stale. At the station, where we were met by the same profound quiet that hung over the town, there was no difficulty buying tickets. When our train pulled in it was almost empty; no Tamils were traveling that day. My father stepped forward to hand me up into the carriage, and I noticed then that his gait was lopsided. I remarked on his limp, and he shrugged, saying, 'Someone threw half a brick at me.' He shook my hand and wished me a pleasant trip.

"The clerk and I had a first-class compartment to ourselves. He was a pudgy young man with an unctuous manner and a jiggling knee. I had disliked him as soon as he came forward to greet us at the station. When our train set off, he asked me an inoffensive question or two. I answered briefly and coldly, buried myself in my book, and ignored him. Later, lulled by the movement of the train, I dozed off. When I woke, he was gone. He returned after a long interval and I said, peevishly: 'Where were you? You're supposed to look after me.' He said that he had been talking to a friend who was traveling third class—he had exchanged his own ticket for one paid for by my father—and assured me that I was perfectly safe. 'You can't be sure of that,' I said. 'There's been a riot. At any minute, I could find myself beset by grave danger.' It was the language of my storybooks, but as I spoke, I found myself swept up in its drama. My mind's eye showed me a solitary hero making a last, gallant stand against an advancing horde. My self-pity brimmed over, and I said, 'I'll tell my father that you left me alone.'

"The fellow's ingratiating mask vanished at once. Years later, when I encountered the term 'class hatred,' I saw that naked face. It wasn't looking at me but at a child with a Batman T-shirt, a leather traveling case, and French sandals. The clerk leaned forward and hissed, 'Nothing will happen to you. Nothing happens to people like you.' The change in him frightened me, and he saw it. He settled back into his seat and, jiggling his knee furiously, told me that a group of about fifty Tamil workers—technicians and clerks, but also gardeners and cleaners—had asked permission to stay overnight in the hospital. Their homes were far away and they were too terrified to venture into the street. The medical superintendent installed them in two rooms on the upper floor of a laboratory that stood near the main hospital building. The lab was locked. But in the night, men armed with iron rods broke down the door and swarmed up the stairs.

"I interrupted: 'Why didn't the police stop them?'

"'The police,' repeated my escort. 'Let me think: did we see the police at all yesterday? You know, I don't think so. It must have been a police holiday.' From his tone, I could tell that his words were as deceptive as a conjurer's silk handkerchief: they seemed ordinary but concealed something startling. I shrank back against my seat, not knowing if I feared a dove or a fist in my face.

"The clerk went on, telling me that most of the people inside the lab escaped by jumping from the windows. A few remained trapped and were bludgeoned to death. He said, 'There was a boy your age who was inside.'

"He stared at me. I saw that he wanted me to ask what had happened to the boy, and I was too afraid of him to resist. I remember that it was difficult to form the words because my lips, my mouth, and my throat were all painfully dry.

"'What do you think happened? He was a cripple. He couldn't jump.' He looked fuller in the face after he said it. More satisfied.

"A week or so later, my father returned to Colombo. We were all back in London by the end of the year."

Ash paused. A few feathers of snow were wafting past his window. He had been about to write, "I've never forgotten that boy." But that wasn't true. The boy was a silhouette at the end of a long, shadowy avenue into which Ash's thoughts seldom strayed. He was in danger of falling into Cassie's error of arranging random facts to make a story. Ash quit his e-mail program without saving the message. The true, lasting bequest of those days in 1977 was not a faceless Tamil child but a sweet, recurrent dream. In it, Ash wandered in innocent perpetuity along grassy paths among magnificent ruins. They were emblems of a past that had no claim on him but was merely available to be studied or ignored. The trees that grew beside the monuments had leaves so large and solid they seemed to have been cut from metal. Ash could see the flat, green surface of the water in the reservoir. He could see the blackish lichen at the base of the stones. Once he had tried to tell Cassie about that dream. He had said something like, "It will explain who I am. It will show you how you might save my life." She had received his revelation in silence—an intimation of the cold-blooded way she would end their affair.

When Ash stretched, his T-shirt rode up to show the brown rise of his belly. On the other side of the world, soldiers were dying in the desert so that people like Ash could stroll about in T-shirts while snow fell outside. These days, when Ash thought of Australia it seemed to belong less to his past than to a time to come, luminous and open-ended. He heard his wife moving about downstairs. In the end, things hadn't worked out with the Iranian-Canadian anthropologist; when you're still finding your way around, you make mistakes. Ash had gone on to marry his head of department. Recently, his wife had taken up the directorship of a research center at Princeton; Ash remained at Rutgers. If he saw a familiar pattern forming, he refused to be disturbed. He left his study and went out onto the landing, where the clean lines in the modern painting that hung there had turned blurry and impressionistic—Ash realized that he was still wearing his reading glasses. He took them off and leaned over the banister, sniffing appreciatively: there would be curry tonight.

III

THE MUSEUM OF ROMANTIC LIFE

THE EXHIBITION OF PAINTINGS AT the Australian Embassy was opened by Professor Wilkes, a stately Aboriginal man. A specialist in international law, he was in Paris to give an address at UNESCO. The embassy, the work of a famous architect, was on a monumental scale. It was rumored that the architect had sought to shrink the French down to size. The echoing corridors that could have passed as tunnels, the reception rooms vast as stations, provided a heroic frame for long-boned Australians while turning the local service staff into beetles.

Introducing Professor Wilkes, Valerie, the cultural attaché, said, "We couldn't get Robert or Germaine or Clive, but luckily Brendon was available." Valerie had the carrying voice and clear, brilliant complexion of someone who lives on an alp. When she first took up her Paris posting, she had lived in the same apartment building as Céleste. The two women got talking at the letterboxes one day; on learning that Céleste had grown up in Australia, Valerie invited her to dinner. Céleste accepted the invitation and controlled herself when informed that the great thing about France was that social class simply didn't exist here—such a change from London, where Valerie had suffered as a girl. Even after Valerie moved to the Sixteenth Arrondissement, where one wasn't subject to constant harassment by the homeless, invitations to ambassadorial cocktails continued to arrive. Céleste met Australian sculptors and language poets and conceptual artists and novelists. They lived at the Cité Internationale des Arts, where they had been awarded residencies by the Australian government. On learning that Céleste was a translator, the writers grew attentive. They would give her their books, expressing the hope that she might translate them into French. Céleste always made it clear that she worked from French to English and not the other way around. That meant nothing to monolingual Australians—at most, it signaled a reluctance that could surely be overcome. The writers invited Céleste to lunch and told her about their trials. No one in Paris had heard of them. They had gone swimming in the pool at Les Halles; the chlorine levels compared unfavorably with Australian pools. Waiters pretended not to speak English—either that, or they made idiotic remarks about kangaroos. Céleste saw that wounds had been inflicted. Setting out from home, the Australians, like fortunate children, had expected to be loved.

Céleste met Pippa at the exhibition opened by Professor Wilkes. The first thing Pippa said was, "Didn't you just die when Valerie came out with that stuff? I felt so ashamed. That poor man, having to stand there and listen to it. I went straight over afterward and told him I loved his speech. He was just so dignified and lovely." Pippa was wearing coral lipstick, a green dress with a stiff, ruffled skirt like a lampshade, and awful shoes. Her head was too small for the massive skirt—she looked like a broomstick at a ball. When it was time to leave, she placed a red beret at a careful angle on her cropped hair. Effort so far in excess of achievement couldn't fail to move. When Pippa looked around at the sound of her name, her skirt seemed to turn more slowly than her hips. Her big teeth, contrasting with her neat little features, would always surprise when she smiled. She agreed readily to meet for a drink near Céleste's apartment in the Ninth.

The spring had been cold, but the appointed evening was breezeless and mild. The homeless man who lived in the tiny triangular square at the end of Céleste's street was singing on his bench. As she walked past, he lowered himself onto the bench and continued to sing. Once he had lived in the telephone box at the apex of the triangle, but it had been removed some years earlier; now it was easier for the street cleaners to hose away the cigarette butts and rotting food scraps that collected around him. He disappeared every year in the depths of winter but returned, with the swallows and the pushy leaves, in early spring.

His song and his smell followed Céleste in gusts. Then came a street that led her past trays of syrupy pastries, and mounds of green and pink marzipan-stuffed dates. Céleste was unmoved by sugar, so the Tunisian cakes held no appeal. But she always paused before the window of the couscous restaurant next door. Here, a diorama in a fish tank presented dunes of pale and red sand, two camels made of polished stone, and a miniature cactus. From the top of the highest dune, a key rose like a standard—a small, old-fashioned key, made of brass, with an oval head. Within the oval, two arabesques formed a sideways figure of eight. It was this key, out of place yet weirdly fitting, that fascinated Céleste. What had it once unlocked? It was easy to believe that it had a message for her—like all charged objects, it didn't belong to the realm of reason but to the empire of mythology and dream.

At the café, the pavement tables had been liberated from the glass box that shielded them from the cold. Céleste sat down at a table that had just become free. The onset of winter was a drawn-out descent into a well, but there was no mistaking the beginning of spring—that was as decisive as the first note at a concert. For the first time in six months, Céleste was wearing shoes instead of boots. The shoes were Fluevogs from eBay, plum and pink with hourglass heels. On her way to the café, Céleste saw men notice her legs and women her shoes. She was wearing them with a boxy blue suit she had found in a flea market when she first returned to live in Paris. The skirt had been a little loose in the waist then; now, thirty years later, it was a little tight.

The waiter, an old ally, rapped on her table with his knuckle and said, "A glass of red?" It was starting to get dark. Lights showed in the apartments across the street, but windows remained open, their curtains hanging down straight. Small children ran about the playground in the square opposite the café; women talked to each other, and admired or scolded the children. That morning, Céleste's diary had informed her that it was Shakespeare's birthday; now she noticed that the chestnut trees in the square were marking the occasion with hundreds of pink candles. The diary, which noted the birthdays of famous British writers and had a picture of the Bard on its cover, was a present from Sabine, who had spent a week in London at Christmas. Céleste could picture her in the museum shop, her cheeks rosier than ever from the damp English cold, carefully choosing a "cultural" gift—hesitating between, say, the diary and a box of William Morris note cards. The diary had probably been marked down in a post-Christmas sale—Sabine had the French respect for money. Afterward, in the street, how wonderful she would have looked in her honey-colored coat. The hair between her legs was the same opulent golden brown. On Facebook, photos showed her going about London in hideous boots with buckles and high, tapering heels. Under the lovely coat, she wore a synthetic blue sweater with bobbles, picked out by Bernard, that the children had been obliged to give their mother for Christmas. Bernard himself always presented Sabine with the latest celebrity perfume from his pharmacy. This year's scent suggested chrysanthemums that had stood too long in graveyards before drying down to sugarcoated mothballs.

The city was full of Easter tourists, but everyone going past had an ironic French face. At the lights, a woman as narrow as a boy was waiting to cross; on the left side of her chest a rectangle glowed. She had almost reached the café before Céleste identified Pippa, imposterish without beret and lampshade dress, her iPod shining through her pocket. At the time, it was merely something else unexpected, an element of the mildly extraordinary evening. But long after the open windows and the tiny running children had vanished, that memory of Pippa would persist. She made her way toward Céleste like a citizen of the future, her heart rectangular and glowing in the dusk.

At the embassy parties, Valerie would introduce Céleste as a translator, but no one made a living translating novels—not the kind that came Céleste's way, at any rate. For twenty-five hours a week, a language school employed her to teach English to its corporate clients. On Fridays and weekends and in the evening, she translated books for a small New York press that published obscure European fiction, novels devoid of spirited heroines, novels that offered no clear message nor any flashing sign as to how they were to be understood, novels whose authors were neither photogenic nor young—sometimes they were even Swiss.

Céleste took a fortnight's holiday every Christmas, staying in cheap hotels. At the mention of Prague, Florence, Lisbon, she saw a curtain of fog. In August, when the language school closed, she stayed in Paris and went on with translation. One summer, about eighteen months before Céleste and Pippa met, friends had asked Céleste to feed their cat while they were away. Every evening, she rode her bike to their apartment behind the Cirque d'Hiver. The light was deep blue and close-woven; whole rows of buildings looked as if they had been cut out with care and glued against the sky. A siren sounded somewhere close at hand. *La police, pleine de malice,* said Céleste to herself.

Waiting at a traffic light, Céleste watched two English girls with pink arms and necks greet each other outside a bar.

The tall one said, "I love your new monkey tattoo."

"It's an owl, actually."

"I always get those two mixed up."

They laughed together, their breasts spluttering happily under their T-shirts in the blue air.

Beatriz and Erica were due back late on the first day of September. Céleste called at their apartment that afternoon. The cat, outraged by this break with routine, refused to talk to her. Céleste changed the litter in his tray, and arranged the grapes she had brought in a bowl. She opened the windows in the bedroom and looked inside the wardrobe. Erica was the same size as Céleste and tired quickly of her clothes. Céleste had her eye on a cucumber-green shirt with buttons made of glass. All winter, she had worn a quilted coat assembled from scraps of Rajasthani textiles—on Erica it had looked like a bedspread. The first time Céleste wore it, she was photographed for *The Sartorialist.*

Céleste was riding back when a lanky redhead emerged from the florist's at the angle with the boulevard: it was the English girl who couldn't tell a monkey from an owl. She was smiling to herself above an armful of purple flowers; she tossed them into an illegally parked car and drove away. The florist had followed her out and was doing something to a bay tree in a tub. When she straightened up, Céleste saw a figure from a painting: heavy gold fringe, wide blue eyes, flesh like solid cream.

"*Bonjour*," said the Renoir girl. She wore a dark apron over a striped blouse. "*Vous désirez quelque-chose?*" Polished little teeth showed in her pink mouth.

Beatriz rang to thank Céleste. "Such beautiful flowers! I adore lisianthus."

"From your neighborhood florist."

"That one! Sabine."

The year Céleste got to know Pippa was also the year her half brother, Dominic, visited Paris with his wife and sons. On the last day of their stay, the Harrisons came to Céleste's studio apartment for lunch. They arrived late. Wendy followed Céleste into the kitchen to explain: it was difficult to persuade her younger son to leave his laptop and his hotel room. "He's been following the Arab Spring. He has all these screens open, watching the protests on different channels, including Al Jazeera. He doesn't say much, but he's a very engaged boy, really."

As she spoke, Wendy was stacking the dishes and pans that Céleste had used in preparing lunch. Holding up a bouquet of dirty spoons, "Where's the dishwasher?" she asked. Céleste said that she didn't have one. "Holy moly!" said Wendy. "Don't tell me you've been washing dishes for thirty years?" She had a halo of bright bronze curls around an oval face. Her emphatic shoulders belonged to a Renaissance angel—the avenging kind with breastplate and sword.

Over apéritifs, the older boy looked around and said, "Why don't you have a TV?"

"I do," said Céleste. "It's right there."

His eyes followed her pointing finger. "Oh, that!" he said. "I thought it was a computer." Neither he nor his brother ate fruit or any vegetable other than potato. They couldn't be left alone together because they hit each other—in Perth, the older one had fractured his elbow when his brother pushed him down some stairs. They were seventeen and fifteen but might as well have been seven and five.

In anticipation of her visitors, Céleste had tidied her room, with its long windows, removing papers and dictionaries from the table and stacking them behind a chair. Sabine's latest flowers, green hellebores and lavender tulips, stood beside the sofa that converted to a bed. Céleste set up folding chairs and laid a stiff damask cloth on the table. The china had been picked up in markets and junk shops—nothing matched, but everything pleased her. She wiped a glass and held it up to the light. It had rained all week, but the day was shiny and cool—perfect for the meal Céleste had planned, *gratin dauphinois* and chicken in a wine sauce. For dessert, she had splurged on the Charlotte Russe that was the local pâtisserie's pride. The sun shone on the jasmine she was nurturing on her balcony, it shone on her pretty table. She had felt buoyant and lucky, grateful to life. Now she saw the room through Harrison eyes. A May '68 poster and a print of Velázquez's *Aesop* were taped to a wall—they belonged in a student's room. The sunlight, brilliant and lethal, showed that the walls themselves hadn't been touched in years. The ceiling, once white, had turned the color of old teeth. Some of the plates had indelible brown stains, and the cloth didn't reach to the ends of the table. Tall Wendy and her rangy sons sat in a row on the sofa, inspecting everything with their knees around their chins. Their house in Perth had a parents' retreat, spas in two of the four bathrooms, a swimming pool, and a guest suite. Wendy was a geologist and Dominic was a mining engineer and there was a minerals boom in Western Australia. Wendy was holding out her iPhone so that Céleste could look at photos of the Harrisons' trip. Every famous monument—Hagia Sophia, the Trevi Fountain, the Duomo—had a geo pick in the foreground. She always included one, explained Wendy, to give an idea of scale.

Céleste poured out wine. Wendy said, "Oh, that's so French, the way you turn your wrist when you've finished pouring." She held up her hand and twisted it, saying, "Did you see that, Dom?"

"It stops the wine dripping down the bottle."

"It's so *French*."

Dominic was dark like their mother, like Céleste. Their mother had died when Céleste was thirteen and Dominic was eight. He had been a shy, affectionate child to whom Céleste fed Milo straight from the can. Sometimes she tortured him, singing, "*Dominique-nique-nique . . .*" while slitting her eyes until his chin shook. He had a present for her now. "It's the new Ottolenghi cookbook. We were worried you might already have it but we decided to take the risk." Céleste examined the beautiful book, the sumptuous photographs. She was wearing her mother's cornelian necklace. She tugged it—a bad habit. Dominic laid his hand on the book, saying, "These are really amazing, these chard cakes with sorrel sauce." When had his fingers grown so fat? A photograph that existed only in Céleste's mind preserved the shapely hand of a small boy stroking a kitten. Dominic went on, "We love this quinoa-and-broad-bean salad—and this one, barley and pomegranate seeds. We lived on this food during the heat waves, didn't we, Wen?"

"Dom's a brilliant cook," said Wendy. "We think he should go on *MasterChef*. Right, guys?"

Her younger son said, I am so weary of these embarrassing retards who pass themselves off as my relatives. He did this by first closing and then opening his eyes with exaggerated slowness. He had Wendy's hectic color, her brazen curls. Pinned to the sofa between his mother and his brother, he looked imprisoned and wild.

Céleste excused herself, saying she had to see to lunch. The younger boy set his elbows on his knees and his face in his hands.

The kitchen had no door—it was scarcely bigger than a larder—but was out of sight of the sofa. Céleste turned on the tap and ran cold water over her wrists. Her life, which she thought of as improvised, anticonsumerist, modestly dedicated to art, now seemed as inadequate as her TV. The meal, chosen to appeal to her nephews, was revealed as heavy and unimaginative. Céleste could rarely afford to eat in restaurants, but when she did the menu offered terrines, roast meats, grilled fish, *canard au sang*—familiar, reassuring dishes. What was quinoa? When had they started eating pomegranates in Perth? Thirty years earlier, aged twenty-two, Céleste had fled barbecued chops and an abomination called salad cream. She had fled the AMP building, the hot, flat streets, the catastrophic light. Roy, her stepfather, had driven her to the airport, with Dominic silent in the back of the car. Not long before that, her brother had started to take an interest in clothes. For the trip to the airport—still, at the start of the 1980s, a ceremonial journey—he was wearing a secondhand rodeo shirt. Céleste couldn't stand the sight of him. She stared out the window. The arthritic eucalypts were an incentive and a reproach. At the airport, she went around to the back of the car to collect her pack, but her brother had got there first. Light struck his eyeballs, the silver points on his collar, his red lips.

Her older nephew came and filled the kitchen doorway. He said tonelessly, "Mum says do you need a hand." A dish of succulent white asparagus stood in the deep porcelain sink. At the last minute, Céleste hadn't been able to resist them. The greengrocer had murmured, "The first of the season"—foreigners, all sentimentalists, would pay exorbitantly for a worn-out tag. Céleste, aware of manipulation, nevertheless pictured herself producing Paris in the spring for Wendy and Dom. Now she feared that the sight of asparagus would ruin the meal to come for her nephew: how repulsive the spears looked, mauve-tinged, like severed fingers. She had just checked the potatoes and was still wearing orange silicon oven mitts. "Quack!" said Céleste, opening and shutting her hands like orange beaks to distract attention from the sink. "Quack, quack!" Even as she spoke she was overcome by shame—why was she behaving like a dim infant teacher?

The boy's face came alive. "Cool!" he said. "Mum! Look at these." He was as dark as his father, his skin the velvety brown achieved by lucky Australian teenagers. His name was Mitch. His brother was called Barr. Modern names, names like bullets, thought Céleste. The story of her own name, told and retold to her in childhood, had the status of myth. Her parents, both Communists, had come to Paris from grim towns in the north of France. Their families had disowned them or were scattered. At the first Party meeting Céleste's mother attended in Paris, a young man, stuttering with nerves, questioned the Soviet invasion of Hungary—he was expelled at once. Yvette stood up and followed the traitor out of the room. She had never given any thought to Soviet foreign policy but couldn't stomach bullying. But three years later when she learned that she was pregnant, she wanted to call the baby Karl—her ideals hadn't faltered, only the Party's. A daughter would be Rosa. Here Lucien, her husband, demurred. He worked at a car factory and had left school at fourteen, but he was a reader. It had begun with *L'Humanité* and was going on with Proust. Swann, the duchess, the band of girls at Balbec, *la petite phrase de Vinteuil* mingled with the international proletariat and dialectical reasoning in a misty, vital realm. Why not call a girl Albertine or Gilberte? Yvette was a reader, too, but preferred facts. To be named after a fictional character struck her as a flimsy start to life. She offered a compromise: they could call a daughter Marcelle, after the great novelist. Lucien vetoed the suggestion—it was his detested mother's name. The argument ran on, not very seriously, for each was sure that the child would be a boy. When she wasn't, her father remembered that Proust had had a servant called Céleste.

From her apartment, Céleste could hear the bells of Notre-Dame-de-Lorette. In the nineteenth century, rich men had installed their mistresses, known as *lorettes*, in luxurious quarters in the surrounding streets. Now their apartments were occupied by the families of lawyers. Céleste thought of the *lorettes* every Tuesday afternoon, hurrying home from teaching to wait for Sabine. They had two hours together: five to seven, *le cinq à sept*, the time slot consecrated to French adultery. Since pundits of the right and left alike were given to thundering that the permafrost of EU regulations and the quicksand of American political correctness had conspired to destroy every cherished French tradition, Céleste had consigned *le cinq à sept* to that lost golden age when it had been possible to blow smoke in the faces of one's fellow diners or rape a cleaning woman without risking reprisals. Sabine assured her that this was far from the case. "It is happening every day. That I can tell you without error. In my work I sell love, you know." When a man entering her shop felt compelled to announce that he was buying flowers for his wife, it was always a lie. On St. Valentine's Day, it was customary for a man to buy two bouquets, explaining that they were for his wife and his mother. "The more expensive one is always for the mistress."

Bernard believed that his wife was at English lessons on Tuesdays. "He likes the idea, he is a snob." It was the kind of cheerful, disparaging remark Sabine made about her husband, saying, "He has no sense of direction" or "He doesn't know the first thing about managing children." At first, Céleste had been somewhat shocked by Sabine's criticism of her husband—quite pleased, too, of course. Later she realized that it was simply the offhand way Sabine spoke about everyone. Her assistant in the flower shop had gone up to a size 42 and she was only nineteen: "She is practically *obèse*." In principle, French was banned from *le cinq à sept*, so that Sabine's English really might improve. "Figure yourself," said Sabine. "Bernard imagines he will start to write songs. He had a band at school. His friends are telling him they could not see a future for him. Now he say he has wrong to listen. He is dreaming!"

Bernard was a pharmacist in the pleasant, lifeless suburb where he had always lived. His father had been the doctor there. Now that his father was dead, Bernard and his family lived with his mother in the doctor's house. Sabine said, "When my daughters will be grown up, I will change my life." Her stubby lashes trembled a little, as Céleste unhooked her bra. Sabine's dark nipples were wild strawberries. All her colors were intense, her hair metallic gold, her lips rosy, her eyes as blue as ink. She lay and shone in Céleste's bed. The only lackluster thing about her was her ring—Bernard's dull little diamond. Sabine's daughters, five and eight years old when Céleste first met her, were now seven and ten. They were called Madison and Jennifer, which Céleste thought peculiar. What was wrong with Albertine and Gilberte? How old were French children when they left home? Bernard the snob, the dreamer, had never left home. On Facebook, he had an intrepid French nose. He didn't look like a failed songwriter but a curly-headed circus poodle, one that knew it was charming and expected applause.

•

Céleste's inheritance, a direct transmission from provincial Sundays spent with *L'Humanité*, was a disdain for guest suites and swimming pools. A recent headline had declared Australia the richest country in the world—Céleste considered it a shameful distinction. The way she lived—in a rented room, wearing castoffs, getting a ride with a neighbor once a month to shop for groceries at a suburban hypermart—enabled her to do work she valued in a city she loved. But now came the thought, Is this all there is? The thought wasn't new, but after the Harrisons' visit it tripped Céleste up more often. That summer, she always felt tired, and there was always more to do. Familiar problems of translation turned insurmountable—what was she to do with *les bestiaux*, for a start? The author was using it to cover sheep as well as cattle, which ruled out both "flocks" and "herds." Céleste would have to settle for "animals" or possibly "farm animals." The sense that something vital had eluded her only grew stronger as her work advanced.

The season progressed, and a new thought arrived in her sixth-floor studio: A swimming pool would be nice. Silently Céleste recited words that meant Australia: sport, veranda, up yourself, teenagers with braces, little battler, the peppercorn tree, provincial touchiness, provincial kindness, dirty wog. Each one was a scene dense with detail, lit in a distinctive way.

Sabine ran her fingers over Céleste's ribs. She said that they looked as if they had been put in by a maker of Japanese fans. Straight black hair and an ivory pallor gave Céleste a faintly oriental look. She had her mother's long lips and diamond-shaped face, and nothing of her father, whose photographed head was a two-handled cup.

He had died on the last day of 1961, when Céleste was two. In October, the police had picked him up on his way home from work. France was at war with Algeria, although war had never been declared. That year there had been terrorist attacks in Paris, so the police did whatever they pleased.

Not far from the hotel where Céleste's parents lived was a café where only Algerians went. The interior, badly lit, gave off a morose brownish glow. On a windy spring evening that year, Lucien paused near the café to light a cigarette. A man came out into the street, a pale-skinned Algerian with crinkly brown hair. Lucien recognized him from the plant and, on an impulse, greeted him. When the man turned, his eyes went straight to the cigarette. At the factory, the Algerian workers had no names—they were all known as Mohammed, when they were not *bicots*, *ratons*, *crouillats*. Lucien held out his packet of cigarettes.

Over the next few months, the two men became—not friends, that was not possible. There was pressure from each side not to fraternize with the other. Céleste's mother always emphasized this distance: "*Ils n'étaient pas copains.*" But on fine evenings, if work hadn't left him exhausted, Lucien liked to go out for a walk. At the factory, he no longer worked on the assembly line but in the paint shop—a punishment. The foreman was a Party man, and Lucien was given to dreaminess. When his bourgeois-imperialist thinking on Hungary had been revealed, it was easy to find fault with his work. He was the only Frenchman in the paint shop, and one of the few whites. His humiliation was to be compounded by working with North Africans and blacks. By the end of his second winter in the paint shop, Lucien had a permanent cough. His eyes smarted at the end of the day, and his head throbbed.

An evening stroll helped his headache. If he ran into Karim, Lucien would take out his cigarettes. In the coldest weather,

Algerians wore thin jackets with their collars turned up, and Lucien was conscious of his padded coat—he was glad to leave it at home as the year grew warm. One Sunday afternoon, although he had never told Karim where he lived, the Algerian was waiting when Lucien and Yvette returned from the park where they had taken Céleste. Karim was in his best clothes, a navy suit and maroon tie. Lucien shook his hand, and so did Yvette. People going past stared. Yvette went inside with the baby, and Karim asked Lucien for a loan: in his village in the Sahara, his mother was ill. It was a small amount of money but not easily spared. Céleste's mother said, "Your father never warmed to Karim, to tell the truth, there was something self-important about the man. But he was Algerian. Your father couldn't refuse."

Autumn came. Karim asked for a second loan—the first had never been mentioned again. This time, Lucien gave less than Karim wanted. Then one evening, when Yvette was preparing dinner, a man came to the door. He was a foreigner—a Hungarian, perhaps, or a Pole. He told her, in a peculiar, tangled French, that he worked with her husband. When they came off their shift that day, the police were checking identity cards at the metro. Lucien had been hustled into a police van along with several Algerians and driven away.

At the gendarmerie, Yvette gave her husband's name. The officer at the desk looked as if he hadn't slept. He opened a file and ran his finger down a list. "That name doesn't appear here," he said.

"In that case, where was my husband taken?"

"His name isn't recorded here."

"He must have been taken somewhere."

"There's no record of his name."

Yvette filled out a missing persons form. The following day, she left the baby with a neighbor and went to the police headquarters on the Île de la Cité. The morning turned into the afternoon. At last, she was seen by a functionary in a soiled shirt. He seemed wretched. Yvette thought, There's trouble at home. The story was the same here: nothing was known of her husband and she was given a form to fill out. When she left the prefecture at the end of the bitter autumn day, Yvette was preceded by two North Africans crossing the courtyard. "I followed them, and we came to a long line of foreigners—Algerians, Portuguese, Spanish—standing along the north side of the building, where the wind was worst. They were there to apply for residency permits. Something about them looked familiar. I recognized a woman's red shawl. Then I realized that most of these people had been standing there when I went in that morning."

Very early on October 16, three days after he had vanished, Lucien was found unconscious in an alley near Austerlitz. One of his wrists was broken and two of his ribs. In the hospital, it was discovered that he had a ruptured spleen. Lying in the open, he had caught a chill that turned into pneumonia. The fumes in the paint shop had ruined his lungs. The pneumonia went away but returned on Christmas Day. Before that, when Lucien could mumble, he told Yvette what the police had said: Karim was a member of the FLN, the Algerian resistance group responsible for the terrorist attacks in Paris. Every time Lucien said that he had known nothing of Karim's politics, a gendarme hit him. Why had he given Karim money? It was common knowledge that Algerian immigrants funded the FLN. Lucien was informed that he was a traitor and would soon be shot. He heard a man screaming on the other side of the wall.

What did Céleste remember of her early life in Paris? An impression of the hotel room remained, a picture half seen through dirty glass: it was vast and shadowy, with a niche for her parents' high bed. She remembered a damp, checked cloth applied vigorously to her face. There was a smell that was not exactly boiled cauliflower but which made it impossible for Céleste to eat cauliflower now. A murky corridor also returned—it must have led to the shared lavatory. The Belleville street in which she was born had vanished, its dubious hotels and squalid houses cleared for Lego-like apartment blocks: forty years on, a modernist slum.

Not far away, steps led up the side of a hill, a shortcut to the street above. Whenever Céleste climbed them, she could have sworn that the upward view—iron railings, an apartment block with curved walls—opened onto the past. She saw herself climbing patiently, her small hand reaching up to a large one that wore a ring. But it was quite possible that steps, ring, and smooth Deco curve simply corresponded to the fragments of a dream. Her memory, a steel plate on which lists of vocabulary, rules governing the subjunctive, and a handful of French poems had been engraved forever, had areas eaten out by rust. Faces fell through it—lately, even her mother's had disappeared. The Belleville hotel room that in retrospect loomed dim and lofty might well have been small and hot. In French, Perth was pronounced *Perte*: "loss." When Céleste was asked where she was from, sometimes she said, "Australia," and sometimes she said, "France," and sometimes she said, "Loss."

Her father was a blank: not even a smell, an aura, a trace. But recently her mother, although remaining invisible, had taken to addressing Céleste. "How fat Dominic has become," Yvette said now. "I always thought we should have spelled his name the correct, French way."

"He and Mitch each ate a whole baguette every day when they were here," reported Céleste, the virtuous child, the sneak.

Her mother's tongue made a noise that signified wonder and dismay.

•

Once a week, Djamila Kateb, the concierge's fourteen-year-old daughter, came to Céleste for an hour of English conversation. Céleste refused payment for this service, saying, "*C'est rien.*" That was both formulaic and true: the hour did nothing for Djamila, who had dreamed of being a hairdresser since she was seven and wanted only to leave school. But a long time ago, her mother had set her mouth in a line. Mopping the entrance hall or vacuuming the stairs, Madame Kateb wore the shapeless, flowery overdress of an elderly provincial housewife to protect her sweatshirt and jeans. Stuck onto her childish torso, her head was a balloon. Her eyes, too, were disproportionate: pits of honey, milky at the rim. Céleste knew that the discoloration was the result of drops taken for a chronic eye disorder. Over time, she had subjected Djamila to a mild interrogation about her family that the girl's English wasn't nimble enough to dodge. It was a technique Céleste had perfected in her language-school classes. Students answering questions in a foreign language, proudly and effortfully deploying grammar and vocabulary, didn't notice what they let slip. Céleste had learned that Madame Kateb was the daughter of Portuguese immigrants, and that Djamila's father had a mobile phone shop *là-bas*—Djamila meant that he had returned to live in Algiers. *Là-bas* was a threat: it was where Djamila would be sent if she didn't do as her mother wished. Djamila's best friend was an Indian girl called Vasanti. Djamila had visited her at home, and seen that Vasanti's mother served her father first, not starting her own meal until her husband had eaten—it was Djamila's belief that comparably primitive arrangements prevailed *là-bas*.

"For you," said Djamila, placing a plastic container on the table. She touched her hair to check it—yes, it was magnificent.

There would be grilled meat in the container or a salad of roasted eggplants or a white bean stew: her mother's way of repaying a good turn. Céleste received these gifts with gratitude but rarely with enthusiasm, for Madame Kateb was an indifferent cook. The dishes she sent up were bland or oversalted, greasy or cooked to mush. They suggested approximations of a folk cuisine, something remembered but remote.

Djamila placed her phone on the table. It was switched off at Céleste's insistence, but had to be kept within sight. At night, Djamila slept with it under her pillow—Vasanti might text her at any time. "A texto is showing she love me."

Céleste said automatically, "'Text' not 'texto.'" Since meeting Sabine, Céleste, too, couldn't stop checking her phone. The temptation was overwhelming: the opportunity for distraction, the hope of reward. Sabine often sent only one word: "*toi.*" She love me! Céleste's heart would stutter like an egg boiling in a pan.

Céleste and Pippa arranged to meet at the Musée de la Vie Romantique. It was a wayward sort of Sunday with a trembly blue sky. Pippa said that when she arrived in France, it had been so cold that the city was deserted after dark. "I went out looking for somewhere to eat on my first night, and the only thing I could see, up and down the street, was parked cars. I thought, Here I am in Paris. It's a garage."

The museum, consciously charming, had green shutters, and a vine around the door. Inside, Chopin rang out without remorse. The same nocturne stood open on the piano; on the public side of the security cord, the carpet was worn smooth. On wall after wall, romantic life took the form of nerveless landscapes. Someone had polished the medals suspended from slivers of ribbon, but all the watches on display had stopped. Pippa and Céleste inspected Nadar's portrait of George Sand, who along with Chopin had attended salons in the house. A plaster cast of the composer's left hand, brilliantly white on the red lining of the cabinet, lay next to a cast of Sand's right arm and hand.

Afterward, in the tea garden, where ivy trailed underfoot, Pippa remarked on the smallness of the plaster hands. She placed her own hand on her breast and said, "To my shame, I'd never heard of George Sand."

"She explored the countryside on a donkey with Chopin," said Céleste. "On the same donkey—poor beast! At the time, George Sand looked like a spaniel. Chopin didn't think much of her when they first met."

For as long as Céleste could remember, tears had rushed readily to her eyes. To counter this affliction, with its suggestion of sentimentality and feminine weakness, she had worked on a way of speaking that showed she had *no illusions*; it came unbidden to her now. She was still unsettled by something that had happened in the museum, where a full-length mirror in an elaborate frame stood propped against a wall in the drawing room as if waiting to be moved. When Céleste glanced into it, *all she saw was a flare of light.* She recovered almost at once—any fool could see that a ray of sun reflected off the surface of the glass produced the phenomenon—and was able to say to Pippa, "If you stand just here and look into that mirror, you'll realize that you're a vampire." But that moment when she had disappeared into an angle of vision remained to disturb. To swat it away, Céleste told herself that the museum, drip-feeding ideas of heightened emotion and extraordinary lives, had long bored her. She came for the trees along the cobbled driveway, for tea on the green perforated-metal chairs.

Pippa remarked that a friend of hers, the novelist George Meshaw, had brought out a new book. "Do you know his work?" When Céleste shook her head, Pippa said, "You know, it's weird, I've met hardly anyone who's heard of him here. He's really well known in Australia." Céleste remained Australian enough to know what that meant: less a partial victory than a far-reaching defeat.

She asked how Pippa was spending her time when she wasn't writing. "Exploring the restaurant scene," said Pippa. In Sydney, where she worked part-time for a publisher of restaurant guides, she dined out once or twice a week with her husband. Matt would be joining her for the last week of her stay, and then they would travel to Italy. An apartment was already booked in Venice—Pippa called it Venezia.

Céleste's mind reached back to dripping, dark streets. "It rained every day I was there," she told Pippa. "Those pink palaces looked like blotting paper." There was also a memory of Sydney, visited long ago. "We stayed in Balmain with my stepfather's sister. If you looked into her front window from the street, you saw straight through the house to the harbor."

"Well, I can't afford to live anywhere near the harbor," said Pippa. "I'm a writer, remember." She had begun the first draft of her new novel, she confided. "It's about a couple who are having problems in their relationship. It's set mostly in Sydney, but the turning point is a holiday they have in France. It's the first time I'm using the past tense and the third person together, so it's a technical challenge." She bit into a *financier* with her big white teeth and said, "It's important to grow as a writer."

She asked Céleste what she was working on, saying, "I'm very interested in translation." Céleste had heard that before: it signaled the rosy mist of low factual density that gathered around an activity both glamorous and obscure. She had already ascertained that the only foreigners Pippa read were North Americans. Now she decided that Pippa might as well be put to use. "Does 'egged on by the enthusiasm of youth and our fervent vocations' sound OK to you?" she asked. "I can't see it straight anymore, so I can't tell if it's clear that 'enthusiasm' applies to the 'fervent vocations' as well."

Pippa asked her to repeat the phrase. Her dark, straight brows, which seemed to have been painted on, gave her the look of a ventriloquist's doll. After a minute, "What about 'the enthusiasm of our youth and fervent vocations'?" she suggested.

Céleste's face, while not unattractive in repose, hinted at severity just concealed. Sabine liked to narrow her eyes and suck in her cheeks, imitating what she called *your white look.* But no one had ever told Céleste about her smile. Through half a century she had remained oblivious to her effect, but now noticed that, while remaining motionless, Pippa seemed to slacken, as if previously she had been tied to her chair.

The wind had stiffened. All around them, forget-me-nots shivered in their beds. Pippa produced a rust-colored jumper from her pack. She pulled it on over her head; her bent elbows, uplifted, were rusty wings. Crew-necked and very possibly hand-knitted, the jumper belonged to a telemovie set in the Depression—an uncharacteristic, piercing nostalgia for the lumpish woolens of childhood found Céleste unprepared.

Pippa had brought Céleste a present of her latest novel. Signing her name on the title page, she said, "It's not very good." One of Pippa's endearing qualities was that she showed outright what others would have hidden: that she had never heard of George Sand, that her novel was a dud. She e-mailed Céleste that evening, adding a PS: "I actually do know good writing when I see it." This, too, had a corrosive effect on defenses. The message ended with an invitation to dinner the following week.

•

Barr, now back in Perth, sent Céleste a friend request on Facebook. Céleste stared at her screen. She couldn't remember her nephew saying a word to her during the Harrisons' stay. At lunch in her studio, Barr had closed his eyes and placed his head on the table next to his untouched plate. Wendy went on talking. She was describing a fish shop she had passed. "There were tuna steaks in the window! I said to Dom, 'When will people realize it's like eating tiger?'" In mid-sentence, two tears started to roll slowly down her cheeks.

When Céleste was herding the Harrisons back to their hotel, Dominic fell behind with her so that they could talk. He told Céleste that Barr set himself tests: to wear nothing over his T-shirt in winter, to refuse food for twelve hours or twenty-four. At Christmas, he had asked for a book called *Kill or Be Killed*. It explained how to break someone's fingers. "Barr's not usually into reading, so we didn't like to say no," said Dominic. "Mitch was fine at that age, just the usual teenage stuff. Was I sort of obsessive at fifteen, do you remember? That period's a bit of a blur for me. There's no one to ask since Dad carked it." Dominic's neck, like his fingers, looked full of blood.

Céleste was Barr's eleventh Facebook friend and the only one who wasn't a teenage boy. "I reckon a girlfriend would sort him out," Dominic had said. Céleste looked at Barr's most recent post: a photograph of a featureless ocean, captioned "Kiting at Woodies." Scrolling down, Céleste saw that all his posts were on similar lines—he hadn't been on Facebook long. She googled "kiting" and then had to look up "kiteboarding" on Wikipedia. His parents hadn't mentioned Barr's interest in it, but she assumed they would be pleased that he wasn't spending all his time watching revolutions on TV. "Yeah, it's good," said Dominic without enthusiasm when Céleste Skyped with him. His voice brightened: "It's really good he's reached out to you."

Wendy appeared and said, "Can you please ask Barr to consider wearing his rashie on cold mornings? Since you seem to have gained his trust." Her carved smile conveyed injury, skepticism, and complete indifference to Céleste's underhand ways.

Céleste sent Barr a brief, breezy message, without reference to rashies, which he quite rightly ignored. She now felt obliged to Like all his posts. Céleste had joined Facebook in order to access Sabine's page—she never posted anything herself. Once a week or so, she checked out Sabine's friends. The tall English girl was among them: she was called Zoe Rosser. Why had she been smiling that day as she emerged from Sabine's shop? Her face was gentle and stupid. Céleste wouldn't stoop to question Sabine, but noticed that Zoe Liked every photo that Sabine posted. Zoe's own page was protected—what did she have to hide?

Every few days, Céleste would receive a text: "Dinner chez moi?" The meals were simple: sometimes Pippa prepared an omelet or grilled chicken breasts, but usually there was only bread, two or three cheeses, and a sturdy, Ottolenghi-ish salad of vegetables and bizarre grains. "I just keep adding to it," said Pippa. "Basically, we've been eating the same salad for weeks."

Pippa's bed was piled with papers and folders cleared from the table. The shaggy piles increased as the weeks went past. The bedclothes looked lumpy—Céleste guessed that the quilt had been drawn over rumpled sheets. In Pippa's studio, she saw the reflection of her own room as work progressed: nesty and smeared. Once, when Pippa was in the bathroom, Céleste flipped through a folder marked "First Draft." Then she went and looked out at the street.

Across the way, a pigeon was shuffling along a sill in front of a window hung with two panels of taut lace. A sense of wasted effort rose in Céleste and quickly spread in all directions, encompassing everything that lay behind her and all she would ever do. The desolation felt physical, as if she were filling up with black ink.

It was understood that these evenings would end early, but on weekends Pippa often opened a second bottle. She had discovered a white Loire wine called Quincy, and now it was all that she and Céleste drank. Pippa talked about whatever she was reading: currently she was making her way through Alice Munro. Céleste would advise her on local material for the Paris section of her novel, saying things like, "You must realize that there are three Seventeenth Arrondissements: bourgeois, working-class, and cool."

Pippa would jump up to identify streets or districts on the map of Paris pinned to the wall. She enthused about a café in the Marais where newspapers hung over wooden holders—exactly the kind of calculated nostalgia to which a tourist would succumb. Wishing to save Pippa from charm, Céleste urged her to track down the places where the metro ran aboveground. "The metro should be subterranean, so when it doesn't conform to its nature, an atmosphere of violation is created. The streets below the line are always depressing. The shops sell ugly, useless things that aren't always cheap. The only flowers you find are those magenta orchids wrapped in clear plastic. Orchids used to be expensive, exotic. Now they're banal—supermarket flowers." This last observation was a borrowing from Sabine that Céleste imagined would be useful to a novelist. "Those neighborhoods are very Parisian," she concluded. "Chinese takeaway places, discount furniture outlets. You should send your characters there."

She had tried, initially, to interest Pippa in the suburbs. Pippa looked doubtful. "What's there?" she asked.

"Showrooms, social housing, pizza joints."

"Why would Australians want to read about that? It sounds like the boring bits of Sydney."

Cycling to dinner with Pippa one evening, Céleste noticed for the first time that every building in her street was fronted with sandstone blocks, with an acanthus carved into the lintel above each paneled door. Those enormous doors looked as if they hadn't been opened in a century. Céleste made a mental note to draw them to Pippa's attention. She was also going to say, "Have you realized that in Paris cats sleep indoors?" Then, on a spike of meanness, she decided, Why should I help her so much? Let her discover things for herself.

When Céleste told Sabine about Barr, Sabine said, "You are his sexy French aunt. Sure he want you for his friend."

"He's doing it to annoy his mother."

Sabine checked her phone before gathering up her clothes. She was thirty-five, sixteen years younger than Céleste. When her bra and camisole were on, she pinched the flesh above her hips. "How will I be on the beach—my God!" Céleste recognized this as a reminder that the summer holidays were drawing near. Sabine's faux silk underwear, and the bright hair streaming over her pearly shoulders, gave her an extravagant, luxurious look. It was easy to picture her dripping and gleaming on a beach.

When she was alone, Céleste took Sabine's delphiniums out of the sink and put them in a vase. Blue and arrested, they splayed against her dingy wall. Sabine's eyes, reborn as petals, would gaze out at Céleste from odd places for the rest of the week. The hour after Sabine left was a slow fall into a bottomless shaft. Céleste looked under her bolster—it was Sabine's habit to leave a card there. The latest showed a teddy bear holding a shiny red balloon. Inside, Sabine had written, "*Un gros bisou.*" With love. Her writing was Frenchly upright, the letter "r" like a backless chair. Céleste put the card with the rest in a shoebox. Her treasure, her evidence of love, was an archive of kitsch. She wondered what the practically obese assistant made of it, Sabine setting out every Tuesday for her English lesson with an expensive bouquet.

Céleste lifted her T-shirt and inspected herself. There was a slight swell across her stomach. Her periods had ceased a month after her last birthday, and now her stomach was no longer flat. Her smooth face could pass for forty, but her left knee turned dodgy if she ran. One evening over dinner, Pippa had asked if Céleste regretted not having children. "To be honest, I don't really want to," said Pippa, "but Matt's pretty keen." Céleste had seen Matt on Facebook—hair going, jawline gone—and concluded that Pippa's big teeth could dispose of him in a single crunch. Pippa was saying that it was difficult for female artists to combine children and a career. "But later on, what if I wish I'd just gone ahead?"

Céleste told her, "Listen, the only immortality you can be sure of is your nose on your child's face." Why had she said that? She didn't wish that she had just gone ahead and had a child, but with the cessation of her periods, a self who had tagged along like a cloudy dream figure disappeared. On Tuesday evenings, with the smell of Sabine still in her sheets, the future shrank to the single point of solitary, penny-pinching old age. She saw herself plainly, one of those skinny old women with a round belly: a spider. In supermarkets, the spider brought her change close up to her eyes, turning over small coins. Eventually, a stranger sitting behind a desk would call a number in Perth. Dominic put down the phone in the middle of the night and turned to Wendy. "Céleste's carked it," he announced.

What are they doing in heaven today? asked Mavis Staples from the apartment across the street. On the boulevard, a siren wailed. *La police, pleine de malice.* Céleste poured herself a glass of wine. She sliced open the end of a baguette, filled it with squares of dark Swiss chocolate, and, chewing, settled down to work. She was on the third draft of her translation. One evening, lying curled in one of Pippa's black vinyl chairs, Céleste had found herself talking about the way she worked. "The first draft is literal—very rough. I end up chucking out most of it, but it has a sort of glimmer of ideas. The second draft is detailed. Lots of dictionary work. For the third draft, I don't look at the original text."

She went on in this vein. Pippa refilled her glass. She waved the bottle at Céleste, asking, "So how many drafts do you do?"

"Four or five."

"Those writers are so lucky to have you," said Pippa. "My editor told me she edited my last book in three and a half days. It was seventy thousand words. I thought it was a confession—that she was asking me to forgive her. Later, I realized it was a boast."

She began to tell Céleste about a party thrown by an Austrian painter who had a studio in the Cité. The painter introduced Pippa to a French journalist, who had sought her opinion of what he insisted on calling Anglo-Saxon literature. "The thing is, I hadn't heard of any of the writers he said were 'of the first importance.' One of them's this Scottish person called Mungo Daniel Daws. There's also a genius American called Mary Bolla. It's nothing to her to wrench metaphysical significance from the spasms of the plastic world."

Céleste put out her hand and grasped Pippa's wrist. They sat on, linked but separate, with their fruity white wine. Paris reeled about outside, its railway stations and clouds. Cars stood trembling at lights. Pippa launched into a disjointed complaint about her father. Her bones lay under Céleste's fingers. Céleste was thinking,

What won't we say to each other? At the end of the street, the Seine rustled on its way.

Céleste came down with a summer virus. Pippa brought her soup made from chicken and leeks. Céleste rarely bothered to cook. She opened tins, ate yogurt and fruit. One of her sayings was "All you really need is a big bowl of bananas on the table." Here, too, the past was at work. Yvette, burning chops while reading *The Feminine Mystique*, would remark that domestic labor was female enslavement. She read Marx and de Beauvoir to her nine-year-old daughter; from *Capital*, Céleste kept a lifelong mistrust of guilds. Her lack of interest in food was a disappointment to Pippa, who had hoped for insights into French home cooking as well as tips on restaurants where tourists didn't go. French coffee, too, was a let-down—all the visiting Australians complained about it. The only drinkable brew, worth crossing Paris for, was found at a café in the Fourteenth run by a couple from Adelaide; they even served decaf almond lattes. Pippa's predecessor in the studio had left the address. So much energy directed at coffee! What was on Céleste's mind as she shivered in bed was a sentence. In her translation, it contained both "possibility" and "fixity," and she couldn't see a way around either—unless "fixedness" would do? The familiar impression that a solution lay just beyond her reach returned to torment.

Sabine had stayed away that week; she had a horror of infection, and there were the children to take into account. But she texted daily and sent a big bunch of silky peonies in shades of pink. Pippa remarked on their magnificence and refreshed their water while the soup warmed. She asked Céleste the French for "free range." The chicken in the soup was a *poulet de Bresse*; the man at the market stall had assured Pippa that this meant it was raised in the open, but she suspected he was laughing at her. She made a comic story of it, repeating the stallholder's assurances of "'Appy chicken! 'Appy chicken!" He had mimed injecting the bird, shaking his head and saying, "No *pshtt*," which Pippa understood to mean that it was free of growth hormones.

Céleste, propped weakly against pillows, watched Pippa adjust the angle of an open window. She replaced the glass beside Céleste's bed with a clean one, and placed a bag of rubbish beside the door to carry down to the bins. She started examining the books on Céleste's shelves, pulling out those that caught her eye—that kind of intrusion was typical of Pippa. She would walk into Céleste's flat, go straight into the kitchen, and lift the lids off pans. Once she had put out her hand and plucked without permission at Céleste's beads. Céleste deduced a large, bold family in cramped rooms where nothing was private. There would be a clutch of sisters in limp T-shirts, lapped by tides of children, who never got around to signing up at the gym.

Small domestic sounds came from the kitchen: the fridge sighed shut, the container of washing-up liquid squeaked. Raising her voice, Céleste began to tell Pippa about an elderly Greek she had known, who cooled his brow with a lump of Parian marble when he fell ill. The story trailed off—she had remembered that the Greek was a character in the first novel she translated.

Pippa went away, and Céleste's agitation returned. The peonies flared as the light withdrew. Their pink aching had entered Céleste's bones. Possibility/fixity: they were the feverish poles of the axis around which her brain twirled.

Céleste recovered. She googled "Pippa Passes," the blog that Pippa updated at longish intervals, and discovered a new post. It was accompanied by two photos. The first showed soup, tiny discs of carrot and golden sequins of oil, simmering in a pan. "I made this soup for a friend who had the flu," wrote Pippa. It was a warm day, but a tree of ice was shooting along Céleste's veins. She realized, astonished, My blood has run cold. "As my friends know," went on Pippa, "I'm a fan of ethical meat." With self-deprecating wit, she described her exchange with the man who had sold her the chicken that might or might not have been free range. A second photo showed hens on a grassy slope. Eleven Australians had already applauded this post. One commented: "The French—lol!! Go you good thing. So kind to make soup for a sick friend."

Sitting up in bed after Pippa had gone away, drinking careful, delicious spoonfuls of chicken-and-leek soup, Céleste had cried. When she tried to wipe her eyes, tears ran down her wrists. It had been a day set apart from the rest like an illuminated letter on a white page. Now something precious that had belonged to Céleste belonged to the world—to everyone and no one. She stared at the photo of the chickens: Why not show them at the moment when their bodies parted from their heads? If Pippa were there, Céleste would have told her, If you're going to eat meat, better not make a song and dance about your ethics. Another thing she wanted to say was, You should have deleted the first sentence in each paragraph of your novel and looked closely at the last. Also, banish the word "beautiful"—it's dangerous for you.

Céleste went onto Amazon and bought George Meshaw's latest book.

Dominic's e-mail said that Barr was no longer going to school. He had turned sixteen, and for the past month had refused to leave his room. At first, Wendy had switched off the modem and told Barr that she wouldn't turn it on again until he talked to her. Barr slid a piece of paper under his door. It said: "YOU ARE PEOPLE OF THE PAST." "Now we just leave food outside his door," wrote Dominic. "We don't want to push too hard. Barr's room is on the second floor, and he's at that age when boys self-harm."

Céleste said, "Do you remember that summer in Perth when the road outside our house cracked and you could see the sand underneath?"

Invisible Yvette pointed invisibly to the poster on her daughter's wall: "*Sous les pavés, la plage!*"

Pippa called for Céleste one afternoon; they had arranged to see a film. A Sydney newspaper had commissioned Pippa to write a feature on eating out in Paris, and she was fresh from lunch at a new restaurant in the Tenth. She read aloud from her notebook by the cloudy light on the stairs: "*L'Atelier: loft-like white space, brushed steel tables, contemporary artworks. Always something fusion on menu: grilled fish with pesto of Thai herbs, scallops with shiitake mushrooms and wild garlic sauce (bright green). Homemade ginger ice cream served with avocado and passionfruit. Dishes here are curated—*"

"Dishes are *what*?"

"Obviously these are just notes."

Céleste kept going downstairs, past the tight little landings, each with its spyholes and doors.

In the entrance hall, Madame Kateb was coming out of her lodge. Its frosted windows gave onto the hall. A light shone within whatever the weather or the time.

"*Bonjour, madame,*" said Céleste.

Pippa said, "*Bonjour. Comment vas-tu?*"

As usual, the concierge gave the impression that she was listening with her eyes. She held out a package to Céleste. "The courier buzzed but no one answered. I was just going to take it up to you."

"I must have been in the shower," said Céleste. She looked at the package—a book from her editor in New York. She asked if Madame Kateb would mind holding on to it until she returned home.

In the street, Pippa said, "That poor woman lives in a cave."

"You should say *vous* to strangers. *Tu* is insulting."

"Oh no—I keep forgetting," wailed Pippa. "I can't believe I went and offended her!"

Panic had turned her face into a scrunched dishcloth. Céleste realized that Pippa would always need to demonstrate her solidarity with the oppressed—indigenous people or battery hens, it scarcely mattered. Now she had added to the humiliations of a working-class cave dweller, and the photograph of herself captioned "A Good Person" had been ripped in half. "Madame Kateb knows you're a foreigner," said Céleste, taking pity. "It's OK."

"I should have it tattooed on my forehead: *Forgive me, I'm Australian.*" But Pippa had recovered. She exclaimed at the tarts in the window of a pâtisserie: the care with which the slices of fruit had been placed!

"Strawberries sold by the kilo," said Céleste, remembering. That had delighted her beyond reason when she first came back to Paris. In Pippa's company, the ghost of that Céleste often appeared. She had smiled at dark men lounging in doorways on trashy boulevards. If she greeted them, they followed her in the street or moved up on her park bench until they were almost touching her. Céleste had arrived with the vague idea of tracking down Karim, or someone who had known him or her father. But the factory that employed them had long since ceased production; a huge new outlet that sold discount sporting equipment had opened on the site. Every

North African woman Céleste saw in the street was doubled by a gold-toothed crone—patterned with henna, redistributing garlic in puffs. This caricatural apparition was Karim's mother, risen from her Saharan village to inquire into the fate of her son. At the time, it was usual to see armed policemen at the entrances to the metro checking the papers of anyone who looked foreign, and this brought the past up close. Very soon, however, Céleste learned to walk through the city like a Parisian, glancing to neither left nor right.

The film, an Iranian one, was playing at a cinema in the rue Gît-le-coeur. "Here lies the heart," translated Céleste. "People used to think that Louis the Fourteenth's mistress was buried under the street. But it turned out to be his favorite cook."

Afterward, sitting on a red leather banquette and drinking kir, Pippa said that she had found the film "really honest." That was high praise—the highest. She had said the same thing about Alice Munro. "I used to try to write beautifully," confided Pippa. "But now honesty's what I aim for in my work."

"But what do moral categories have to do with art? Doesn't one aim for precision above all?" Céleste believed this, but it was also intended to open a discussion—any one of her French friends would have understood that.

Pippa ran her finger along the edge of the marble-topped table. "I'm useless at talking about this kind of stuff. I'm no intellectual. My education was rubbish. Country high school and crap university." Then she said, "No, the thing was, at uni I used to have this part-time job that started at four, so I always chose morning classes. But all the cool lecturers were night people who liked to sleep in. Like in the English Department, the theory seminars were always timetabled in the afternoon. I'm the only person my age with an arts degree who hasn't read those guys like Foucault."

"Does it matter?"

"Everything changed in the Eighties," said Pippa. "The big division used to be between people who were born before the Second World War and people who were born after. Now it's between people who know about poststructuralism and the rest of us. It's a different way of seeing the world."

She produced a printout that she passed across the table. It advertised a weeklong, live-in cooking course in the Jura in which she had enrolled that day. Céleste read: "For lovers of the authentic cuisine, full of rustic flavors and grandma secrets." "But it's in the Jura," she said, as mystified as any Parisian by this desire to exchange the city for the provinces. "Why would anyone want to go there?"

"Aren't the mountains something else?"

"Oh, the mountains!" said Céleste, dismissing them.

"All the real Parisians go away in August."

Céleste, stung, said, "That's a myth, like saying the French are always on strike." Pippa looked as if she had been slapped. Céleste wanted to shout, What makes you Australians think you can blunder about, expecting people to be *nice*? The silence between them stretched. It swelled to encompass August, and Céleste, abandoned even by Pippa, sitting at her keyboard in her shuttered room with only the daily statistics about holidaymaker fatalities to console her. A pivoting electric fan blew papers from her desk. Summer, like Sunday, could last as long as a life. To fend off that vision, Céleste began talking about the latest knot in her translation. "The narrator's describing his childhood in a village during the Second World War. One of his neighbors has gingham curtains. In French, 'gingham' is '*vichy*.'"

Pippa looked blank.

"Well, so it's a word that immediately evokes Vichy. You know—the regime. Collaboration with the Nazis."

Pippa seemed to be trying to remember something.

"Which 'gingham' doesn't."

"I don't see what anyone could do about that," said Pippa. "Some things you just have to let go."

Céleste looked out the window. When she first met Pippa, she had mentioned "my girlfriend"—it was essential to make that clear. But Pippa knew nothing about Sabine and never would. It had been a possibility once, but not since the post about the soup. Nevertheless, Pippa was the sole receptacle of certain confessions decanted in the course of a long dinner in her studio when they had finished the Quincy and were making do with red: for instance, the overwhelming relief that Céleste had felt when her mother finally died. Pippa's grandmother, too, had died after a lengthy illness. "I used to look at her lying there, out of it but not especially in pain or anything," said Pippa, "and over and over in my head, I'd say, Just die. *Just die.*"

She began to laugh wildly. It set Céleste off as well. "How awful we were," cried Céleste, when she could speak, writhing in her chair. "I really mean that." In Pippa's mouth, squared off in terror, her tongue showed, darkened by wine.

In the café after the Iranian film, Pippa placed her elbows on the table like a judge. She said, "You told me you translate into English because that's your native language. But if you were four when you left here, you must have spoken French first."

Taken aback by this evidence of Pippa's mind working behind the scenes, Céleste said coolly, "Of course. But I started to think in English when we moved to Perth. My mother used to speak to me in French and I would answer her in English. I had to learn to speak French all over again, at high school and university."

"Something must have remained. A pattern."

When Pippa and Céleste went out into the street, the atmosphere of the film, which the brightness and bustle of the café had dispelled, returned. The light, now down to its grotty underwear, was cinematically sad. The two women walked slowly across a square, as if responding to direction. They might have been coming away from an event that had changed their lives, although they had yet to appreciate its weight. Céleste was wearing a glossy vinyl jacket over a lace dress that reached to her calves, and grubby lilac tennis shoes. A stranger would instinctively have addressed her in French, just as no one would have spoken anything but English to Pippa. The streetlights had come on, and the people crossing Pont St.-Michel had the look of messengers, coming toward Pippa and Céleste out of the dusk.

A river of cars poured along the quai. Then there was the river itself, moving just as purposefully, and a tourist boat lit up and noisy like the memory of a party seen from afar. All the lights along the embankment shuddered in the water. The last of the day was slithering off fairy-tale towers that proclaimed the city of spectacle and romance.

The sky over the river, curdy and vast, was a Dutch painting. Sometimes it was an Italian one, brilliant pink and gold. They crossed the first half of the bridge, and Pippa decided that she would walk home along the lower path beside the water. She paused to read a brass plaque near the head of the steps. She was still collecting details for the French section of her book. In the café, Céleste had watched her write "kir = 4 euros" and "American girls with sluttish eye shadow" in her Moleskine notebook. Pippa had spent four months in France without progressing beyond "*L'addition, s'il vous plaît*" and "*Je ne comprends pas,*" but the events memorialized on plaques tended to the world-historical. She proved it now, saying, "I know about Jews being deported during the war and Parisians liberating their city in 1944. But what happened on the seventeenth of October 1961?"

Céleste said, "A curfew had been imposed on Algerians living in Paris. On the evening of the seventeenth, hundreds of them came out into the streets in a peaceful protest. It had been organized in secret, but someone tipped off the police. They beat some of the demonstrators senseless and threw them into the Seine. Others were taken to the police headquarters just over there and killed."

Pippa's fingers, spread out across her mouth, belonged to a child. She said, "I had no idea."

"Don't worry, plenty of French people know nothing about it either." Céleste didn't add that she had been present when the mayor of Paris unveiled the plaque. Some people carried white cardboard cutouts of men with their hands on their heads. Céleste had read the official statement, issued forty years earlier. It mentioned "gunfire" in the course of which two Algerians had died. Her mother had said that everyone talked privately of atrocities—it was rumored that hundreds of bodies had been pulled from the river—but there was nothing in the media. All that week, Algerians were rounded up and disappeared. Hurrying past their café on her way to visit her husband in hospital, Yvette was startled to see it closed up. The following spring brought independence for Algeria and peace. What Parisians wanted then was to seal up the events of 1961 in a lead container and drop it into the Seine. Their imagination had never been stirred by the Algerian conflict. Its corpses, its reprisals, its clandestine networks were only the warmed-up leftovers of the old war, the real one—toward the end, even de Gaulle had reappeared. Somehow, though, the second time around everything had been reversed in an evil mirror, and the French were no longer the brave heroes of the resistance but the agents of oppression. No wonder there was relief when it was all over. "Nineteen sixty-two was a fresh start," said Yvette. "Everyone wanted a fridge and a white nylon shirt."

"My first winter here," Céleste told Pippa, "someone wrote *Ici on noye les Algériens* on this bridge. 'They drown Algerians here.' The word 'drown' was spelled wrong." She kissed Pippa on both cheeks, and marched on alone, into the arcade of plane trees that led across the island: she was stepping over waterlogged bodies all the way to the gilded gates of the Palais de Justice.

Céleste had once asked what Djamila knew of the events of 1961. The girl looked away—she felt only boredom or horror for anything to do with *là-bas*. "That was the old-fashioned time," she said.

"You should say 'the past.' What happened in the past is part of your history."

"I am French."

"It's part of French people's history."

"No," said Djamila. "That is not true." She spoke slowly and distinctly, as to a fool.

Yvette called from the kitchen: "*Ma grande*, it's one thing not to fetishize housework and quite another to have cockroaches under the sink."

Every August, Bernard, Sabine, and the girls spent three weeks at his uncle's holiday house in Brittany. On the second Sunday they were away, Céleste received a text: "Skype?" When they were online, Sabine told her that everyone else had gone out to lunch. "I said I had a *crise de foie*. So I could have lunch with you." Her voice was bland, as it always was when describing her actions, as if stating something she had merely happened to observe. Céleste spread *biscottes* with goat's cheese, while Sabine microwaved a Weight Watchers meal of asparagus and fish. They toasted each other, cautiously touching their glasses to their screens. "*Les yeux dans les yeux*," instructed Sabine, bringing her face close. Céleste leaned forward and kissed her. Improbably, all the bells of Notre-Dame-de-Lorette started ringing out, peal after peal. "Someone is getting married," said Sabine. She ate neatly, cutting her salmon into squares, and talked about a cousin's wedding that had taken place the previous weekend. This cousin had won the lottery, marrying the son of a *richissime* Jordanian. The wedding was held on his horse stud in Normandy, the five hundred guests seated in a crystal marquee designed to represent a Bedouin tent. There were three official photographers, and a drone that filmed everything from overhead. Madison, Sabine's seven-year-old, had been a flower girl. At the last minute she refused to wear her dress, saying it pricked under her arms. She was bribed, eventually, with the promise of a mini iPad. "She is like me, that girl," said Sabine, complacently. "She knows what she wants and she gets it." She showed a container. "Low-fat strawberry mousse."

Céleste held up an apricot. She told Sabine about Barr's latest Facebook post. "He wrote, 'Mum's birthday today. Maybe Dad'll let her wear a strap-on.'" Céleste said, "This kid's barely sixteen!"

"He's gay," said Sabine, licking a teaspoon.

"You think so?"

"Sure. He wishes for his father what he dreams of for himself. It explains his behavior, his unhappiness. Australian men are so macho, it must be awful to be gay there." Sabine's picture of Australia, a violently dramatic comic strip, took its inspiration from a wildlife documentary about the culling of brumbies that she had watched as a child. For her, Australia would always be a country where stone-hearted killers leaned from helicopters to shoot horses. Once, she had asked Céleste, "In Perth, is it possible to go out into the street alone if you are a woman?"

"No, they send a helicopter to kill you."

"I am serious!" Then Sabine said, "It is such a long time you are away, you have forgotten what life is like for an Australian woman." It was her standard response. Contesting Sabine's wilder claims—"It is quite impossible to raise sheep there. They sicken on the inferior grass." "Even the little children drink beer."—Céleste would find all discussion routed by a firmly smiling "You have forgotten."

Sabine had found it utterly incredible that Céleste's mother should have married an Australian. How could such a thing have happened?

"They met in the metro. Roy was visiting Paris. He'd missed his stop and my mother helped him," said Céleste. "He was a nice man. Anyone could see that straightaway."

Sabine looked dubious. "To go and live in Perth!"

"My mother had no reason to love France."

"In her place, I would have made a complaint about what happened to my husband."

"She did. Before I was born, she'd worked in a factory that made cardboard packaging. The owner, Monsieur Kahn, was married to a woman whose father had been at the bar. Madame Kahn wrote one of those lawyer-type letters filled with unspecified threats to the Ministry of the Interior, and her husband took a copy to the prefecture himself. He went back twice, and each time he had a new letter." Céleste said, "Monsieur Kahn also went with my mother to the car plant where my father had worked. They wanted to talk to the man who had seen him being picked up by the police. But he didn't work there anymore. No one could tell them what had become of him."

"And your mother and this Jew—they stop there?"

After a moment, Céleste said, "The Kahns were old and unimportant. What did the ministry have to fear? And then my mother met my stepfather. I'm guessing she was tired of her life, tired of struggling. It was time for a fridge and a white nylon shirt."

"In Australia. My God—such courage!"

This Jew. Céleste knew that Madame Kahn couldn't have children because her ovaries had been removed without anesthetic in a camp. The cornelian necklace had belonged to her, a farewell gift when Yvette left France. The beads were ancient, valuable, Chinese. When Céleste touched them, they were warmly alive. She told herself that it was important not to exaggerate what was only a dismissive manner of speaking. What Sabine had said was level with He can't read a map. At the same time, Céleste knew that there were people who wouldn't even think *this Jew*—Pippa, for one, or Wendy.

In Brittany, Sabine rotated her head as if her neck were stiff and said in her offhand way, "Imagine what Bernard has decided. He's going to enter the lottery for a green card. He says Europe is finished, except for Germany, and he doesn't like Germans. He spent two weeks in Hanover on a school exchange. His host family ate smoked fish at breakfast. The mother's feet were bigger than the father's."

The hollow opening under Céleste's ribs informed her that everything vital there had been scooped out. "And you?" she managed to say. "Do you want to live in the States?"

Sabine's eyes were fixed on her screen, her creamy lids at

half-mast. "Jennifer and I like Los Angeles or New Orleans, but Madison and Bernard prefer New York."

"Even the little children have guns."

Wendy was in the habit of sending Céleste small, fragrant presents that Céleste characterized as *suitable for a maiden aunt*: geranium-scented hand cream, a carved sandalwood box. When Wendy came to Paris, she had brought Céleste an air freshener made from mandarin peel and cinnamon. Céleste sprayed her room after her Skype lunch with Sabine. It was wasteful—the windows were wide open. Across the road, Mavis Staples was on repeat: *Peace abounds like a river, they say.* From Notre-Dame-de-Lorette, the Virgin peered at Céleste over rooftops, through the smog. A storm was on its way. It came every August, on or around the Feast of the Assumption. After that, whatever the weather, summer was done.

At five, the downpour came. Soon after, the doorbell rang. It was Djamila: like Céleste, the Katebs stayed at home and sweltered out the month. Where could they go? A hotel was out of the question, and neither side of the family wanted them. Slouching in, Djamila began at once to complain that she was misunderstood by her mother. "Of course you are," said Céleste. "It's the fate of all teenage girls. Mothers are so limited. Take yours: she doesn't want you to repeat her life. As if you would—can't she see your generation is already so much more advanced?"

"Exactly." Blessed with a total absence of irony, Djamila was armored against self-doubt. Her expertly made-up eyes inspected Céleste: she was assessing her hair. Every few weeks, she would sit Céleste at the table with a towel over her shoulders and scissors to hand. The handle of a comb prodded now and then at the creeping gray. "Chestnut?" pleaded Djamila. "Or a nice mahogany? Blended highlights, not streaks."

"Only if you say everything in perfect English."

Usually, however, the conversation hour began with a personality quiz (*What could be more fascinating than you?*) that Céleste had found on the net. Djamila loved these tests: they were clues to secret selves. She had learned which Kardashian she was, which fashion decade, what she looked for in a date, and her hotness rating out of ten. Her archetype was the Warrior (dynamic, ambitious, organized, thrives on challenge) and her soul animal was a bat (fun-loving, loyal, methodical).

As a little girl, Djamila had been in the habit of bouncing her ball against a wall in the courtyard. Céleste, going to and from the communal rubbish bins, would see her there on the coldest afternoons: jacketless, the wind putting color into her beige cheeks. Even in summer, the courtyard gave off the chilly, ancient smell of stone. Djamila's small, round arm swung tirelessly, her unwavering gaze was a glare. Then a man who lived on the second floor complained of the noise. After that the child was confined to the concierge's lodge.

When Djamila had left, Céleste checked her phone—nothing—and Sabine's Facebook page. Then she looked at Bernard's page, which was protected, so that all she could see was his profile picture and cover photo. The latter had been updated: it showed Bernard and Sabine, his arm around her shoulders, sitting behind glasses of wine. A child's face was an unfocused smile in one corner.

Madame Kateb's latest offering was a slimy sort of soup. Here and there, pieces of zucchini formed a vegetable flotsam. Céleste took the container into her kitchen and saw that rain was flowing from the benchtop to the floor—she had forgotten to close the window. Cursing, moving a cloth in circles over the tiles, Céleste was peering at a terrace in Brittany. Sabine, Bernard, assorted members of Bernard's family, and the children were eating dinner. There was a tureen on the table, and bones. Bernard's mother had prepared a couscous—the children had left chunks of underdone carrot on their plates. Lit by drunken candles, Sabine was describing a drama that had taken place at work. A gentleman, *un monsieur très distingué*, not a regular customer, had ordered a funeral tribute, a pillow made up of white roses. He paid cash and said no message was required. A few days later, a woman came to the shop. A floral pillow made up in this very shop—she held out the card that proved it—had been delivered to her husband's funeral. She wanted the sender's name. When Sabine said she didn't know it, the woman cried that she had a right to be informed. To send a pillow—it was blatant! She demanded to know the bitch's name! Here, Bernard's mother gave a meaningful cough: *Pas devant les enfants*. Sabine moved smoothly into a story about her assistant's new boyfriend. "He's tighter than any Jew. You know what they say about Savoyards, always throwing money through the windows—they throw it inside from out!" Everyone laughed. They sat back in their chairs, easygoing and full of food. Bernard caught his wife's eye: later, he would glide about inside her.

In the early days of their love, Sabine had presented Céleste with a flowering cactus. "This is you," she announced, handing over the pot with its stiff red bloom. The cactus would have looked well in a domed glass case, the centerpiece of a creepy Victorian collection. Céleste couldn't bring herself to throw it away, so settled for keeping it on top of a cabinet in the kitchen. Over time she grew used to it. The glowering red flower died and was eventually replaced by another. Céleste addressed it now, addressing her fierce red self: You know you chose this freely. Like so much that is true, it was of no help at all.

Pippa e-mailed Céleste from the Jura. She couldn't get phone coverage and had to pay for Wi-Fi. It had been raining for three days—now hail was expected. The mountains were invisible, draped in mist. Pippa wrote, "I wanted France to be more beautiful than this." The weather had cleared briefly one afternoon, and then the mountains were topped with a sinister band of rock. Viewed from the corner of an eye, they seemed to rise and fall as if breathing. The local delicacy was a dish of mushrooms that were out of season. All the food was light brown and drowned in cream. "No one's cooked like this in Australia since the last days of disco. Roger, the chef, expects us to call him *Maître*. Last night he got pissed and told us that his father is Belgian. His childhood was ruined in the effort to ward off the accent. There's an ancient American woman here who tells Roger he is *terrible*—it means she's in love with him, apparently. Her name is Miss Gertrude Sauer. Her grandparents emigrated from Germany. She wants to learn French cooking because in her family, at the end of a good meal, the old people would say, 'We have eaten like God in France.'" Pippa had added a PS: "Miss you!"

Céleste told herself, That's what you represent to Pippa: an afterthought.

Pippa had a new automatic sign-off: "I acknowledge the traditional owners and custodians of country throughout Australia and their continuing connection to land, culture, and community. I pay my respects to Elders, past, present and future. Sent from my iPad."

•

Yvette said, "See this: you've written, *It only has to be expressed to cease to be a secret.* So clumsy!"

"*It ceases to be a secret as soon as it's expressed,*" said Céleste, correcting the page.

"Is this really the way you want to spend your life? It's so secondhand. I really don't understand why you want to live here. You should have stayed in Australia. You could have been a cleaner in a hospital. A noble life of labor."

"I'd rather be a cleaner for a mining company. Fly in, fly out. Dom says they clear twenty grand a month."

Her mother made that noise with her tongue.

Pippa had a dinner party to celebrate her birthday. The other guests were an Australian couple who were over from London for a few days. Céleste arrived to find everyone looking at photos of famous French writers in a handsome book that was Pippa's present from Kirsty and Will. Simone de Beauvoir, with an armful of newspapers, had just stepped out of a car. "This one's my favorite," said Pippa, showing Céleste a small woman in a big chair behind a desk—she was laughing, face and body contorted. "Marguerite Duras," said Pippa, sounding the final "s" in the writer's name.

"Have you read any Duras, Pip?" asked Will. He left the last letter silent. "Some of it's quite passable."

"Oh, is that how you say her name? I'll never be able to speak French," said Pippa.

"You were right, in fact," said Céleste. She smiled at Pippa. "It's Dura*s*."

Will dug into the white bean dip with a cracker. He studied a photo of Camus.

Céleste had brought Pippa a vintage scarf patterned with

playing cards and dice. "I love retro," said Pippa, tying the blue silk square around her neck. She was wearing the lampshade dress—how on earth had she squashed it into her suitcase? Her hair had grown and now curled about her ears. Her head no longer looked like a golf ball, but nothing could help that dress. I would put her in a dress the color of eggshells, thought Céleste. Bias cut, close-fitting, three-quarter sleeves—very simple. There would be touches of clear but not hard blue: a belt, perhaps, or a line of piping on the cuffs. She saw Pippa strolling ahead of her in the street: inexplicably, Pippa was now in a silky skirt and long boots. With each step, a stripe of flesh behind her knees showed, was hidden, showed.

Pippa went into the kitchen and Will followed. Kirsty stretched out her legs; her toes, strapped into red Birkenstocks, were dusty and straight. She asked polite questions that Céleste answered mechanically—she was listening to Will quiz Pippa about her novel.

Kirsty began to describe the morning's tourism. She and Will had walked up to Montmartre for the view and then kept going, choosing streets at random. On a boulevard lined with clothing stalls, Kirsty had felt like such a white girl. Within ten minutes of the Sacré-Coeur, the tourist city disappeared. "We came to railway lines, and everything looked desolate. It looked like London." Céleste grew distracted, gazing at Kirsty. There were hollows at her temples and under her cheekbones, making her face look dinted.

Pippa served a lamb curry, a dish of spicy beans, coconut chutney, and eggplant in mustard sauce. She said, "I really got into Indian cooking last year."

"See, that's the great thing about globalization," said Will. "You can get into Thai or Malaysian or Indian cuisine without ever having to know any Indians or Malaysians or Thais."

Will and Pippa had done the same creative writing course in Sydney, Céleste learned. Will worked in finance now but hadn't given up on fiction. He had written a novel but was still perfecting it. "So many terrible novels get published and three months later they've disappeared forever. I don't see the point of rushing into print." His manuscript was long and boldly experimental. "I'm going to insist on it being published loose-leaf, in a box. No pagination—it's so authoritarian. Real literature interpellates the reader in active meaning-making. I mean, what's the point of writing if you're not going to push the game along?"

People drank and chewed.

"I've just bought your mate George's new book, Pips," said Will, helping himself to more beans.

"I'll have to get around to reading him sometime," said Kirsty. She asked Pippa, "Do you like his books?"

"They're very intelligent."

Will turned to Céleste: "That means 'No.' Intelligence is un-Australian."

After they had eaten, the inevitable lament about coffee began. "That was the best thing about being back home at Easter," said Will. "There's nothing like being able to go into any café—even in the airport—and get a great latte."

"Did you really order lattes in Sydney?"

Will's thundery blue eyes turned on Pippa.

"It's just that the coffee scene's changed since you left Australia," she went on. "Only people from the 'burbs have lattes now. You're no one if you don't ask for a flat white."

Kirsty told Céleste that she worked for an NGO that monitored human rights. Soon she would be going to Sri Lanka, where she would address members of the armed forces on why the use of torture should be banned.

"How will that work?" asked Céleste. "I mean, what do you say to people like that?" She intoned robotically: "Torture is bad." And added, "If they don't know that by now . . ."

"The government's invited us. So they must be interested in change."

"In foreign aid, more likely. Don't Western governments tend to link that to favorable human rights reports?"

"You can't get anywhere without hope." Kirsty said, "I believe in the ethics of possibility."

In the days that followed, she often appeared to Céleste: *such a white girl*, calm as a queen in her dusty sandals. She stood at a lectern in a darkened room, addressing men whose medals gleamed like blades. Kirsty pressed a key on her laptop, but the image that flashed up on the screen belonged to Céleste's past. It showed a hospital room in Perth. Yvette patted her bed, saying, "Sit." She informed a child in a school uniform, "Today I'm going to tell you why the police released your father." The air-conditioning unit shuddered on the wall. Then the soundtrack went silent, because that was all that Céleste could remember. She was thirteen years old. She loathed the bald yellow woman who had replaced her mother. The bald woman's soundless voice went on and on, speaking French, which Céleste detested. Over the road from the hospital, a building was going up. Céleste watched the activities of men in orange hard hats. What happened if one of them needed to scratch his head?

Years later, she would write to Roy, "Did Mum talk to you about my father when she was dying?" But Roy couldn't help. It was Céleste who knew and Céleste who had forgotten. There were days when it seemed straightforward: the police lost interest in her father because they had been informed of the Algerian demonstration. *La police, pleine de malice*. But why would Yvette, knowing that she was dying, return to that well-worn tune? Céleste answered herself: To stop me imagining worse. *Worse* meant her father telling his torturers what the Algerians had planned. This scenario was simply there when Céleste woke up in Paris one day, waiting like the blue stain that had spread in the washbasin from the base of the taps. It was absurd—the demonstration was a secret no Algerian would have shared with a Frenchman. Not even Karim? asked the tireless vigilante in Céleste's brain. Karim who was self-important. Karim who wanted money and might have offered a secret in return. "*Ils n'étaient pas copains*," said Yvette, emphatically—why was she so insistent? What was certain was that someone had betrayed the Algerians. The police records of the protest and all that pertained to it remained classified; Céleste had checked.

When she returned to live in Paris, Céleste had been accepted into a postgraduate degree in French literature. Enrollment at a university, which had required half an hour in Perth, took three weeks in France. During that time, Céleste waited in line outside a variety of offices to which prospective students were allowed entry at arbitrary, obscure, and clashing hours. From each office, usually on a second or third visit, she collected a piece of paper or a stamp. At last, she had everything she needed. In the final office, she handed her dossier across a counter to a hunchback. He accepted it without returning her smile and checked through each page, unhurriedly ticking items on a list; his fingernails were rimmed in black. Satisfied at last that no document lacked its authorized triplicate, he transferred the contents of her folder to a large manila envelope. With practiced grace, he tossed the envelope over his shoulder into the metallic yawn of a filing cabinet that contained dozens of identical, unmarked envelopes. That meant Céleste was enrolled.

Whenever she thought of the police records, Céleste saw a basement the size of a principality in which streets of filing cabinets stuffed with plain manila envelopes were stacked ceiling-high. One of the envelopes contained a sheet of paper that told the story of her father: it was stamped "Informant" or "Fool." If you held it up to the mirror, the stamp read "Collaborator" or "Victim." But the information could never be retrieved. Céleste studied the two images she owned of her father. In his wedding photograph, where he seemed to be smiling at neither his wife nor the photographer but at an invisible onlooker, his face was partly shaded by his hat. The second photo, taken on some momentous provincial occasion, was the one in which his head looked like a cup. What could photographs say? Their testimony was useless, mute.

Céleste had once visited a soft-palmed hypnotist who recovered buried memories. Fragrant oil burned on his desk. When he told Céleste to picture herself descending a flight of steps, her pulse picked up. She listened, hyperalert, to his lavender-scented evocations of grassy meadows and gentle, bath-warm streams. He ran Céleste's credit card through his machine and informed her that she was an unsuitable subject. On her way home, she discovered that she had the answer to a translation problem that had teased her for weeks.

Pippa was running a Facebook poll on whether people preferred their freekeh toasted or not.

Céleste asked her mother, "Why do Australians go on so much about food?"

"Because they live in a country of no importance."

•

Céleste texted Pippa, proposing a visit to the Rodin Museum. Matt was due in a couple of days. They would all have dinner together before Pippa and Matt left for Italy. But this would be Céleste and Pippa's last outing together.

It was early September, and the wind was sharpening itself on the edges of buildings in readiness for what was to come. When the sun put its head out, the day turned ruffled and golden, like Sabine's hair in bed. Céleste was wearing a dark jacket with dropped sleeves that had belonged to Yvette before she married, and a round tweed hat. The homeless man at the bottom of her street hailed her from his bench. His heavy woolen coat, encrusted with dirt, must have once been expensive. When Céleste put her hand into her pocket for coins, he cried, "Go on, lady, get out your checkbook!" His merry red eyes danced in his knotted face.

Céleste had finally got around to starting George Meshaw's novel. It described an average kind of man, married to a thorny sort of woman, who had run into difficulty at work. One of his co-workers, an Indian passed over for promotion, had accused him of racism. There was trouble at home, too: his daughter had failed her scholarship exams, and now money had to be found for her schooling. Her father was in favor of her attending the local high school, but her mother disagreed.

Translation had taught Céleste that every book had an internal rhythm: energetic or languid, jittery or calm. That was its *hum.* The novel she was translating at present was arterial blood: oxygenated, pumped out. It had something in common with George Meshaw's sentences: metrical as marchers, they pushed Céleste forward. Meanwhile, the problems closing in on his protagonist were a weight, growing heavier with each paragraph, which pressed down on her chest.

At the museum, Céleste waited beside an urn that held a

ruthless topiary shape. All at once there was Pippa, the suddenness of her face. Her hair was in pieces from the wind. She wore a belted green coat and a red scarf—had she never seen a garden gnome? Her cheeks were icy under Céleste's lips. Nodding at the urn, she said, "That belongs on a grave."

What had Céleste imagined? That Pippa would wail, I can't believe I'm going away? She told Pippa, "You sound exactly like me," and led the way inside.

The parquetry squeaked as they moved from one exhibit to another. Céleste lingered before a strange assemblage called *L'Adieu*: a woman's marble head set on a rectangular plinth with two bony hands touching her mouth—the eyes were wide with fright. The museum was crowded with weekend visitors, and a couple came up beside Céleste—one of those couples that populate Paris, a man with silvery, swept-back hair, a worshipful, thin-wristed young woman. A cardigan in a docile color was draped around her shoulders. Her hips, streamlined in cunningly cut linen, nevertheless promised the production of sturdy heirs in a selfless perpetuation of family and nation. Anyone could see that she would prepare a light, delicious savory flan that evening. While trimming slender green beans—she had risen at dawn to haggle over them in a market—she would comment intelligently on the latest developments in the Middle East. After supper, it would be time to draft the next chapter of her doctoral thesis, write the footnotes for the man's forthcoming book, put on a load of his washing, and practice the pelvic-floor exercises that maintained his sexual pleasure at an optimum.

"Now this, you see, is fascinating," said the man. His voice was sonorous and clear, the voice of an educated Frenchman, designed to instruct. "One recognizes the model, of course, she is Camille Claudel. Rodin added those hands—they have nothing to do with her. Notice the title." His companion's eyes rolled to do his bidding as if they had come loose in their sockets. "It refers to a painful episode in the life of the couple. But what is of ontological interest is obviously the plinth."

Céleste moved away. She was standing near *Fugit Amor* when the sun slipped free of clouds. Light, flowing into the room through the tall windows, polished the parquet. *It entered the marble lovers.* Marble lips, toes, nostrils turned translucent, individual crystals sparkled.

Later, walking with Pippa in the grounds, Céleste said, "Did you notice that someone had kissed the bust of Clémenceau? An atrocity—magenta lipstick."

The hedges, savagely pruned, were giving off a cold green scent. Céleste ran her palm along one, discovering how the sharp little twigs pricked. Pippa's shoes were dusty from the gravel while hers remained immaculate—how come? She told Pippa that she was reading George Meshaw. "His sentences are like gunfire." Céleste aimed two fingers at the hedge. "*Bang bang bang.* And the way everything is closing in on that guy—I feel I can't breathe, reading that book."

"I know what you mean," said Pippa. "George's writing's sort of . . . abstract but oppressive, isn't it? You never learn what his characters look like, but by the end of the novel you feel like you were stuck in a lift with them for hours. But a lot of critics—men, I mean—really like that kind of thing. You can only get so far if men don't like your work."

"Oh, don't get me wrong. I couldn't say I'm enjoying his book but I think your friend's *great,*" said Céleste.

It was true. At the same time, she was aware of drawing blood.

Light rushed down the avenues, fleeing into the distance. Two women went by, in beige trenchcoats with tinselly saris underneath; the younger one's mouth was colored an appalling pink—Céleste's eyes met Pippa's. A roaring child followed a few paces behind. When the lipsticked woman turned and spoke to him, he shouted, "Don't interrupt! I'm crying."

"To be honest, museums depress me," said Pippa. Her red scarf lent a rosy cast to her face. "What am I meant to *feel* looking at all that stuff? Paris is so crushing." She broke a sprig from a hedge and began driving her thumbnail into each leaf. "I'll be glad to get back to Sydney," she announced. "Everything hasn't already been done there."

Céleste realized that she could see Pippa in ten years, even fifteen—she was wearing leather trousers. She no longer wrote novels, but had a weekly television show in which she cooked a meal for a celebrity. Over dinner, eaten on a penthouse terrace overlooking Sydney Harbour, they discussed the book the celebrity had written. They mostly talked about the food, which was just as well. Pippa said, "Cooking with fresh, organic ingredients is my way of honoring life." She gazed out over the billionaires' view and added, "It's the simple things. Always." Now and then she thought of Alice Munro.

"Incredible!" said Céleste. "Look at this—I've translated *en effet* as 'in effect.'"

"Also, your shoes need polishing," said Yvette. "It's not a question of vanity, it's a matter of looking after your belongings so that they last. When I think of what you squandered on those shoes!"

"Why won't you tell me what I want to know about my father?"

"Ridiculous child! Always looking over your shoulder."

•

Sabine's widowed great-aunt, who lived in an old people's home in Besançon, had been ill, and it was decided that Sabine ought to visit her. Telling Céleste, Sabine said simply, "She is rich." Fortunately, the old woman had never been fond of children, and in any case Jennifer had a ballet exam, so the girls were to remain at home with their father. Sabine said, as if it had already been arranged, "We'll have a whole night together at last."

On the train, Sabine played Sudoku on her phone—she was training her left brain, she explained. "My work is creative, so it's necessary to compensate." She interrupted her game to google a test. Céleste saw the silhouette of a ponytailed woman on the screen. As she looked, the woman began to spin on her heel.

"Which way is she turning?" asked Sabine.

"This way." Céleste drew a circle in the air with her finger.

"You're left-brained. I knew it: logical, good with words."

Céleste stared at the phone. "Do you really see her spinning the other way?"

"Oh, yes."

"That's amazing. I can't believe that we're looking at the same image and registering two different things."

"That's because you're left-brained—you're uncomfortable with anything you can't explain straightaway. I'm the opposite, creative and intuitive, so a little chaos doesn't disturb me at all."

Céleste watched hedges blur in the window of the TGV. George Meshaw's novel lay unopened on her lap. She felt predictable and dull.

In Besançon, their hotel lay at the end of a cobbled yard. Their room was ready, but the manager asked if they would mind returning in an hour or two—the hotel's website was being updated, a photographer was expected, and she didn't want her best room disturbed. She led Céleste and Sabine up two flights of white-walled, paint-smelling stairs and unlocked a door. The room behind it swam in green light from the wisteria climbing in over the balcony. Here, too, the smell of paint prevailed. "It's the most charming room in the establishment," said the manager in her thrilling smoker's voice. She looked no older than Sabine but had paused to wheeze on each landing. She inserted a mauve plastic fingernail into a keyhole and hooked open a door that was flush with the wall. "Leave your bags here for the moment," she said, indicating the closet, which contained two pillows. Near the window hung a picture of what appeared to be a bright blue bird trapped in orange branching coral. Sabine was studying it intently. Céleste realized that she, too, was looking anywhere except at the bed.

The town was built of a pale stone that looked dingy even in the sun—in winter every house would have a gray face. Saturday shoppers crowded the streets. A man with his arm in a cast was surveying the window display of a unisex shoe shop called Ladyboy. Like all the young men these days, he had a beard and hat that made him look like an Impressionist painter. Sabine stopped to cast a professional eye over the offerings in a florist's shop. "You see?" she said. "People here don't mind roses that have opened. In Paris, nothing will persuade them to put their hands in their pockets for anything but a bud. They're so limited." Having lived in Limoges until the age of two, Sabine often assumed a detached, Olympian view of the deficient Parisian mind.

They strolled on, past the market, past a motionless carousel in a square. In a park beside the river, a woman was wheeling a whippet in an old-fashioned pram. "Is it an accident? Does she need help?" Sabine hurried forward. The woman explained that the dog had grown too old to walk but still enjoyed *un petit tour de la ville*. Stretched full-length, the whippet was beached wood: gray and motionless, his adventures behind him.

Vauban's citadel, overlooking the old town, could be seen from the path that ran beside the water. Sabine pointed the other way, to her aunt's house. It lay across the river on a wooded hill, a gleaming white cube with windows that were mirrors in the sun. "After dinner, the two of us used to sit out on the terrace, drinking Irish whiskey and singing. Once there were soldiers in the citadel and they sang with us. Tante Rosalie didn't like soldiers—she called them vulgar." Sabine lifted her arms, stretched. She had taken off her jacket, and her halter-neck dress displayed the square shoulders that even quite recently would have been thought ugly. "That was the summer I turned sixteen," she said, and sighed.

"What did you sing?"

"My aunt's favorite was David Bowie. What does it mean exactly, 'funk to funky'?"

"No idea."

"But if you had to translate it?"

"I wouldn't."

Tante Rosalie, like her husband, had been born into a colonial family, explained Sabine, leading Céleste across a bridge. Her husband had seen what was coming in Algeria. He sold his hotels and his cork factory, and the orchards his grandfather had planted, and pulled out in '53. In France, he bought commercial real estate in three cities, including Paris. Certain phrases, such as *springtime in the Atlas Mountains*, would cause him to tug his mustache. Tante Rosalie always made her own couscous, the grains incomparably fine. All through the difficult winter of 1961, her husband lived for a weekly radio broadcast called *Algiers a Hundred Years Ago*. He died on the same day as de Gaulle, who had betrayed him and every Frenchman by granting Algeria independence. All this was family legend, but Sabine herself could attest to the smell of the house. In widowhood, Tante Rosalie started to keep cats—by the time she went into the home, she had thirty-six. "She used to put down bowls of meat and forget about them." Sabine's hand made the tipping gesture that signifies drink. "She was old, even twenty years ago. And so thin. Her rings were superb, these enormous stones. They slipped around on her fingers. Once I found a ruby in the cats' meat. After that, I checked the bowls every day." Sabine added, "What they say is quite true, you know: Algeria was never just a colony. I know it for a fact, from my family."

Céleste didn't say, Funny how you never hear an Algerian say that.

The road curved and began to climb. Presently, they turned off onto a narrower road where logs had been stacked under blue tarpaulins, ready for winter. Trees grew close to the verge and filled up all the distance. The town had disappeared; it might never have existed. Céleste's notion of space having been formed in Australia, she still thought of France as a small, urbanized country—the claims of its trees, swift and far-reaching, were always a shock.

A broad track led up through the woods. It took them to a gate, spiked and chained and set into a long brick wall: *Propriété privée. Défense d'entrer.* Beyond the gate, the beech trees stretched. Sabine said, "I was sure we could see the house from here." She passed her hand across her eyes, a magician's gesture, and then stared around, as if a fresh arrangement of their surroundings might have been conjured into sight.

"Wait here," she commanded. Explaining that she recalled a smaller gate, around to one side, she was already moving off. At first Céleste could see her stepping through ivy; then she disappeared. By the time she came back, Sabine had remembered cherry blossom. "At the back of the house. There was no garden to speak of, and no one had pruned the cherry tree since my uncle died, but it blossomed every year." She combed her fringe with her fingers and said, "It was a waste of time to come here."

"It doesn't matter," said Céleste. For several minutes, the only picture in her mind had showed Sabine arrayed on leaf mold with her pink dress ruched about her hips. A snail with a butter-yellow shell passed in close-up; a cartridge case lay beside Sabine's spread hair.

"The whole place is overrun with nettles," said Sabine, as if answering a silent entreaty. "We'll just have time to get back for lunch before I visit my aunt."

She talked incessantly on the way down of what Céleste would never see: the view from the terrace of the house, the room that had been hers—its two awkwardly spaced windows, "like eyes set just a little too far apart."

At the bridge, Céleste said, "See that guy over there? He's the second man I've seen here with his arm in plaster." Then she asked, "What happened to your aunt's cats when she went into the home?"

"She had a friend who used to visit her. He might have rescued one of the kittens."

They dined in a restaurant by the river. The foyer held a tank of trout, who had turned their tails to the room and were nosing at the darkest corner of the glass. Sabine was rather silent. She had spent the afternoon with her aunt, who seemed pleased to see her. Very soon, however, the old woman slipped away into a different world. "Over and over, she said, 'Please don't, Alain, please don't.'"

"Who's Alain?"

"Some bastard." Sabine went on, "My aunt shares a room with a lady who has MS. The only visitor she has is her mother.

Her mother's ninety and lives in Clermont-Ferrand, so she can't manage the trip more than once a year." Sabine had counted nine shades of brown in that room. All the time she was there, a voice farther along the corridor shouted, "Help! Help!" No one took any notice. "But you know the worst thing in that place? The staff wear T-shirts that say, *We make each day the best it can be.* My God!"

While Sabine was at the nursing home, Céleste had showered and turned down their bed. But when Sabine returned, she had to call each of her children as well as Bernard. A text from Jennifer had informed her of a crisis: Bernard's mother had fixed Jennifer's hair in such a way that four strands had stuck out of her chignon all morning, and Jennifer's life was ruined. After a soothing conversation that went on and on, Sabine called her mother, to report on Tante Rosalie. Céleste, lying on the bed, could hear Sabine's voice on the balcony. The words "incoherent" and "disgusting" recurred, but Céleste could think only of the long night they would spend together, the long waking. On the back of the door, a list of instructions on what to do in case of a fire had survived from an earlier era: *Gardez votre sang-froid*, it began.

That night Céleste woke at around two. The mattress sagged, and Sabine was lying more or less on top of her. When Céleste stroked her shoulder, Sabine rolled away, heaving herself out of the dip. She put out a hand, very white in the darkness, and moved it across the wall. Céleste breathed quietly, listening as Sabine settled back into sleep. Half an hour later, she was still thinking of trout and cats and the empty, frightening years that waited. Sydney appeared: it was a wooden house opening onto blue water. That led to Pippa, who had left Venice and was traveling south. Pouring wine on the last evening in her studio, Pippa had said, "Did you notice that, the way I twisted the bottle? I learned that from you."

Céleste rose and dressed. Passing the reception desk, she almost upset a bowl of water set in the middle of the floor—to absorb the smell of paint, she supposed. She was carrying George Meshaw's book, with the vague idea that she would find somewhere to sit and read for a while. But the breakfast room was locked, and the lobby contained no chairs.

She crossed the yard and the vaulted carriage entrance, and pressed the button that opened the heavy street door. The night was cool, and Céleste had dressed hurriedly in whatever came to hand. She walked briskly to keep warm, and when she came to a crossroad, chose the street that led uphill. It took her past a church, and the walled gardens of villas. Where it came to an end, a single streetlight showed a flight of steps. They ran up through trees and then—Céleste could sense rather than see its bulk—to the citadel. She climbed up to the road that ran past the fortifications. There was another streetlight, and a watchtower in the angle of a wall. Céleste went inside and peered through a deep-set, slitty window. Lights pricked the town below; they showed her the glistening vein of the river.

Pictures of Sabine appeared and faded in Céleste's mind like stars. She saw her that afternoon by the river, her exact shoulders, with hills behind her face. In the restaurant where the two of them had dined, the trout would still be looking for a way through glass. Sabine, glancing at their tank as she passed, had murmured, "*Pauvres bêtes.*" She avoided the fish on the menu and ordered grilled lamb.

They had arrived as the restaurant opened, wishing to return early to bed. When their plates had been cleared away, the waitress said, "*Alors—un petit dessert, mesdames?*"

Céleste glanced at Sabine and replied, "No, thank you."

"I shouldn't," began Sabine.

"*Allez!*" said the waitress, in a tone of huge indulgence. "What are holidays for?" And then, as Sabine still hesitated, "I'll bring you a menu."

She brought one for Céleste as well and went away again. Sabine read through the list of desserts with care. "*Ganache au chocolat*," she murmured. Then she snapped the menu shut and laid it aside, saying, "I mustn't. When I wore my polka-dot skirt last week, I had to leave the button on the waistband undone."

"Let's just get the bill, then," said Céleste.

"You don't know how lucky you are not having a sweet tooth."

Céleste looked around, but the waitress was busy elsewhere.

"If you ordered something, I could have a spoonful."

"Sure. What would you like?"

"Anything. It doesn't matter. I'm only having a spoonful. Get whatever you want."

Céleste consulted her menu. "The apple tart, I think."

The waitress was bearing down on them. "I would have ordered the *île flottante*," said Sabine. "Of course, it's more fattening."

Céleste asked for an *île flottante* and two spoons.

In her lookout, the smell of old stones grew overwhelming. Moist cold was seeping up through Céleste's sneakers as if she were standing in an invisible stream. A distant car shrieked like a bird. She made her way back to the stairs and started down between trees that were soft black walls. Almost at once, in the flowing dark, she missed her step and dropped her novel. Her weak knee raged as she crouched, low-growing branches in her face, her fingers encountering only damp leaves and earth. The dark world closed around her, ribbed with tree trunks. At last she found the book. Afterward, walking through the lighted, silent town, she clutched the novel as if it were a talisman, an object with no use but whose loss, standing in for all others, would be vast.

In the hotel lobby, the stainless-steel bowl on the floor shone silver; the surface of the water gleamed. Céleste could easily have walked around it. But it was like stepping over the moon.

On Sunday morning, Céleste was woken by the outbreak of civil war. That was what it sounded like—either that, or a reconstruction of the Battle of the Somme for an educational film. When she opened the shutters, the golden autumn weather of the previous day had vanished, and it looked as if they were in for rain. Céleste had envisaged a slow, luxurious rising, but Sabine was already in the shower. When she emerged from the bathroom, she announced that between calling home and visiting Tante Rosalie, she wished to take "a violent walk." She said, "I ate so much last night. And there'll be no time for the gym when I go home." Strands of her hair, darkened by the shower, were stuck to her breasts. She turned her back and began to drag clothes from her case. Below her shoulder blades, her flesh was dimpled. Céleste went into the bathroom, where a hag with red eyes peered blurrily through the condensation on the mirror. She had drunk only three glasses of wine the previous night, so why was a mud-brown river flowing through her skull? When she sat on the lavatory, a fart sighed free. Would the bowl have contained it, or would Sabine have heard? Céleste bowed her head and spread her hands over her face. She remembered that, returning from her excursion in the night, she had opened the door on robust snoring. Sabine lay on her back in the middle of the bed, a white figure on a tomb.

In the breakfast room, the gunfire was even louder. "Hunters," said the manager, placing a basket of croissants on their table; her varnished toenails shone through her tights. "Dentists and bank clerks. Sad bastards. They think a gun makes them interesting."

She picked at her tongue as if removing a stray hair and yielded to her matted cough.

After breakfast, Sabine went to their room to make her phone calls, and Céleste steadied herself with a second cup of tea. When she went upstairs, she stood outside their door and listened to the *plink plink plink* that was Sabine texting. Sabine sprang up when Céleste entered, saying that there was something she had to see. She herded Céleste back to the stairs, then up and up: "I was dreaming and climbed too far."

At the top of the house, a tight corridor wormed past attic rooms. Céleste found herself in front of an oval mirror. What was left of its silvering had dimmed: her face showed simplified and strange. Sabine placed her cheek next to Céleste's as if posing for a selfie. They saw themselves as they might have looked to an artist who scorned the present, painting for the centuries instead.

Tante Rosalie's house stood white as a ship on its hill. Here and there, where a track ran through the trees, hi-vis jackets dabbed fluorescent orange on an adjoining hillside, but the woods all around were still unbroken green. "They'll be hunting boar," said Sabine. She had sprayed herself with Bernard's perfume—with the addition of fresh air, it turned into unwashed feet.

That year there had been a craze for brooches fashioned from resin or lightweight wood to resemble birds. Soon it extended to dogs, cats, horses' heads. When the trend spread to clothing, woodland animals—foxes, rabbits, deer—appeared, appliquéd or printed across young women's breasts. To ward off the morning's chill, Sabine was wearing a cotton scarf, and a sweatshirt on which a hare crouched in grass. What did the fashion for these creatures signal, wondered Céleste. Shyness? Wildness? An invitation to the chase?

The women continued along the riverside path, the wind at their backs, and so reached the outskirts of the town. Webs strung on bushes masqueraded as the skeletons of LPs. The busy spiders had also stretched snares across the path, so that every few minutes one of the women had to pluck a sticky thread from her face.

Ducks sat on their watery doubles where the mist had lifted from the river. There were houses now beside the promenade; long, raked gardens boasted walnut trees, eggplants, cabbages as big as heads. A dog came along the path at a trot: her ears, blown sideways, were mussel shells lined with pink. "Oh, the gorgeous little doggie!" cried Sabine, stooping, her hand out. The dog, collarless but sleek, went by without a glance. Her smell made it plain that she had rolled in something foul. Céleste was lost in a future where she and Sabine lived beside the river in a creepered villa with green shutters; in a bed that ran beside the fence, dahlias grew like weeds. Their leeks flourished and their pear tree, and they kept a boat tied to the bank. The dog entered this idyll and passed through it, lending it fullness and truth.

"It's a different story when the river floods," remarked Sabine, continuing an uncanny conversation. "I've seen ducks swimming about in dining rooms here."

Céleste's imagination widened to take in a duck paddling past a sideboard. Or a swan gliding by, its smooth white curves ghosted in oak wood—why not?

"When the water goes down, everything is streaked with filth. The doors are twisted off their hinges. And the stench—my God!"

Westminster chimes played; Sabine took out her phone. She read the text that had just arrived and, without comment, returned the phone to her bag. Céleste fingered her cornelian beads. The phantom swan had vanished, leaving only a horse chestnut tree that dropped diseased brown leaves on the path.

They had turned back toward the town when a plump young man with his arm in a cast came into view. The wind ran past and twitched his beard. When he was out of earshot, Céleste raised her eyebrows: "Another one! What does it mean?"

"But is it another one? Or the same man, in disguise? I think he's stalking you. The cast is a fake. He wants to tell you, 'I would risk my limbs for you.'" Sabine's hand slipped like a snake through Céleste's arm. She said, "When we get back to Paris, we should get off the train separately. In case Bernard takes it into his head to come to the station."

So that was the text she had received.

Barr's Facebook posts now consisted of images from the Occupy movement. Céleste Liked every photo of protesters crammed into Zuccotti Park. One held a sign that read, *The Revolution Will Not Be Televised*—how did Barr feel about that?

Dominic e-mailed: "Will you get in touch with Barr? You might get through."

"I've no idea what to say," said Céleste to Sabine.

"Tell him you know why his father marry his mother."

Céleste looked at her.

"To have someone to attract the mosquitoes." Sabine rolled over in bed, laughing. Jennifer had brought the joke home from school. Sabine grew serious. "Teenage is a difficult time. It is so important to have a good home environment. Mother, father, everything very regular. *Les ados se perturbent facilement.*"

This was plainly a warning that Céleste would be sacrificed to ensure Madison's and Jennifer's smooth passage through their teenage years. She said coldly, "There's nothing wrong with Barr's home environment. It's entirely what you call regular."

"Ah, but the poor boy struggle with his sexuality. He know his parents do not accept it."

"Barr's never shown the least sign of being gay."

"No, he must be secret, the brave child."

"If he were gay, his parents would be nothing but supportive. They know I'm a lesbian. It doesn't matter to them in the least."

"You live at the other end of the world. You are not their only child."

"Nor is Barr, actually."

"The youngest is always the most precious." Sabine stroked the inside of Céleste's thigh. One of the drawbacks of *le cinq à sept* was that there was no time for both sex and talk. A great deal went unsaid.

Wendy wrote: "I never apportion blame, but I wonder if Dom's provided an adequate model of masculinity for Barr. Can it be helpful to a young boy to see his father in an apron every evening? There is still time for Dom to take up a sport. Fencing develops poise and should come naturally to him, since he is half French. I've always explained to the boys that your side of the family is eccentric and that we must try to understand without judging, but Barr is just much more impressionable than Mitch. It's so difficult to remain hopeful and so easy to imagine the worst. Last night I dreamed that Barr came out of his room and told us he'd become a Christian."

Céleste sent Barr a haiku Djamila had written:

Autumn is here.
The big moon high up in the fur tree
Is stuck like me.

As usual, Barr didn't reply. Céleste's last e-mail to Pippa, sent two weeks earlier, had also gone unanswered. During that time, Pippa had uploaded a blog post about her travels in Italy as well as posting several new photos on Facebook. She also Liked or left comments on various friends' pages. Reading these supportive remarks, Céleste was fifteen years old, standing alone at a party: defeated by connections that were invisible, exclusive, hip.

Barr posted a photo, taken earlier in the year, of a crowd packed into a Cairo square. The striped flags in the square were clearly visible, while the people wielding them were colored blobs. Barr had captioned it: "I want to be a pixel."

On Skype, Wendy was wearing a sleeveless top. She said, "Barr is manifesting a desire for self-effacement that's perfectly normal for sensitive boys at his stage of development." Her left hand slipped up through the armhole of her blouse as she talked and began to caress her chest; the creased skin there, below her neck, was twenty years older than Wendy's face. Then the video froze. With her mouth slung sideways and her eyes showing their whites, Wendy appeared to have suffered a stroke. Her hand, arrested, was a caramel claw, fashioned into a brooch and pinned to crepe. Céleste thought, Summer in Perth. She closed her eyes and summoned grevilleas that were past their peak. In the vast innocence of air-conditioned bedrooms, becoming a Christian was the worst fate people could imagine for their children. A freeway warbled in the distance, where cars ran through the night like rats.

". . . global phenomenon." Wendy dissolved into life. "Young people in Japan, boys mostly, shut themselves up in their rooms all the time."

"How long do they stay there?"

"Forever, sometimes." Wendy's voice was level. But any fool could see that she was screaming on the inside of her face.

Céleste and Djamila were determining whether Céleste was a Healer, an Analyst, an Adventurer or a Commander. Djamila read out: "'Which statement describes you best? (a) People say you are inflexible; (b) You are happy being the center of attention; (c) Your home environment is very tidy.'" As Céleste hesitated, "The answer is *a*," said Djamila. "*C'est évident.*"

Pippa's blog announced that she was pregnant. The baby had been conceived in Italy. "If she's a girl, we're going to call her Roma." A photograph showed a piazza, a fountain, bougainvillea tumbling over a burnt-orange wall. Rome was where Céleste was going at Christmas. Now a ghost who had yet to be born would track her like mist among the ruins, through the icy, empty palaces. The update had been posted while Europe slept—Céleste read twenty-seven congratulatory messages from Pippa's Australian friends. What she had just fully grasped was that she was now one of the many people to whom Pippa told one thing at a time: there would be no more sharing of many things with only her. That was modern life, it was stupid to mind. Céleste told herself, You are a person of the past. She remembered the way Pippa would yawn hugely, making her eyes shine. That first evening at the embassy came back, the slow-mo swirl of a big green skirt.

It was Friday morning. Céleste stayed in bed and worked. Then she got dressed and left her flat. On her way down, she saw Madame Kateb coming out of a door on the fourth floor. She fixed her atrocious gaze on Céleste. "Monsieur Alessi is away," she said. "He asked me to water his plants."

Her voice followed Céleste onto the metro, onto the train. *Monsieur Alessi asked me to water his plants.* It would never have occurred to Céleste to question what Madame Kateb was doing in their neighbor's apartment, but the concierge had judged it necessary to explain. Consequently, it was Céleste who felt accused of something sordid. She took out her phone, accessed her bank account, and checked her savings. It would soon be Christmas. Every year, there were residents who presented Madame Kateb with a scarf they didn't like or a vase that clashed with a new couch. Céleste, being short of money, knew the value of it and always left the concierge an envelope that contained notes. So why turn her into a class enemy now? She wondered if she could get away with shaving twenty euros off the sum she had set aside for Madame Kateb, or at least ten.

Céleste got off the train in a suburb to the west of the city. A mall stood across the parking lot in front of the station, but her destination lay farther out. Winter had gripped the day like a lover. Céleste's ears ached, and her eyes. Her made-up face was compacted sugar. She walked along what had once been a village street, past a boulangerie that had closed and a pizza place that was serving lunch. There was the soft sound of tires in the road. Electric stars had been strung between lampposts, and the middle distance was a fuzzy sort of blue. Céleste came to a pair of flat-faced village houses, one a beauty salon, the other a funeral parlor, their windows outlined in colored bulbs; then, on the far side of a bridge, the houses grew imposing and were set back from the road. Silvery, leafless branches impersonated frozen lightning behind high stone walls. There would be big dogs there, padding beside the exhausted earth in the flower beds. Two men came out of a gate that one of them locked with a remote. On this sunless day, both wore rapacious dark glasses that curved around the sides of their heads. Céleste passed them with her white stare.

The medical center was on the road that led to the highway. There was a sports ground across the street, overlooked by daunting blocks of flats. Céleste waited for a van that was pulling out of a service station; the center, built of sand-colored bricks, lay just beyond. A flight of steps with turquoise railings led up to the pharmacy, which was signaled by a trembling green cross. Its window framed a frightening, giant close-up of a fat-mottled thigh. Fortunately, all any woman had to do to avoid that fate was to massage her flesh with the firming lotion on display.

Inside the pharmacy, Céleste undid her coat and unwound her scarf. A sales assistant was serving a customer, an old man with hippyish hair, who was complaining of the cold. A woman accompanied by a child in a stroller was examining a range of herbal teas—the child gave off a violent smell of sour milk. It mingled with air freshener to suggest that plastic roses were being boiled down with a goatskin at the back of the shop.

"It's the Internet," said the old man. "It interferes with the weather. My nephew, the one who works for the post office, can explain it all to you. His family is scientific, his father bred English setters."

Céleste picked up a tester for an expensive lipstick and drew a stroke on the back of her hand. She drew another, in a different shade, and mimed indecision, frowning slightly, angling her hand. Her performance was wasted. The assistant, a gaunt brunette, was listening without impatience as the old man aired his views on Corsica, where he had never been. Whenever he paused, "Quite so," she murmured. "Quite so."

The pharmacist emerged from his dispensary. He nodded to

the young mother, and began to run through her medication: her sore throat required the application of a spray, a syrup with which she was to gargle after meals and at bedtime, and anti-inflammatory suppositories. The child gurgled and flung out a fleece-clad arm; the pharmacist leaned his elbows on the counter and clicked his tongue to return the salute. Céleste had drawn closer and was peering around a display of organic skin care. When Bernard appeared in his white coat, reality had stretched like a balloon. A phantom solidified instead of melting away—Céleste's head filled with light. She thought, I know so much about you. As if he had heard, Bernard glanced her way. He resembled his Facebook photographs exactly. Life closed over and absorbed the wedge of eeriness. Céleste shoved the lipstick onto a shelf and left.

There was a long wait for the next train. Céleste checked her messages: nothing from Sabine. It was drizzling as she crossed the road to the mall, where she found a café and ordered tea—her mouth felt stiff when she spoke. When the tea arrived, there was still a faint tingling along her arms. Why had she come here, what had she imagined the sight of Bernard would change? She noticed that she had dressed up for the encounter in a slinky black Agnès B. rip-off that one of her students, a buyer at Printemps, had sold her at a knockdown price. Since the dress had been pretty much hidden under her patchwork coat, its effect was lost except on Céleste. She turned her hands over on the table and saw two stripes, one coral, one rose. Her nails were unpainted. She owned no rings. Sabine appeared to her, examining the contents of a bowl, plucking a ruby from a lump of rank meat.

A girl entered the café, bringing the chilly smell of outdoors—there was rain on her shoulders. She had Djamila's hunched look, the same short neck surmounted by elaborate waves of hair. Tiny stones sparkled along her eyebrow, ran down her dark ear. A group of girls, the children or grandchildren of immigrants, all dressed in bright, synthetic clothing, hailed her. The pierced girl raised her hand in greeting, and Céleste saw that her fake fingernails were set with shining chips.

At the end of George Meshaw's novel, his hero was diagnosed with an eye disease that would soon destroy his sight. His wife had left him. His house was for sale. The conflict at work had been smoothed over, but he knew that he would be eased out at the next restructuring—his Indian colleague, meanwhile, was promoted. The novel ended with the man going into St. James Station, on his way home from an appointment with a Macquarie Street ophthalmologist. *It was his usual station, the one he had arrived at and departed from every day of his working life. For the first time, he noticed the glitter of mica in the granite under his feet. It kept catching his eye, as he fed his ticket into the turnstile and started down the stairs.*

Céleste had read these sentences, the last in the novel, over and over. Sometimes the mica offered the only pinpricks of hope in a merciless book. Then she would change her mind, deciding that the sparkling stone was a last, mocking cruelty: soon the man would be denied the sight of even that modest splendor. Céleste googled reviews of the novel—they were useless. On the wall-mounted TV in the café, the hit of the summer started up. A few of the teenagers sang along: "*She's got two lives . . . Lonely Lisa!*" The pierced girl was tearing at a croissant with her glittering nails. Céleste took out a Kleenex and wiped the lipstick stripes off her hand. She found coins for the tea she had left untasted, and removed her coat from the stand in a corner. It was time for her train.

When it pulled in, she glimpsed her reflection in the doors. What had she been thinking of, making up her face, zipping up her boots, twisting up her hair? Soon she was speeding toward Paris. A woman sitting across the aisle took a picture book from her bag and handed it to her daughter. The child examined the book, turning it about in both hands. Her downy brows drew together: "*Maman*, what is the password?" she asked.

On the journey back from Besançon, Sabine had retrieved her case from the overhead rack as soon as the first grimy Parisian apartment blocks appeared. *Fugit amor,* thought Céleste. Sabine put on her jacket, drawing in her stomach as she did up the buttons, and smoothed her skirt. Her aunt had been much livelier that morning, talkative and alert, and Sabine returned from the visit elated. She told Céleste the news at once: "She's left me her jewels." Sabine smiled and bit her lips. Her aunt had said, "With those eyes, you should wear sapphires." Sabine's excitement lasted all the way back to Paris. On the train, she began to tell Céleste about a customer who had come into her shop to complain that the lemon tree he had bought was fatally diseased. "You won't believe this, but it's the fourth time he's come in with this kind of story. The first time it was a bouquet of gerberas and lilies. I gave him a refund—it can happen, why not. But four times! The lemon tree cost a hundred and fifty euros, and this creep says it's as good as dead. So I told him—" Here Sabine broke off. She said in her unemphatic way, "Tante Rosalie came out with a strange thing today. We were talking about her jewelry and she described it all perfectly, even a little pearl brooch. Then out of the blue, she said, 'Do you remember that colonel who used to come to dinner in Algiers? He had one of our gardeners tortured to death.' It must have been a dream she'd had," said Sabine. "She went on talking about the brooch, telling me to be careful because the catch isn't reliable."

At the Gare de l'Est, "Until Tuesday," said Sabine, planting brisk kisses on Céleste's cheeks. She was among the first passengers off the train. By the time Céleste followed, only a few stragglers remained on the platform. There was the clatter of wind on the roof. Céleste looked up and saw rain running slowly down glass—it made her long for gin. Bernard had probably brought the children with him to the station. Sabine would have kissed them all, and complimented Jennifer on her hair. Later, at home, there would be champagne—the girls, allowed a sip, would beg their mother to describe Tante Rosalie's rings. Sabine would tell them, "You can look into a sapphire forever."

Remembering that endless walk to the head of the platform, Céleste relived the onrush of despair. When the black mist lifted, something remained: a pattern. She would always accept what she didn't want so that Sabine could enjoy a spoonful of sweetness. The motive for her ridiculous expedition to the pharmacy was plain. What she had needed was not to inspect Bernard but to display herself to him. Dress, boots, upswept hair proclaimed, I exist. The reality of Bernard had never been in question. It was her own presence that could be wiped out by a flare of light.

At St.-Michel, Céleste decided to get out and walk. On the escalator, she spotted the girls from the café. Two of them, the pierced girl and one whose long, unbound hair was dyed yellow, were sharing an iPod, each with a bud in one ear. "*Lonely Lisa*," they burst out together, arms linked, swaying on their step. Their greedy young faces were turned upward. Céleste smiled at them, but they didn't notice her, absorbed in each other and the song.

In the street, she resolved on a whim to follow the pack of girls. They led her along the quai, past a bridge. The rain had stopped, but people still had their umbrellas out and were casting glances at the sky. A faint brightness in the air, as if the sun were pressing close behind the clouds, created a peculiar, greasy light. The girls shoved along the crowded pavement, their shoulders thrusting sideways in the puffy jackets they wore over their skimpy tops.

On Pont de l'Archevêché, they came to a halt. Céleste loitered as if admiring the view downstream. The river, running high between its stone embankments, magically evoked the approach to Tante Rosalie's house—Céleste saw beech trees stretching away. There were no gardeners: they had all been left behind in Algiers. In spring, the cherry blossom assumed the shape of a dead man—but that was only a bad dream.

The pierced girl unzipped her backpack and took out a padlock that she handed to the blonde. Cameras and phones appeared. The two girls posed, holding up the padlock between them. Hundreds of locks were already fastened to the bridge, some engraved with two names and a date, others plain, some rusty—there was a handsome golden one shaped like a fish. The girls began to search for somewhere to add their own padlock; the blonde's hair bounced down her spine. Presently they had attracted quite a little crowd. A space was found at last, inconveniently low, near the pavement. The girls crouched, attached their love lock to the mesh, posed for their friends' cameras. "Vandals!" cried a woman, leaning from a pillion. When the girls rose, the pierced one hurled the key over the bridge. The river received it—it received everything. The girls kissed. *She love me!* Faintly ironic cheers rose from bystanders, a horn sounded. "Congratulations!" said Céleste. The girls didn't notice. They were looking through her, at a future locked into place.

Céleste walked on, over the island, past the fizzing, Christmassy shops. A zigzag of back streets brought her to a doorway filled with a family of Roma, the sharp-faced children huddled against a calm brown dog. Farther along the boulevard, a couple approached, arm in arm, the woman carrying a bouquet. The flowers were obscured by their wrapping, but as the pair drew closer, molecules of eucalyptus wafted past. Céleste held her head high: if she looked down, the old, stupid tears would fall. They were there, hard as beads, lined up behind her lids. For their first Christmas together, Sabine had brought her a sheaf of sweet-scented dollar gum. Later, Céleste made tea, and toast spread with butter and Vegemite. Sabine took one bite—"My God!" In the card she left that day, Céleste placed a round blue leaf.

The couscous restaurant lay on her way. The street was the kind where the buildings breathed into each other's faces, and evening arrived at half past three. As Céleste paused in front of the restaurant, a light came on inside. At once the room with its white-draped tables was transformed into a stage. A man carrying a metal cash box entered from the rear, like an actor, and crossed out of sight. Céleste asked silently, *Maman*, what is the password? The brass key in the diorama seemed to grow larger, as if she were seeing it under water. Behind it, that other key traced an arc through her mind: it glittered like the ethics of possibility, like the girl who had thrown it into the Seine.

Someone called, "Céleste!" in a commanding trill. What was Valerie doing back in her old neighborhood on a working day? "I was just about to text you," she told Céleste as they kissed. "What's happened to Didier?"

"Didier?"

Valerie jerked her chin over her shoulder. "Didier. Who lives in the square."

"Oh—that guy." Céleste said, "He always disappears in winter."

"A charity picks him up. They take him to a hostel. But it's too early for that—they only stop by a day or two before Christmas. Didier's just vanished, and none of the shopkeepers can tell me what's become of him."

Céleste saw that the environmentally responsible carrier bag on Valerie's wrist held a foil package of the type used for roast chicken. The corner of a takeout container showed underneath. She said, "Did you come all this way to bring him food? That's so great."

"Of course not!" said Valerie. Her high color intensified, as if she had been caught out in a minor barbarity—double-dipping in an ambassadorial tapenade, perhaps. She said, "I always have my suede jacket dry-cleaned at that place near the metro—you must know the one. I wouldn't trust anyone else in Paris with it."

"There's a Roma family begging back there, on the boulevard," said Céleste. "You could give them the food."

Valerie's curls were solid brown bubbles against her camel-hair coat. She said, "Are you kidding me? That lot are all thieves."

"There were two children. With braids. And a dog."

"They'll be fine, then. They'll eat the dog."

Rain began to fall, the first heavy coins. A secret channel of association caused Céleste to recall the interior of the Katebs' lodge. It contained a leather couch that Valerie had handed down when she moved away: mid-century modern, a little grubby but with good Danish bones. Valerie's pug had chewed a corner of the upholstery, but the damage looked far less conspicuous than it had in Valerie's big white empty flat. The light in the lodge, which seemed to glare through the frosted glass into the hall, was in fact quite dim. There was a fluorescent tube above a partition wall that didn't reach the ceiling, but Madame Kateb preferred to set shadows floating by switching on a lamp. Céleste knew that on the other side of the partition were twin beds separated by a closet. There was also a wardrobe, mirrored on one door, which Djamila and her mother shared—it was one of Djamila's grievances. Nowhere was there enough natural light for her to make up her face, and the electric lights threw shadows in all the wrong places.

Whenever Céleste entered the lodge, she expected the smell of stale cooking—either that, or the reek of floors washed down with *eau de Javel.* In any case, she would brace for something unpleasant, unconsciously holding her breath. But every time, against logic and instinct, the airless room smelled clean and fresh.

IV

PIPPA PASSES

SIX MINUTES LATER, PIPPA CHECKED her Twitter feed again. @warmstrong said, "Reading Martin Amis's latest. Losing the will to live." That was her friend Will; Pippa retweeted him. The self she had curated at @pippapasses was warmly supportive of other writers, at least those on Twitter, but Amis, having contrived to find fame without the benefit of social media, didn't count.

On Facebook, Rashida had posted a photo of homemade labneh with citrus zest and truffle oil. The labneh sat on its blue plate like a fat white turd flecked with orange. Pippa Liked it, and so did nineteen other people, three of whom were Rashida's sisters. Photos showed that all four Afzal sisters had the same pudgy face embedded in long, amazing hair. In Rome, Matt and Pippa had seen a hairdressing salon called Capellissimmi. "It means hairy hair," said Matt, putting his arm around Pippa. Hairy hair! said Pippa to herself whenever she saw Rashida. The Afzals made red velvet cupcakes for one another's birthdays and wrote "Gorgeous girl!" under their sisters' chubby selfies on Facebook. The latest post on Ferial Afzal's page informed Pippa that Ferial's baby, Iggy Syed, had celebrated his first birthday that weekend in Melbourne. Under damp-looking curls, Iggy Syed looked starey and haunted. Rashida wrote, "Aww. My big boy! So happy I could celebrate with you."

@gloriahallelujah tweeted: "Amazing party on friend's yacht. Finally met @JoshKapoor. Be still my beating heart." A photo showed Gloria clutching a bottle, her flushed, kittenish face turned to a man who was smiling at someone else. Gloria was Pippa's agent and she had had Pippa's new manuscript for four weeks now. Pippa texted Matt: "Won't hear from G today. She's hungover again." Matt was teaching all morning, so Pippa sent the same message to George. He texted back: "Bummer. Were onesies 2012 or 2013?" That was George: your classic narcissist. His latest novel contained a line about the Nineties being when there were more dogs called Max than people—that was something Pippa had said, and George hadn't even thanked her. He never thanked anyone: his novels were published without acknowledgments, which Pippa considered a typically male move. George's agent would never be photographed pissed with her tits falling out of a two-sizes-too-small designer dress. George's agent was part Japanese, part Finnish, and part vampire. Back in the day, when Pippa was looking for an agent, George had suggested Minako. Minako lived in New York, and according to George she was really shy. In Pippa's experience, shy people didn't send e-mails that said, "George showed me three chapters of your novel. I'm afraid I didn't get past the first."

From Monday to Wednesday Pippa worked for a company that published restaurant guides. Today was Thursday; part of Pippa's brain murmured that she should be planning out a new book or at least putting the sheets on to wash. She picked up the postcard from her mother that had come the previous day. Her mother ran a B&B in New Zealand, but the postcard showed garish flower beds in a nondescript Spanish square. Somewhere, Pippa's mother had acquired multiple copies of this card with its out-of-focus fountain. Pippa received three or four a year. They said things like "The lake is complicated today." Or, "Try to live life from beyond the grave as it were. Imagine what you will have been"—the last three words underlined twice.

On Twitter, @warmstrong asked: "What is the point of historical fiction? #banHilaryMantel." Someone had a photo of the view from her Airbnb room in Porto. Someone else linked to footage of Syrian refugees pleading to be granted asylum in Australia. @gloriahallelujah followed @TheEllenShow. She retweeted a hilarious cartoon about the plight of cats trapped in folk music environments. Pippa retweeted it too.

Hank the Tank came and looked at her from the door of her study. "I hear you," said Pippa. "Soon. We'll go to the park soon." Hank produced a noise like a teddy whose growl had worn down to a wheeze. His eyes were large and dark and believing. Pippa checked her e-mail: an invitation from Matt's mother to lunch on the weekend, a special offer from FragranceNet, nothing from Gloria. Pippa retweeted @MargaretAtwood urging the donation of books to prisons. She followed every famous writer she could find on Twitter, but so far none of them had followed her back. Someone posted a photo of a dog on a skateboard. @warmstrong linked to a screening of *Hotel Monterey*. "Chantal Akerman: wonderwoman or wanker? You decide." Pippa read a Lydia Davis story on the *New Yorker* website. She googled to see if Lydia Davis was on Twitter. She read a *Crikey* piece about arts funding, followed a few links, and some time later bought a swimsuit. Her e-mail chimed; it was an overdue reminder from the library. Anyway, Gloria would call, not e-mail. Gloria's voice was always low and exhausted. Of Pippa's previous novel, she had whispered, "Everyone here really, really loves it. The scene with the endives is amazing! I've never read anything so raw. It really amazed everyone. But we ran it through SIMS, our amazing new reader-response software, and it says readers are over the whole

French thing. I hope you're not expecting much in the way of an advance."

Pippa's phone rang and she snatched it up. But it was only a former neighbor, so she let it ring out. She e-mailed Matt's mother: "Hi Eva, Thanks for the lovely invite. Lunch would have been great, but a few people are coming over on Sunday. xxP." "A few people" meant Rashida and Steve, an old friend of Matt's. Steve was freshly single because his wife had repartnered with a divorce lawyer. Pippa had also invited Will and a friend of hers from work so that the setup wasn't too blatant.

"Steve's perfect for Rashida," Pippa had told Matt.

"Can't see it—they've got nothing in common."

"They're both into, you know, environmental stuff."

"You mean Steve's an eco-fascist. He spends his holidays killing poplars."

"Well, Rashida's a vegetarian."

Matt said, "Steve's hardly her type."

When Pippa moved to Sydney to go to university, she missed the town in northern New South Wales where she had grown up. In Sydney everything was strange: noises, intersections, buildings, views. Someone had put a dimmer switch on the stars. The city was daredevil, filthy and full of people who knew where they were going. Driving to a party in Leichhardt, Pippa couldn't get off Parramatta Road: every intersection displayed a "No Right Turn" sign. "It's like a Communist Party convention," said Vince, peering through the windscreen. He was from the country too, a different part of it, and no help with navigation. Later, when Pippa was living in a shared house by the beach, she would lie in bed at night listening to the surf. She felt how easily the city could pound her, too. It was shocking and thrilling. Her thoughts ran with its rivers, flinging themselves into the sea. Sydney was a place where everything piled up behind you. All its windows watched and shone. Those sad palm trees—their broken green spokes! The city's beauty, like its money, was self-important, calculated to stun. It judged all who came its way according to silent, iron rules. If you were not rich, you were nothing: that was the first rule. She was part of this place now, its snappy answers and impersonal brutishness. She set her teeth. She was going to be a writer. When she was famous, Sydney would be obliged to place commemorative plaques outside the houses where she had lived. Her future was as vast as the light beating its wings in clifftop parks.

By the time Matt and Pippa became friends, she was living on the other side of the city, and the Pacific was nowhere near. Not far from her house was a park where they would meet—Matt wouldn't go to the house, because a woman who had no further use for him also lived there. The wreckage of that relationship was what Pippa and Matt picked through that spring, sitting under a lemon-scented gum. There were scribbles of sun on their faces and arms. Until then, Matt had been the subject of stories told by Pippa's housemate late at night as a joint passed back and forth—they were rather scathing little stories. In the park, he grew real to Pippa, emerging from a pack of boys who jingled coins in their pockets.

On a sticky November day, she arranged to meet him there in the late evening. They arrived at the same time, each bringing beer, and exclaimed at the same thing: the ghostliness of a white flowering hedge at dusk. Matt did most of the talking. As he spoke, he moved his hands, which were nothing like Pippa's idea of a musician's hands: they had dimples for knuckles. After a while, lying on her back in her thin cotton dress, Pippa wanted to take one of those fleshy hands and place it between her legs. At home, she would write down things Matt had said. "She doesn't care about people, she classifies them." "Her words pour out and her heart never moves." What mattered to him was music, not books, but what he said struck her with the force of poetry: formal, wise. Pippa thought, He'll be good for my writing. Then, lusty young animal, she drove fast through the fumy night to the disgusting Marrickville flat that Vince shared with two other guys. Vince already belonged to the past, but for different reasons neither of them could forgo the visits that Pippa still paid him that spring.

One evening, she arrived early at the park and took a novel from her bag. She wanted to appear occupied, not waiting for Matt. Having read a page or two self-consciously, she grew absorbed and didn't see him arrive. He slipped his hand into her hair—his fingers lay coolly against her scalp. Intense feeling caused him to smile. He glanced down and sideways, which made him look cagey.

After that, Pippa had to find somewhere else to live. Matt, who happened to be between houses, was back home with his parents. But at once he came up with a place for them both. He was a Sydney boy: he had friends or at least mates or at least phone numbers all over town. Someone gave him the keys to a flat at Kurraba Point. The flat was on the ground floor: the living room window was twenty-two inches above the harbor. The bedroom was uninhabitable, and everywhere ponged of drains and damp. Work on the flat had been delayed, and Matt and Pippa lived there, paying almost nothing, all summer. The wiring was suspect, so they made do with torches and candles. The white shirts Pippa needed for waitressing had to be ironed in batches at a friend's house. In the mold-stippled bathroom, her toothbrush went mushy. She and Matt rolled about in bed, as lively and purposeful as lions.

Whenever they touched, a horizon widened. Pippa dreamed that she had drawn the night into their room: looking up, she met the cold, mineral gaze of stars.

No matter how late they fell asleep, Matt would wake before it was light, shut himself into the kitchen, and play his violin. He would soon be auditioning for music schools in London and the States. "No one'll come right out and say it, but an overseas qualification's still the royal road to a permanent gig with a professional orchestra here," he told Pippa. Each audition piece was a problem he needed to solve: that was how he thought of music, as something strict and technical stripped of the fuzzy notions about self-expression that people brought to art.

There was always a breeze licking out that flat. About a week after they moved in, a storm swooshed water up past the tide mark to the level of their sill; they had to drag their futon away from the window. The building, white-painted and curvy, had once been a house and was now three flats, set one above the other. It suffered from subsidence and was a little lopsided—that, and the curving walls on the upper stories, gave it the air of a ship that had been scuttled and was slowly sinking. They told each other, "It's just like Venice," where neither had been. Italy was suggested also by the white colonnade that stood at a right angle to the building. It must have been designed for vines or flowering creepers, but its pillars were bare.

There was something vaguely dodgy about Matt and Pippa's presence in the flat, and they were under instruction to say, if questioned, that they were related to the owner and visiting Sydney for a short stay. As it turned out, they rarely saw the other tenants, and no one spoke to them. On the first night, Pippa had woken up, certain that a dinner party was taking place upstairs at three in the morning—she could hear cutlery against plates. The next morning it was still going on. Matt said, "It's that chinking sound made by wind in rigging." He had—of course—a friend with a boat. They watched the fireworks from it on New Year's Eve. Long pink lilies of light swooned over the harbor, and they drank bubbly from a bottle as big as a baby. By the end of the display, they were alive in a new century, and the word "Eternity" was flowing across the bridge.

Matt knew why a clothing store in Oxford Street displayed only three identical white dresses in its window from time to time, and the significance of the modernist apartment block on Balmoral Beach. He could tell Pippa where to find the ghost platforms at Central Station, and which lane to take when driving over the harbor bridge. All through their first year together, Sydney concertinaed out before Pippa. Matt had visited mythological places—New York, Delhi, the Greek islands—and believed in glimpses, in the unexpected view. He said, "Anything memorable should take you by surprise." Strolling to a restaurant in Balmain, he touched Pippa's arm. She slid her eyes sideways and found herself looking down a street that seemed to rise directly from the harbor. Thickset trees stood like guardians between the land and the water. Spring came around again, and Matt drew her attention to a Newtown cul-de-sac where freshly green plane trees led the eye to a blue mist. The jacaranda and the seagoing street found their way into the stories Pippa was writing when waitressing hadn't left her exhausted. They were stories about growing up, part record-keeping, part revenge, but Pippa set them in Sydney. She could remember her old ambition to bring the city to heel, but not exactly why she had felt that way: Sydney before Matt was the view from a car speeding through fog. By the time he and Pippa had been together a year, even that memory had faded and vanished from the sky. It amazed her how quickly everything had fled into the past. The white flat beside the harbor, the park with its spotty, eucalypt shadows were already as remote as photos. It was as if, not having much common history to carry into the future, they needed to stock up fast.

Matt didn't get a place at the Juilliard School, the New England Conservatory, or the Royal Academy of Music. It was the end of his dream of a performance career. He said, "That was my mother's dream, not mine." His mother had instructed Loreto nuns to offer up prayers for his success. Matt's hands, shapeless and full of music, plucked at the shoulders of his T-shirt—the hands, the gesture, these too belonged to his mother.

"There must be other schools," said Pippa.

"Not for me." At the time, Pippa didn't realize that this meant, Not for my mother.

Meanwhile, Pippa had sent her three best stories to magazines; they were all rejected. It was her night off from waitressing, so they got dressed up, went into town, and drank vodka shots at a harbor bar. Matt said, "I'm not afraid of teaching. It's something I do OK." Pippa leaned across the table and kissed him: a slow, openmouthed kiss to show that she trusted in whatever might come. "We'll have kids, won't we?" he said. "Beautiful kids." She took this, like her kiss, as a statement of faith rather than intent. When Pippa thought of motherhood, she saw something like a swamp. She saw heavy, veined flesh, worn-out women enslaved by miniature despots, a barnyard functionality in which every ideal mired and drowned. Each woman was wrapped in a large apron on which was embroidered "For Daily Use." It was a vision that originated in observation but drew its power from slippery, frightening, invisible things: the passing of time, the thinning of possibility.

When she rose to leave the bar, Pippa teetered on her strappy red shoes. Matt took her arm. She folded her hand over his. Around them, people went on drinking in tight, laughing circles. Matt and Pippa strolled away, a couple in the balmy, iconic evening, backed by an opera house and a bridge. Each was aware of space, its milky vacancy, swinging around them. This was how it would be, Pippa decided, they would hold each other and step out as if there was nothing to fear.

The floating world of student parties and shared houses had detached Matt from his context. It was obvious that he had been ground out by a private school; for the rest, he was just another guy in cargo pants smoking a joint with his long feet up on some girl's balcony. They didn't sit in chairs, those boys, but lay in them, like children, with glasses, bottles, and ashtray within reach.

It turned out that Matt belonged to a family as hierarchical and splendid as an army. He had four older sisters. One was a partner in a commercial law firm, and one was an architect in Chicago, and one was in Cambodia with Doctors Without Borders, and the fourth did something amazing and digital, the exact nature of which Pippa could never pin down. They were girls with ponies in their past. All four took after their father, a whippy, sparrow-colored ophthalmologist. The family home in Bellevue Hill had a music room that held the gleaming, concentrated presence of a grand piano and, in a shadowy corner, an angel without a head. Closer inspection revealed a dust-sheeted harp. It had belonged to Matt's grandmother, who once played it at the Albert Hall. She was half Irish, Matt confided—Pippa was never to let on that she knew.

Two remarks defined the Elkinsons for Pippa. Over her first Christmas lunch with the family, the conversation led to the beach house in Jervis Bay where various Elkinsons would be spending time in January. Ronnie, the digital sister, looked up from her portion of colorless, flavorless turkey breast and asked Pippa, "Where do your folks have their beach house?"

"We don't have one," said Pippa into the sudden silence. She added, as if it were an explanation rather than a non sequitur, "My parents are divorced."

Talk flowed on around the table, over the dismal food. All the Elkinson girls had their mother's searching face, but Ronnie's gaze was the most intent. She was the first middle-class person Pippa knew with serious tattoos. From elbow to wrist her arms were the exquisite green-blue of mold, except for an uninked heart shape on each. When introduced to Pippa, Ronnie had kissed her at once on both cheeks: hard kisses, like knocks at a door. And here she sat, smiling and doing her best to make Pippa feel welcome—it wasn't possible to hate her, realized Pippa, with dismay.

The second remark dated from a party thrown by the Elkinsons to celebrate a great-aunt's ninetieth birthday. The old woman had translucent green teeth and a doddery spaniel. The spaniel lay on an antique rug and was fed cake. When Eva, Matt's mother, stepped too close to the dog, he snapped at her ankles. "Isn't he sweet?" said Eva. She added hazily, "You hear such sad stories. Most old dogs drown in the family pool."

When Matt announced that he was going to train as a teacher, Eva said that she wasn't surprised. "Becky was always the musical one." Becky was the doctor. Matt had his mother's wavy hair, blocky torso, and secretive smile. Eva was Polish, spoiled her fortunate Australian children and forgave them nothing. Her way of punishing Matt for failing to become a professional musician was to behave as if the mere mention of a violin now affected him like a fatal wound. Music came to Matt from his father, Keith. Arranging Matt and Pippa's wedding, Eva announced that Keith would play at the reception. Keith looked at his son. "'Légende'? Or shall we treat them to Bach?"

"Obviously I meant just you, my love," said Eva, her voice creamy with inner meaning. "It's Matt's day—he doesn't want to do anything upsetting."

Pippa said, "But you'd love to play, wouldn't you, Matt? It would be great. I'm counting on it."

Matt smiled at a corner of the floor. Eva's eyes, widened at her husband, said, How could you be so insensitive! At the wedding, Keith took off his jacket, rolled up his sleeves, and sat at the piano. The notes seemed to run up through his elbows. If not for Keith, the lowest step on the family pyramid would have been reserved for Matt. Keith filled the role of a pet: tolerated, even loved, and of no importance. One of his daughters confided, "It's so embarrassing going out with Dad—he smiles at everyone."

Keith drove a rackety powder-blue Beetle in defiance of his wife and children. The cry of "Carbon footprint!" arose whenever it roared up the drive. Eva said, "When that man wants something, he wants it violently." Her surfeited smile, angled at the rug, informed her audience that she knew what it was to be wanted like that.

Pippa put the Beetle down to a rich man's infantile tastes—what was a Beetle if not an egg laid by a Ferrari? Then Keith told her, "Pretty much all other cars look aggressive. This one seems defenseless, don't you think?"

Pippa said that the Beetle looked more human than most humans. Her own car, an ancient Peugeot, refused to start in wet weather. "It's ironic, isn't it," said Pippa, "a car that won't go when the weather's bad?" The Peugeot had belonged to Aidan, her brother, dead at twenty on a surfing holiday. Keith and Pippa were allies, although it was an alliance with no outward sign. On parting, he would grasp Pippa with the firm, unsmiling embrace of a man about to go into battle or to the scaffold. His hands, always chilly, were shaped like the heads of snakes.

There was a history of heart trouble in Keith's family, said Eva, so he had to watch what he ate. Keith obediently made his way through pale boiled potatoes—he wasn't allowed baked—and a piece of skinless chicken. Pippa believed that food should smile on a plate. When her parents-in-law came over for meals, Pippa made salads that contained radishes and pomegranate seeds and dark red leaves. There was chicken cooked with yogurt and golden raisins and spices. There was fish and seafood garnished with fistfuls of herbs, and spiced honey served with fat purple figs. The first time Pippa cooked for him, Keith said that he had never eaten so well in his life. A while later, Eva remarked that nowadays people seemed to make a cult of eating. "It's considered normal. I was raised to value things of the spirit."

Eva was the kind of woman who could carry off a fine knit. She referred to herself as "a citizen of conscience" and was in favor of sculpture in malls. Twice a week, she attended mass in a hat. Unbelievably, she had a tame priest, a Jesuit who could be found murmuring with her on a couch. The Jesuit was breezy and soft-shoe, always dressed in jeans and a creaseless dark shirt. He had a loose, manly laugh that made Pippa fear he was about to drop into a boxing feint. "I suppose it all seems very *Brideshead Revisited* to you," said Eva to Pippa. "Or Graham Greene, perhaps? This hut and so on." Eva's English, an artifact polished to a high sheen, was not altogether free of cracks. For "hat" and "heart" alike she said "hut." She had returned from mass minutes before Pippa and Matt arrived for lunch, and was standing before the hall mirror, removing her hat. Her dress, a dreamier blue than the hat, bloused over at the waist. Hydrangea bush, thought Pippa. She said cheerfully that she had never read Graham Greene. "But I loved *Brideshead.* Anthony Andrews—where are you now?"

In the mirror, Eva's eyes rested on Pippa's reflection. She raised a hand to her hair. Her spongy fingers glared with a sapphire, a band set with turquoise and pearls, and an aquamarine the size of a swimming pool. "I am one kind of Australian," said Eva to reflected Pippa, "and you are another."

The Elkinsons were well informed about kinds of Australians. Pippa learned that Bondi was favored by South Africans and Russians, Rose Bay by Jews. Chatswood had gone over to the Chinese: "It barely qualifies as North Shore these days." Bellevue Hill, where the Elkinsons lived, was another Jewish stronghold. "Very decent people," said Keith, as if reassuring someone. He had a light, deliberate way of speaking that Pippa associated with judges in British television dramas; she was pleased when she learned that his father had been on the bench. She had thought of Matt's connections as silvery spider threads webbing Sydney but was discovering that they were stout cables attaching the Elkinsons to politics, banking, the judiciary, the upper reaches of the public service. Caroline, the lawyer sister, was married to a man whose cousin played cricket for Australia. At Caroline's wedding, this cousin had followed the bride into a bathroom and groped her. She swiped at him, causing his nose to bleed. Blood ran down the front of his shirt and onto her dress when she tried to stanch it. "So there we were, blood all down us, and the dickhead goes, 'No need to mention this, doll.'"

•

Something not immediately apparent about the Elkinsons was the way they picked up and echoed one another's remarks. When Ronnie was refusing to fall in with one of Eva's schemes, Caroline told her, "You only have one mother."

"Thank God for that!" cried Ronnie, startling Pippa, who had once heard the same exchange between Matt and his father. What she had thought singular and noteworthy was merely recurrent. She began to hear the repetitions that looped through Elkinson conversations. "You're making my life dark." "White flowers are the most beautiful." "What this situation requires is a fresh pitcher of martinis." It was a form of birdsong: communal, serving to identify and bind.

Caroline's older boy was at the piano, attacking Bach's "Minuet in G." He played the way the Elkinson women went at life: with great verve, ignoring wrong notes. His little brother lay on the floor, alternately sniffing the pianist's feet and lightly chewing a rose.

In the living room, Keith was saying, "Did you see the local paper on Australia Day? That photograph of a Greek got up like Byron. What do they think is the point?"

"I'm amazed they could find a Greek in Bellevue Hill. Must've been someone's pool guy," said Matt.

"Please, Dad," said Ronnie. "You're being a pig and a bore." Ronnie had fallen off her Birkenstocks and fractured an ankle. She had moved home to recuperate and was lying on a leather daybed with her foot in a cast.

"So you say, Veronica, but can you tell me why a newspaper would choose to display a picture of a man in fancy dress smashing a plate on its front page?"

Eva and Ronnie spoke together. "It's multiculturalism, darling. You know that perfectly well." And, "Because there are plenty of fascists in this country who think only Anglos have the right to be here."

"I'll tell you another thing about this country," said Keith. "I had tea at the Sofitel with Geoffrey Carlton the other day. You remember Geoff, don't you? Ear, nose, and throat. He's been in Boston for—oh, it must be a good twenty years now. Anyway, there we were, offered those enormous menus, length of my arm, and Geoff waves his away and says, 'I'll have a Bushells, please.' Well, now, you see the waitress is barely sixteen and I would say Middle Eastern. Probably come into town from somewhere out west on a train." Keith pronounced "Middle Eastern," "out west," and "train" with care, as if borrowing from a foreign language. "Well, this lass has absolutely no idea that Geoff wants a cup of tea. She starts to say that they've only got what's on the menu, and I see poor old Geoffrey's face. It's just dawned on him that in this country today, you can't count on everyone knowing what a Bushells means."

"Oh, oh, oh," said Eva. "Be careful, my darling. Soon you'll be complaining that the peasants are wearing velvet trousers and playing accordions." She raised her voice and called "Bravo!" in the direction of the music room, where the assault on Bach continued. "Bravo, *chéri*!" The pianist's brother appeared in the doorway: he had caught the admiration in his grandmother's voice and knew that it had to be directed at him. He entered the room, smiling hugely and walking on his knees.

Keith's eyes snapped—he was delighted with himself. They were blue eyes, blameless as clocks. They looked very keenly; Pippa had the impression that they were inspecting her bones. Once a year, Keith spent two weeks in the hill country in Vietnam working for a medical aid organization. In the teeth of Eva's injunctions, he insisted on traveling around on a motorbike, and often said that he would spend half the year in Vietnam if he could. "Absolutely wonderful people. Straight as a die. Unspoiled."

"Dad, you come across like those brain-dead Pommy colonels who carry on about the good old days with the Mau Mau."

"The Mau Mau were the enemy, son. Sometimes it's impossible not to wonder where all those school fees I paid went."

In summer, waxy frangipani always lay on the Elkinsons' dining table and beside the basin in the powder room. "This is a city governed by flowers," said Eva. "When I first came here, I couldn't believe it: beautiful, scented flowers just lying there on the pavement. People stepping on them! I used to pick up as many as I could and take them home." Now Eva had a tree that dropped frangipani in her garden, but she was still unable to pass the fallen blooms without gathering them up.

"Eva likes rescuing things," said Matt, "don't you, Eva?" One of the things Pippa found creepy about her mother-in-law was that her children were required to call her by her first name. Eva had worked as a nurse before she married, but now went in for philanthropic boards, volunteering at the Art Gallery, attending talks on watercolor painting or the conservation of wildflowers—what Pippa thought of as "pastimes for ladies." The chief pastime was causes. Easily the most annoying thing about Eva was that her politics couldn't be faulted. She circulated petitions protesting against Indigenous deaths in custody, Australia's treatment of asylum seekers, the live export of sheep. She chivvied her children to attend rallies and visit detention centers. Once Pippa had spotted her in the television footage of a Palm Sunday rally: her hair girlishly down her back, her jaw square with virtue, her Jesuit beside her.

For a while, the finger food at Elkinson parties was provided by a not-for-profit catering group that employed only asylum seekers. Pippa ate Guatemalan empanadas, Burmese dumplings, Iraqi croquettes, and Eritrean fritters that all had the same texture (paste), the same color (mud), the same flavor (nothing), and came with the same tongue-stripping sauce. They were handed around by beautiful, spindly African women, who moved silently about the room like etiolated gods dropping in on the human race. Passing among her awestruck guests, Eva offered an authenticating purr: "They're refugees." The citizen of conscience presided over these gatherings in garments stiffened with embroidery and beads. At throat and wrist she wore silver set with gems, some the color of butter, others the color of blood. These tribal ornaments lit Eva's face and proclaimed her solidarity with the wretched of the earth.

In Poland, Eva's father had been a cameraman. He was employed on the official documentary when Stalin visited the new People's Republic in 1952. Some months later he was arrested: in one frame of the film, a pillar cast a shadow across Stalin's face. Eva never saw her father again. Her mother was arrested soon afterward for failing to denounce her husband; she would die in prison the following year.

Before that happened, a family friend stepped in and saved Eva from an orphanage. In time, Mateusz Holz emigrated to Australia, taking Eva with him. It was officially impossible to leave Poland, but Mateusz was an ethnic German: an "unwanted individual," like the daughter of traitors. "We didn't fit the template," said Eva. "In a totalitarian system, that means a bullet or a passport."

On hearing this story for the first time, Pippa had thought, I could use that. She saw Europe, momentous and world-historical, magnifying eventless Australia. Scenes from a backstory came ready-formed to mind: the midnight ring on the doorbell, a child's wan face under a black hat, leafless trees along an avenue where it had never been spring. Out of consideration for Eva's feelings, Pippa would substitute the Soviet Union for Poland. Her mother-in-law already seemed both larger than life and paper-flat: a character. While the sun beat down on her Sydney boardinghouse, this paper woman ate the food of her cold, dark homeland: pale dumplings, boiled meats, sour pickled vegetables drained of color.

Pippa asked Eva a tactful question or two, saying that she was working on a novel about a Russian woman who had grown up under Stalin. Eva said, "That is a story without interest."

"*E*va!" said Matt.

"Everyone knows that story," went on Eva, buttering a slice of squishy bread. "It was summed up long ago. A novel should be new, it should bring us messages from the world. What we need to hear today is what is happening in China, in the Middle East. Those stories are formless: they haven't already set into shapes."

When they were alone, Matt told Pippa, "Write whatever you want." His father had said much the same, only in a more roundabout way, while stacking the dishwasher with Pippa. "When you know Eva's background," said Keith, "you understand why she wants everything out in the open. No shadows. Even if the light is blinding at times."

Handing Keith a smeared platter, Pippa was aware of the scab of shaving foam on his ear. She couldn't conceive of life with Eva as anything other than a punishment—the woman was as heartless as a mirror. An image of the not-Eva waiting to be written arrived: she was looking at the silky Pacific, her arm raised to protect her eyes. In her other hand she carried a brown cardboard suitcase stamped "Old Hat." When Pippa returned to her laptop, it was the same thing: every scene with the Russian woman was a stiff cutout. Pippa deleted them all. She had Australia. It was enough. She possessed the native genius for making do and easily concocted an aesthetic from a snub. Her mind drew a border, a magic line, between Australia and the world. Her books would be island continents: self-sufficient, self-enclosed. History, benignly neglectful, had handed her the small picture. Why seek to enlarge it with histrionic strangers? Long ago, George Meshaw had encouraged her to look inward for material. He was smart, George. Pippa never forgot that he had set her on her path. She was his student at the time and she had gone up to him at the end of a tutorial to tell him how much she was enjoying the course. Over the scraping of chairs and the clatter of departing students, George told her, "You should write." He looked directly into her face as if issuing a command.

Eva, connoisseur of Waugh and Greene, theorist of the novel, excused herself from reading Pippa's books: "Only history and philosophy have meaning at my age." Keith wouldn't accept presents of Pippa's novels and bought his own copies, which he would ask her to sign. In time, a note would arrive: "Thank you for a most enjoyable book. The people struck me as very true to life. I was particularly impressed by—" The note, printed on letterhead that listed Keith's degrees, was always signed with his full name. That "true to life" was a little disconcerting. Pippa always tried to twist whatever she borrowed out of recognition, and anyway, she only borrowed from people Keith didn't know. Basically, she borrowed from less-than-real people: either they were no longer part of Pippa's life or they weren't on Facebook, which came to the same thing. Pippa told herself that Keith intended only to pay her a compliment. But sometimes she wondered about currents under his pondlike surface. Around the time he met Eva, Keith's parents had made him a present of their Arts and Crafts house. Keith had it demolished, replacing it with modernist glass and stone designed by a disciple of Harry Seidler. The new house had a stepped concrete roof from which a panoramic harbor view could be admired and the dollars it added assessed. It was a lovely building, light-ridden, slick with mid-century cool, but Pippa hadn't thought of Keith as someone who pulled down the past. As for Eva, she had visited the old house once and still mourned it. "You should have seen the fireplace tiles: De Morgans." The frangipani tree was all she had managed to save. She begged Keith to spare it, although the architect raged.

Pippa was of the opinion that people disliked the kind of house in which they had grown up. That was why she couldn't hack fibro, or louvers at which leggy hibiscus knocked, while Keith's children had things to say about split-levels and exposed bricks. But Keith claimed that his aversion to old buildings was impersonal: they were dark, expensive to maintain, unhygienic. "Who can say how many people have been there over the years, touching things with dirty hands?"

There were mornings when Pippa woke as full of fear as a hospital. It was occasioned by the cold realization that she had grit, longing, imagination, a capacity for hard work, a measure of selfishness, a shot of insanity—in short, everything needed for greatness except talent. Elsewhere in the house, Matt would be playing his violin. He rose at six and practiced for half an hour: scales, followed by something testing like a Paganini caprice, and ending always with Bach. He was preparing for an audition that would never take place. Eva was the judge—she looked away, bored. Her scorecard, prepared long in advance, said, "Disappointing."

On good days, Pippa believed that Matt was wrong—and worse still, wasteful—not to accept that art was also the near miss and the flawed. When she told him so, he said, "Near enough is good enough—is that really what you think?" What Pippa really thought was that he should have persisted with performance, auditioned for a third-tier music school, played with a municipal orchestra. Or why not an edgy sort of band? Look at the Dirty Three! Matt's vision of music as nothing if not celestial was thin and high and useless. It was also secondhand: a crippling European ideal of purity and achievement that Eva had imprinted on her children.

On bad days, Pippa was afraid that Eva was right: the worst humiliation was being not quite good enough. In Paris, under a gray felt sky with stones underfoot, her fear had reached its high-water mark—there were afternoons when its dark salt silted up her throat. Every Sunday, the church bells gave her a headache. A few weeks into her residency, the future in which Pippa had trusted assumed the form of a gentle downhill slope. This was the depressive effect of a city where the past—its monuments, its battles, its vintages—had a strut that the present couldn't match. History could spring out there at any time like a mugger. In an endless, unmoving queue at the post office, the man waiting behind Pippa told her firmly, "We need a new Napoleon." For the rest of the day, Pippa couldn't tell if she felt sorrier for herself or for France, where a young man's idea of progress was a costume replay in a silly hat.

She told a friend that no Australian would come out with crap like that. Her friend said, "That's because Australians are ashamed of the past. You have no choice but to look forward."

Pippa, looking forward, saw a life that had drained away in the service of novels no one wanted to read. She came to a decision. When Matt joined her in France, she sat astride him, placed his hands on her breasts, and told him that she had thrown away her diaphragm. It marked the end of a long, invisible, unbroken campaign conducted mostly without words. Like many a seasoned soldier, Matt went to pieces when victory was at hand. A tiny voice in Pippa's head hoped that their child wouldn't have his coloring: he had those cautious blue eyes that turn red at once with tears.

He cried again, helplessly, soaking hankies, when Pippa miscarried. The hankies were another of the preposterous things about Eva: she hemmed them by hand and embroidered Matt's initials in one corner. He received half a dozen every Christmas. As for Pippa, the first thing she did when she came home after the curette was to delete all her posts and close down her blog; she had announced the pregnancy there just a short month earlier. Her eyes were solid glass balls and remained that way, although over the following months she would dream repeatedly of having lost something ordinary and essential: a credit card, keys. Sorting through a box of oddments, she came across a photograph of their harbor flat from that first summer. The bare colonnade looked prophetic, a missed warning about something that could have been fruitful but wasn't. Pippa told Matt, "I can't go through that again." She was conscious of a great strategic advantage: untold centuries of female suffering, casually inflicted by men and fate on women's bodies, pressed up behind her and strengthened her case. The mild elation this caused made her voice kind: "It's hopeless—I'm sorry. I think I'm just not meant to have kids."

They both heard the echo of something she had said a long time ago, soon after they married: "I'm not sure that I want children. I'm sorry."

On that previous occasion, Matt had said, "Sorry! That's what someone says when they step on your foot." This time around, he said nothing. The conversation remained suspended. Like a blade, thought Pippa from time to time.

Mateusz Holz was Matt's godfather. When he died, he left his house to Matt. Pippa and Matt were living in St. Peters at the time, in a renovated semi they had found through one of Caroline's friends. The rent, paid in cash, was below market value, but Pippa had always disliked the house. The renovation was your classic bodgie job: the breakneck stairs violated every regulation, handles collapsed into hands. The rooms were cramped, drafty and full of dust. A long time ago there had been brickworks in St. Peters, and Pippa believed that a ghostly brick dust still blew through its flat streets and found its way into houses, where it velveted everything with a fine, pinkish grit. The houses in Pippa and Matt's street had been given names like Dunroamin and Bullecourt, although the people who lived in them now came from places where those jokes and battles meant nothing. One house, a stark orange-brick Seventies rebuild, was called Stendhal. Matt said that it had been named for the antipodean version of Stendhal's syndrome: "If you look at it too intently, you faint from the ugliness."

Traffic raged through St. Peters, and planes flew so low that Pippa wore noise-canceling earphones when she was writing. In Glebe, in Mateusz's street, commotion was the prerogative of birds. His house had been untouched in forty years, but it had big, airy rooms opening to right and left of a central hall. The doors were solid; they closed with an air of finality. Things were different at the rear of the house, where brick gave way to weatherboard: kitchen, dining area, and laundry had been tacked on there. The corners of these back rooms stayed shadowy even when the light was on. Long ago, damp had colonized them unopposed.

That part of the house was entered through an archway hung with a thick damson-pink curtain on a brass rod. The curtain concealed and revealed: its decadent, Venetian hue was a declaration in code. "It's like visiting someone's unconscious," said Matt, parting the heavy folds and going into the kitchen. The cooktop was rusty, and one of the burners didn't work. They replaced the stove, and when the plumber's apprentice was wheeling the old one out, the back flew open and oil lurched out to lay a rancid scarf across the vinyl. None of this mattered. There was an overgrown backyard with an orange tree and a pomegranate and a single, superb lemon gum—the orange tree was heavy with fruit. Pippa, seeing the zestful weeds, thought, Veggies! They debated the matter of chooks.

The house stood on a hill, and the back door opened onto treetops and sky. Great clouds passed there. Pippa looked down on trees with clustered leaves, like flowers with huge green petals, and frondy ones with leaves like whips. Trees stood in gardens farther down the slope, and in the park at its foot, and along streets everywhere—they were the glory of Glebe. They set light and shade moving on pavements, so that to walk there was to think of rivers. The suburb was moneyed, boho chic, although not when Mateusz had moved there in the Sixties. "Bloody lucky he bought up here," said Matt. His Elkinson instinct for stratification was at work: farther down Glebe Point Road, the suburb began its social slide, its Victorian terraces given over to students and social housing. Not all the graffiti was licensed. Sizable rats made merry in its cafés. This proximate squalor was prized: it added an authentic sheen while leaving house prices unharmed. Pippa understood this language now, and that it lay under everything, and understood also that it was not a language but a form of thuggery. On learning that he had inherited Mateusz's house, Matt told Pippa, "We don't have to save for our own place now, so I could go casual if that was ever necessary. Your writing wouldn't be interrupted." He meant if they had a child. He was so supportive—it complicated everything. Children and money and work: these things triangulated her marriage. Each represented a different kind of power, a different kind of satisfaction, and a different kind of jail.

Matt had taken to reading out the real estate auction results listed every week in the local paper. Everything had a price, and the prices were amazing. Glebe was amazing! Even the dumps got amazing results! The trees remained aloofly benign throughout the suburb, calm jamborees enjoyed by creative directors and the long-term unemployed alike.

It was windy on the crest of Mateusz's hill, and soil and seeds blew onto roofs. In her first spring there, Pippa would look up and see pink poppies against the sky. The yard put out a white embroidery: arums, daisies, and something like moonlight, which climbed and shone and claimed everything in its path.

Eva and Keith came to lunch. His children claimed that if Keith was obliged to venture west of the city, he stocked up on water-purification tablets and checked that his tetanus shot was up to date. His map of Sydney was a densely cross-hatched eastern suburbs ghetto surrounded by a trackless steppe. Neighborhoods that had been ruthlessly gentrifying for two generations were canceled with an indelible stamp: "Slum." Keith told Pippa, "When I was growing up, my mother told me never to stray south of Foy's. I've stuck to that, pretty much." He had been born, educated, employed, married, had raised a family, and would no doubt be buried within the space of the same few square miles. Pippa delighted him by asking, "What's Foy's?" demonstrating the witlessness of the young.

When Pippa opened the door, Keith handed her a bottle and asked whether the sea breeze penetrated as far as Glebe. Mateusz had been something of a recluse, and it was Keith's first visit to the house in years. He walked through the shabby rooms, his eyes bright and hard; like his measured voice, they were made for summing up. Noticing the absence of insect screens, he told Pippa, "In summer, you'll have butterflies in every room."

If Keith filled the role of a pet, Eva was a child. She wore her hair like an old-fashioned girl, drawn back from her brow without a parting and fastened behind her head. Her children teased her lovingly—it was quite different from the mild disdain Keith called forth.

When Pippa dropped a spoon one day, Eva announced, "We will have an unexpected visitor."

"And remind me, please, what it means if my nose itches," said Ronnie. "Will a man with no teeth ask for my hand in marriage or is a ghost present?"

"No, the toothless guy is if your forehead itches, isn't that right, Eva?" asked Tess. She was the architect, back from Chicago on holiday. "An itchy nose means you'll drink currant-leaf vodka on Wednesday. But only if it itches on the right side. On the left, you will find fulfillment with a three-legged cow on a collectivized turnip farm. But do you remember what you must never do on any account?"

"Place your handbag on the floor!" chorused Eva's children.

"That's right, make fun of your old mother," said Eva placidly. She knew she was unassailable, the keeper of the castle.

Like a child, Eva was permitted to say what others only

thought. On that first visit to Matt and Pippa in Glebe, she paused on the veranda as she was leaving: "It's a perfect house for children." The remark hung about, like the smell of stale oil, sliding into Pippa's consciousness at intervals.

Ronnie and her new partner, Siobhan, dropped by. There was a potted bay tree in Ronnie's blue arms. They were arms that travestied and honored the blue jewels on her mother's fingers. "Bay keeps witches away," said Ronnie, presenting Pippa with the pot, "so with luck Eva won't visit too often." It was one of those golden July afternoons stolen from spring, and they sat outside in T-shirts drinking beer. Ronnie was telling Siobhan about Mateusz's succession of male "tenants"—Ronnie's fingers made scare quotes—the last of whom had died not long before Mateusz.

"That generation." Siobhan shook her head. Briefly, they were all contemplative. They were looking at the past: a cavernous hall filled with light like gravy, where all the furniture was ugly or broken, people got around with embarrassing hair, and a violent, senseless film with a soundtrack by Bread played on a flickering screen. Silently, they gave thanks for their escape.

The way Pippa saw it, Eva was to blame for Rashida. Eva, who had a scoliotic spine, swore by an osteopath in Surry Hills. Rashida practiced at the same clinic, and Eva met her when she was filling in for Joe one day. It was inevitable that Eva would befriend Rashida. At one time or another, her collection of ethnically diverse people included a Balinese interior decorator, an Aboriginal photographer, a Timorese nurse, an Iraqi housepainter, a Korean cardiologist. The Jesuit brought her some of these specimens; others, Eva dug out for herself. They were deployed at parties, like her tribal jewelry, and served to impress in conversation: "According to Tony, my Indigenous friend . . ." For two happy years, Eva was able to say, "Anh, Tess's Vietnamese partner . . ." Anh—buzz cut, sleek-toothed—exhibited his ethnicity in the largest photo on the grand piano. Then he and Tess split up. "It's not something I like admitting about my own daughter," said Eva, "but Tess has always been intolerant."

"The guy was a douchebag, Eva. He was dating someone else on the side."

"Your sister is so inflexible. In any relationship, there has to be give and take."

Rashida turned up for the first time at the Elkinsons' not long after *French Lessons*, the novel Pippa had written in Paris, was accepted for publication. That was the occasion the lunch was supposed to mark, but Eva kept the conversation focused on her new guest. She urged Caroline, who had strained her back activating her core at Pilates, to visit the clinic where Rashida worked. "Joe's known all over the country. Rashida moved up from Melbourne just to work with him. They practice such a gentle form of osteopathy. There's none of that terrible crunching of joints. The osteopath simply holds the injured part, supporting it."

"And it works?" asked Pippa.

Rashida looked at her. When Rashida's gray eyes shifted, light ran in her face.

Eva told Pippa, "Rashida is a Muslim." Her tone was reproachful, as if Pippa's question could be construed as anti-Islam. "Her family emigrated from Mumbai when she was eight."

Keith informed Rashida, "You prefer it here, of course."

"Keith and I honeymooned in India," said Eva. "It was the most wonderful experience. Transformative."

"Marvelous people. Remember our driver? Straight as a die."

"We went back with the children when they were little. Early exposure to other cultures is so important. And there's such spirituality in that country."

"I had the most amazing diarrhea," said Ronnie. "Seven days straight." She asked Rashida, "Why did your family leave?"

"My parents thought that India wasn't the best place for Muslims," said Rashida. "I love these potato pancakes, Eva. Could I have the recipe?"

"Were you persecuted for your faith?" asked Eva, hushed and hopeful.

"Not really."

Keith said, "So you were privileged migrants."

Rashida said nothing. She seemed to be turning the sentence over in her mind, trying to work out its shape.

Eva didn't attend the launch party for Pippa's third novel, but Rashida came. Keith was there, too, with a giant, funereal bouquet that he handed to Pippa when the speeches were done. Pippa didn't think that white flowers were the most beautiful—that had to be Eva's joyless aesthetic at work—but submitted gracefully to Keith's strict embrace.

"You're showing me up, Dad," said Matt. He cast his sly smile in Pippa's direction, and she blazed at him in return. Required to describe their marriage that night, each would have thought of a mirror: a bright steadiness at the center of their lives.

Everyone was looking at Pippa, from her flowery arms to her beautiful shoes. Rashida's look said, Those shoes are stupid. They're wrecking your feet and your back. Rashida was wearing chunky black ankle boots scuffed across the toes, and a loose gray shift that reached halfway down her shins: she looked like an extra in a period drama about a TB sanitorium. Personally, Pippa couldn't see the point of a dress-up dress that wasn't sexy. She loved her launch parties: sometimes she wondered if they were the real reason she wrote books. Gloria always whispered, "Is a launch really necessary? You know Parrett and Wezel will say their marketing spend doesn't run to one"—although she showed up, of course, and put away liters of Pippa's booze. Pippa gladly paid for the parties herself. Each time, she treated herself to a new dress and shoes. Before setting out that evening, she had been standing in front of the mirror admiring her outfit when Matt came into the bedroom. He put his arms around her from behind, saying, "You're gorgeous." He lifted the clingy fabric of her dress and slipped his other hand down the front of her panties. Afterward, Pippa had to change them. She felt so sorry for Rashida, standing there in her daggy clothes, clutching her signed copy of *French Lessons*. "You're looking gorgeous, lovey," said Pippa. "Have you had something to eat? Half the rice balls are vegetarian."

One morning Pippa heard Matt break off in the middle of a piece. That was unprecedented. She found him in their dingy kitchen, his face quenched. He said, "I couldn't manage a fingered octave. It's happened before, when you were in Paris. I was never good enough and I'm getting worse."

"It doesn't matter. You've always said the stuff that's tied to what you can do physically is only a surface thing—that music is in the structure of a piece, not in showmanship."

"The surface doesn't matter if you're up to it. If you're not, it's everything."

Pippa put her arms around him. He stood inside them, as rigid as a stake. He spoke softly: "I'm an instant closer to death." What frightened her was that he hadn't said "we." It was useless to ask him to abandon his daily ritual. Under his friable surface ran a vein of adamant. It had transferred itself to his music—it was the clenched-teeth music of someone hanging on. A little flame of scorn shone blue in the pit of Pippa's mind. Of course his playing was falling off—what did he expect? Art wasn't a half-hour diversion; it defined your life or it was nothing. In Rome, Matt had told her, "I knew that if I kept up my playing, we would have a baby." That was what music represented to him now: a bargain he had sought with fate. In a less anemic age, he would have sacrificed virgins or immaculate lambs.

Matt often complained of pain and stiffness in his neck: the violinist's ailment. When his osteopath moved to the Gold Coast, he decided to try the clinic to which Eva went. "It was pretty amazing," he told Pippa that evening. "Totally worth the schlep to Surry Hills. Joe just sort of held my head between his hands, and now my neck doesn't hurt anymore." He added, "It's probably psychological as much as anything. Everyone just wants to be held."

Some months later, Matt's shoulder was giving him trouble. He went back to Joe, who suggested he try the Alexander Technique and referred him to Rashida, who taught it. Matt told Pippa, "One of my teachers at the Con taught AT as well. There were people I knew who had lessons with her."

"But you didn't?"

"That Alexander crowd—" Matt said, "They weren't my tribe." He meant that he hadn't wanted to sleep with the girls.

He came home from his first Alexander lesson and said, "Rashida says the way I hold my neck compresses it, and that's why the pain keeps coming back. We did a visualization exercise: I thought about my vertebrae and imagined inserting a little cushion of air between each one. It was amazing—I could feel the tension easing off and my spine growing longer. You should try it. Rashida says it's a great exercise for anyone who spends a lot of time sitting."

Matt stood against the frame of a door and asked Pippa to mark off his height with a pencil. On the Internet, there were people who claimed to have grown taller as a result of the Technique. After his second session with Rashida, the pain snarled under Matt's shoulder blade went away and didn't return. He bought a yoga mat and lay on it on his back every day for fifteen minutes, with his knees drawn up and a book under his head.

One day he brought his phone into the kitchen. "Have a listen to this."

Pippa looked up from the salmon steaks she was marinating. "Is that you?"

"Rashida recorded me during our lesson."

"Yeah?"

He said, "Oh, Pips, it sounds so beautiful. I'm playing with such ease." His voice was shaky. "How is it possible? She knows nothing about music. The first time I took my violin in, she called the bow a cue." He repeated, "How is it possible for someone like that to release this music in me?"

Words like "release," "lightness," and "ease" recurred when Matt spoke about Rashida. Pippa reminded herself that he was talking about the Technique.

•

Rashida told Pippa, "Eva's so kind. She knows I miss my family and she invites me over for lunch with you guys all the time." Pippa didn't think that kindness came into it. A recent poll had announced, "Most Australians are anti-Islam," and Pippa guessed that Eva wanted to display "my Muslim friend, Rashida"—the Iraqi housepainter having melted out of view.

Eva asked Rashida why she didn't wear the hijab. "Those soft folds frame a face so beautifully."

"My mum doesn't wear it. No one does in my family. I don't want to get involved in religious stuff."

"Of course, it could make you a target for anti-Islam feeling." Eva said, "I am so ashamed of this country these days." Her eyes were darkly dreamy. She had taken to appearing in a salwar kameez and silky, embroidered shoes. Pippa thought, Eva would love to be taken for a Muslim. For the first time, she saw the glamour of oppression. Eva would always be that small girl on whom suffering had conferred distinction. Now she thirsted for it in its pure form, wrapped in a free-floating, decorative orientalism unhampered by history and geography alike.

Pippa asked Matt if Rashida had a partner. "Wouldn't have a clue," he answered. "When we talk, it's about AT." He would come home from a lesson with advice on how to breathe—"Picture your lungs as balloons, gently filling and lifting sideways in your chest"—or how to get up from a chair—"Let the neck be free. Allow the head to lead the body into length." He told Pippa to keep her feet flat on the floor when she was sitting down and to resist crossing her legs. Watching TV, he pointed out the tense angle of an actor's head. It got irritating pretty fast.

Pippa probed Eva for information. "That sweet girl!" replied

Eva. "I don't know what's wrong with men—she's hardly overweight at all. But they only look at the surface."

"Nothing wrong with the surface," said Matt.

"Swipe right!" called Ronnie from the next room, where she was picking out something bluesy on the piano.

"I know she wants a family. She loves children." Eva said, "It's hut-breaking."

All the Elkinsons had a thing for Rashida, it seemed. When Eva was describing a new rug, woven in Afghanistan, that she was thinking of buying, Ronnie said, "Well, I hope no children went blind weaving it."

"This is nitpicky, but technically those carpet-slave kids don't go blind from weaving," said Rashida. "It's malnutrition that causes them to lose their sight."

"Exactly right!" said Keith. "Optic neuropathy brought about by a deficiency of B_{12}. A point I didn't succeed in getting across to my own children, as you see."

"That reminds me," said Rashida. "Next month, this guy's giving a talk on how the Alexander Technique can improve eyesight. I wondered if you'd be interested, Keith?"

"I daresay it wouldn't do any harm."

There he sat, all smiley indulgence. Pippa thought, Oh, Keith—even you! She had believed that he reserved a certain kind of approval for her.

At Eva's one Sunday, a conversation arose about what people were reading. Rashida, who had never said a word about *French Lessons*, announced that she loved George Meshaw's latest book. "There's this really great bit where one of the characters wonders what happened to squash. And where all the courts went."

"I've read that book," said Caroline. "I liked the bit where he describes the sound made by a Polaroid camera shutter: Cuh-*chunk*-click."

Eva murmured, "Once you have read Gombrowicz . . ."

Matt told Rashida, "George is an old friend of Pippa's."

"Really? Cool. I listened to a podcast of him talking about that book the other day—it was great." Rashida asked Pippa, "Have you heard that interview?"

"Not sure," said Pippa. "Yeah, he's very smart." She remembered the interview perfectly. When George was asked why his protagonist was referred to only as "the man," he had replied that it linked the character to the millions of nameless animals delivered up for slaughter. George, who was the biggest carnivore since *T. rex*.

"I bought two more of his books after reading that one," went on Rashida.

"I'm not sure I totally loved it," said Pippa. "I mean, didn't you think the way he wrote about the Indian guy was a bit racist?"

"Not at all."

Right there was the problem with Rashida: that unshakable assurance. There was a whisper in Pippa's brain, like a subdued, left-hand accompaniment to her thoughts, and this whisper was of the opinion that Rashida should be grateful that white people overlooked the double handicap of her religion and her race. The whisper said that Rashida should be a little bit sort of humble. It lived in a folded, reptilian corner of Pippa's brain, and she was scarcely aware of its existence. She was always for the underdog and would leap to protect. What caused turmoil were underdogs who failed to respect their allotted rank. Then the whisper thundered like an ancestor roaring out of a muffled past.

"That was classic with Rashida, wasn't it?" Pippa said to Matt on their way home from Bellevue Hill. "Doesn't know the first thing about literature but she knows what she likes."

"She's a pretty big reader, actually." Matt added, "Her mum was a poet in India. She works in a carpet showroom now."

"And you know all this how?"

"She tells Eva stuff."

"You know the only thing your mother's ever said about my writing, don't you?" Pippa plucked at her shoulders and Eva-ishly inflected her voice: "'I don't understand, Pippa, I was taught that the simple past tense of 'sink' is 'sank' not 'sunk.' She just randomly opens a book that she doesn't bother to read and—" What Pippa really wanted to say was, Your mother is a woman who can't tell her heart from her hat.

"That's got nothing to do with Rashida."

"Don't start defending her as well."

There was the time when Eva was telling Rashida about an NGO that promoted female literacy in Asia. A fund-raising event was coming up. The Jesuit had suggested that Rashida would make a good speaker. "That man has such a genius for connections," said Eva. "What do you think, Rashida?"

"No, thanks. It's not my kind of thing."

"But you wouldn't have to speak for more than a few minutes, and it would be so wonderful to hear from a young woman like you about the importance of literacy in the developing world."

"Actually, I never want to speak for the developing world."

Finding herself alone with Ronnie not long afterward, Pippa said, "Wow! Rashida can be pretty abrasive, can't she?"

"Oh, it doesn't do Eva any harm if her plans for the human race occasionally come unstuck."

"I just think Rashida could make a bit more of an effort to be likable."

Ronnie rolled her eyes. "Likable's overrated, if you ask me."

"It's fairly crucial if you want to be liked."

"Why should Rashida want to be liked?" Ronnie said, "Maybe she just wants to *be*."

Out of nowhere a realization arrived—or rather, not a realization but that far more powerful thing, an intuition: Pippa saw that Eva had set out to bring Rashida and Matt together. ("My Muslim daughter-in-law.") Eva mentioned Rashida's love of children so frequently that Matt couldn't have failed to take it in. And Rashida was at it as well: always getting out her phone and showing Eva photos of her sisters' children, or asking after Caroline's and Becky's kids. Pippa had heard her tell Caroline, "If you're ever stuck for a babysitter . . ."

Another time, Rashida led the conversation around to Twitter in the most blatant way, asking Eva—Eva!—if she had thought about signing up.

"You don't want to go there, Eva," said Ronnie. "Trust me. Oversharing, ephemera, schmoozing, and cats." Ronnie was addicted to Twitter, of course. "Not forgetting the transparently curated selves. And did I mention cats?"

"People have always done that," said Rashida.

"Shared photos of their chia porridge with the world?"

"Presented selective aspects of themselves. Twitter's also about connection," said Rashida. "And activism. That's why I think Eva would like it."

"The advances in technology over the course of my working life have been nothing short of staggering," said Keith. "The things that imaging can do today—unimaginable even twenty years ago."

Pippa looked at Rashida. "I didn't realize you're on Twitter. What's your handle? I'll follow you."

"Oh, I'm speaking generally, not from personal experience," said Rashida. "I don't fit the Twitter demographic: it mostly appeals to people aged between thirty-five and fifty-five. My generation's more Facebook and Instagram."

That's right, Pippa thought. Remind everyone you're the youngest person here. Up to her thirty-fifth birthday, Pippa had always known immediately how old she was. These days she had to pause before she could remember her age—but she was still young, she was sure of that. Rashida was thirty-three, only five years younger than Pippa, but Pippa realized that they were five critical years. She decided that Rashida's remark was aimed specifically at Matt. She was letting him know that, unlike his wife, she could still have two or three kids; or a whole battalion, given that twin thing that was going on.

Teaching kept Matt busy and unhappy; he had changed employers twice. Now he was at a school that wasn't far from his parents' house. He began arriving home late once or twice a week, saying that he had dropped in to see Eva after work.

Pippa said, "We spend practically every weekend with your family. Do you have to see Eva after work as well?"

"She's worried about Dad. Thinks he's pushing himself too hard, working late, conferences, whatever. She wants him to cut back, maybe work four days a week, but he won't hear of it. And yesterday he told her he's going to spend an extra week in Vietnam this year. It helps if I have a glass of wine with her and let her natter."

"Isn't that what she keeps a priest for?" Pippa felt queasy. She could sense something shimmering yet precise: Matt was having an affair with Rashida, with Eva's knowledge and connivance. She had agreed to provide her son with an alibi, should one be required.

One evening, when Matt was supposed to be with Eva, Pippa rang the clinic and was told that Rashida was "with a client"—who? She called Matt. He said that he was just leaving Bellevue Hill. How was Pippa to know if that was true? She looked through the folder where he kept his Visa statements—nothing. Nothing proved nothing. She went back to her laptop, deleted a sentence in her novel, then pasted it back in. @gloriahallelujah retweeted a list of the ten best pigs in literature. @pippapasses did the same. She tweeted, "So humbled by lovely email from reader about French Lessons. Favorite novel—aww!" Her publishers had forwarded the e-mail some weeks earlier. It began, "My book group did your novel *French Lessons*. We found it unbelievable and boring. Why . . . ?"

It was Saturday. Pippa was reading the newspaper over breakfast, and Matt was watching *Game of Thrones*. The books section in the paper was largely given over to an ad for an opulent new residential development called Parvenu. A profile of a bestselling American novelist had been squeezed in: "He was raised by his father, a general, and has magical memories of childhood holidays in Panama, Haiti, and the Middle East."

Across the table, Matt was on to his second croissant. Birds sang loudly in the yard. Pippa noticed that her toenails needed cutting—she was way overdue for a mani-pedi. Was her marriage normal? she wondered. Was this how other people lived? The American novelist, bespectacled and cleft-chinned, brought Clark

Kent to mind. Pippa imagined, idly, being in bed with him: their clumsiness, his soft lips. It would be mess, plunder, gambling, excess. It would be nothing like proficient married sex—the kind she could look forward to for the rest of her life.

She nudged Matt with her foot. "Ever think about having an affair?" She had intended to add, "with Rashida," but the words refused to come.

"Mmm."

"Matt!"

He took out his earbuds, but the screen still pulled his gaze. Pippa repeated her question.

He looked at her at last. "Bad writing week?"

"Just *say*, will you."

"The answer's no."

It had the weakness of truth. At the same time, Matt had been sort of evasive. But the air between them felt clear; the invisible barrier that descended in the aftermath of an argument or the buildup to one wasn't there. Pippa was the one who had difficulty speaking Rashida's name: there seemed to be a kind of danger about it. She decided: He's not actually on with her now, but that doesn't mean he won't be. Her friend Liz, who had plenty of experience to call on, always said, "If you really set out to get a married guy, you will." Pippa saw Eva's hand pushing things along, its feverish blue stones. Afterward, she would murmur, "I have such a genius for connection," beaming at Rashida and Matt.

There were new scatter cushions on Eva's couch. "How great are these!" said Caroline, picking one up. The fabric was handprinted with yellow leaves, stylized and black-veined, on a gray ground.

Eva said, "That shop in Woollahra is having a sale."

"Really? I'm so ready for new cushions."

"These are down to eighty-five each."

"That's so reasonable. I really need a couple of cushions. Do they come in red?"

A visor had descended over Rashida's face. One of her recent Facebook photos had shown Iggy Syed with Rashida's father. On a clothesline in the background, a bath mat could be seen: it was lime-green loop-shag chenille. Pippa knew that bath mat: its purple twin was embedded in her past. Pippa's grandmother had installed it in the bathroom when her daughter and the children moved in after the divorce. Her daughter ticked her off: such a waste of money, the household couldn't afford it, there was nothing wrong with the old rubber mat. Pippa was only nine at the time and had no words for what she understood at once: the bath mat was an assertion of spirit. Every time she stepped out of the shower and felt that fluffy coziness between her toes, Pippa knew that a four-room box wouldn't contain her for long. Her life was going to bring her everything anyone could ever want: an audience with Boy George, chocolates, a strapless satin dress, admirers, heaven, a long envelope containing a check, flashes going off.

When she moved to Sydney, Pippa and one of her new housemates had gone shopping at Kmart for stuff like tea towels and reading lamps. Spotting a cheerful pile of loop-shag chenille, Pippa cried, "Look!"

The other girl looked. "Hilarious," she said. Her flat hair whipped as she turned away. "Genuine bogan." Pippa lowered her outstretched arm.

Eva's three bathrooms, updated with floating vanities, contained nothing but thick white Egyptian cotton. Pippa pictured herself running into the nearest and returning with a snowy mat that she placed in the middle of the floor. Rashida and Pippa would squat on it together and urinate, supporting each other lightly under the elbows and laughing.

Caroline said, "These cushions are really great. I'm thinking it would make sense to get four."

Despite Eva's concern that he was overdoing things, Keith looked well: fit, relaxed. His hair was white now but still sprang closely all over his head. He had the kind of body that was unassertive but unyielding, the chest not hollowed out and no sausage of fat at the waist. A tiny grandchild racing around a table with elbows lifted and carroty locks flying was seized by Keith and kissed. The child put her hands on the places that would one day be her hips and spoke to him in a quiet voice: "No one is allowed to touch me without my permission."

"Quite right," said Keith, and sent her on her way with a soft smack. He noticed Pippa watching and asked about the progress of her new book.

"Oh, you know." Pippa said, "I'm trying to write really honestly about a marriage. It's tricky."

"I thought you did that very well in *French Lessons*."

Pippa could have hugged him. Also, inexplicably, she might have cried. She said, "Things might have gone downhill since then. In the marriage, I mean."

He said formally, "I'm sorry to hear that."

"What's up with Rashida?" Pippa asked, one Sunday. "I haven't seen her for ages."

"I believe she's been spending weekends in Melbourne. She tells me her father hasn't been well." Eva smiled at her plate and changed the subject. The air turned into a sort of gel: slimy, veiling. Something was going on all around Pippa—it was everywhere but hidden—something shameful and mean.

She checked Rashida's Facebook page every day, but found only links to Alexander stuff, or photos of Rashida's family or of food. Rashida wasn't a very active Facebook user, although she had almost six hundred friends there. Matt used Facebook just to keep up with Tess in Chicago, and with Becky, now working at an Indigenous health center in Darwin; he never commented on Rashida's posts.

Rashida posted a YouTube link: James Carr's "The Dark End of the Street." She wrote: "Can't get this out of my head lately." Ferial commented, "Sending so much love your way." What Pippa saw when she opened her eyes in the morning was what she had seen when she closed them: Rashida pressed against her lover in a doorway, his hands inside her coat. Pippa was working on the final draft of her novel but kept returning to Rashida's post. She played and replayed the song.

There came an evening when she jumped up from her laptop and went fast down the hall—the red curtain screamed on its rings. She said, "You were whistling 'The Dark End of the Street.' I heard you."

Matt was doing the washing-up in a dorky pose that Rashida had taught him: spine straight, legs bent at the knees, he was hinging forward from the hips. With the po-faced, cultish sincerity that characterized all his pronouncements about the Technique, he had told Pippa, "Young children naturally assume the Monkey

Position. It keeps the spine long and the neck free when carrying out everyday activities." The song and the stance now added up with arithmetical certainty to one thing: *proof.*

"Why were you whistling that?" Pippa repeated, "I heard you," as if he had denied it.

"You've been playing it. Over and over." Pippa remained in the doorway, tight-faced, rampant. Wiping his forehead with a sudsy hand, Matt said, "What's up? Is it your book?"

In bed that night Pippa told him, "I want to try again."

"Are you sure?" And before she could answer, "Let's wait till your book's done, OK?"

Pippa's veins turned to wire. She thought, He's going to leave me. Matt and she had sudden animal clashes, sudden shared intuitions. One morning they discovered that they had dreamed the same thing: a large blond cow had leaped from a death truck and escaped along a city street. It was one of those strange, bright moments that illuminate a marriage. The first time they looked out at the view from the back door, Pippa had said, "Callan Park." In Callan Park, if you left the path that ran beside the bay and scrambled up the embankment to the oval, space suddenly opened before you. The soul widened too, responding to clarity and expanse. Matt had taken Pippa there in their first year together; it had been one of their places. Lying in bed, Pippa knew that no one else on the planet would have understood why she had looked out at the yard and said "Callan Park." She thought, I'm impossible to live with. She rolled onto her back, away from Matt.

As it happened, Steve the poplar killer came down with bronchitis and pulled out of the lunch that was to bring Rashida and him together. Rashida wasn't well either: she had caught a cold. Her face seemed to have shrunk into her hood of hair. She took a tissue from her bag and dabbed at her glazed nostrils. Her nails were painted a pale pink that matched her shirt: the color darkened her face, her hands.

It was a breezeless day at the end of summer, the sky that firm Australian blue. They were having lunch on the deck, but Hank the Tank had to be shut inside because Rashida had announced that she didn't like dogs. When Hank wished to complain, he neither barked nor whined but produced noises like grinding machinery interspersed with strangled squawks. All through the meal, he stood with his nose to the screen door and made his noises. They sounded prehistoric, said Will: "The sort of noises a wounded pterodactyl might have made." Rashida didn't apologize, as Pippa would have done in her place, for bringing about the situation. She wiped her nose on the stringy Kleenex, and ate Pippa's tomato salad tossed in pomegranate syrup without saying a word.

"An aversion to dogs is a cultural thing," said Liz, an athletic-looking woman with a long, soft face in whom Pippa had confided her matchmaking hopes. On finding only one eligible man present, Liz had grown confused and now believed that Pippa was trying to set Rashida up with Will. It was necessary, therefore, to embellish Rashida's bald statement about disliking dogs. "It's Islamic. Like not drinking alcohol." She radiated ecumenical understanding and upended the prosecco over her glass.

"No, it's me," said Rashida. She blew her nose. "My parents have a poodle that my little sister rescued. And the reason I'm not drinking's because I've got a cold." She repeated, "I just don't like dogs."

Matt said, "Who does when they carry on like Hank?"

Rashida smiled at him and dropped what was left of her Kleenex onto her lap. At least she didn't laugh or touch her hair when Matt spoke to her: infallible signs of sexual electricity, according to Liz. Nor had Matt given Pippa any unexpected, expensive presents—jewelry, for instance, was tantamount to a confession of adulterous love.

Will asked, "Why don't you eat meat? Muslims do." His long neck gave Will a high-up stare, which he now bestowed on Rashida. It informed her that she was either a fake Muslim or a fake vegetarian, and that either way, she had been found out.

"I don't eat meat because I don't like the taste. Most things I do aren't related to being a Muslim."

Liz, continuing to exude benevolence, said, "I think what Will was getting at was that we've learned from other cultures and are all eating less meat these days."

Will was preparing his smile that was really a glare. Before he could unleash it, Pippa told Rashida, "I bet you picked up that cold in Melbourne. I came home with one the last time I was there."

"Melbourne!" said Will, glaring around. "Can you believe that place? They wear black to the beach."

"How did you know I've been to Melbourne?" asked Rashida.

Unable to answer, I've been Facebook-stalking your relatives, Pippa said, "Eva mentioned that your dad's been ill. I'm sorry to hear that. I hope it wasn't anything serious?"

Rashida looked down. She shook her head. Somewhere in the depths of her hair were dangly earrings set with stones that glittered when they caught the light. Their tackiness, like the nail polish, was at odds with her muted style. Pippa thought, She's dressing with someone in mind.

Liz began talking about the digital marketing guy at work. "Ever since he went to Burning Man, he starts every meeting by giving everyone a hug. I end up stinking of his beard oil for the rest of the day."

Pippa gathered up the salad dish and empty bottles, refusing help. All the knives flashed in the sun. Inside, the kitchen was black—it was amazing how much darkness could collect in a room on a bright day. Hank placed himself in her path and gazed. He had the square chest and round head of a dog on a gatepost. "It's not fair, is it?" said Pippa. "Have a tomato." She checked her phone: there were a couple of texts that could wait, and a missed call, also unimportant. Pippa arranged zucchini fritters on a platter, poured a herby yogurt sauce into a shallow bowl, and lined them up for a photo. She would post it on Facebook and Twitter to show her support for vegetarianism. It was important to show it. When it came to domestic violence or same-sex marriage or climate change, Pippa knew, unequivocally, that she was on *the right side.* That was the side of people who drank fair-trade coffee and attended vigils for murdered asylum seekers and had rescue pets and shopped at farmers' markets and said no to plastic bags. It was not the side of Pippa's father, who blamed feminism for the breakdown of his marriage, and believed that Australia was for Australians, by which he meant people who looked like him. He held these opinions not meanly but casually: his bigotry was the laid-back Australian kind. Choice by choice, his daughter planted her flags on the highest hill—they proclaimed her distance from him. But now and then that sunlit peak dwindled to a little mound, and a shadow fell. Vegetarians were Falun Gong to Pippa's Chinese embassy: they just stood there with their lives. To counter the criticism that no one offered, she sought out ethical butchers and tweeted about it at least once a month—the shadow shrank and the peak rose again, shining. What was more, if Pippa had vegetarian guests she catered for them magnificently, as she was doing with this meal. Long before the advent of Rashida, Becky had brought a man who didn't eat meat to dinner at her parents' house. As she laid his plate before him, Eva said, "We are having grilled fish and steamed vegetables, and you are having steamed vegetables." Pippa watched the poor guy fill up on slice after slice of limp white bread. While here was she, piling a feast onto trays: as well as the fritters, there were butter beans with feta, and a salad that mixed ancient grains and nuts.

Rashida chose that moment to come in from the garden. Hank lumbered forward, smiling—he always wished to demonstrate his admiration of the human race. "Sorry!" said Pippa, grabbing his collar.

"It's OK," said Rashida. "I'm not scared of him. I need the bathroom."

As she spoke, she glanced around the kitchen. Pippa felt compelled to say, "We've been meaning to fix up this place ever since we moved in. But renos are such a nightmare!"

"That's the problem with old places," said Rashida. "Everything needs fixing. And you need a light on in the middle of the day."

"The cooker's new," said Pippa. "And the surfaces are a bit worn but they're really clean, actually." The idea that Muslims were big on hygiene had suddenly ballooned in her mind. "Hank's not usually allowed in the kitchen," she went on. "I'll just put him outside for a minute so he can have a run around the yard while you're gone."

"I'd love a yard," said Rashida. "But the best I can do is some herbs in a window box."

"You're in Earlwood, aren't you?" Pippa improvised, "Friends of mine just moved there. Elswick Street, I think, is that near you?"

"I don't know it. I'm in Ashmead Place, near the river."

"Sounds nice."

"It's just a small flat. But the building's new, and everything works, and I can walk to the bus."

Pippa was repeating silently, Ashmead Place, Ashmead Place.

When she was alone, Pippa picked up her phone. She hadn't looked at Facebook for a few hours. Rashida had posted a new photo since then: a spectacular arrangement of white lilies, lisianthus, stock, and what seemed to be sweet peas. No one bought flowers like that for themselves. Ferial had already responded: "Love, love, love!" Did that mean that she loved the flowers? Or that they were an expression of love—whose? Pippa's brain sang: White flowers are the most beautiful. How many times had she heard Matt say that? Not that he ever gave Pippa white flowers. Every year on their anniversary, he produced a gaudy wheel of tropical blooms, because she had once said that she loved cannas as a child.

Will's voice insisted: "Any writer who consents to publication has compromised their literary integrity *by definition*."

Pippa put her phone on to charge, shifted the tab that locked the screen door to open, and picked up the tray.

A few days later, Pippa's phone rang. Gloria whispered, "I really, really love *The Kitchen Diaries*. The castration scene is amazing! We were all really blown away. SIMS said it was like a punch to the head."

Pippa said, "Oh my God! That's unbelievable. That's *great*." Then she said, "Do you really like it?"

"I love it. It's so brutal and sexy and unforgiving and raw. Sort of Cormac McCarthy and *The Girl on the Train* and just the right amount of *Kitchen Confidential*."

"I haven't actually read any of those," said Pippa faintly.

"The timing's so perfect: we'll be able to springboard off the domestic violence campaign." Gloria's voice almost rose with excitement. "Get yourself a good accountant, girl. This is going to go *off*."

•

Matt and Eva were having dinner with Ronnie, so Pippa stayed back late at work. She studied an e-mail from a newish restaurant reviewer that had come in that afternoon: "Hi Pippa, I've read through your edited version of my review and I have some concerns. 'Comprehensive wine list' has become 'fully fleshed wine list.' You've changed 'minimalist mains' to 'naked mains,' and 'mussels' to 'plump mussels.' 'Clean-tasting' has become 'succulent,' 'toothy, left-field pairing' is now 'toothy, provocative pairing.' ('Toothy' was a mistake. I meant 'toothsome,' but you didn't pick that up.)" The e-mail went on and on, and concluded: "So what do all these plump, provocative, glistening, coral pink, naked, fully fleshed, firm, yielding, succulent, yadda yadda changes add up to? Porn. You guys are selling porn. I'm writing restaurant reviews. Please reinstate my original (see Track Changes in attachment)."

Pippa e-mailed, "Hi Anastasia, Thanks for your feedback. Moving forward, we'll definitely think about taking it on board. Cheers, P." She sent the review, in her version, not Anastasia's, to production. She dallied on Twitter and Facebook, and spent a little time googling George Meshaw. A translation of his last novel had won a prize—an obscure one, in a country no one would live in if they had a choice. Pippa shut down her computer, touched up her lipstick, and left the office, heading for Surry Hills.

The osteopathy clinic was in a dingy neighborhood where the rag trade had once flourished. Pippa wandered around while she waited for Rashida to finish up for the day. There were signs of hipsterdom—beards, warehouse conversions, a cocktail bar—but the area remained transitional. Pippa passed a brothel, and two cops bent over a boy who was lying on a wall. Something about the way the boy's stringy arm lay across his chest reminded Pippa of her brother—he had been dead now for longer than he was alive.

The streets were noisy with traffic and bustle: office workers cutting through on their way to or from the station, a pub stuffed with drinkers, a woman pulled along by a tiny dog, two men sitting on old car seats on a veranda with Bollywood pouring out of the room behind them. Pippa turned into a street lined on one side with plane trees whose leaves had started to change color. The European trees, the grotty buildings, the workers in dark jackets streaming past all looked cinematic and remote. This feeling of estrangement crept over her now and then, triggered by lights coming on in windows, the impersonal push of people and cars, a four-wheel drive squeezing around a corner, the realization that she wasn't sure which way to turn. Sydney denied all knowledge of her. The past opened like a lit corridor, and Pippa saw the city as it had once been: an enemy. It was a sensation that had grown more unsettling with time—not because Pippa feared that it would remain but because she knew it would not. A different way of being in the world—ignorant, braver—had been lost.

Just before seven, she positioned herself across the street from the clinic. Presently, a young man came out the door, soon followed by an older one. Two women emerged together—one was Rashida. The other woman came up the street, toward Pippa, who crossed over to Rashida's side. She called softly and hurried forward. Rashida turned: her hair was twisted up behind her head, which made her face look naked.

"Amazing!" said Pippa. "They say you never run into anyone you know in a city. How *are* you? I've just had a meeting with a freelancer near here."

"Hi," said Rashida.

"So great to run into you." Pippa wondered, Has she been crying? She offered the female code for "You've lost weight": "You're looking well."

"Thanks." After a moment, Rashida said, "How're you going?"

"Yeah, good. Listen, do you want to get a drink or something?"

"I've got to get home. Sorry."

"I'm heading toward Central," said Pippa. "You, too? Shall we do that walk-and-talk thing?"

They set off together. Rashida walked briskly, looking straight ahead. Her sneakers squeaked with each step. Pippa remembered her grandmother saying that squeaky shoes hadn't been paid for.

"Hard day?"

Rashida shrugged. "The usual."

"Just about everyone at my work's on the five-two diet," said Pippa, "and it's one of their fast days. I had a team meeting after lunch and for like a whole hour I was trapped in a room full of bad breath."

That made Rashida laugh. She asked, "How's the book going?"

Pippa said that it would be published the following year. "My publishers seem pretty excited about it, which is a first."

All this information had been on Facebook for weeks, but Rashida acted as if it were news. "That's great," she said. "Congratulations."

A phone was ringing. "You should get that," said Pippa.

"It doesn't matter."

The Elizabeth Street lights were against them. As they waited, Pippa said, "Matt and I are planning to start a family. Now that my book's out of the way. Matt's really keen." Her voice, raised against the traffic, sounded stagey and aggrieved.

The lights changed, and they were caught up in the river of

people rolling forward. When they had crossed, Rashida said, "My bus is that way."

Pippa was wondering, Do we kiss? when Rashida turned, and her face could be plainly read. What was written there was dislike—nothing extreme, just a moderate aversion. It struck Pippa like a blow to the breastbone: shocking, bodily. Somehow it had been for her to assess Rashida, not the other way around.

Rashida raised her hand: "Ciao," she said, and was gone.

Pippa headed for the light rail. She had said what she had come to say. She was damp under her arms. Who had been calling Rashida? She got out her phone to check her messages. Matt was at Ronnie's—it would have been easy to have left a room and made a call. Sometimes, when he was in the shower, Pippa would try out different passcodes on his phone but she hadn't cracked the right one yet. She texted him now and checked her Twitter feed. @gloriahallelujah followed @victoriabeckham and @russellcrowe. Someone linked to a photo of Beckett on his haunches contemplating a dog and a cat. Someone else was transforming her house into a space of serenity and inspiration with Marie Kondo. @warmstrong asked, "Seriously, Jonathan Franzen, what were you even thinking?" Pippa remembered that she had forgotten to change "toothy" to "toothsome." She opened Facebook and forgot again.

"Four," announced Vern. "Possum again." He felt obliged to keep track of roadkill. The B&B was closed for winter, but the McLeods had risen early for the drive to Wellington. Vern was going into hospital to have a benign cyst removed from his bladder; his overnight bag was on the backseat. Glenice was at the wheel.

Every time Vern burped, he followed it up with a little cough: a marital substitute for "Excuse me." He was hungry, having had to fast since the previous night; Glenice had fasted too in solidarity and felt resentful now.

A line of pale green light appeared along the wintry horizon. After a while it gave way to a line of honey, but the air remained dark. Headlights approached. Glenice glanced into the ute as it passed and saw Vern sitting in the cabin with his old gray beanie pulled low over his ears. That meant he would come safely through the procedure. She wasn't surprised by what she had seen: the anniversary of her son's death was only two days away. Aidan's birthday and deathday brought disturbances, presages, twisty, memorable dreams.

Vern was whistling something without a tune between his teeth. He had whistled like that the night before, on his way to bed. It meant he was afraid. He had wrenched Glenice's nipples and fastened her hand around him. While she labored, he whispered, "Slut," "Tart," "Stinking bitch," and—repeatedly—a savage, private name, "Thessaly." For many years, Glenice had heard "Cecily." Who/what Thessaly was she had never asked or even wondered. Vern groaned and whispered in his happy anguish, and let Glenice rub herself against his shin.

A month after her son's funeral, when Glenice was still going around staring at faces and trees as if waiting for them to explode, she had realized that she was going to marry Vern McLeod. He had looked after her car for years, and now he was going to look after her. He had, too—she had no complaints there. A speckled, easygoing man with firm hair, he brought her cups of tea in bed. As soon as her daughter left home, Glenice had informed Vern that they were moving to New Zealand. She felt sorry for him, in the impersonal way that characterized her inner life after Aidan. She was what he had got.

Glenice kept her eyes on the road and spoke into the heated darkness: "Everything will be fine."

Vern let out a long breath as if he had been waiting for her to say exactly that, but resumed whistling as the car heaved itself up to the top of the pass and they saw the grainy amber glow that announced the rim of the city. Then he said, "Your side. Five."

Vern's operation was scheduled for eleven. They had agreed that Glenice wouldn't wait with him, as there were errands to run in the city. So when she had handed Vern over to nurses, Glenice had breakfast at a place near the hospital. Afterward there were the various bits of shopping, and then she drove to Cuba Street. A southerly was on the loose, and everyone was dressed for a polar expedition: beanies, down jackets, fleece. Before the McLeods moved out to the lake and took over the B&B, they had lived in Wellington. Every August, gales laid waste to the rose-red camellias that were Vern's pride. The wind could turn ferocious in any season; Glenice had seen summer hedges shiver like shorn lambs. Wellington gardens had misty English flowers—forget-me-nots, snowdrops, daphne—and shrubs that Glenice valued not in their fullness but when the lively red claws of leaf buds appeared on their bare branches. The wooden city met some need in her: its frank weather, its cold green hills.

Four years in, she had discovered the gallery when a hailstorm chased her off the street. The door stuck—it still did—and was set back from the street between two shops that sold vintage clothing. Glenice climbed the stairs and went in. A gray-faced man peered out around a curtain at the far end of the room. He nodded and returned to his heater and his laptop. He knew Glenice of old: she wouldn't buy, steal, or vandalize anything, and he had no interest in her. His lumpy black cat strolled out, inspected Glenice, tested the patch of light that the window threw on the floor, and stalked back into the office.

Quite often there was something here for Glenice. Today it was a room with a table, a vase, a dish of fruit and part of a window. The hungry blue of the window frame clashed perfectly with the blue of the tablecloth without taking it over. The vase held flowers, mauve, pinky yellow, pale red, blackish—Glenice tried and failed to call up the names of black flowers. The wall was a quiet, mortal sort of pink, and there were sleepy-looking pears slumped on a green dish. It looked to Glenice like the kind of room in which someone had gradually recovered from a long illness. She stared at the painting until her feet died from the cold and then she left.

The café had an inner room, out of drafts from the door. Glenice chose a table by the window and closed prayerful hands around a skinny cappuccino. A baby sent her a radiant smile from the next table. It was Aidan. *It was Aidan.* Then quite gently it was not. Not-Aidan laughed at his mother's striped sleeve. He pointed his fleecy toes and gurgled at the waitress hurrying forward with a cloth. The waitress came back with a fresh cup for which she later wouldn't charge Glenice; her weather was calm, unruffled by ambient turbulence.

Glenice's daughter had Skyped on the weekend to say that she was expecting a baby. Glenice received the news with detachment: a child would complicate a divorce. At Easter, she had looked out at the lake one morning and seen Pippa having a meal with a man who wasn't Matt. The slouchy way they sat at a table floating just above the water made it clear that their bodies were familiar with each other. What had drawn Pippa to this fair, fading man, who was plainer than Matt and at least ten years older? But one of the things Glenice had lost along with Aidan was her curiosity about other people. Pippa, and even Vern, were at the back of her thoughts, which were carrying on their involvement with the painted room. It was those jarring colors that had kept Glenice looking. She was looking at a vanished Australian summer when the children were small. It was the summer when her husband had embarked on an affair with a travel agent called Sandy. Sandy's mother was Malaysian, so Don called her Shandy: half and half. Before Shandy, there had been Maeve, who had a big, hard spray of golden hair, and before that, Anita from the bank. Glenice kicked up a stink, and Don was hurt. It was only sex—he had thought even she could see that. He had kindly gone on having sex with Glenice, too, so it wasn't as if he was taking anything away from their marriage. In fact, the sex had improved: Maeve and Anita had been instructive. The improvement was what gave Don away every time. Glenice enjoyed the attention he was paying her body but continued to make scenes, and eventually it was curtains for Anita, and later for Maeve.

With Shandy, Glenice wasn't sure that she could be bothered. But her unhappiness must have been plain: a student counselor at the agricultural college where Glenice worked in the office invited her on holiday. Lorna was a single mother whose son, Ricky, was in Aidan's year at school, and Glenice had had coffee with her once or twice. In January Lorna would be driving down to the Central Coast, where an old friend lived. "Why don't you come with us?" she said. "Bring the kids. Patonga's great, and you'll love Trish."

Trish lived in a fibro shack at the end of a row of houses that faced the water. She was nothing special to look at, Trish—thick brown hair, thick brown body—and her house was a mess. Glenice sat on the couch, eating a cake baked by Trish and taking in the room. In those days, contempt came readily to her—it was one of the things she had in common with Don—and contempt was what she felt as she glanced around. Pieces of rich-looking cloth, some set with little mirrors, were draped over chairs and the back of the couch, and none of the cushions matched. The walls were painted a dusty yellow, and the table was painted red. The floor was gritty with sand; a blue-and-red rug looked guaranteed to harbor germs. A floral chamberpot held a cheese plant, and glass vases in shouty colors stood on the windowsill—all the vases, like the window itself, needed a good clean. The standard lamp had a fluted satin shade like a little girl's stiff party skirt. Glenice's eyes went from thing to thing, and her mind turned them into patterns. She knew from magazines that a room should look nothing like that: it should be neutral and low-slung, ivory and beige. It had crossed her mind that she might very well get a taupe leather-look three-seater couch out of Don over Shandy.

After the holiday, when Don asked what Trish was like, Glenice wrinkled her neat nose. "Bit of a hippie," she said. "Incense and that." She felt a strong if obscure need to protect Trish from Don. Something important had happened in Patonga—but what? It was the usual sort of beach holiday. The women ate toast and avocadoes for breakfast, and the children ate toast and jam. Everyone went swimming. They lay on beach towels and ate cut-up mangoes. Lorna produced a bottle of polish, and the three women painted their toenails a vampish red. The children joined up with other holiday kids and played cricket on the oval that lay at the foot of a forested hill: a charmed place that remained cool on the most boiling afternoon. Time seemed to slow there, in the shadow of the hill. The big grassy oval lay in plain sight, but struck Glenice as secret, a discovery; an ordinary place that was instantly memorable. There was nothing much to the rest of the village: fish-and-chips joint, bakery, general store; the fish came from the day's catch.

Boats moored in the shallows swung gently about with the tide. When Glenice closed her eyes, the sea was still there, a silvery dishevelment at the back of her mind.

Dinner was barbecued sausages or hamburgers. Lorna, who was generous, you had to give her that, bought ice cream for the kids, bought wine in the small, classy kind of cask. When the light sank in the bay, and it grew too dark to play outside, the children watched old movies that Trish had taped off TV. The women sat out on the porch, drinking wine. They all smoked: Peter Jacksons for Glenice, Alpines for Lorna, and roll-ups for Trish. Now and then a child would find a reason—thirst, a card trick, an injustice—to run out to the porch, wishing to assert a prior claim on the women's attention.

Trish and Lorna liked to talk with light, good-natured scorn about men they had got the better of, or who had got the better of them—there was no middle way. Whenever they paused, Glenice felt but refused to see the glance that Lorna sent her way like an invitation. Glenice mistrusted the oozy exchange of revelations that served as mortar in female friendships. Betrayal was never far off. On the drive down, Lorna had told Glenice that when Trish lived in Sydney, she had been involved with a no-hoper for years. Lorna's voice was hushed so that the kids couldn't hear, but the note of silky satisfaction at a friend's idiocy came through. Sitting on the porch, Glenice swatted a mosquito, drank wine, and looked out at the blank, bristling water. She could tell that Lorna was dying to hear her say that Don was a bastard, and no way was Glenice going to spill her guts. When Glenice thought that, she didn't see the pinky spillage of intestines but a fire extinguisher pumping out foam. The foam smothered everything and ruined it and could never be retracted.

Lorna and Trish had Trish's bedroom, and the boys had the

sleep-out at the back of the house. Glenice and Pippa had the pull-out couch in the living room—except Pippa wasn't Pippa then but Narelle. Narelle yearned for the sleep-out, but Aidan had made an urgent face at his mother. That face remained as clear to Glenice as if it were pressed against the café window: it was pleading and angry, a characteristic male face, and it was the first time she had seen it on her son. Glenice knew that Aidan was afraid of what Ricky would say. She should have insisted—Ricky was a manipulative little shit, if you asked Glenice—but she didn't want trouble with Lorna. Lorna had sharp edges on which you could scrape your shins. When Glenice pronounced "patio" to rhyme with "ratio," Lorna pretended not to understand. Then she said, "Oh: PAT-io, you mean," and slid a smile at Trish. Lorna's voice was bright and dauntless, so why did she need so much makeup? That makeup spoke to Glenice of deep-rooted fear, and the frightened are dangerous. So Glenice controlled herself. She was doing a lot of that, at the time.

After everyone had gone to bed, the moon appeared in a round mirror with wavy edges that hung in Trish's living room from a silver chain. Glenice was awake, claimed by black, bitter thoughts. She was also conscious of shame because she was craving Don. When Glenice thought about what he was probably up to with Shandy right now, she filled up with rage but also with starry prickles of lust. Narelle flung out a dreaming arm and caught her mother on the breast, and Glenice tried to focus on the reflected moon. She had been impervious to the charms of Anita and Maeve, but sourly acknowledged that Shandy was pretty glam with her bouncy black ponytail and her pert aqua dress. When Glenice watched her children running across the beach to fling themselves at the sea, she couldn't help thinking of Shandy, who was so young and so perfect and offered herself so fully to adventure.

Trish had worked for a publishing company in Sydney but now she was freelance. She showed Glenice a book whose cover featured Ned Kelly, Donald Bradman, and an Anzac. It was called *Australian Heroes* and had never been out of print; Trish was preparing a new edition, updated to include Alan Bond. In the sweaty afternoon, while Lorna had a nap and the children were on the oval, Trish cleared the table, put on soft, jazzy music, set out her reference books, and went on editing. The blinds were closed against the heat. A fan turned slowly. Glenice lay on the couch, leafing through a magazine but aware of Trish. It was deeply reassuring to be in the presence of peaceful, concentrated labor. Glenice listened for the *kreek-kreek* that meant Trish was sharpening her pencil. Sometimes Trish said, "Bugger!" and sometimes she snorted. Sometimes she read aloud: Glenice heard, "Bond's entrepreneurial vision has shown the world there is more to us than cricket and sheep." Trish knew heaps of stuff and also nothing much. Why didn't she do something about the silver lines running like the diagram of a nervous system through her hair? It occurred to Glenice that while she often felt sorry for women, she didn't much like them. She went into the kitchen, made tea, and placed one of Trish's colored cups at her round brown elbow. "You're a champion," said Trish, without looking up.

One day, Glenice asked, "Weren't you afraid? Giving up your job and everything?"

"Petrified. Still am, sometimes." Trish said, "I'm always dipping into my savings. When I have to get my car fixed or the insurance comes around, it's panic stations. I don't want to think what'll happen if I get ill and can't work."

Glenice's face was a question.

Trish picked a shred of tobacco from her lip. She lit up the cigarette and said, "I was living a sort of double life: there was the life I kept fantasizing about and there was my life in Sydney. One of those lives was never going to happen, and the other never stopped." She added, "Sorry. That's not very clear."

"No, it is," lied Glenice. "Now you're living the way you used to dream about."

"Oh, no. This is nothing like I used to imagine."

On the last night, they bought shark and chips for dinner. Trish produced a bottle of Gilbey's and mixed up G&Ts. Over dinner the women went on with wine. Trish was a boozer; for the first time, Glenice matched her glass for glass. They had all dolled up a bit: Lorna was wearing an off-the-shoulder dress, Glenice had put on earrings and perfume, and Trish was in a sea-colored blouse with bat-wing sleeves. The children went to bed in the sleep-out—Trish said, "Seeing as it's the last night, you boys are allowed to have Narelle in with you as a treat," and Ricky hadn't dared to so much as roll his eyes. Farther up the beach, toward the creek, some teenagers had a fire going. The moon rose, and the sea kept running up to the land for a gossip. The moon was only a day or so away from fullness. Glenice imagined it hanging, round and silver, in the round, silver mirror. She wouldn't be there to see it. She felt slightly sick and also on edge. Instead of relaxing her, the alcohol had keyed her up. She kept thinking, Something is going to happen tonight. She lit up another Peter Jackson and hoped that she would be equal to whatever it was.

What happened was that Trish and Lorna started reminiscing about the community choir where they had met. It was boring: people Glenice didn't know, ancient disasters; someone called Warren who was a bass, and then he went on his honeymoon and came back a tenor; and that time the sopranos led the altos astray. Then one of them, Trish or Lorna, started singing, and the other joined in:

And all I've done for want of wit
To memory now I can't recall
So fill to me the parting glass
Good night and joy be with you all.

It was some time since muffled excitement had drifted from the sleep-out, so it was to be assumed that the children were asleep. But a few weeks later, Glenice heard a clear, untuneful voice as Narelle bounced on her trampoline in the backyard: "*So fill to me the passing glass.*" Evidently she could remember no more and went on repeating: "*So fill to me the passing glass.*" Glenice, at the sink, was transfixed. The picture in her mind showed her a glass of wine passing from hand to hand. She was on that porch with Trish and Lorna in the lantern-lit night at Patonga, and they were taking turns at drinking wine from the same glass—Glenice saw Lorna's rings, and Trish's kind, squashy face. But the three women had never handed around a glass like that, Glenice knew: the picture had been summoned by a child's mistake. She also knew, with equal certainty, that she was looking at *transformation*. The scene on the porch was trivial, fanciful, alluring, and it told her plainly: What has been isn't all there is. A vast amazement came over Glenice, quelling every petty emotion. Something of the same sort took hold of her every time she waded into the sea.

It took her another two years to leave Don. When she did, she wanted to tell Trish. Her mind reached for words like "wreckage" and "dream," but she ended up sending a Christmas card with a brief PS. There was no reply. Ricky and Aidan were in different schools by then, and Lorna had switched to part-time and moved in with a bloke who owned a tree farm. Glenice hardly saw her anymore.

In the café in Cuba Street, Glenice took a postcard from her bag—she always kept one there in case. She borrowed a pen from the waitress and wrote, "When your brother was born, he had small, mauve hands." What was that about? She had intended to say: Go to Patonga. You will see what you need to imagine. Glenice's life since Don had been nothing like she imagined, and she could see no reason why things should be different for Pippa. But imagination had nothing to do with reason: its promise of change came from the same hidden, tidal source as catastrophe and luck. It was a lever that would provide whatever shift Pippa required. There would be cracking open and mess; things would be different, if not necessarily better. After a while, life would return to its monotonous groove.

Glenice was addressing the card when her phone rang. It was the hospital—she'd almost forgotten about Vern. She was completely unprepared for what she was about to hear.

Keith died that year, just before Christmas. By the time it was diagnosed, the cancer was in his lymph nodes and his lungs. The last time Pippa saw him alone was in November, when he was still at home in Bellevue Hill. Eva answered the door; she had just come back from the shops, she said, kissing Pippa.

Pippa said, "How is he?"

"You know he's refused any more treatment?" It was a sunny, breezy day, and Eva was wearing a cardigan. Her boneless hands, dangling from the sleeves, had the look of outdated appliances. She picked up the gardenias lying on the hall table and brought them to her face. "White flowers. His favorite."

"I brought him some soup. Organic chicken and veggies, very light."

"How kind," said Eva without interest. "Go in and see him. I'll put these in water."

"Actually, I need the bathroom first. After the drive here . . ."

Eva glanced at the globe pushing out Pippa's dress and looked away. "Of course." She said, "Ronnie was here yesterday. She insisted on crying. It was very upsetting. I hope you aren't going to cry."

Keith was in the living room, on the daybed by the window with a cashmere throw over his knees. A tiny white dog, with muddy stains under its eyes, lay in the crook of his arm. This animal, who was given to uncontrollable trembling, had been adopted by Eva from a shelter just days before Keith's diagnosis, as if she had known that she would soon need a new pet.

On the wall was a photograph of Keith's father in his judge's robes and one of his mother at her harp. Larger than either of these was a portrait of Eva, painted when she was seventeen, wearing white. The room was full of music and the smell of florist's ferns. Pippa realized that she disliked every object in it. The music was a sonata for violin and piano. She told Keith, "I'll always be sorry you and Matt didn't play at our wedding."

Eva came in with the gardenias and a cup of the raspberry-leaf tea that she had decided Pippa should drink for an easy labor. "Pippa has brought you soup," she told Keith.

"Really? How very kind."

"I'll heat some up for your lunch. You must say if it's too rich."

Keith said, "I'm sure it'll be just right."

He could have eaten all the roast potatoes he wanted, thought Pippa. It seemed the worst injustice.

"The Zeldins are downsizing," Eva told Keith. "I ran into Marcie at the shops. They've put their house on the market and bought a place in Bronte. Only four bedrooms, but there's a lap pool."

Eva looked rather wonderful that spring: her face was more finely drawn, quieter. She had squared up to specialists, dietitians, nurses, hospital administrators. There were the Loreto nuns to direct as well. Once a week her children received an e-mail with links to cancer websites, summaries of discussions with medical staff, and bulletins on their father's progress. Eva had found a cause under her roof—a lost one, the best kind.

"Marcie says they won't have an ocean view," she went on.

"Really? That *is* a shame," said Keith.

Eva said that she had e-mails to send. The wider world still had to be kept up to the mark, and she was organizing an open letter to the prime minister that called for an end to the offshore detention of refugees. It was to be signed by leaders of the business community: "Every time I sit next to one of those people at a dinner, I take out my phone and show them photos of refugees who have sought asylum here. Then I ask them to guess how many are still alive. The correct answer is none."

"How tireless you are, my dear." Keith made it sound like a compliment.

Eva favored him with her furtive smile. The gardenias, placed on a table near him, were crowded by a carnival riot of lilies and tight orange tulips. "I'm going to move Bethany's flowers," said Eva. "They're not very restful, to my mind." She picked up the vase and placed it on a cabinet where Keith couldn't see it. She drew out a tulip, frowned at it, reinserted it at a different angle, and still she didn't go away. Looking at Pippa, she said, "You know about poor Rashida, of course?"

The previous day, Rashida had posted a photo of raw pork ribs on Facebook. She wrote, "Left outside my door the day after the Paris attacks." Pippa took to Twitter at once: "Lovely Muslim friend the target of abuse. #hate-crime." While Pippa was typing this out, tears came into her eyes: she was watching herself place her arm around Rashida's bowed shoulders. Her tweet drew eleven responses expressing sympathy and asking if Pippa was OK.

"I've tried to call her," went on Eva. "But she's not picking up."

"I left a comment under her post. I made Matt leave one too. It's so horrible—how can people do stuff like that?"

"Joe tells me poor Rashida won't take time off. She's insisted on going in to work."

"People are sending heaps of support on Facebook."

"She'll come through it, I know. She's a very determined young woman." Eva plucked at her dress. Her rings burned recklessly blue. "Do you know what this husband of mine said when I told him what had happened? 'I'm afraid Muslims have to expect this kind of thing as long as jihadists go about murdering innocent people.'" Eva's voice was bright and amused. It was the voice a mother uses to her children to downplay something of which she's frightened herself. The voice went on, "It's not as if poor Rashida could ever be a threat to anyone."

Throughout all this, Keith lay inert, his eyes turned to the window. He gave the impression of listening intently to something faint and far away. After Eva had spoken, silence fell, far louder than the music in the room. It swelled out from the room and from the beautiful, sleek house, and silenced everything that it didn't wish to hear. At the center of the silence stood Eva and Keith, glued hand to hand like wedding-cake figurines. The silence said: What happens outside this room is only manageable novelty. There is give-and-take in every relationship. Hush now: a young woman with bare white arms is playing civilized music on a harp.

Eva went away at last. Keith cleared his throat. He said, "The first time I met Bethany she was six months old. She had a turned eye. She's twenty-seven now, and her eyes are perfectly straight. It's immensely satisfying." He shifted on his pillows as he spoke.

Pippa said, "Are you comfortable? Can I get you anything?"

"I've always felt a very strong attachment to the world. I'd prefer not to leave it yet. Then again, I've seen my children grow up and I'll die in my bed with as little pain as medical science can manage. That's more than most people on earth can say."

On one of the cancer websites to which Eva's e-mails linked, Pippa had read that patients sometimes experienced a foul smell at the back of the throat. You would think "a foul taste"; but no, it was "smell." Keith's face was the color of mushrooms. He said, "How are you, my dear?"

Pippa patted her stomach. "He can kick like anything these days. I wonder if he'll arrive early." There was a spot where her stomach was sore from the kicking—she could barely remember when her body had been empty and tight.

"And your book?"

"The marketing campaign's already getting into gear. There's even going to be this amazing Pippa Reynolds app. People will be able to download all this stuff about me."

"I've been wondering if the marriage worked out all right, in the end."

"It worked out just fine."

"I'm so pleased." Looking hard at the wall, Keith said, "You know, Matt takes after his mother: loyal through and through. It's all you'll ever have to fear from him."

Pippa made a noise that could pass for a laugh. The little dog stiffened and began to shake.

Keith said, "Come here, boy." He shifted the dog to his chest, holding him close to his heart.

"Look at that—he's calmed right down," said Pippa.

"Everyone just wants to be held."

When she left Bellevue Hill, Pippa drove to Earlwood. It was a long drive. All the way, an excited whisper ran through the undergrowth of her mind, pointing out that Rashida no longer existed for the Elkinsons. There was only "poor Rashida": a victim, pitied and without power. Stuck in traffic, Pippa turned her head and saw three tailor's dummies in the window of a shop, each wearing an identical white dress. It meant the shop was holding a sale. Pippa had known that for a long time but now saw death in the three headless figures, in the folds of the crisp white clothes.

In Earlwood, she found a café off Homer Street where she ordered homemade moussaka and salad. She checked her messages and did some other things on her phone. The food arrived. A real estate lift-out from the local paper lay within reach: "Colonial Mansion Has Twenty-Eight Car Spaces." Pippa barely noticed. She was thinking about Keith: his ceremonial embraces, his light, decisive voice. It was easy to picture him roaring up Vietnamese mountains on his motorbike, smiling at everyone he passed. As she was leaving, he had said, "Cairo. I never got there, you know." His eyes had kept their X-ray intensity, but now their concentration was turned inward. Pippa guessed that he was following some prolonged, cottony thought, the consequence of illness or drugs. It was leading him to a river, domed buildings, a life running out over thick, sweet coffee in the lacy shadows cast by a cutwork brass lamp. There were pearls of sweat along Keith's upper lip. Medical science had left only a sparse white garland around his head: a prefiguration of the wreath that would lie on his coffin. Tangled up in all this, somehow, was a memory of Pippa's father, with whom she now quarreled whenever they met: until she was nine, when her parents split, she had always run to meet him. He never entered the house without calling her name.

After lunch, Pippa went looking for a florist. Then she drove to the street in which Rashida lived. It wasn't her first time there.

In May that year, Matt had told Pippa that he was going to spend a couple of nights in Bellevue Hill. "Dad's away in Canberra for a conference, and there was a break-in across the street last week. Eva's nervous, although you'll never get her to admit it. Caro's doing a night as well, and so's Ronnie."

Pippa went out to dinner with Eva and Matt on the first day he was away. On the second, she was at work when a familiar itch started up. She called the clinic, and was told that Rashida was on holiday that week.

"Has she gone to Melbourne?"

"To be honest, I wouldn't know that, honestly," said the receptionist. "Would you like me to schedule you for next week?"

The next morning, Pippa woke at five. Rain was pounding the roof. Fear rolled through her with the force of a flood. There had been a dream—in the dream Matt had been on a train in the company of a shadowy figure. Teeth were involved, and the ten of clubs. On her way to the kitchen, Pippa saw herself in a mirror: her jaw and nose had strengthened with age. She pulled a few faces to banish the one in front of her, but it persisted—for the rest of her life, she would look like a skinny man.

She put the coffee on, opened the back door, and switched on the outside light: rain was falling over the edge of the roof in an unbroken sheet. Pippa slid her hand under her sweatshirt and scratched—between her breasts, her flesh was still warm with sleep. She was sure that she was pregnant but every day she put off confirming it. Every day Matt didn't ask. His not-asking deafened Pippa. She crossed her arms over her chest and wondered, What have I done?

The air in the kitchen felt solid on wet mornings: Pippa had to dig her way through. Tess had drawn up plans for renovations ages ago, but Matt and Pippa still hadn't even taken down Mateusz's grotty curtain. Now there would be a baby; the work would have to be postponed again. The espresso machine shuddered, and Pippa knew that she would always look for reasons to keep these rooms as they were. When they disappeared, a door that had remained ajar would swing shut. Pippa didn't want to walk through that door, but she wanted to preserve the landscape that lay beyond. Otherwise, there would be only this life: willed into being, shipshape and all around her.

She took her coffee back to bed, and Hank ambled along with her. Pippa told him, "I think I should tell Matt today, don't you?" Hank leaped up onto the bed, which was forbidden, collapsed against Pippa, and began to purr. No one was able to decide whether Hank was incredibly stupid or incredibly good. When Pippa had proposed adopting a dog, a long time ago now, Matt agreed at once. Months after Hank arrived, they were waiting for the bill in a restaurant when Matt said, "A dog isn't what we need." He was never unkind to Hank, but their relations were without humor.

Pippa texted Matt: "Happy news. Love ya." His tracksuit pants and a T-shirt were laid out on his side of the bed like clothes whose owner lay in a morgue. A different dream rose to the surface of Pippa's mind, one from earlier in the night: she was in a deli, buying a kind of cheese that cured jet lag. That would make an excellent tweet: #middleclassdreams. @warmstrong said, "A detailed, nonironic review of a coloring book. *facepalms*." Someone had a video of a kangaroo pushing a man into a billabong. Someone else asked whether Norwex cloths were worth the $$. @gloriahallelujah tweeted, "So blessed to represent @JoshKapoor. Stunning food memoir out next June! Form an orderly queue."

By half past six, Pippa and Hank were dashing through the rain to her car. When she returned from France, Pippa had finally conceded that the Peugeot had to go. Leaving the car dealership, she began to cry—Aidan had spent entire Saturday afternoons lying in the driveway with his head under that car, and now the Peugeot was cowering in a corner of a car yard, a defeated animal destined for the slaughterhouse. The tedious red Honda she had traded it for never failed to start: its meekness still took Pippa by surprise. Wipers dutifully manic now, it was carrying her through the early-morning traffic, heading for Earlwood. Hank breathed hotly on the backseat. He experimented with his harness, stepping to the left and to the right. He made pitiful noises: why couldn't he lay his head in the beloved female's lap—why, why? If a different human had been present, Hank would have loved her, too. His love was God's love: it overlooked no one, and the specific could not be expected of it.

The silhouettes of cranes rose all along the manipulated suburban skyline: giant fingerposts directing This Way to Megabucks. The names of property developers were offered to the sky like modern prayers. Pippa had reached Marrickville when her phone rang—that would be Matt. She took a wrong turn and ended up heading down a hill toward the river. On the far side of the valley, the brick-and-tile ranges of Earlwood loomed in charcoal shapes, their brightwork of windows hellfire yellow, like a sinister allegory of city life. A text came through; Pippa knew that Matt had guessed her news. She drummed her fingers on the wheel and said, "Bye bye, Rashida!": a grim, happy thought.

When she turned in to it, Ashmead Place was black with rain. It was a short street, a dead end, with only one apartment block; Pippa slowed as she drew near. She pictured Rashida luxuriously awake, watching her streaming, beaten windows. She saw herself running up the stairs. Rashida's door swung open at her touch, as had the one to the street. Pippa switched on every light she passed. In the bedroom, she dragged Rashida from the bed where she lay folded into Matt. Rashida didn't offer any resistance: she was guilty, and Pippa was invincible. Grasping her by a hank of hair, Pippa slammed her head into the wall: once, twice. The repeated thwack of Rashida's skull against the bricks, the sludge of her blood and brains on the plaster—how satisfying!

Pippa turned her car around at the river end of the street and drove slowly back the other way. The thick sort of day that was breaking obscured as much as it revealed, but there was no mistaking the powder-blue Beetle parked under a dripping tree.

Now, six months after that morning, every jacaranda in the street had lilac hair. Pippa peered through massy blossom at Rashida's building: its rendered brick bulk looked as composed and still as a ship that had pitched through a storm and lay serenely in harbor at last. In Rashida's Facebook photo, part of a word, printed on her doormat, showed beside the pork ribs: "ME." Pippa parked and walked up to the entrance of the building. She was carrying a colossal bouquet—roses, carnations, wax flowers, stock—that she intended to leave on Rashida's mat: obliterating, scented flowers that would cry, "Welcome! Welcome!" But the thick glass security door was locked. Pippa buzzed a few apartments but got no answer. It was very frustrating: the flowers would have made a spectacular photo on social media. Seeing it in their Twitter feeds, people would think: Pippa Reynolds is such a warm, generous person!

The bright afternoon had relaxed into warmth. The river was an invitation at the bottom of the street. Pippa left the flowers in her car and made her way down to the water. She followed a path that led to an avenue of blurry she-oaks. A mild contraction brought her to a standstill in the shade of three Moreton Bay figs, and she thought, as she had thought every day since that rainy May morning, I didn't have to do this. Now having a baby was something there was no going around, only through. Pippa felt as she did when she had spent days cooking a meal, and the guests were about to arrive: anticipation, a light euphoria, and the wish to be transported to a hotel with excellent room service where she could remake her life. During her first, brief pregnancy, she had asked Keith, using a flip sort of voice to mask fear, "What if I don't love this baby?" Everyone else on whom she tried that out had answered, "Of course you will!" Keith said, "That must happen sometimes. But in my experience people suffer much more from the promises they don't make than the ones they can't keep."

The last time Pippa had seen both Keith and Rashida was, as usual, over Sunday lunch in Bellevue Hill. It was a celebratory occasion: Pippa had announced her pregnancy, and Caroline had embarked on a new career. The previous year, she had decided to resign her partnership: "I'm fed up with commercial law. I want to live differently, get some of that edge back." Now she had gone into investment banking. Ronnie said, "So here's my sister's idea of living dangerously: she's swapped the Beemer for an Alfa Romeo." Pippa barely noticed the joshing: she was watching Rashida and Keith. They ignored each other, pretty much, but not in a pointed way, just as they had always done. Rashida looked up and saw Pippa inspecting her—her gray eyes looked straight back. She was wearing her trashy earrings: they shone like frozen rain against her hair. A beat later, Pippa realized, They're *real*. Keith, of course. Pricey bling would be exactly his notion of a gift that would appeal to the primitive mind.

Rashida turned to Eva: "These cabbage rolls are your best ever." Pippa thought, Wow! You're good at this. She hadn't told Matt what she had discovered—how to explain what she had been doing in Ashmead Place? Running alongside that difficulty, and not entirely acknowledged by Pippa, was a desire to protect Keith. The secret, held close, felt potent and dangerous, a magic amulet—it lit up inside Pippa from time to time, delivering a small, shocking thrill.

Keith touched her wrist: "May I trouble you for the bread?" He smiled at her: a buffoon, a cheat. Pippa realized, *You're* good at this. Rashida's learned from you. She remembered, "When that man wants something, he wants it violently." Pippa picked up her glass of sparkling water—she felt wobbly inside. As it turned out, it would be the last lunch of its kind. Two days later, Keith consulted a doctor about the pain in his chest.

As Pippa made her way along the river in Earlwood, she saw trees hanging their heads, sodden with blossom. Bougainvillea had dragged its hefty colored swags over fences; honeysuckle wandered between gardens, perfuming and strangling as it went. A cyclist rode past with a hound coursing beside her, and Pippa resolved to bring Hank here one day soon. She had left the path and was strolling along the broad grassy verge. It was the time of year when the light—even in squalid Sydney—was a pure, inquisitorial gold. It laid bare the world that Keith was leaving and Pippa's child was entering: the world of the "Minuet in G" and *Game of Thrones*, the world of sarcomas and adult coloring books and full-throttle spring afternoons. In that world of appetite and detail, Matt got a son and Pippa got a bestseller and Rashida got a slab of pork ribs, and to be honest, honestly, Pippa was neither wholly glad nor wholly sorry about any of those things.

Beyond a playground the trees ended, and the way ahead ran open and radiant beside the varnished membrane of the river. Pippa was about to turn back when a procession appeared in the west—at least, a procession was what she thought of at first. The sunlight, shining into her eyes, seemed to warp around the figures, who now brought pilgrims to mind; and then formality and purposefulness gave way, and Pippa thought of a carnival troupe. Each successive impression was of something archaic because the scene before her seemed to have fallen out of time. Something cold crawled between Pippa's shoulders. But the strangers were closer now, and she saw that they were just people enjoying a walk along the river. It was their gaudy clothes that had confused her—they were like costumes borrowed from a different age. Five men led the way, in bright shirts that reached to the knees of their baggy cotton trousers. Some wore flat-topped skullcaps bordered with embroidery; one had on tracksuit pants, and a waistcoat woven with metallic threads. A dozen or so women followed, dressed in ankle-length skirts and loose shirts in flamboyant combinations of color: pink and emerald, purple and mustard, turquoise and clear red. Like the men, they wore sandals or chunky sneakers, and walked nonchalantly, swinging their arms. Their speech, by turns piercing and watery, carried messages from the world. They cried out to one another and to the men, who answered over their shoulders. One woman held up her palm and snapped her fingers, another hurried forward and tugged at a sleeve—the whole scene was emphatic with gesture and talk. Pippa saw flat golden-brown faces. They were old and young, and they had square, un-Australian teeth, some of them broken. Strung out across the path, the men and women surged past Pippa as if she were invisible, their raucous exchanges passing through her. They flowed on and vanished into the trees, and Pippa remained where she was. The heat pressed about her like a pelt; she glanced down, lightly aware of her beating heart. When she looked up, a troll had materialized in the punishing light; the squat figure approached, half skipping, half running, waving his arms. He called out, and a burst of laughter floated back from the trees. The child pranced on: a fattish boy of about ten, wearing an orange T-shirt over those baggy trousers. Unlike his elders, he paused when he drew level with Pippa, and his lively eyes passed over her. Then he laughed in her face and lolloped away.

It would become a story that Pippa told her son (and, in time, her stepgrandchildren): the story of how she went for a walk one afternoon and met a band of strangers, passing through Sydney on their way to curious lands. "You were there with me," she would say to her son. "We were keeping each other safe. But you were invisible."

The river story proved a favorite with Pippa's son, and she added to it with each telling: an embellishment of high, clear music, symbolic fish leaping in the water, and a kookaburra whose cracked laughter was a code. One of the strangers played a flute, said Pippa, and another beat a drum, while a girl with a wing of black hair juggled three silver cups. Men and women alike wore broad bangles of beaten metal, set with flashing stones, that reached halfway up their arms. The people on the river path had left an impression of earthy coarseness, but in Pippa's account, they seemed to have been spun from music and gold. Their sleeves flared from their elbows like flags. A dog with a round head and a square chest ran forward to inspect them. Hank was dead by then; Pippa's son remembered him only as a sort of threadbare shadow, but he loved the dog in the tale. Hank was persuaded by the golden people to join their band, said Pippa, and saw wonders in their company. According to the vet, Hank's kidneys had given out, but Pippa knew that he had died of a broken heart. Long after they buried him under the orange tree she went on hearing him, separated from the human companionship he longed for, pleading outside the back door to be allowed into the house. Hank became the hero of her story, a gallant adventurer. He visited kingdoms deep under the sea, and tucked away in the bush, and hidden among the starry lanes of outlandish galaxies. His new friends could be fierce, but Hank kept them from quarrels and steered them into gentle ways. As time passed, Pippa came to believe that he really had been with her that day, moseying along in the bold urban grass. Her life had leafed out; it wasn't always possible to see past the experiences it carried like obscuring blossoms. No memory of that meeting by the river could match the confusion of the event, and gradually her mind reworked it so that everything—the boisterous strangers, the judgmental light—took on a kindly tint.

She forgot that well after the boy in the orange T-shirt had disappeared into the trees, the shock of their encounter continued to vibrate: the way he had laughed so brazenly, showing all his bitey little teeth. There was such lightness in him! As he capered away, the day seemed to darken. Pippa's dress, of printed cotton, sat heavily on her encumbered body; it seemed to be sending an ache down to her calves. She took a bottle of water from her bag and drank from it, tilting her face to the sky. The sun knocked all the leaves into light, transforming them into birds.

There had been barbecues and picnic tables by the playground; Pippa returned to it and sat down. She gave a little, unconscious shake—it was useless, she couldn't rid herself of what she had seen. That rowdy visitation didn't belong to the past but to the future. There were no memorial plaques in the future, only a daunting horde to which Pippa was of no account. It called over its shoulder as it rammed past: "You missed everything important."

Pippa's phone rang. It was no one who mattered; she let voice mail pick it up. What she needed was the reassurance of a virtual new world that offered the hope all new worlds extend: an unlimited expanse in which she might live out her best idea of herself.

Her profile picture on Facebook was overlaid with a transparency of the French flag, and there were 193 responses to Rashida's post. On Twitter, @gloriahallelujah's pinned tweet was a photo of the opera house lit up in red, white, and blue with the caption "Vive la France!" Someone quoted Christina Rossetti: "Does the road wind uphill all the way? / Yes, to the very end." Someone else wondered why cats just allowed themselves to be stereotyped like that. @warmstrong said, "Patrick White was a genius. Up to a point."

V

OLLY FAITHFUL

SEVENTEEN MONTHS HAD PASSED SINCE Bunty died, and she had been living at Waratah Lodge before that, but Christabel still woke daily to a feeling of surprise—or rather, bewilderment and resistance on finding herself alone. Bunty's bed with its candlewick coverlet was still there across the room. Christabel woke early and slept lightly, unlike Bunty, who had snored—how many times had Christabel cried, "Bunty!" in the middle of the night? Sometimes it was necessary to get out of bed and prod until Bunty turned onto her side. She maintained that she didn't snore, or hardly ever, and would accuse Christabel of exaggeration. Another thing that they couldn't agree on was the cold. Bunty didn't feel it and refused to have a heater in the bedroom. "That's because you're fat," Christabel said. The memory of that kind of remark was a torture, although Bunty had merely observed that Christabel ought to dress more warmly—ignoring her flannelette nightie and ribbed red socks.

On the morning of the Sydney Writers' Festival, Christabel sat up in bed and reached for an old jumper with a loose roll-neck; it had wide sleeves, making it easy to get her arms in before dropping the rest over her head. There was no one to object to a radiator now, but without Bunty to share bills, Christabel couldn't afford to heat the room except in the coldest months. She switched on her clock radio and caught the forecast: "A medium chance of showers, clearing to a fine afternoon." What help was "a medium chance"? Christabel used to say, "Bunty, do you think I should take an umbrella? A coat?" Whatever Bunty answered was right some of the time, which was no worse than the weather bureau and inspired more confidence because it had been customized for Christabel. Whether the official forecast said "Partly cloudy" or "Thunderstorm developing" or "Strong southwesterly winds turning light in the evening," what it was really saying was, "Now you are alone in the world."

Bunty and Christabel had met in Ceylon when they were girls. Fa took one look at Bunty: "The Mediterranean type: exquisite at seventeen, overblown at twenty, fat at twenty-five." Christabel was twelve when Fa said that, and Bunty was fourteen, and the Sedgwicks had just moved into the street. Mr. Sedgwick was English—the wrong kind, who drank. He had failed to manage a tea estate in the hills. In Colombo, he was employed as some kind of clerk.

Kiki Mack informed everyone that Bunty's Italian mother had run off with a Creole bandleader when Bunty was only five. Excitability, too, came with the type, said Fa.

When Bunty turned up at Christabel's school, her white skin was admired, and the way her breasts crowded her uniform; but her strong features were judged rather plain. Her real name was Alfrieda, but very soon not even the teachers called her that.

The two girls had little to do with each other, being in different grades. Outside school, it was the same thing: the Sedgwicks' house was screened by tall flowering shrubs. It was known that there were older boys, who had been to school in England. One had gone to the dogs: he had been seen around the place with a Chinese girl.

Fa ran into Mr. Sedgwick at a club where Englishmen didn't go. Christabel heard him tell Moth, "Trim Sedgwick has the sincere blue eyes of a born liar."

Trim!

Moth was no longer strong enough to play the piano. When Christabel was small, people had come to the house every evening to hear Moth play. Years later, Fa would talk about those evenings. "A brilliant company" was the phrase that recurred. It encompassed a local diva, and a Danish painter, and a former prime minister who believed himself in love with Moth. Fa described them all. By then he and Christabel were living in a flat where rats ran behind the walls. What Christabel recalled about the early part of her life was a morning when she was four or five. She had risen while it was still dark and wandered out of the house. The crows were already calling. The lawn lay in deep shadow, but the upper part of the air was full of light. It announced the approach of something loose and strong and expansive. Christabel sat on a step and waited for her life.

Rehearsals for the carol service began. The choir was ruled by Miss Felton-Fowler, who taught music throughout the school. At every rehearsal, the Old Fowl interrupted the choir to cry, "All ye faithful! Enunciate! E-nun-ci-ate!"

"O come, Olly Faithful," sang the girls, as they did every year.

The carol service always opened with the first verse of "Once in Royal David's City" sung by a sixth former. But the Old Fowl chose Bunty as her soloist that year.

With the first notes, all the girls hushed.

The Old Fowl rubbed her crabby red eyes and addressed Bunty: "There were Sedgwicks at Horsley Hall in Derbyshire. Are you related to them?"

"I wouldn't know," said Bunty. "I've lived here all my life."

That was the way she spoke. There were teachers who went on giving her lines for failing to say "Miss." But Christabel saw that Bunty wasn't rude, only indifferent. It was as if her mind were attending to matters known to her alone, far removed from the petty laws of school. Punished, she remained large and placid, and blinked with no discernible sense of disgrace. Her teeth looked sharp and were surprisingly small. She gave no sign of the perfection she carried inside her. At netball, she threw powerfully from the shoulder, like a boy.

Moth died. She hadn't left her bedroom in years. A delegation of girls came to the house and pressed Christabel's hand.

From the corridor a step led down into Moth's room, setting it apart. Long before Moth became ill, the sunken back bedroom had made Christabel feel sad. Even when the curtains were open, the dressing-table mirror swallowed all the light. Moth's books still lay by the stripped iron bed. Christabel looked through a few. A pencil line marked a sentence: "We should live life neither as it is, nor as it should be, but as we see it in our dreams." How beautiful that was! Then she realized that it wasn't "live life" but "show life."

In time the pieces of the world came together again. But now all the seams showed.

•

A Sedgwick roared up and down the street on a motorcycle at inconsiderate hours.

Fa's lecture "The Romantic Imagination" was disrupted when a group of undergraduates invaded the amphitheater to chant, "Sinhala only! Sinhala only!" A very low class of student was being admitted to the university these days.

Bunty had to repeat a year at school. She was only one grade higher than Christabel now but remained remote. It wasn't clear whether she sought solitude or was shunned. She was as tall and radiant as a queen, and like royalty had no need to be kind.

On her way home from her elocution lesson at Kiki Mack's Academy of Speech and Drama, Christabel practiced vocal clarity: "Parp-pope-poop-pawp-pape-peep. Barb-bobe-boob-bawb-babe-beeb." Very fast, she recited, "He hits his fists against the posts and still insists he sees the ghosts."

The street was lined with shade trees. Birds grumbled as she passed. Out of the green gloom came the blare of Bunty's arms, Bunty's face. A lanky black-and-white dog materialized, too, running up to inspect Christabel.

The girls drew close and halted—uncertainly, as if they might yet pass each other without a sign. The face Christabel saw was as white as a bandage and as blank. For comfort, she thumbed a hard object in the pocket of her skirt. The sweet, held out, was round and orange in a cellophane twist. For a frightening moment, she thought Bunty would strike it from her hand.

They still hadn't spoken. Having accepted the butterscotch, Bunty just stood there. The dog, sniffing about, lifted his leg against a wall.

Bunty said, "He's called Oliver." She gave a barking sort of laugh: "Olly Faithful!"

At dinner, Fa said, "The Sedgwicks' dog has a boy's name, and the Sedgwick boys are named for dogs."

It was quite true that Bunty had a brother called Sizzle. And another who answered to Raven. A third, who had been in the war, went out to Nyasaland around this time and was never heard of again.

In January, Bunty wasn't there when school began. It was learned that she would have had to repeat the year a second time if she had stayed. A boarder whose family lived up-country reported that Bunty had been seen in a hill station; she looked well and had put on weight.

By the end of the year it became known that Bunty had gone abroad. Kiki Mack decided that she had gone out to join her brother in Africa. She launched her gentle, throaty laugh and said, "Girls are in demand in places like that." Thereafter, if Christabel's thoughts turned to Bunty, she pictured her on horseback with a white hat and a gun. Men with categorical jawlines—also hatted and armed—buzzed in her wake.

Christabel began teaching in Kiki's academy as an amusement, to pass the time until she married. There was Len Raymond, Fa's most promising student. Len took Christabel to the Varsity Ball. On a veranda strung with Chinese lanterns, he had opinions about

Yeats. Afterward, in the shadowy garden, the length of their bodies pressed.

Another time Len came to the house and sat with Christabel for over an hour, drinking tea with his knees sideways. One of his socks had lost its elastic—out of compassion Christabel looked away. They discussed modern literature and agreed on the importance of the subjective view. A weighty silence followed. At last, Len gazed into the crotons that jazzed in the garden and announced that an uncle in Canada had paid his passage there. He said, "This is no country for young men." His voice shot up, and he laughed to cover it—it was obvious that he had rehearsed the line.

Christabel discovered that she was sensible and practical. "You'll need warm, waterproof clothes," she said. "And it's said that seventy percent of body heat is lost through the head. You'll find a hat essential. Preferably fur." This newfound briskness lasted years, at least where Len was concerned.

News of Sedgwicks—though never of Bunty—reached Christabel now and then. Sizzle married a well-to-do Sinhalese girl. Soon afterward, Raven and his father returned to England. Fa said, "They should have left in '48." He meant with the rest of the British. Fa was a patriot. All through the Sixties, there were departures; Len Raymond was only the start. Looking back, Christabel would never understand how things could have come to an end so quietly and so fast. People she had known all her life queued for the gangplank. Later, they walked in line across the tarmac to the waiting plane. A world collapsed in an orderly way. Christabel realized, We are going down with it.

At every farewell party, Fa found an opportunity to say, "My own, my native land." Christabel, standing off to one side, saw the smiles and recognized embarrassment. Serves them right! she thought. They had been reminded of a beautiful and noble sentiment. But as the years passed, she moved away when she saw Fa getting ready to speak. He wore a weak, foolish smile on these occasions. Afterward she wanted to go over and place her palm against his—she never did, believing this assault of tenderness to be an admission of his defeat. In fact it sealed his victory, since pity fastened her to him more securely than any lock and chain.

The farewells always seemed to take place on particularly lovely evenings with attentive breezes and a giant moon. Christabel liked to find a vantage point beside a window or on a veranda where it was easy to look away from the faces of those who were to leave. They were the faces of victors, gleeful and exposed. A girl Christabel knew from school said, "Why are you staying? They don't want people like us here." She meant people whose European surnames—Portuguese, Dutch, British—were studies in empire. They had no place in the modern nation: they embodied shabby bargains, old defeats. "If your father won't leave, you should go," said the girl, fingering the ripe pimple on her neck. "I'll write when we get to Melbourne. You can stay with us when you come."

She never wrote. Or maybe she did; Christabel and Fa were no longer at their old address, having had to move to two fourth-floor rooms in a slummy wilderness on the wrong side of Colombo. Fa's illness had intervened, and the spiteful magic of inflation. His savings disappeared while his pension bought less each month.

Christabel inserted herself into a bus that would take her to work. Upright in the crush of bodies, she became aware of a peculiar pressure in the small of her back. The bus braked, causing her to stagger. The pressure increased, shifting to her buttocks. As her stop approached, she squirmed around to begin the slow journey to the door and saw, through lowered lids, a trousered leg. Western clothes: A gentleman, she thought automatically. That evening, she read to Fa after dinner: "*Nothing in the world is single; / All things by a law divine / In one spirit meet and mingle.*" After a while she excused herself, pleading hoarseness, and went out onto the landing. The barred window there was open, but the air in the stairwell was always foul. Christabel was conscious of an urge to touch her tongue to the rusted flakes on a bar. A gentleman! She couldn't have said which was more painful to contemplate, the foolishness of her reflex or the depth of her need. She was thirty-four. She had believed, briefly, that her life could be joyful. Now a clutching in her ribs told her that she was moving toward defeat.

Fa died—awfully, among the opals of phlegm on the floor of a public hospital. Some hours earlier, he had opened his eyes and said, "What is done is done. And what is not done is not done."

Without his pension, Christabel could no longer afford the flat. That was when Kiki Mack offered her garage. "Many would call it luxurious," said Kiki. Her eyes grew larger and dreamier and closer together. She said, "You'll find the rent very reasonable. Even though I've had shelving put in."

Christabel placed Fa's Keats on one of the shelves. All the other books, with which Fa had steadfastly refused to part, had been sold. Silverfish had infiltrated all seven volumes of Gibbon. "They're leather-bound," said Christabel to the bookseller standing over Fa's trunk. He scratched his head; his yellow mustache was sorrowful. "No demand," he told her. She agreed at last to his price. His assistant came forward, and the two men began wrapping the books in old newspapers. Christabel saw a headline about insurgents. Another announced that Charles Manson had been sentenced to life.

At Kiki's, Christabel had to use the servants' bathroom, the servants' lavatory. She learned to walk past the kitchen veranda as if going to a ball, clutching her cake of Lux.

Kiki supplied her meals, deducting the cost from her wages. Christabel put on weight. For years, she had fed Fa nourishing, expensive chicken or fish while dining on bread sprinkled with sugar. Now she was well and strong, and her mind was very clear. When she remembered the moment on the landing, she felt only scorn for her former self. A gentleman! Christabel looked into the square of mirror on the slimy wall of the servants' bathroom. She watched her eyes slip all over the place and brought them back to face facts. "No demand," she said.

Calmly, she tidied the garage and set out for the station. She should have had only a minute or two to wait, but the train had been delayed. From the edge of the platform, she watched the direction from which it would come. People had walked out to the end of the tracks and were standing there, smoking to pass the time: blue ringlets hung in the sunny air. Christabel's bag was over her arm, and her arms were crossed at her waist. Her small, sharp bones were full of light. She looked down to check that her shoes were clean. She heard the train and felt its breath, and turned into a column of lead. Commuters pressed forward around her, while others attempted to alight. She was shoved aside and stumbled. Her bag slid from her arm. The clasp broke when it struck the platform and everything fell out. Everything was a piece of paper with Kiki's name and phone number. A thick brown sandal stepped on it as she watched.

Leaving the station, she realized that her first class for the day, at a school in Cinnamon Gardens, should have started ten minutes ago; there would be trouble about that. Also, she would have to pay someone to mend her bag.

Backed up against a wall, a kitten was arching itself at a crow—a small kitten and a large crow. Barely interrupting her stride, Christabel picked up the kitten by his scruff. "You are sentenced to life," she said, and stowed him in her broken bag.

Kiki's house was in a lane that ran off a busy road. If Christabel walked to the top of the lane of an evening, there were always people standing around. She would look up and see the moon riding high, as white as a life cut back to the bone. There was usually a scattering of sugary stars. Farther along the road, several small buildings had been razed to make way for a multistory office block. Fa used to say, "We are being demolished into the future," whenever he saw an old place pulled down. But work had come to an indefinite halt on the construction site. People would hang about across the road in the evenings, staring at walls that had risen no higher in months. These people were servants, or kept huddled shops, or emerged from the huts that lined a nearby canal. The clearing of the site, the work of construction, the uncertain outcome—in short, the drama of the office block—provided a distraction from hardship and need. Suspended between optimism and melancholy, the building stood for life itself. And then, the incomplete walls and jutting steel rods consoled with proof that the rich, too, had their difficulties and deserved compassion. Christabel thought, All around me are ordinary people and I am ordinary like them. For some weeks, this immersion in humanity brought intense satisfaction: a radiant exaltation, in fact. The smell of cheap cigarettes, the whining folk song issuing from a radio, the workers clinging to buses like maggots to a carcass, even a panting, wooly dog who appeared from nowhere one evening and sped along the pavement, scattering bystanders: everything inspired the joyful exclamation, I am ordinary!

After a while, however, there was no comfort in the thought; on the contrary, it was a blow directed at Moth and Fa. Christabel remembered "a brilliant company." But that life had gone forever. She could barely recall it; it was Fa who had harped on about it when it was over, like someone determined to recount a dream. There was really only the future: unfinished, looming in the dark. Christabel told herself that it would hold happiness as well as sorrow—in books, it held everything. "Life is long," she murmured, as she walked back down the lane. She was not even forty. There was still time for everything to change.

But there were evenings when a terrible, silent cry filled the garage: Oh, my life! It was before her eyes, a clear spring leaping from its source, winding aimlessly downhill and gathering murk until it disappeared into a cleft where it surged and moaned unseen. No one used or directed its power. Napoleon mewed silently on her lap, showing her the roof of his mouth. Christabel asked him, "Do you entertain illusions?" She kissed his cruel, furry cheeks.

A servant ran out from the house to say that Christabel was wanted on the phone. Kiki was waiting with both chins held high. "How you disappoint me," she said to the air beside Christabel's left ear. "You know very well that this number is for business purposes only." She pointed to the thick black receiver waiting on the desk and glided out to eavesdrop in the hall.

"But how did you know where to find me?" Christabel asked afterward, when she was installed in Bunty's house in Sydney.

"Sizzle."

"But how did *he* know?"

"I don't know."

Where had Bunty, who had failed everything at school, learned bookkeeping? When Christabel arrived in Sydney, she found Bunty overseeing the accounts of an Italian who imported tiles. Every Christmas, Mr. Valente gave her a panforte and an envelope stuffed with cash. "I usually leave the panforte in a park," said Bunty. "But I thought you might like it."

Christabel didn't.

They thought greedily of the Christmas cakes of home: stuffed with sweet spices, moist.

Christabel had three excellent, useless A levels. "I've taught elocution since I was twenty," she said. "And I can do invisible mending." Bunty borrowed a typewriter from work and gave Christabel a book called *Teach Yourself Typing*. Christabel practiced at the kitchen table, feeling out the home keys with a tea towel over her hands.

Mr. Valente, sleek in a close-fitting purple shirt, arrived at their house on Saturday with orchids to match. He was shiny all over: shoes, teeth, eyes. Bunty came up the passage in one of the tidy blouses and jail-colored skirts she wore to work; her insteps overflowed her shoes. She was going to the races at Randwick with Mr. Valente. As soon as they left the house, Christabel scurried to the front window and spied. Mr. Valente touched Bunty's elbow and unlocked the passenger door of his Mercedes. His gleaming head was half the size of Bunty's.

"He wants to marry you," said Christabel when Bunty

returned. Hadn't she seen his juicy eyes? Her life with Bunty, barely begun, was already at an end. She had spent the day picturing herself banished to Bunty and Mr. Valente's garage: it had amenities, being Australian, and shag pile. He only comes up to her armpit, she thought, full of spite.

"He already has a wife," said Bunty, removing her watch. It had a plain brown strap and was the only jewelry she wore. She had kept the silent repose Christabel associated with large things: mountains, cathedrals. What she did say—like the revelation that Mr. Valente was married—often pointed only to a wider and obscure story. Once, when they were making their way home through a green uninteresting park, Bunty looked across the road to a building with a rickety balcony and said that it reminded her of the shop-house in which she had lived in Kuala Lumpur. Somehow it was impossible to ask what she had been doing there, and when.

Bunty called her front room the soft room because the chairs in the other rooms were hard. The soft room was where she watched TV, listened to her radio, and kept her bottle of scotch. She never indicated by word or sign that she wanted to be left alone, but sometimes the air around her would grow cold. Then she existed, just as she had done at school, in the center of an inviolable ring.

They would lie in their beds and talk across the dark. Christabel spoke about Len casually, calling him "an old flame." She described him as "one of those men who have their head in the clouds." "One of those men" pleased her, suggesting depths of experience and worldly wisdom. "His socks sagged," she told Bunty. "I wonder how he managed to withstand those winters."

"In Russia," said Bunty, "the peasants drape themselves across stoves. I was told that in Hong Kong by a girl who had grown up in Harbin. Her father was Chinese, and her mother was Russian. She was very subtle. She could express an opinion and its opposite, and believe both. She pointed out such a frightening thing once: 'The only life in which you play a leading role is your own.'"

It was an informative speech for Bunty. Christabel wanted to know: What happened to the girl? Was she beautiful? What were you doing in Hong Kong?

"She knew the strangest people," went on Bunty. "There was a Chinese student who believed he was a genius, marked for stupendous things. One summer he was visited repeatedly by a ghostly monk. These visits inspired him to do great—"

"That's a famous story!" interrupted Christabel. "A Russian story. When the man is cured of his visions, he becomes ordinary and dull. Your friend obviously stole the whole thing."

"She was happy telling it, and I was happy listening."

"Was it Raven who had a Chinese girlfriend? Or Sizzle?"

"Raven had a motorbike," said Bunty.

Weeks went by.

Bunty said, "Raven rode his bike into a tree. He killed himself and his girlfriend—she might have been Chinese."

"How awful!" cried Christabel. "Your poor father!"

She heard the creaking that said Bunty was settling herself to sleep.

The sunglasses were the first pair Christabel had owned. The lenses were shaped like black glass eggs. Bunty's had thin gold frames and Christabel's were tortoiseshell. "How glamorous we are!" cried Bunty. They lay on recliners in the yard, wearing their sunglasses, and couldn't stop laughing.

•

On Wednesdays they went to the pictures after work.

That was what they said: "the pictures."

Jone from Payroll handed Christabel the small brown envelope that contained her wages, and said, "We're having a few people 'round for a barbie Sunday."

Christabel prepared for the adventure with Touch and Glow, and a dress with a circular, gypsyish skirt. In Australia she was no longer Moth and Fa's daughter but merely Christabel. She could wear three clashing bracelets, and no one would care.

"*The lovely lady, Christabel,*" quoted Bunty. She had slept late and was just coming out of the bathroom. Her dressing gown, carelessly fastened, showed a long, pale slit from neck to thigh. "*The lovely lady, Christabel / Whom her father loves so well.* When we read that at school, I thought my name should have been Christabel."

Jone and Rob had two fox terriers and half a house in Arncliffe. Christabel tasted champagne punch for the first time—delicious! She knocked it back, and picked the last white-hearted strawberry from the bottom of her glass.

Rob placed a thick chop and a thin sausage on Christabel's paper plate, saying, "Wrap yourself around that." Sally from Customer Service passed the tomato sauce. She had spilled a thousand satin ruffles down her shirt.

When there were only a few blackened mint leaves left in a puddle of punch, Jone led Christabel to a cardboard cask. Christabel bravely said that the wine was lovely—suddenly, magically, it was. Without waiting to be asked, she refilled her glass. "Cheers, big ears!" said Jone. She was glorious in a peacock-and-lime maxi, and a necklace of enameled pink flowers.

Jone's neighbor Mike was a small, handsome Englishman with square knees. He was in electricals. There were more Australians around the barbecue and lolling under a gum tree. The fox terriers went around licking toes. Mike had one of those new computer watches. Teeth fortified with fluoride bore down rhythmically on chops.

Everyone watched Christabel trying to vanquish a sausage with a splade.

"Christabel's from Sri Lanka," explained Jone.

With the moselle funneling down, Christabel admitted, "I still forget to say Sri Lanka. Even though it's been called that for seven years."

Mike's wife knew it had had a much nicer name once.

"It was Ceylon until '72."

"Oh, but Sri Lanka is lovely!" said Jone.

"I was born in India," said Mike. "That was when it *was* India, mind."

"Mike's awful," said Jone to Christabel. "You're awful, Mike!" she cried, and touched her hair at the rim. There were curls there, round with light.

"Would you call that a stack perm?" asked Mike's wife. "My hairdresser suggested a stack perm. But I've never been a slave to passing fashions." She called, "Here, doggie!" and dangled a length of snot-gray fat. A terrier snatched. "Manners!" cried Mike's wife. "Naughty, naughty boy! But so sweet to eat it all up!"

Sally strummed her ruffles. She was considering Transcendental Meditation.

Mike had a hamstring.

It was nothing to his wife's underlapping toe.

"What I'm wondering," confided Rob to Christabel, "is why you're not wearing a sari."

"A sari is so feminine," said Jone, topping up Christabel's glass. "Can you show me how to drape one, Chrissie?"

"See, the great thing about your Asian bird is that she understands what a bloke needs. None of that libber rubbish," said Mike.

His wife said, "Well, excuse *me*."

The flat-petaled flowers on a sprawling shrub were exactly the same shape and shade of pink as those around Jone's throat. This correspondence between nature and art struck Christabel as nothing short of miraculous. Her eyes swiveled from necklace to flowers—a mistake. She sloshed the funny feeling down with more wine.

"No one's got any business making you feel ashamed of your heritage," went on Rob. He twisted his mustache and admitted, "I know we Aussies can be pretty crude." He refilled Christabel's glass.

The flowers were open-faced, unsecretive. Christabel longed to know what they thought of her dress. Did the color suggest boldness and originality? Or shellfish? One of her hooped earrings kept moving, so that a flash of silver rested on the rim of her eye.

Mike's wife couldn't go past a pavlova. She shattered meringue with a dreamy air.

Christabel felt really splendid. The sun came dazzling through the leaves. It commanded her to set down her plate. But she held on to her glass as she floated across buffalo grass to the beckoning pink. Rob followed, murmuring, "If you've been the victim of racial prejudice, Chrissie, you've only to let me know."

Mike's voice swelled like the afternoon. He had returned to India; it seemed to belong to him. "Take your Brahmin—a bundle of superstitions." He grew louder and more ecstatic as India gripped him, streamed through him. The porters! The drains!

A force larger than Christabel compelled her to kneel before the flowers. She drank to them, upending her glass. Her bracelets pulsed on her wrist. The flowers grew bigger and pinker and swirled.

Rob hosed away the vomit while the terriers danced around, now and then darting in for a slurp. His hands were big and cleanly formed. Later he placed Christabel across the backseat of his car, with a damp washcloth for her brow, and drove her home to St. Peters, being careful how he took the curves. Power lines poured past the window. The pounding in Christabel's head said, The brazen greaves. The brazen greaves. By the time they had reached the Princes Highway, it was saying, The blazing grief.

"No trouble at all," said Rob, although she hadn't spoken, shifting down into second to accommodate a bus.

Bunty came out of the soft room roaring, "O come, Olly Faithful!" Her horse had won—she was joyful and triumphant.

Bunty's voice had darkened. It was still full and true but no longer suggested other, limitlessly great things.

Jone's sister was ill, and Jone was required in Cairns. Christabel came out of the lobby after work and into a stiff harbor breeze. She loved Sydney but not the few crooked miles that made up its chilly heart. Drawing her cardigan tight, she heard her name. Rob's eyes were wild blue beams. His hand touched her arm, then settled on the nape of her neck.

A mate of his had a place near Chinatown. Christabel's breasts were warm, round apples as she followed him up the stairs. Doors opened off each narrow landing: it was like climbing up through a hive. In one room, there seemed to be a party going on. On the next landing, Rosen's Wholesale Buttons faced off against the Structuralist Bunyip Gallery. Rob unlocked a door, and they entered a room furnished with a piano and a couch. He took firm hold of Christabel, murmuring, "Teach me to explore darkness, Chrissie." She took it as a reference to the lack of light in the room.

As he jiggled, she decided that it was very odd and very nice, this business that outstripped ordinary existence without being quite like a dream. It was charged with the power and strangeness of novels: at once removed from and more vivid than life.

Rob's hair was soft, thin, of an indeterminate color. Fetus hair, Christabel thought, examining it from above.

Afterward, he rose and parted the curtains. Christabel's breasts were deflated balloons lying on her ribs. She fumbled for her cardi as Rob informed her with a touch of jubilation, "You're the first." At which he grew shy and ducked his head. "My dark lady," he mumbled, straining the words through his mustache. Christabel understood then that she constituted an experiment. He had demonstrated, if only to his own satisfaction, that he was unburdened by racial prejudice. He grew expansive, offering her a cuppa—a gentleman! His ears, seen from behind as he investigated a cupboard, were innocently ajar. She lay there picturing all the chops he would eat, slab after red slab, over the course of his life.

No experiment is valid unless reproducible. Four times more, they climbed up through the hive. Rob's eyes continued to emit streams of lunatic blue light. Between their meetings, time passed in a daze—Christabel's movements were heavy and slow, as on an afternoon of stupefying heat. Then Jone came back from Cairns.

•

The back door of Bunty's house was directly in line with the front one. When the southerly brought relief at the end of a summer day, wind dashed through the house like a child.

Christabel had discovered the municipal library. She would go out to do some shopping and return with a bag of books, with which she would settle down at the kitchen table. In bad weather, whole weekends passed in the outrageous happiness of reading. When pain corkscrewed down her spine she walked up and down the passage. The neutral passage, running from the kitchen to the soft room, linked her domain with Bunty's. They were connected but apart. Each, unconsciously, paused an instant on the other's threshold. Rain came over the house, and the house took on the dimensions of a palace. The windows faced the wrong way or were shaded with verandas; daylight entered diffidently, slithering into the small rooms. Christabel didn't notice: there was the soft brightness of candles and lamps. It was a house suited to the interior life, to dank winter afternoons and summer downpours. It surrounded Christabel, an echo of the old, warm world she had shared with Moth and Fa.

Bunty had bought it from a Mr. Kingsley, who was going to live with his sister. He assured Bunty, "No one has died in this house. You won't find any ghosts." Christabel knew that without being told. The house was friendly, scoured, all its noises were kind. In those days, she believed with Mr. Kingsley that no one wanted ghosts.

Set into the back door was a stained-glass window arched at the top. It was just wide enough to hold a saint who held a book: in his round hands, it had the look of an object from a story. Bunty said, "I couldn't think where else to put him." She was vague about the provenance of the window, but Christabel gathered that Mr. Valente had been involved. She would glance up from her book and see the saint, in his deep blue robe, looking down at his. If she turned her gaze to the window above the sink, she would see a tree with a bare trunk and a cylindrical green head, some kind of conifer, sticking straight up in the distance—it was an overgrown, living version of the bottlebrush on the draining board. These doublings sealed the sense of rightness in the room. Christabel wished for nothing more than to look at that saint and that tree for the rest of her life.

They were on their way to the Blue Mountains. When the train started to climb, they were on the wrong side of the carriage for the view. There were hardly any passengers, so they changed seats. Then the track wound around, and once again they found themselves looking into the stony face of a mountain. They changed back to their old places. A man stared. And then—unbelievable!—again the window was full of bare rock. They clung to each other and stumbled across the aisle. Bunty had kept her big, chesty laugh. The man got up and moved to the far end of the carriage. They were as giddy as girls. They had only to look at each other to start up.

Thoughts would pass between them. Also: a comb, socks.

They had brief, heartfelt quarrels. Why did Christabel wait until the train was drawing in to wonder aloud if she had switched off the iron? Why did Bunty wash the eggy plates first?

•

Bunty kept a secondhand school atlas in the soft room. Studying maps and guidebooks and the brochures of travel agents, she calculated and dreamed. When Christabel learned what was going on, she wanted to go with Bunty, of course. "Italy?" she asked, already placing herself on friendly piazzas. "France?"

Bunty had visited those places long ago. She said grandly, "I never go back."

What that meant was that they ended up in countries where the toilet arrangements left a great deal to be desired. It was not the kind of thing Bunty noticed: she had no sense of smell, shoveled down whatever food was put in front of her, snored on stony beds in mosquito-haunted rooms. Delivered to their destination, she took no further interest in the practical. All the detail of itineraries and timetables was left to Christabel. She was also in charge of first aid. It suited them both very well.

The usual things happened: sunsets, pickpockets, gastro. Away from home, reality was ice cream molded into fantastic shapes: transient, astonishing, quickly devoured. But for a long time after coming across it, they used to remind each other of an ancient threshing floor they had seen on a Greek island, a white marble disk on a dry hill.

They snapped up bargains which, unpacked at home, were magically revealed in all their foulness and quietly, after a decent interval, deposited in charity bins.

Kiki Mack's latest aerogram reported kidnappings, communal murder, and the price of eggs. Old women Christabel had called Auntie were dying of hunger. She sent Kiki banknotes in an envelope for distribution. Kiki would write, eventually, that it had never arrived.

When she thought of home, Christabel saw a grimy stretch of wall, split by the sun, where lizards ran in and out of the cracks. Pictures like that were always there, running invisibly under her Australian life, appearing now and again like snatches of an old videotape that a later recording had overlaid without entirely erasing.

A girl at work, freshly returned from a holiday, said that Sri Lanka was "really welcoming." Christabel wanted to shout, I used to breathe that air!

Every month, an aerogram came for Bunty. Christabel peered at the sender's name: "Who's C. Sedgwick?"

"Sizzle."

"What's his real name?"

"Sizzle. C-e-c-i-l."

It was too late: he was Sizzle. He telephoned Bunty twice a year, at Christmas and on her birthday. When direct dialing came in, his greeting in Christabel's ear—"Sizzle Sedgwick here"—was an insect's tinny hum.

Bunty said, "I'm never going back." The coldness came over her like a white shadow. She said, "I have no use for the past."

They had a toast: "To the buffalo!" One morning a buffalo had escaped from a stationary train and run amok near their school. A constable was gored. The buffalo yearned to lie down in water and was frightened and crazed. By the time reinforcements arrived, it had vanished—but it was there, somewhere. The headmistress lost her head. Instead of ordering the gates locked, she sent everyone home. Sensible girls sobbed and clung to friends as they were released into the street, but Christabel and Bunty were among those who rushed through the gates. They were joyful and triumphant. "To the buffalo!"

Christabel left her first workplace for another almost as dull. When she looked up from her desk, screen after screen of luminous green letters stretched away; the monitors were the grubby beige of old bras.

The new office was in a tower block on the edge of the city, next to a motorway. Cars rolled past Christabel's ankles as she proactively monitored her competency framework. From a corner of the tinted window that occupied a wall, it was possible to see the stubborn cobweb of the harbor bridge. Freshly recruited, Christabel had liked to stand at that window while eating her lunch. She would imagine herself on a ferry with bright, wet wind around her face. Bunty was with her; it was Sunday, and they were on their way to Manly: "Seven miles from Sydney, a thousand miles from care." One of their treats was fish and chips from the Corso. They would picnic on the seawall, their bare feet dangling—it allowed the ozone to work on their corns. The Pacific chuckled softly: it was insane, twinkling away in a violent blue dream.

Opposite Christabel's concrete-and-glass cliff stood its twin; within it, prison light shone on men and women stacked above one another and looking into screens. A tiny, spotless white garment, suited to an infant, always hung in a window on the fifteenth floor. Why? How Christabel loved the baffling, marvelous world! Then a man whose desk was near her vantage point complained that she was watching him as he worked; there was also the matter of crumbs. No one was allowed to touch the potted peace lily this man kept on his desk, nor his framed photograph of Torvill and Dean. Fantasies of surveillance—the wish to be of interest—flourished like viruses in the overheated office. On Christabel's first day there, a girl had followed her into the bathroom to confide that one of her co-workers was monitoring the number of times she took a tampon from her drawer. The fluorescent lighting, pounding all day, ground down nerves. The lily man was quite mad, of course, but only in a normal sort of way, and very popular. Their supervisor got out her high-heeled manner. Christabel ate her sausage roll at her desk after that.

"We should get a kitten," Bunty said. They were picnicking in the disused graveyard at St. Peter's Church, in their favorite corner, where the grass was long. Saturday morning had been metallic, but then the day turned glassy and clear. It was too late to take a train to a headland or a bay, but the graveyard, with its stately trees, was only a short walk from home. Children accounted for most of the dead who lay around. They were nameless, numerous, colonial, folkloric. Like children in cautionary tales they had fallen into fireplaces or down wells, or died with feverish scarlet cheeks and white-ringed mouths.

A tribe of cats lived in the wilderness beyond the rectory. Slouching between headstones that tipped in every direction, a long orange beast had provoked Bunty's remark.

Christabel watched Bunty's sharp little teeth bite into a crescent of mandarin and release the juice. She said nothing. That meant no.

They could sit at the kitchen table, close and opposite, without speaking to each other. There was no need. The bulb dimmed whenever a plane passed overhead. The sash rattled. A freight train bleated. Wind scraped the house.

"Body" was not a word they felt comfortable using, not even to a doctor.

Making her way to the highway on blurry winter mornings, Christabel could believe that she was walking toward the sea: if the mist lifted, she would see it there, trembling. The old brick-works chimney stacks, looming in the distance, served very well as stand-in masts.

At work, the screen on her desktop had turned black and white. The new technology had already achieved classic status: like print, old photos, old films.

The African violet on her desk flowered once, magnificently, then yielded to the air-conditioning. Her co-workers, too, bloomed and dropped away. Conversations about football, like the pocked gray ceiling tiles, were repeated endlessly. For ten minutes or so toward the end of the day, sunlight sneaked into the windowless photocopying room, having first crawled through the office across the passage. By the time it reached the photocopier the light was the color of cement. It said, Everything accomplished here is a waste of time.

When she sat down to work each day, Christabel took off her gilt watch and bangle and left them on the edge of her desk. That double golden coil, catching now and then on a corner of her vision, was the assurance of a different life. She accepted, humbly, that it might never exist for her ("I am ordinary!"), but she needed to know that it was there. It was enormous and astonishing.

Sometimes it lay in the future, like an infinitely suspended wave. Sometimes the wave had already broken and receded, leaving only darkly gleaming sand. The work she did was tedious yet required concentration, like a standard-issue dream. And as with a dream, any attempt to describe it sounded implausible and weak. "Provide ad hoc clerical assistance and action paperwork arising from financial systems (Oracle)." That other life, hazy in outline, acquired solidity by comparison. It rose, glittered, and sank back.

On their first day in Jakarta, they found a clean room at the back of a thick-walled house. The room had two interior doors. One opened to reveal a cell that contained a toilet and a shower—of course the toilet was a hole in the concrete floor. The second door gave onto another room, hardly bigger than the first, with a heavy beam that ran across the ceiling. All it held was a wooden chair and a dead cockroach. "I suppose it's to put our luggage in," said Christabel.

Bunty came and looked over Christabel's shoulder. She retreated to the main room. "We can't stay here," she said.

It was the first time the white shroud had settled over her while they were on holiday.

"Why can't we stay?" Christabel asked, knowing all questions were useless.

They had paid for the first night. Their landlord smiled and smiled and refused to refund their money—reasonably, since they could give no reason for wanting to leave. They dragged their cases along filthy streets. The room with the chair took on a clear outline in Christabel's mind, as final and defined as an ending. Bunty lumbered ahead, an icy block in the equatorial afternoon.

By the next morning, in their new room, everything was all right.

•

Bunty was finding sleep elusive. She would get up and change her sheets, carrying the discards silently out of the bedroom to dump in the machine. "It's the change," said the GP Christabel consulted after she, too, began waking up slimy with sweat. It was her rostered day off. When she came out of the doctor's surgery, it was noon. Across the street, a doorway was solid with darkness. In the twelve years since Rob, there had been six men—secretly, Christabel folded down a finger for each. Behind each man was a wife or an ocean or merely reluctance for more intimate engagement. She supposed that all that was over now.

At the end of an evening, after what she thought of as one of her *interludes*, Christabel had always refused a taxi or a lift. As her train curved toward the midnight suburbs, the city shone like rubble from the Milky Way. Christabel would get off at St. Peters and walk up to the main road, past the pub with a rail opposite the door to save drunks from stepping in front of cars. King Street swept off to her left, blank and hungover, beerily illuminated. Even when it was busy with buses and shopping, the southern end of King Street looked bleak and unloved. That was because it led only to a highway. Christabel turned off it as soon as she could, exchanging the flare of headlights for black, empty streets. There were deserted factories with flattened cardboard boxes protruding from bins. She unbuttoned her jacket to that enemy the wind. Her flesh, damp and alive, answered the night with ease. How extraordinary that she should possess this talent for the calm taking of pleasure, the calm leaving of it! Certain streets were so narrow that she passed along them like a pea slipping through a pipe. Leisurely rats crossed in front of her. The night rushed up her sleeves.

•

Mr. Valente was diagnosed with cancer of the throat. He gave up the races at once, hoping to soften God's heart. It was understood that "the races" meant Bunty. God was in the mood for deals, and Mr. Valente went into remission. Bunty came out with the story on the day he was given the all clear. She and Christabel were watching TV with a giant slab of Cadbury's Rum 'n' Raisin on the couch between them. Bunty said, "Poor Enzo," in a disinterested way, never taking her eyes from the French planes flying in formation to celebrate the fiftieth anniversary of D-day. In the darkened room her calves, propped on a footstool, were thick white boots.

Christabel said, "You don't have to go on working for him."

"I have no qualifications. Bookkeeping's just something I picked up."

Christabel couldn't see how bookkeeping was something you "picked up" like the flu. "Another thing," went on Bunty, "is that Enzo lent me the deposit for this house. Interest free. I'd never have been able to afford it if not for him."

"But to have to go on seeing him every day!"

"That will be difficult for him."

This conversation was taking place around midnight, because after the late news they had stayed up watching a Turkish film; Bunty enjoyed the foreign films on SBS almost as much as westerns. Once she had come down the passage to tell Christabel, "If we had been born in Sweden, say, I might have been a filmmaker. You might have written books." Christabel made a noise but didn't look up from her page. What was the point of a dream like that? It was all right to have no use for the past, but it was what they were stuck with.

The Turkish film went on forever. It showed a well on a hillside, the shadow of a leafless tree slanted across a courtyard, a man in a dark suit making his way along a street of houses, workshops, and little stores. Bunty ate the last square of chocolate, sucking it noisily. Christabel knew what was coming. Bunty said, "Let's go to Turkey next."

They went to Turkey and came home again. Now the white shadow often crept over Bunty as she prepared to leave the house for work. She still followed the races on her radio and stopped by the betting shop of an afternoon. But alone in the soft room, she no longer sang.

Mr. Valente announced that he was going to retire. His son-in-law was to take over the tiling business. Bunty decided that she, too, had had enough. She said of the son-in-law, "He makes my teeth itch."

After Mr. Valente and his wife retreated to their house on the Central Coast, the phone started to ring at unusual hours. Bunty and Christabel would hear the pips that signified long distance; silence followed before the caller hung up. "Enzo has always been a consistent person," said Bunty when this had been going on for some time. "All those awful cakes, year after year."

A terrible, terrible thing happened to Kiki Mack: she was strangled by a servant, who had only meant to steal her car.

The CEO informed his assembled staff that the company had been taken over by another, which would be moving its operations offshore. At the end of the month they would all be unemployed. By way of compensation they could sign off for the day, although it was only ten past four. A data-entry clerk standing next to Christabel began to cry silently, the tears slipping under her glasses and down her cheeks. But in a way the announcement was a relief, decided Christabel on the train home: there had been rumors and redundancies for months. Only a few short years ago, she had thrashed about under the realization that she was growing old—how much more restful, as her sixtieth birthday approached, to *be* old. The end of her working life would be like that, a release from dread. Underpinning her cheerfulness was the unsquashable sense of reprieve that came from leaving work early. To the buffalo! Christabel overflowed with affection for the cramped, no-pool backyards sliding past under inflamed clouds.

Bunty was in the bedroom cutting her toenails; they grew fast and had been known to rip sheets. She was dressed in one of the velour tracksuits that were more or less all she had worn since giving up work. The coldness was on her—she peered at Christabel as if looking out from an icy hood. After Christabel, too, had changed into comfy clothes, she sat at the kitchen table explaining about the takeover while Bunty boiled potatoes. As Christabel talked, her exuberance dropped away. She was wrung with tenderness for something both immense and touching that was already behind her, for lighted buildings around whose feet a dark stream of workers was hurrying home, and herself a tiny part of all that.

Bunty microwaved fish fingers and slid them onto two plates. They took their dinner and the sauce bottle out to the little patio beyond the kitchen—it was the first mild evening of the spring. The sun having knocked off for the day, what was left was the kind of light that magnifies everything, including the din of a plane. All around the yard, red roofs approached antiquity, even the emerald tiles with which they were studded taking on a subdued glow. It was the magic hour, burdened with human dreams, webbing everything in strangeness. Anything might appear against the sky: an angel, a sniper, King Kong. The bottlebrush tree was holding its breath.

Bunty said, "Sizzle's dead." Her knife screamed against her plate. Chewing, she said something that might have been "Stroke."

The Hills Hoist had assumed prominent, solid lines as the light withdrew. It was the pendant to a stunted lemon tree—ancient, untended, and burdened with thick-skinned fruit—that persisted in a diamond of earth. Three eskies, respectively colored red, green, and blue with white undertones, provided the only other decorative touch. Bunty had salvaged them from a Dumpster, planted them with succulents and set them on half bricks stacked to different heights.

"Oh, Bunty," began Christabel, and couldn't remember what to say next. Once, as she was leaving a hotel with a man, he had caressed her cheek, grazing it lightly with his broad golden ring. "I don't think much of your face," he said. Then, as now, Christabel felt the blood recede from her fingers. She summoned up the paper Sizzle that Bunty kept in a frame in the soft room: he looked waxy and bland, like a murderer on TV.

Bunty said, "I had a dog when I was growing up." She was probing her potatoes with her fork as if they might conceal a foreign object. "Oliver used to follow me around and breathe on me. One morning, Sizzle came into my room and told me he'd had a nightmare. He said, 'I dreamed there was something awful inside Oliver.' We looked at Olly, stretched at the foot of my bed. He thumped his tail. His black fur was as shiny as paint. A week later he was dead. He had a kind of cancer that only became apparent right at the end."

Christabel wanted to put her arms around Bunty; she could

see herself doing it, but someone had shackled her to her chair. She tried and failed to meet the appalled purple faces of succulents. "I'm so sorry," she told Bunty at last, locking her hands—life seemed to end at her wrists.

From the depths of her chilly cowl, Bunty said, "My father hanged himself." She went on talking, but another plane blasting across the sky blanked out the rest. Christabel's eyes were on the shapes made by Bunty's mouth, but the yard had given way to a Javanese room as final as a grave. When the roar overhead faded, Christabel heard, ". . . all dead now. Pombo, Raven, Sizzle. And Dad, of course."

Pombo!

"All my brothers were useless. But Sizzle tried to help."

"I had a cat," said Christabel, "when I lived in Kiki Mack's garage."

The traffic along the highway was as murmurous as the sea. They were having lunch in the graveyard again. These days they lowered themselves cautiously onto the grass. Getting up could also be tricky. Bunty, being fat and strong, had devised a method that involved clambering onto all fours. Christabel preferred to grasp one of the iron railings in the fence and *heave.*

A succession of pips sounded. Children rushed out of low buildings as if shooed with a broom. They were of all nations, a human assortment. A few drew near the fence and stared.

"I dream of him," said Christabel. "In the dream, I'm at the cinema watching a film. Ann-Margret is in the film, feeding Napoleon strips of roast beef. He scratches her arm. Only I know it's an accident, that he doesn't mean to hurt."

"Ann-Margret!" said Bunty. "I'd completely forgotten Ann-Margret. How about that!"

"When I was leaving, Kiki wouldn't have Napoleon—she was very firm. She'd never liked me keeping a cat in her garage. I asked everyone. I put notices in the papers, even the Sinhalese and Tamil ones. In the end, I sold my mother's ring that I'd been saving to pay for my funeral and gave the money to the man who picked Kiki's coconuts. He promised me Napoleon would be happy and well looked after in his village."

Bunty was transfixed by a cloud.

"I'd been in Sydney five months when Kiki wrote to tell me Napoleon had been run over. She said there was no mistaking his corpse in the gutter. She wrote, 'At least its suffering is over now. An animal who has been petted and spoiled cannot survive as a stray. I simply cannot understand your cruelty.'

"Oh, Bunty!" cried Christabel. "From the time you sent me my ticket, Kiki told me I should have Napoleon put down. But he was only four years old! And I thought, Life is long."

Bunty ate the last corned beef sandwich. She began the maneuvers that would bring her to her feet. Halfway up, she resembled a great cow.

Christabel dusted her skirt free of little pieces of leaf. A child was watching her from the other side of the fence. In his peaked cap with its long neck flap he looked like a small colonial soldier. His lips moved. Christabel waved in return. She put her face close to the railings and smiled. The child's voice reached her, bold as a bell: "Bitch!" he shouted. "Bitch!"

The old women took a gummy sort of smell with them into the street. With a powerful hand, Bunty snapped off a branch flowering over a wall. She presented the clotted pink blossoms to Christabel.

Weeks passed.

"My mother smelled like pencil shavings," said Bunty. "Dad

used to say that it was cruel of her to abandon her children. Especially me."

"Did you hate her for it?"

"When I think of her, even now, what I remember is feeling loved."

New people moved into the adjoining semi. Christabel saw the young woman in the street and stopped to admire her dog. The dog was stumpy and smiley, with a back as broad as a shelf. The woman said that he was called Hank, adding, "And I'm Pippa Reynolds."

Christabel gave her name in return. Bricks quivered in the midday haze. Farther along the street, a man from the council was mowing a nature strip. The young woman's smile didn't change. An odd little silence fell. Christabel had the impression—ridiculous, glancing, unshakable—that she had made a mistake.

"I have to get going now," said Pippa at last. "I like to be back at my desk by half past one."

"Oh, do you work from home?"

"Only two days a week. The rest of the time, there's the day job. Because, frankly, it's impossible to make a living writing novels."

The council worker carried on mowing as if the afternoon hadn't just executed a pirouette.

When Christabel told Bunty that their new neighbor was a writer, Bunty said, "Ah." It sounded like a stone dropping into a well.

Pippa and her husband were to attend the wedding of an old friend. "It's a Wiccan ceremony in a rain forest up north," Pippa told

Christabel—they had come out to collect their mail at the same time. "My friend's never really recovered from being raised by hippies. She's being married by a white witch." But what was to be done with Hank? He was such a people dog—Pippa hated to board him. At once, Christabel offered to mind him for the weekend.

When she got back from the wedding, Pippa invited Christabel to afternoon tea. Matt was always late home on a Thursday, she said, he played tennis after work. Christabel sat in Pippa's red leather armchair. The floorboards had a watery sheen: a skylight had been let into the ceiling. Christabel's soul expanded, pulled upward by the light. She asked questions, ardent and clumsy, about writing books. Pippa said that she thought of each book as a problem that required solving. "It's the way an engineer might think about a technical drawing or a mathematician might approach a proof. It's strict, not dreamy."

A routine formed: Hank came to stay whenever Pippa and Matt went away, and every few weeks the phone would ring on a Thursday. "Only me," said Pippa. "I'm done for the day and I've just taken a cake out of the oven. Would you like to come around?"

Matt and Pippa's semi had an upstairs extension that served as their bedroom. Their spare room, which corresponded to Christabel and Bunty's bedroom, doubled as Pippa's study. "This is where the magic happens," said Pippa, holding her study door open with her arm. Christabel admired the messy desk with its ergonomic chair, the photos and postcards pinned to a corkboard, the day bed covered with a slaty blue throw. There was a jug of lilies by the window—they made sharp shadows in an oblong of light on the floor. The books from which Pippa was currently drawing inspiration were grouped between two bookends. "My touchstones," said Pippa, running a finger along their spines like someone checking for dust.

At home, walking down the passage, Christabel ran an imitative hand along the wall. She felt tender toward it: it was the wall that attached her to Pippa. On the other side of those bricks and plaster lay a different world: one where there was nothing remarkable about polished wood, little tangy lemon tarts, and flowers making a sunset in a vase. She had made the tarts herself, said Pippa. "Pastry isn't difficult really but it's an art. You have a cool, quick hand or you haven't. It can't be taught."

Whenever she thought of her afternoons with Pippa, Christabel saw a scene in a paperweight: something perfect, sealed-off, round.

The local library didn't stock Pippa's novels but ordered them in for Christabel from a different branch. Christabel read both books straight through. She had no opinion about them as literature; they were miracles worked by someone she knew. Until then, her imagination had been stirred by words rather than by writers. Writers were dead or distant: haloed in unreality. A sense of this found its way into how she thought about Pippa. Anything might happen between them. It was unnerving and thrilling. Christabel recalled their first meeting, the moment of panicky suspension. She had misunderstood its nature, she decided: now she saw it as the necessarily precarious moment before a far-reaching change.

Pippa needed a name for a character in the novel she was planning. "It has to be something ordinary," she explained. "Nothing fancy-schmancy but not too far the other way either. It's just not possible to create sympathy for someone called Marlene—or any -een, really." Louise was perfect, and so was Cathy, but Pippa had already used both. She had friends called Mandy and Liz and Tina, so they were all out. "All I can think of is Carly, but that's a bit close to Cathy."

"Helen?" suggested Christabel after some thought.

"Helen! That's total genius!"

It was one of those winter afternoons, lamplit at four, that encourage confessions, the windy cold kept at bay with an unflued gas heater that produced drowsiness and unbuttoned ease. The one drawback to tea at Pippa's was the tea itself. Pippa drank only coffee, which caused Christabel's heart to race, so the first time Christabel visited, Pippa had dug around in her pantry and found a packet of citrus-flavored rooibos left by a houseguest. It tasted of nothing, but Christabel had politely praised it, so now Pippa bought it just for her. Christabel was getting rid of it with quick, birdlike sips when Pippa, stroking a cushion, said, "It's lovely having a friend who's a reader. Matt isn't, not really." Then she told a long story about a bookshop where the sales assistant had failed to recognize her. "I paid with Visa, so she saw my name, but she obviously didn't know I'm a writer. I don't expect to be mobbed in the street or anything, but this was someone who works in a bookshop. It's a little wounding—you know?" Her voice was charged; Hank, who had been making the noises that meant he was dreaming of barking, lifted his head. Christabel saw a Pippa stripped of the hard lacquer of glamour. Oddly, it was she, Christabel, who felt exposed.

When Christabel was about to leave, Pippa said, "Hang on! I still haven't paid you for Hank's leash." Hank had been staying at Christabel's when the clip on his leash broke and she had to buy him a new one. Pippa unzipped her wallet and produced a fifty-dollar note.

"It only cost thirty."

"I don't have anything smaller. You know ATMs. Don't worry about it, lovey. You can give me the change whenever."

Christabel said that she would return with it at once; to her, twenty dollars was a significant sum. "OK, I'll go with you then," said Pippa. "I don't want you to have to come out again in this weather." At this proof of Pippa's concern for her well-being, a lit candelabra branched in Christabel's chest.

An ad break was leaking under the door of the soft room when they entered the house. A buttery voice said, "At Planet Travel we specialize in unique tourism experiences." Instead of continuing down the passage to wait for Christabel in the kitchen, Pippa followed her into the bedroom. Ignoring the upright chair, she plonked down on Bunty's bed. Beds are not for sitting on! Christabel couldn't decide if the casual contravention of what she had taken for a universal and eternal law was exhilarating or upsetting or both.

Pippa's face was alive from the wind and something else uncontrollable. "Who has the wardrobe?" she asked. "Bunty or you?"

"Bunty has a couple of coats in the hanging part."

"So where does she keep the rest of her stuff?"

"In the chest of drawers. And she has some things in the cupboards in the other room."

One of Bunty's undergarments—vast, pig-colored—lay on the chest. It whispered of old, stewy, female life. The candelabra had been extinguished as soon as Pippa entered the room. Now a lumpy object that grew larger with each question was making its presence known inside Christabel. On Pippa's side of the wall, their conversation had unrolled in the intimate glimmer of strategically placed lamps. Here, the overhead light was sinister and flat. The unheated room smelled of used pillows. Reproach was a faint blue aura rising from the mismatched beds, the dressing gowns hanging behind the door, the neglected chair. A thought—a realization—came forward fast but swerved and faded. Christabel stood with her face and breasts in the wardrobe. She took notes from her purse and handed them over. Shouts of television laughter followed Pippa out of the house.

Pippa and Matt were lunching with friends at the table set up under their grapevine. Determined red tentacles from the vine curled over the fence, and voices, too, found their way into Christabel and Bunty's yard. Washing up, with the window open, Christabel heard Pippa say, "I can't stand that kind of competitiveness."

Bunty came into the kitchen. She opened the fridge and took out a beer. "Have you seen the . . . thing?" she asked, glancing around.

"A glass?" asked Christabel, wishing that Bunty would go away.

"The *thing*," said Bunty, clattering drawers.

A chair scraped on the pavers next door. At last, Bunty took her beer outside.

A man said, "So is it true that George has come out? I heard he's living with this guy called Tran."

People started laughing. "That one's been doing the rounds for a while," said Pippa. "George used to have this housemate called Fran. She moved out ages ago, but I'm guessing that's how the rumor got started. Half of Australia has him down as a rice queen now."

"It's his own fault," said the man. "He won't give personal interviews, he's not on social media. People fill in the blanks."

"Oh, look, I agree," said Pippa. "He told me his agent said he should take control of his brand. She was trying to get him to sign up for Twitter. You know what he told her? 'Twitter's all about drawing attention to yourself while pretending to draw attention to something else.' Hey, Matt, we're out of wine at this end."

Bunty came back into the kitchen. “The thing,” she said, “like the thing we had at home.” Her hands sketched a shape in the air.

“Cushion?”

Bunty went away up the passage, moving with weighty, serious grace. She returned almost at once: “Found it!”

“Oh, your *radio*!”

“We used to call it a wireless. It was much bigger. The lights inside were like a city at night. They were talking about those Aboriginal children this morning. The ones who were stolen from their mothers.”

“Your beer’s outside,” said Christabel, because Bunty had sat down. The table was scattered with gum leaves in muted, sensational colors: dim green and lilac, milky coffee splotched with chocolate, a faded red inlaid with gray.

“My child was stolen,” said Bunty. Her radio was on the table and she was holding it with both hands. “I signed a paper. But I was barely sixteen. It was stealing, really.”

A woman cried, “Pippa, these quails are a-MA-zing!”

“I don’t understand,” said Christabel.

Then she did.

“The nuns at my old school up-country arranged everything,” went on Bunty. “They were very kind. It made me long to run away. Afterward, it was decided that it would be best if I went abroad. The nuns took care of that, too. There was a branch of the order in Hong Kong.”

Questions crashed around Christabel’s mind. Was it a girl or a boy? Who was the father? Did he know about the baby?

“For a long time I used to tell myself stories about her. She was living with my mother in a house with nine windows. My mother was plaiting her hair.”

Christabel heard herself say, “I’m sure a loving family was

found." It came out sounding as if her mouth was stuffed with socks.

"There are no secrets left now," said Bunty. "Only mysteries." A quick, frightening smile passed over her face. She lifted her arms, examined them as if they were foreign objects, and lowered them, saying, "What are you talking about?"

Christabel looked closely at her. "Did you really have a baby?"

"There's no time for that. The car's too long."

"What?"

"The car needs cutting. It's too long."

"Whose car? What do you mean?"

Bunty said, "Why are you talking about a car?"

A bewildering notion wriggled to the front of Christabel's brain: the impression that her friendship with Pippa had cooled. It wasn't a sustained conviction but a bleary sensation that came and went. Months had passed without an invitation to tea, and Pippa no longer got in touch about minding Hank but sent Matt around to make the arrangements instead. The feeling of unease was compounded by something that had happened earlier that year when Bunty was in bed with a cold, and Christabel, too, felt germy and weak. The phone rang. Pippa said, "Look on your porch, lovey." A note stuck to the lidded dish said that it contained lamb cooked with saffron and carrots and fennel. Christabel almost cried. She rang Pippa back at once and thanked her. "You didn't have to call, lovey," said Pippa. "Just enjoy and get strong."

A week or two passed. Christabel ran into Pippa and Hank on their way to the park. Hank clasped Christabel lovingly about the knees and grinned—he had just consumed a pavement turd. Greetings, my stinky darling, said Christabel silently, massaging his ears. A small girl going past told her mother, "That dog looks *zactly* like a tiger." She snarled and bared her teeth, making a tiger face.

Pippa tugged Hank down and asked, without inflection, "So did you like that tagine I left you?"

"It was delicious," said Christabel, wondering why Pippa's eyes seemed darker than a moment ago. "Thank you so much."

"No need to thank me again," said Pippa in the same flat tone. "Just checking that you liked it."

"We loved it. We got at least a couple of meals out of it. I keep forgetting to bring your dish around. I'm sorry—"

"I've got plenty of dishes. But when you cook for someone, it's good to know if they liked it."

"Oh, we loved it! I'm sorry—"

"Listen, I've really got to get going. Hank doesn't walk himself, you know."

It was like their first meeting: Christabel relived the sensation that she had failed a test. Earlier, rain had exploded, and now every scraggy callistemon in the street was wrapped in brilliant, watery light. The light turned up the gory in geraniums but did nothing at all for the unfortunate trees. Christabel heaved her shopping bags past them, biting her lips. The power lines across the street were noteless staves interrupted only by the crotchet rest of a decomposing bat.

Confusingly, there was a reassuring memory to counter that one. When Christabel saw Pippa near St. Peters Station one afternoon, Pippa paused to explain that she had been flat out of late. The wind, swimming past, shoved her hair to one side. "Let's catch up soon," she called, walking backwards over the railway bridge and waving. Christabel went on her way, straight-backed, springy with hope.

•

The year stumbled on, the winter softened: it had been a fierce one that frosted the streets. Spring brightened and strengthened—suddenly it was the bolshie Sydney spring. The phone rang. "Hellooo!" yodeled Pippa. "I've got amazing news. Can you come 'round?"

She had baked a poppy-seed cake, and there was a new cushion with a cover made from a vintage tea towel on the cherry-red chair. The tea towel, a souvenir of the Great Barrier Reef, featured tropical fish. On the couch, with her feet tucked up, just as Christabel always pictured her, Pippa announced that she had been awarded a six-month residency in Paris for the following year. She felt really honored and humbled because competition for the residency was keen. Beyond her shoulder, yellow roses were assertive in a jug. Matt would join her near the end of her time in Paris, went on Pippa, brushing crumbs from her T-shirt. "I'll miss him like anything, of course. And Hank. I'll be counting on you to keep an eye on them for me, Christabel."

Christabel looked away. If only Pippa could see into the mirror across the room: it held part of a bookcase, half a painting of a ferry passing a headland, and the crumpled light from the roses. Who could want to abandon that view? Pippa confided that her new novel was called *French Lessons.* The long middle section would be set in Paris; she had already begun reading guidebooks in preparation. "It's important to do your research in advance and then bury it while you write." That was the kind of window onto the creative mind for which Christabel believed she came. She didn't notice it, because she was thinking of an afternoon when Pippa had said, "Whenever I try a new hairdresser, I secretly hope my whole life will be different." Christabel thought, Who will she tell her secrets to in Paris? What she meant was, What will my life be like without her? There were things she longed to hear Pippa say that she couldn't precisely name.

It was not until the next day, or perhaps the one after—in any case, after the wedge of poppy-seed cake Christabel carried home had been eaten—that she realized, I was right. She *was* avoiding me. The reason was plain: Pippa had been trying to prepare her for the parting to come. At this proof of Pippa's sensitivity and consideration, Christabel was so overcome that she laid out the whole story for Bunty that night.

There was a long silence. A bedspring protested as Bunty shifted her weight. She said, "That hillside on Santorini where I thought I'd sprained my ankle—do you remember? It was flowery and stony. Pippa reminds me of that."

So that forever after, the idea of Pippa would come to Christabel accompanied by creamy spires of asphodel.

Bunty was saying, "But who dislikes someone just for their faults? That girl smiles at you as if she's chosen you out of all the world."

Christabel avoided missing Pippa too acutely by conducting long, silent talks with her while she was in France. They were peaceful conversations, very detailed in some respects and hazy in others. Sometimes Pippa said, "You're like a sister to me, you know," and sometimes she asked Christabel for help with her writing. Christabel had noticed all kinds of small wrinkles in Pippa's work, and she smoothed these out with great tact, waving away thanks. They told each other about books they had read and anecdotes from their lives. Christabel was reluctant to talk about herself at first, but gradually the person she was describing gripped her, and she spoke eagerly about a Christabel who was at once very well known to her and not quite real—someone who belonged to "a brilliant company."

No matter how they began or expanded, these conversations were characterized by warmth and friendliness and the delicate pleasure of feeling understood. One part of Christabel's mind knew very well that all this was the work of her imagination. That part of her mind was of little account. But it existed, and that gave her permission to imagine anything. There could be no harm in it; it was like watching a film and being in a film at the same time. The film seemed truer and more compelling than life while it was going on, and cast a cinematic glow on her relations with Pippa when it was not.

Pippa came back from France at last. The phone rang one evening while Christabel was defrosting peas. Matt had spotted Bunty walking along the highway dressed in her knickers and vest—as he braked, she was stepping into the road. Rushing up the passage, Christabel discovered the TV on, Bunty's clothes on the floor, and the front door standing open. A few minutes later, Pippa came out onto her porch; Matt had called her, too. She was carrying a quilt and looked very pretty in a green shirt with a hood. When Matt pulled up, Pippa opened the car door and handed Bunty the quilt—it had an embroidered white cover. Bunty climbed out with it draped about her like a swansdown cloak. Pippa tucked in a trailing edge. Her hand, with its short nails painted red, rested on Bunty's arm.

"The thing is, this . . . thing," said Bunty, as they came up the path together. There was no color in her face. She said, "Am I making myself plain? Your age is against you."

Pippa gave a little cry. "Oh, lovey, you sound just like my nan. She used to say life turns against you when you grow old."

"I am talking about *your* age. What can you know?"

The next day, the phone rang. "Only me," said Pippa. "Lovey, this can't go on." Pippa knew about everything: assessments, social workers, waiting lists, forms. "It all takes ages, so you've got to start right away." Everything she said was wise and clear and depressing. There was a really helpful website; Pippa would bring her laptop around. She asked, "Do you have Bunty's power of attorney?"

Christabel wanted to say, You're talking about Bunty. She is she. She has favorite colors and weather and game show hosts. But what came out was, "I see that she takes her pills."

"Pills! Lovey, I didn't like to say anything, but I was shocked by the change when I came back from Paris. You've been amazing but you can't look after Bunty now. She needs professional care. It'll be best for you, too: you're so thin, Christabel, when's the last time you got a proper night's sleep?"

It was a fatal question. Christabel had been about to say, "I can't imagine my life without Bunty." But that was a lie: she could. There would be no toaster stuffed into the rubbish. The electricity bill wouldn't disappear, along with their toothbrushes. Christabel wouldn't find a library book soaking in the sink. Best of all, there would be uninterrupted sleep. The prospect floated in front of Christabel, as dangerous and irresistible as a gift from the gods. Her mind circled it. The word "sleep" entered and took possession of her, clouding her thoughts.

Just the night before, a sixth sense had woken her. She found Bunty in the kitchen, in front of the open fridge. With midnight clarity, Christabel thought, The light in the city is like that, white and cold, like the light from a fridge. Bunty was taking things out and dropping them onto the floor. Christabel saw that a pack of butter had been unwrapped and placed in the sink.

"What are you doing?" she cried.

"I'm looking for the queen."

"The queen!"

"They've lost her," said Bunty, tossing out a packet of cheese slices. A patch of skin on her hand was bubbly from the time she had trailed it in a flame on the stove. "She's not to be found."

Inspiration arrived. Christabel said, "The queen is in the parlor, eating bread and honey."

Bunty took her head out of the fridge. "Is she really?"

It was a period Christabel survived by lying on her bed in the afternoon, while Bunty snored on the couch. Christabel was usually too tired to sleep, but she wore her high-necked blue dressing gown over her clothes and lay there thinking how she would like to give Bunty a good kicking. She liked to picture it: Kick! Kick!

On the phone, Pippa was asking about Bunty's next of kin. Pombo and Raven. Sizzle. Trim. Dead men with dogs' names, Christabel said, or intended to. But Bunty was standing in the kitchen doorway. "Why are you whispering?" she asked. She looked cheerful and well. Her blouse was an old one from the Mr. Valente days. The buttons were done up wrong.

Curtains hung between the three beds in Bunty's room at Waratah Lodge, but Christabel usually found them pulled back and Bunty there alone. In the dayroom, where the TV was always on, old people sat with their backs to the wall. If she was led there, Bunty would get up and walk away. In her bedroom she sat by the window, listening to her radio. She talked to Christabel. She talked a great deal, as if making up for a lifetime of reticence. "I'm very well, thank you," she might say. "But I wish they'd do something about the sun. It's broken down."

"You're right—it's been raining since dawn. Did you hear it on the roof?"

"Yes, he'll be back soon. That's right."

"Would you like me to brush your hair, Bunty?"

"I was under the impression it was a ladder. All the boats went this-way, that-way, this-way, that-way. Why does she . . . ?"

"A huge new block of flats is going up in Illawarra Road."

"When does the train leave?"

"Where would you like to go?"

"There's nothing wrong with this invoice."

"I wish they'd wash the curtains in this room."

Bunty said, "I'm older than you now."

"You've always been older."

"Is that so?" said Bunty with astonishment.

Every afternoon for eight days in a row, she sat at a table in the dining room, coloring in flowers—she pushed away pictures of animals or fruit. All around her, old women murmured and twisted their hands. Bunty chose lively colors—emerald, magenta, electric blue—and took great care, her crayon hardly ever straying over one of the thick black lines. "Look!" she cried. She sounded eager and amazed.

The music video came on. An aide joined in with "You Are My Sunshine," dancing slowly past with a human husk in her arms. That was Jian—sweet Jian, who kissed pleated old cheeks, and offered words that were immediately grasped by those who now understood only two things: kindness and its absence.

Bunty raised her voice: "O come, Olly Faithful."

"Joyful and triumphant," went on Christabel encouragingly.

Bunty insisted, "O come, Olly Faithful."

A kitchen hand arrived with fruit. Bunty fell silent and eye-balled the cart. She scooped cubes of watermelon into her mouth with the panicky greed of old age, as if time would run out before everything could be eaten up.

The movers were due at Pippa's at seven. Christabel left her house at twenty to. All night, a figure with an electric head had stood grinning outside her window. Now the day stretched before her: a tightrope. It was a matter of getting to the other end.

The sky was still dark, inset here and there with a low-wattage star. It was the third week of winter. The first drops came as Christabel reached the station. By the time the train was crossing Tom Ugly's Bridge, the rain was vengeful. When the Pacific slid into view, it was a colorless smudge. Christabel had seen herself on the shore at Thirroul, eating her sandwiches against a backdrop of pines; when she rose to leave, she whacked sand from her skirt.

This vision had the propulsive force of reality, so when the express pulled in to Thirroul, she got off and made her way to the beach. The rain had turned gentle and unrelenting. Christabel's mouth had tasted muddy all morning; now her jaw began to ache. She peered out from the severe canopy of her umbrella at a sea of gray wool. Silent reproaches flew up around her like moths. Today, for the first time since Bunty had gone into care, Christabel wouldn't visit her. Not that Bunty would notice—her wheels went around independently. One afternoon, when Christabel told her, "I'll be back tomorrow," Bunty had said, "Why?"

In a fish-and-chip shop, Christabel's shoes were soaked. She burned her tongue on a potato scallop while reading Keats. When she came to *And, little town, thy streets for evermore / will silent be*, she had to close the book. It was her favorite ode because it mentioned Tempe, which was just down the highway from St. Peters. But now Keats's empty, silent town lay outside Christabel's front door.

Nothing was the same since Bunty had moved to Waratah Lodge, but at least Pippa had still been there. Sometimes, of an evening, Christabel would set a chair in the passage and lean her head on their shared wall. There were companionable noises: music, a toilet flushing, Hank racketing down the hallway. The waitress had gone into the room at the back of the shop, where Christabel could see her spooning egg into a toddler in a high chair; each time his mouth opened, so did hers.

After a cup of tea, Christabel caught a train back to the city. She had her all-day senior's travel card, so from Wolli Creek she went south again. There were muddy footprints on the floor of the carriage and puddles left by umbrellas. She ate her sandwiches. As the train passed through Coalcliff, the rain changed to crystal strings.

Coalcliff! There had been a time when Christabel spent every Saturday and Sunday there. She came to be with a man: the last one, the one who turned up after she had thought sex was over. He had a shack tucked up against the escarpment at Coalcliff. What a place for a beach house—a child could have looked at the name and known that the sun set there at three! At first Christabel couldn't understand how he was able to get away from his family every weekend. Then she realized that his marriage was a fiction. He didn't want her to know where he lived in the city, that was all. It didn't matter. On a flannelette sheet, in the inky afternoon under the escarpment, Christabel saw the world arch: the harbor bridge spanned a dusty sports ground where girls in white uniforms were playing netball. She flew upside down over the coconut palms of childhood, her veined legs reckless, her dress slippery, a bride.

One spectacularly sunny Saturday she arrived at the house and found all the blinds down as if someone had died. Christabel waited a while, pulling leaves off the lantana. She felt bright and unusual.

She went around to the back and peered through the laundry window. A pair of rusty secateurs lay in the trough. What was really annoying was that she had lost the thin gold chain she used to wear at the time—she was sure it had come off in the man's bed. One day soon a faceless woman would slip her hand under a pillow and fish out a broken chain. For now, someone using Christabel's voice was speaking: "What is done is done," she declared. The voice was like the look in Len Raymond's eyes when he had said goodbye: helpless and hard.

Coalcliff belonged to the end of the old century. No one had wanted to touch Christabel since then. From time to time, she would engineer a momentary contact: her fingers brushing a cashier's, her hip swaying against another on a crowded train.

She traveled on in her lumpy, desiring body.

Still the rain fell.

She read "The Eve of St. Agnes" in the waiting room at Wollongong Station.

The rain stopped while Christabel was walking home, and the wind came up out of the west. The sky, carelessly wiped, showed a thumbprint of moon. When Christabel turned into her street, pellets of rain fell onto her shoulders out of a tree. She had been quite wrong, she realized: the tightrope stretched without an end, there was no other side. Life is long! How had she missed the warning in that? The empty parking space in front of Pippa's gate was as conspicuous as a missing tooth. Her house looked back at Christabel with blind black eyes. A hydrangea still bloomed, rotting by the steps. Christabel went to her door and slipped her hand under the rubber doormat. It had been Pippa's idea to thwart burglars by swapping keys. "The magic switcheroo," she said, taping Christabel's key to the underside of her own windowsill.

Christabel unlocked Pippa's door and went inside. From the

head of the passage, she looked into the naked house. The doors had been left a little open and let in panels of dusty light. They produced a ghostly kind of shimmer in the plaster flowers overhead. The first time Christabel stood in this passage, Pippa had said, "This place is so small, there's nowhere to do a star jump." She spread her arms to show that her fingertips brushed the walls on either side.

That night Christabel was woken by a voice at the door. She flung off her coverings and rose with the liquid movements of a girl: Pippa called out like that, ignoring the bell. She hugged Christabel and explained that it had all been a mistake or a test of character or a baffling game: she had never really intended to move away. Christabel drew back the bolt and opened the door wide. The wind rushed into the house like someone bringing news.

Christabel arrived at Waratah Lodge with a foil container of macaroni cheese. She was filling out the Food Book kept at reception when Sister Reena appeared. "We're trying to keep Bunty's weight down, you know," said Sister Reena.

"Just this once," said Christabel.

"I don't like to think what Dr. Metaxas will say."

An old woman in a knife-pleated flannel skirt approached, trailing a shitty sheet like a bridal veil. She kissed Christabel's hand and said, "I want to go home with you."

"Watch out for that one," said Sister Reena. "She's a biter."

An aide came around the corner, pushing a wheeled rack of clean laundry in shades of pink. "I'm doing Oz Lotto tonight, if you're interested," Sister Reena told her. "And Powerball on Thursday."

"I really don't know how you keep track of all the things you do," said the aide. "You're a wonder." She was new, Christabel saw: the tag still dangled at the back of her logoed shirt.

"Live while you can, that's what I say," said Sister Reena. Her hair was bronze and fabulous. She thumped her chest: "I never forget I've got a heart."

Christabel said, "Macaroni cheese is Bunty's favorite. A treat."

"We get the blame, you know."

The old woman shouted, "Be quiet, you fool!" Her breath tasered them; no one had brushed her teeth in days.

Heat was seeping from the container, condensing on Christabel's fingers. She told Sister Reena, "Oh, but you do such wonderful, caring work."

Pleading and flattery were her tokens in this game. When there were enough tokens on the board, Sister Reena would relent. Sister Reena's bright brown gaze diminished everything on which it rested. She had a small head, muscled calves, feet that pointed outward: once a ballerina, always a duck. Christabel told Bunty, "I would like to kill her. Just once."

On the wall near Bunty's bed was a picture of a vaulted room with a checkerboard floor. Its painted walls went up and up, dwarfing the people in their heavy, draped clothes. The cold interior light that filled the picture had seeped out into Waratah Lodge. Ceiling fans turned in empty rooms. Televisions talked to no one. Disturbingly credible flowers stood in transparent vases of fake water. For a dreadful week, the dayroom contained a clear-sided brooding pen in which chickens hatched out from eggs. An overhead lamp, shining into the pen, provided heat and lit the activities of the chicks. These were few. Newly hatched, they fluffed up their damp feathers, then stood dull-eyed. What they knew of the planet was sawdust; their sun was a lamp. Soon they would be taken away and killed. Christabel read the publicity brochure: "A hassle-free and cost-effective way to provide residents with hours of fascinated enjoyment." She read it twice before realizing that what counted was "cost-effective." All the old people, including those whose minds were furthest eroded, instinctively turned away from the birds.

Bunty was concentrating on macaroni cheese. She hadn't spilled much on her bib. When she had eaten it all, she nodded off. Christabel picked a dried fleck of pumpkin from the mobile tray-table with her nail. Bunty woke with a long, shuddering breath. She stared—she was developing a stare. The stare wasn't directed at Christabel's eyes but at her chin, which made Christabel feel uneasy. It had been a long time since Bunty laughed. Christabel was glad about that; she feared that Bunty's laughter, once a joyous weapon, would have unraveled into something baleful.

She told Bunty, "Pippa's freesias are out. I still think of them as hers."

"I couldn't say what he was doing there."

"There are new people at number seventeen—you know, the house with the lions at the gate. They have a small girl. She has one of those stern, humorless faces you sometimes see on young children."

"Thank you." Bunty's mouth was hanging open. A glob of macaroni cheese could be seen inside it. New nurses marveled that she still had her own teeth.

Across the passage, an ancient man shouted, "Mum! Mum!"

"O come, Olly Faithful," sang Christabel, "Joyful and triumphant." She persisted for a bar or two but got only the stare.

After Bunty died, days slid into one another like the colors in a sunset. Whole afternoons passed as Christabel drank tea in the kitchen under the saint's glassy gaze. If there was a book in front of her, she would look away frequently and forget to turn its pages—she no longer read in the old, urgent way. The taste for reading had started to withdraw from her; she felt it pulling gently away, like a tide. Books contained hard truths, waiting like splinters in their pages. Over the years, many had lodged in her unnoticed. Little anticipations of life's awfulness, they might have served as a defense against it but pierced instead with knowledge of damage, error, waste.

As each afternoon wore on, and the blue of the saint's robe intensified, the book in his hand would come to look like a reproof. "Little man," said Christabel. "What do you know?" Her hairdresser, hearing the news about Bunty, had said, "I'm sorry for your loss." Studying Christabel's face, she proposed a new hair spray: "It creates a lighter, fuller effect." Christabel's GP suggested Vegemite: "Packed with vitamin B—excellent for the nerves." Christabel erected her own shaky ramparts. Every morning she cleaned the house. She washed windows, scrubbed spotless benchtops; every surface knew her unforgiving hands. Spraying the mold in the shower, she recited names: scribbly gum, crepe myrtle, magnolia, all the ordinary, lovely trees. The courage of birds was exemplary: small hearts pulsing, small wings working in the endless, transparent air. All the while, she understood that nothing could save her from the emptiness of the years that still had to be lived. Days passed, and weeks, and no one said her name.

Long after the kitchen had grown dark, there was still light outside; it was after sunset but before the stars. It was the hour, remembered from childhood, when clocks ticked loudest: a long moment of suspension when boundaries blurred. That was when Christabel expected Bunty to appear—each time, she was sure she would come. She might take the form of an out-of-season cockroach or a shudder in a pipe. Christabel would accept anything. What was unthinkable was that Bunty, clasped so close in memory, might have wandered unreachably far.

Christabel had got into the habit of keeping the door to the soft room closed, even though it darkened the passage and necessitated a light in the middle of the day. On a sunless afternoon, she realized that Bunty was trapped in the soft room. The unheated passage was a river of cold air. She went quickly along it and opened the door. The room looked all wrong, zigzag and black. Christabel returned to the kitchen and waited. She sat there for so long that when she got up, an abacus clicked in her hip. She thought, I'm closed to ghosts. When Kiki Mack's husband died, Kiki had commanded him to appear in her dreams. He continued to obey her as he had done in life, advising her on business matters and whether to replace the car or keep it going for another year. But Christabel's nightly entreaties vanished into her pillow. Nonsensical dreams came. She climbed out of a bus and crossed a deserted parking lot on a snowy evening. A low building appeared, with icicles hanging from the eaves like bluish white combs. She was carrying a bag with a shoulder strap and tried to walk quickly in fur-topped boots. There were also the nights when she had to sit an exam in a subject she had never studied—chemistry, or was it Dutch?

The telephone mounted on the kitchen wall rang. A man said, "Madam, there is an urgent problem with your computer." Christabel let him go on talking: it was lovely to hear a human voice. The oven was on, with the door open for warmth. But these days there was always a long, drafty corridor at her back.

Pippa came back once to show Christabel her baby: a wobbly infant who left a long strand of spit on Christabel. Christabel had bought a wooly blue bear for little Ben. At the sight of it, he screamed and turned his face to his mother's breast. When Christabel brought out the expensive kind of Nescafé that made cappuccino, Pippa said, "My naturopath has me on a caffeine-free protocol." She asked for herbal tea. There wasn't any, so Pippa said a slice of lemon in a cup of hot water would be fine. Christabel had to admit that she had no lemons either. Pippa resettled the baby. She said, "Just some water, then." Her hair had been dyed as black as a piano—it turned her face gray. Another upsetting thing was that Christabel had forgotten to bring in the washing. From the kitchen table, Pippa had an unimpeded view of a towel and a bath mat that had faded and dried hard. Kindly ignoring them, she told Christabel that she had another novel coming out very soon. It was called *The Kitchen Diaries*, and Pippa had written it in barely three months. "It was amazing, Christabel, I set self-criticism aside and just experienced *flow*." The novel was a really honest description of an adulterous affair set against a backdrop of corruption in the restaurant business. The early reviews were so good they were humbling. Pippa had brought Christabel a print-out of the cover: a headless woman in a mauve dress faced away from the reader, holding a cleaver behind her back. Christabel read, "Brutal and brilliant, this fearless account of forbidden . . ." She put her hand to the side of her head—was the ache there or in her teeth?

It was one of those changeable autumn days, cutting and caressing by turns. Pippa was wearing a denim jacket over a dress splashed with flowery red—she always had beautiful clothes. Her new hair was angular and asymmetrical, slashed off above her ear on one side of her face and swooping down to a point beside her chin on the other. Pippa saw Christabel looking at it. "What do you think?" she asked, in a way that made it clear only one answer was possible. "I got it done for my publicity photos. Matt's not so keen, but I think it ups the cool factor, don't you? Anyway, I've decided on my epitaph. Hang on, take Ben." Pippa passed him to Christabel as if transferring a package. She shrugged out of her jacket and placed one hand behind her head in an actressy pose, declaring, "Her hair was a talking point." Christabel, cradling the baby's head, noticed that the tops of Pippa's arms had spread. The baby curled his long fingers. His fixed, wide-open stare had been borrowed from a thinker or a corpse.

Pippa explained that she couldn't stay long because she was having a really social week. She reclaimed Ben and went on, "My agent took me out to lunch yesterday. We went to this amazing new Asian place at Darling Harbour. It's been quite controversial because they do live sashimi. But Gloria and I talked about it, the cruelty aspect, and we decided that it was a Japanese cultural tradition, so it was OK." She stretched sideways to sip her water, holding the cup away from Ben. He had been grizzling placidly but chose that moment to turn rigid and roar.

Pippa was on her way out when she said, "Where's my head, Christabel? It's called milk brain, apparently. I took this photo yesterday specially for you."

Hank's moon face smiled from a screen. Christabel realized that what she wanted most in the world at that moment was a photograph of Hank—a real one, a paper one—but one of the useless commandments that had been drilled into her was never to ask for anything for herself. It was one of Moth's rules. Her daughter owned a stiff, dark photo that showed Moth as a bride: she looked out flintily as if staring down an assassin. The weight of that photograph was immense.

"Hank's an outdoors dog these days," said Pippa, tucking her phone away. "Matt put his foot down. Because of Ben. We really miss having you next door, Christabel. We're going up the coast next week, and poor old Hank'll have to board at the vet's."

"You could drop him off here. I'd love to have him."

"That's so sweet of you. But it would mean going completely out of our way."

"Does he mind living outside?"

"He made his noises at the start but he doesn't do that so much now."

"But what about when there's a storm? He's afraid of thunder."

"He has a kennel," said Pippa in a patient, curved voice. "He's fine, Christabel. I'll bring him next time I come around."

Christabel saw a stack of *The Kitchen Diaries* in the window of a bookshop. She went in and looked at the price. She thought about waiting for the library to acquire a copy, but that would mean a delay before she could ring Pippa to tell her how much she had enjoyed her book. Also, if Christabel had her own copy, she could ask Pippa to sign it. Pippa would come over, bringing Hank and Ben, and this time Christabel would be prepared with peppermint tea.

Pippa no longer had a landline, so when Christabel had read *The Kitchen Diaries*, she had to call Pippa's mobile. While Christabel was still talking, Pippa said, "Oh, Christabel, you don't get it—fiction isn't real life. Eileen's a character. She's made up. No way is she you, just like Margot's not me and Patrick isn't Matt." She said a few more things. Christabel pictured her face: melting at first, then sharp. "Have to go, lovey," said Pippa. "I'm at the pool and Baby Swim's about to start. Talk soon, OK?" But whenever Christabel called, a stranger told her to leave a message, and Pippa didn't ring back.

•

At Christmas Christabel sent a card.

In January she sent another one, for Ben's first birthday.

There were letters, elaborated over days, that couldn't be sent: they weren't written on paper but in Christabel's head. They had replaced the old, silent conversations with Pippa, because Christabel had discovered that she could no longer imagine what Pippa would say.

One letter offered, "It would be no trouble to me to take Hank off your hands. I would be glad to help, and glad of his company, to tell the truth." Another began, "When my mother died, I went into the dining room early one morning and found my father there, crying. At once I told myself that it was only a dream. Fa looked up and saw me, and there was a convulsion in his throat: he swallowed his tears like pills. He spoke to me, saying something about breakfast, and his voice was steady. There was no room in either of our minds for his tears—they were simply not possible. In the same way, it wasn't possible for Fa to imagine leaving Ceylon. When I tried to, the pictures that came were as flimsy as ghosts. They were whitish and see-through, the way the souls of the dead are depicted in comic books. People said, 'Australia' or 'Canada,' and I saw ghost cars traveling past ghost buildings, ghost trees.

"Bunty was different: she could imagine me in Sydney. When she offered to pay for my ticket and sponsor my application to immigrate, it was as if someone had knocked a hole in a brick wall that stretched forever: I watched a herd of antelope pass through.

"The incredible thing was that Bunty and I hardly knew each other. As soon as I saw her again I asked why she had helped me. She said that when we were girls, I'd given her a sweet. A sweet!

Why give it such weight? But I'm no longer sure that people's motives can be understood and expressed.

"When I arrived in Sydney, I hadn't slept for thirty-eight hours. Suspension had taken hold of me, a belief in magic. It soothed fear. Everything familiar belonged to the past. I had stepped onto the plane and was suddenly modern.

"On the way from the airport, I saw the strangest, most wonderful tree I had ever seen, a tree from another planet, with a smooth mauve trunk. It was summer; the sky pealed with blue. I walked down our street for the first time, and there were wavy lines in the air. The houses moved in front of my eyes. Much later, I learned that those small houses had been built for workers at the old St. Peters brickfields and were considered little better than slums. They seemed perfect to me, people-size houses with good-tempered faces. Everything fitted, everything was in proportion. Another lovely thing was the path to Bunty's door. The paint was fresh then, glossy and red. At the sight of it I felt something like a victorious expansion. Although this is a dark, poky house, exactly as you describe it in your novel, standing at the front door for the first time I might have been about to enter a palace: a sequence of rooms awaited, gilded, mirror-hung. My father used to say that books opened doors to other worlds; but it was Bunty who did that for me, who opened up those bright rooms.

"All my life I had been waiting for something wonderful to happen, and when I came to live with Bunty, I thought, Here it is. What I didn't realize was that there would be no more big, unexpected changes like events in a book; at the back of my mind, I went on waiting for another transformation. By the time you arrived next door, it was your life that seemed brighter and fuller than reality, and I believed I could walk into it, as I had walked into Bunty's house."

•

A month after Ben's birthday, a postcard arrived: "Thanks for the beautiful cards and thoughtfulness. We've been in New York! Book out there now. It's also been translated into Catalan, Hungarian, and French. Must catch up soon. With love from us all." A PS written by an ant trailed around the edge of the card: "Benjamin means 'child of my right hand.' My right hand might as well be tied to Ben. He still wakes up twice a night. I've written nothing since he was born."

Christabel turned the card over: hardy Australian flowers bristled on the front. She put it into an Arnott's shortbread tin, where it joined the two postcards Pippa had sent her from France. Fa's voice said, "*Farewell, thou child of my right hand, and joy; / My sin was too much hope of thee, loved boy.*" The tin also contained a copy of *French Lessons*, a gift from the author. Christabel knew the inscription by heart: "For dear Christabel, Thank you for being such a great neighbor! Big love from Pippa." There was a girl called Edie in *French Lessons* and another named Renée, but no one called Helen. The tin went into Christabel's wardrobe, next to a blue bear discovered under the kitchen table after Pippa and Ben had driven away.

Among the brochures by the library door was a stack of programs for the Sydney Writers' Festival. Christabel thought of Pippa at once. But at home, on checking the list of writers, she discovered that Pippa wasn't there. She read the list all the way through again, and this time she paused at a name. Not long after Bunty had gone to Waratah Lodge, Christabel was coming home from visiting her when Pippa and a man came out of Pippa's door. "Christabel!"

called Pippa, running lightly down the steps, smiling at Christabel across the sloping garden wall. "I came around to see you earlier but you weren't there." She was dressed for going out into the scented summer evening, in a wafty frock and fragile golden shoes. "It's about Christmas," said Pippa. "The good news is we've managed to dodge Matt's family this year, so we thought we'd do what we've always fantasized about and just have a few friends over for a quiet lunch."

There were the damp smells of gardens, and a wave lifting under Christabel's heart.

"The only thing is, is Hank," went on Pippa. "My agent's coming and she's allergic to dogs." She looked at the man and said, "You got over that allergy, didn't you? But Gloria passes out, or chokes or something, if she's around a dog. Also her lips swell if she eats blue cheese." Turning back to Christabel, Pippa continued, "So I was wondering, lovey, if you'd be able to have Hank on Christmas Day? I know it'll be the first time you've minded him on your own, so if you think you won't be able to manage it without Bunty, no probs. We can always board him at the vet's."

Christabel's smile was stuck in her cheeks. A glance at the man waiting beside Pippa showed that he knew what Christabel had thought. Christabel's spine had been replaced by an icicle, and a reddish mist was fuzzing the lemon gum across the street. The mist swelled and made the top of her head hot. All she wanted to do was to lie down on the path, close her eyes, and burn with shame. The flames would melt the icicle and consume her, and she would disappear.

"Hi," said the man.

"Oh, Christabel, this is George. The *famous* George Meshaw."

The famous George Meshaw shook Christabel's hand. She directed what was left of her awful smile at his chest.

"So do you want to have a think about Christmas, lovey? If you could let me know by the weekend . . . ?"

Christabel said, "Hank's no trouble at all."

"Very good to meet you," said the man.

Finding his name now, in the festival lineup, sent Christabel to the soft room. She retrieved *The Kitchen Diaries* from the cupboard where it was hidden so that she could try to forget what it said. She had remembered correctly: George Meshaw described it on its cover as "an unforgettable novel." Christabel looked around as if the room might instruct her on where to hide. It had the drained feeling of all unused spaces. The window reflected a square of meaningless light onto a wall. George Meshaw, who had spoken kindly to Christabel, despite having looked into her and seen that she was a fool, approved of Pippa's book. The book contained a character called Eileen. Eileen, Margot's elderly Sri Lankan neighbor, was introduced on page thirty-one as "a closet lesbian with a mannish face." These words, when Christabel first encountered them, had simply not entered her brain. She read on to the end of the novel, and what it had to say about Eileen, as if drugged. Days later, while cleaning the bathroom basin, she realized that something had happened. She searched her mind and found new things in it, solid and plain.

Standing in front of the fridge on the morning of the writers' festival, Christabel ate three spoons of jam. It was apricot jam, the clear, deep gold of the cairngorm brooch she intended to wear to the festival—she had pinned it to her jacket before going to bed. The cairngorm had belonged to Bunty's grandmother, and Bunty had lent it to Christabel one day. "Keep it," she said when Christabel tried to return the brooch. It was summer: Bunty was in the yard, lying on a recliner with bright plastic webbing that made a red rectangle on the concrete. She had spread a towel over her shoulders and was drying her hair. The cairngorm, round and golden, shone in Christabel's hand. Time made a loop, hauling back the years: Christabel was offering a butterscotch to the schoolgirl peering from Bunty's face.

Christabel drank her first cup of tea for the day while it was still dark outside. Birds were talking to one another: tuneful, scratchy, or liquid conversations, all coiled through with energetic chatter and throaty shrieks. She closed her eyes and ticked off the contents of her bag: purse, reading glasses, keys, Panadol Osteo, festival program; also *The Kitchen Diaries*. Should she add an umbrella? wondered Christabel. A scarf?

The oven was on, door open against the early morning chill. It was an old oven with a hoarse flame. Christabel ate two spoonfuls of eggplant pickle and another of jam. At the end of each day, a collection of teaspoons marked out her meals: strawberry yogurt, soft-boiled egg, half an avocado pear. She ate a third spoonful of pickle and reboiled the electric jug.

After she had showered and dressed, Christabel went out into the yard. A few succulents persisted in Bunty's eskies. They had been joined by tufts of grass, and weeds with delicate pink and yellow flowers. Christabel held out her hands, palms up, trying to assess the weather. It was going to be one of those shapeless days that knocked about between seasons. Would she be warm enough at the festival? Or too hot? She was wearing her smart navy trousers—they had a waistband, not elastic—and a long-sleeved blouse under the jacket with the cairngorm brooch.

Below the reproachful blue saint, the back door carried a bolt on a chain. Christabel fastened the bolt and looked at her watch. It was too early to set out; she sat at the table to wait. A debate that had been going on all week started up again: should she make herself a sandwich to take along for lunch? What if people glanced away smiling when she produced food from her bag? A bowl on the table contained moldy lemons; Christabel had felt obliged to harvest them, and now they were turning into soft green brains. She looked away and straightened the tea towel on the handle of the oven door. Her reflection confronted her: the sour muscles around her mouth. They drove her out of the house.

A flyer protruded from the letterbox. It showed four undertakers in sharp black suits—why were they smiling? Then Christabel realized that they were real estate agents. As she slipped them into her bag, she remembered that she hadn't checked the phone; someone might have called while she was in the shower. She unlocked the front door, went inside, and dialed *10#: "No unanswered call is registered. You have not been charged for this call." No sooner had she hung up than the phone rang. That would be Pippa—it had to be. Reaching for the receiver, Christabel heard, Let's have lunch at the festival. I have so much to tell you. A stranger spoke distinctly: "There's no one here to take your call. Please leave a message after the tone and we will get back to you as soon as possible."

"One of the things Bunty and I shared was a mistrust of disclosure." Christabel was composing a letter to Pippa while waiting for her train. "When we were growing up, silence was considered mannerly. Later I came to think of it as the outward sign of a fear that struck to the heart: the same fear I saw in Fa in the dining room that morning. It was a fear I came to associate with the English. I thought of it as one of the dreadful consequences of their war—the one we had stopped calling 'Great.' When I discovered the poetry of that war, I recognized the anger and reined-in terror of Englishmen. By 'Englishmen,' I mean Bunty's father. I saw him in the street now and then, with his hat and his hurt, angry face. The only strong feeling that men like that could display was rage. Once Mr. Sedgwick was sitting near me at the cinema. The film was a comedy, and I wish I could describe the way he laughed—I want to say *with delighted fury*. He had no idea that we were neighbors. If I had been brought to his attention, it would never have occurred to him that we had anything in common. But we had both been raised to believe that there were simply things of which no one spoke, emotions no one showed; if you did, everything would fall apart. What was 'everything'? It was the world arranged for the benefit of gentlemen.

"Do you feel that there are hidden ties between people, not always readily explained? At school, I always linked Bunty with a teacher we called the Old Fowl. They shared a feeling for music, but their true connection ran deeper. They were two people of great dignity and little importance. The day I saw Mr. Sedgwick at the cinema, I thought, If we were shut up together in a darkened room, you would take me for one of your own. We would be silent together. His hands were narrow and as white as tripe. Suddenly the notion of finding myself in the dark with Mr. Sedgwick made me want to giggle like a madwoman. Then it made me afraid.

"One of the wonderful things about living with Bunty was that she changed the nature of silence. It was no longer rooted in fear, but in an important courtesy. In our house, silence was gentle and grave. Now that I'm on my own, silence is different again."

At Circular Quay, Christabel went carefully down the station stairs. When had she started walking like that, watching her feet as if expecting a trap? She made her way up to the top of George

Street, past the Harbour View Hotel. Bunty had taken Christabel there for lunch on Christabel's sixty-fifth birthday. It had been a day as sharp and yellow as a lemon. Halfway up the hill, Bunty halted. Her lips had gone thin. She said, "My heart's always with me now."

At their table on the terrace, a waiter fetched wine that sparkled like the view. When their glasses were empty they were still full of golden light. Bunty had exchanged her tracksuit pants for stretchy trousers. Christabel's fingernails were painted a festive pink. Her napkin, shaken loose, caught the wind like a sail. The harbor was so blue that if they looked at it too long it turned black. The waiter brought out potato wedges, baked tomatoes, and fish cooked in banana leaves. When they couldn't eat another thing, Bunty ate an Eton Mess.

It was a day that bulged into the present: Christabel could look across time and see the two of them perched there on that terrace, immortal in the afternoon, while another Christabel headed to the festival down an endless flight of steps. The water lifting in the harbor was the dull gray of a bloated tick, and the word beating in her brain was "gone."

There were people all along the wharves where the festival was taking place, talking, queuing, clustered in cafés and along the blustery walkways. Against the sunless sea glare, all that casual clothing had the Technicolor appearance of a crowd in a film. Christabel moved through it, as historical as a fax. The cheery, fit-looking elderly, decently upbeat, seemed particularly remote from her: as staunch and twinkling as distant stars.

The young man at the information booth consulted a list, murmuring, "George Meshaw, George . . . OK, so that's *Would I Lie to You?* It'll be over on that pier, over there, and you go in that third door. See?"

What Christabel saw was a queue that stretched the length of the wharf and around the corner of a building. "I'll never get in!" she cried.

"It's OK. That's the queue for Josh Kapoor."

Christabel looked at him. He smiled back, nicely. "He's a celebrity chef. He has a show on TV. Your guy's just a writer, right? He won't pull anything like that many punters. Get there fifteen, twenty minutes before it starts and you'll be good."

In the nearest café, Christabel lined up for a cup of tea. It cost four dollars fifty—four dollars fifty! For a tea bag! The ham-and-cheese croissants were ten! She could have murdered a sandwich—egg and lettuce, or mustard and silverside—but there were only the croissants. Pippa's voice rose behind her: "*Hi.* I've been looking for you everywhere." Christabel's heart turned inside out. She looked around to see not-Pippa embracing a man with a soft ginger beard.

There was an empty table near a window. Christabel stirred sugar into her tea, in a crossfire of ringtones. Everyone in the café had the tense, resolute face of a shopper at a Boxing Day sale: they were faces that hadn't renounced hope but were prepared for disappointment. Christabel's lips, too, were pressed together—she patted them with the Kleenex she kept in her sleeve. She wondered, Did I bring my lipstick? She began to scrabble through the contents of her bag.

A girl carrying a cup approached; around her neck, like a penance, hung a string of weighty wooden beads. "Is this chair free?" she asked, placing her hand on the back.

"Yes!" Christabel smiled her gratitude at this chance companion.

The girl picked up the chair and walked away.

The queue for the Ladies' was even longer than the one for the celebrity chef. By the time Christabel had used the bathroom and crossed to the next pier, she was almost the last in line. A woman standing behind her sighed, "It's always like this when it's a free event." She asked her friend, "What's this George Meshaw written?"

"I've never heard of him."

"Hang on: didn't he write that memoir about running a restaurant in Paris? My book club did that one. He got food poisoning and almost died—we laughed *so* much!"

"All I know is Ryan will be worth the wait."

"You know, I don't think the restaurant man was called George. It was a name like that but a bit different. Tony. Or Rafael."

Seated at last, Christabel found that her view of the stage was partially obscured by a pillar—still, she could see George Meshaw if she leaned to the left. He was fatter than the picture she had carried around in her mind. That would come from running a restaurant, she thought, seeing him in a white jacket, spooning up a creamy sauce. Then she remembered that that wasn't George after all.

The chair of the panel, a birdy woman dressed more or less entirely in scarves, introduced the three speakers. "I thought it would be fun to get going by asking each of our guests to share a lie they've told," she concluded. "Would you like to start us off, Ryan?"

An Irish comedian who had written a memoir sprang to his feet. He strolled about the stage for the next quarter of an hour, telling hilarious tales about alcoholism and child abuse in his quilted Irish voice. Christabel wept tears of laughter with the rest.

"Thank you so much, Ryan," said the bird woman when he paused. "That was really, really insightful. And now . . ."

"Just one wee minute more," wheedled Ryan, running a hand through his charming curls.

A black-haired woman rose from her seat on the stage, strode forward, and announced, "You are sitting down, Ryan." Then she addressed the audience: "Hi, you will know I am Marta. For Australia I perform my cross-genre work narrated by a cell phone. It is called 'Death of a Young Child.' Unhappily, the English translation is no good at all. It gives insufficient sense of the smallness of the child and the very horror of her trauma. So you will know the authentic dread of my work, I am reading the Estonian original."

Christabel drifted into a private conversation with George Meshaw. They were sitting in the café; he had insisted on buying her a croissant. He said, "Very understandable" and "You're quite right." He would do all he could to explain everything to Pippa, he assured Christabel. "It's pretty clear to me that she's avoiding you because you remind her she's been hurtful. But have you never thought of simply going to see her and talking it all over face-to-face?"

Christabel told him that she had planned out the route to Glebe. "I know which bus to take from Central. The light rail is also an option. But then I see myself opening Pippa's gate and going up to the front door. There are two portly shrubs there, the kind Bunty used to call ever-yellows. Matt inherited them along with the house. Pippa calls them Awful and Cheerful. Pippa's car is in the street, so I know that she's at home. But she doesn't answer the bell. Hank barks and barks. He makes his Hank the Tank noises: strange, harsh cockatoo squawks. They're his way of pleading. The curtains hang down, solid as wood. And then it's impossible to go on believing that Pippa wants anything more to do with me." All the time she was talking, Christabel kept finger-writing the word "please" on her knee.

George said that he could see the difficulty. Rubbing his chin, he told her, "I spend half the year in Paris now. Why don't you visit me there? You would meet my friends: poets, scholars, artists, chefs . . ."

A voice from the stage broke in. The chair was saying, "Really, I'm very sorry, but I really feel I must intervene. Marta, we have twenty minutes left and—"

Marta said, "That is very sufficient. I need only eighteen."

The chair said, "But—"

Marta resumed her reading.

Christabel stood at the prow of a boat skippered by George Meshaw and was carried down the Seine. Hank was there, too, barking at French seagulls. But it wasn't Hank at all, it was Bunty—she smiled on all fours in her bright fur. People riding their bicycles beside the river waved. In the cabin of the boat, preparations were under way for a party: a waiter hurrying past with a tray of glasses balanced on his palm winked at Christabel. The boat drew level with a palace where Moth and Fa leaned from a round window under a silvery roof. That kind of thing went on very pleasantly for a while. Then something strange happened, and the scene went quiet and froze.

Marta had fallen silent. George Meshaw cleared his throat. He leaned over and murmured something to the chair. But the chair had changed strategies and was gazing out over the room with a serene, yogic smile. It announced that she had found herself in this world by chance—its earthbound strife couldn't touch her.

A man with a goatee rose from his seat in the front row. "Brava!" he shouted. "Encore! Encore!" He stamped his feet and applauded.

"Thank you," blushed Marta. A five-year-old had taken her place on the stage. The audience saw the face under Marta's face. The black spikes had given way to yellow pigtails, the black leather sheath to a frilly skirt that stuck out. Above the apple cheeks, the round eyes begged, Please be kind. Marta shoved the child behind her. She spoke with simple dignity: "Now I am available to sign my works."

In the bookshop, a drafty, makeshift affair at one end of the pier, a long, long line of readers was waiting for Ryan. Waves of merriment rolled from his signing table. Christabel joined the much shorter queue that had formed in front of George.

A very tall redhead was moving down this line. When she reached Christabel she snapped, "Please have your book open at the title page."

"My book?"

"Well—George's book, obviously. All of them, if you'd like him to sign more than one."

"Can I just speak to him?"

The redhead looked at her. It was the kind of look an ocean liner casts at a paper boat.

Christabel left the queue. "Her scarves were so aggressive!" she heard, as she passed Marta and her fan club of one. "Hostile interruption . . . psychological assault . . ."

"Make representations . . . embassy," soothed the goatee man. "Magnificent reading in the face of . . . such reserves of strength . . ."

George Meshaw's book cost thirty-five dollars. Thirty-five dollars! Returning with it, Christabel saw Marta and her courtier leaving together. "Private reading" and "diplomatic channels" hovered in their wake. Ryan's fans were departing too, clutching their books, half-dead from laughing. His queue still reached to the door.

Christabel found herself standing in front of George.

"Hi," he said, looking her in the stomach. His cushiony fingers turned a pen that had leaked onto some of them.

"You won't remember me," began Christabel. "But Pippa Reynolds used to be my neighbor in St. Peters."

George looked up. His outsized glasses made it seem as if dark circles had been stamped around his eyes. "Oh, *hi*," he said. "Hi."

Christabel took *The Kitchen Diaries* from her bag. "I wanted to ask you—" But it was easier to hand Pippa's book to George. "Where the bookmark is. I've underlined it."

George Meshaw scanned the page. "*A closet lesbian with a mannish face*," he murmured.

"I didn't take it in when I first read it. Then it upset me so much."

"Yes. A gross stereotype."

"It's not *true*," said Christabel.

George looked up again. "I see," he said. He closed the novel and placed it on the table.

"If it were true, we wouldn't have been ashamed of it. But we shared a house, and now Bunty's gone. I mean she's no longer alive. Why would Pippa write something like that?"

"You must ask her."

"She said I was confusing life with fiction. She said, 'I know you're not a lesbian. Right there's the proof that Eileen isn't you.' But there are all kinds of things later on about this Eileen, silly things she says, even the 'dirt-brown splashback' in her kitchen . . . Pippa's describing *me*." Christabel stopped. She tried again. "How could someone reading this book know what is and isn't true? It's Pippa who's mixing up fiction and life."

After a moment, George Meshaw said, "How can I help you?"

Christabel had no idea. She couldn't remember why she had come, only what it had cost. She thought about saying something like, Tell me how to live without illusions. Pippa's book stared up from the table. As plainly as if it had spoken, it told Christabel why she had sought out George: it was to punish Pippa by exposing her betrayal. Look at me lying here, said *The Kitchen Diaries*. I am the exact measure of the dimensions of your soul.

It was appalling information. Christabel glanced left and right but couldn't avoid the charge. Her eyes returned to Pippa's novel, and she saw Eileen genie up from its pages. Eileen wafted about the room and spiraled out the window. She was only a minor character on the margin of the lives that mattered, and it was impossible to feel sympathy for her: Pippa had seen to that. From the top of the harbor bridge, Eileen's whining voice called to Christabel, "I am your other life. You are immortal!"

George Meshaw was waiting for an answer. Christabel managed to say, "You called it 'an unforgettable novel.'" Her voice seemed to have to push past her teeth.

"It is. In a way."

"I'm not hurrying you, George," said the redhead. "But that student journalist's waiting to interview you in the greenroom. And I've got to collect Josh Kapoor and take him over to Channel Nine."

"I'm sorry," said George to Christabel.

Christabel took the long way back to Circular Quay, past the water, carrying her face like a mask. Ferries glided meekly as if pulled on a string. The sun came out: what a dreadful old hack it was, routinely switching on that blinding charm. The harbor fizzed a slavish blue. Towers flashed their eyes, their logos blazed. The wasted day turned headachey and aureatic, the outlines of buildings, trees, lampposts flickering into a yellowish smudge. There were blooms of sweat in Christabel's armpits. She struggled out of her jacket—it seemed to weigh more than she did. Folding it into her bag, she avoided the cairngorm's accusatory eye. The bag dragged at her arm as she went up the stairs at the station. Her good black shoes preceded her, obedient, snub-nosed little animals.

On the platform, tourists were photographing the view. The view was designed to drop you to your knees. That! thought Christabel and turned her back. She sat down between two people who were reading their phones and opened George Meshaw's book. But she stared at the print blindly: she was writing to Pippa.

"People say approvingly of someone, 'He never pretends.' But pretense can be deliberate and life-giving. A long time ago I had a friend with whom I spent several evenings over the length of a winter and a spring. He had a wife, a daughter, and two sons; the younger boy was ill, his father's accent sharpened when he spoke of him. We told each other about the countries we had come from. He described a town by a lake, an old resort. I saw boulevards lined with palms, a yellow clock tower, an avenue of catalpas leading to a bandstand. The biggest hotel had a glassed-in veranda. That was where we would stay, he told me, we would eat ice cream on the veranda. Ice cream! It was a child's vision of happiness. He had left when he was a boy and never returned. There had been a war. The town no longer existed—it had been destroyed or transformed. It was plain from the outset that we would never go there or anywhere else together. But he made me a gift of that town. In winter, there is snow on the palm trees. I can still find my way to the square by the station where the old men played dice.

"I have a talent for pretense and, since our strengths easily grow unbalanced and tip over into faults, I fall readily into illusion. Have you ever noticed that we're the same height? We're straight up and down, both of us, and our faces are the same shape. These are only trivial resemblances, of course. But one day I saw Matt in the supermarket. I went up to him and touched his arm. He looked confused. I thought, He took me for Pippa! What madness—the truth was that for a moment, in an unfamiliar context, he couldn't remember who I was. But there was no limit to my fusing of our lives. At best I might have conceded, He took me for her sister. You see how it was? Once when you were cutting up a chocolate babka you had baked, I willed the knife to slip. The cut wouldn't be deep but it would bleed profusely. You would have to lie on the couch, and I would wrap my hanky around your finger; blood would seep through the cloth. I fetched a blanket and tucked it around you. One of your feet slipped out, and I sat with it on my lap, warming it in my hands. Oh yes, I treasured you and damaged you without hesitation. That's how it was."

When her train came in, Christabel chose an upstairs seat and settled down to George's novel. Stations passed slowly: Redfern, Erskineville. The train was crooning to itself as it eased out of Sydenham when Christabel looked out the window. For a moment, the graffitied Victorian walls and billboards advertising mobile phone plans had escaped from a film; then she realized that she had missed her stop. It didn't matter, she could double back at the next station. But when she got off at Marrickville, instead of going around to the other platform, she went out into Illawarra Road. She hadn't been back there since Bunty died.

In the last months of her life, Bunty had stopped speaking English. She had discovered a language of her own: strings of sounds like water running over pebbles, like elusive, archaic songs, like an unmusical bird. This language welled up fluently in Bunty. Now and then, something that resembled an English word might stand out: "Murr-mmm-mmm-nnnnn-mlk-luh-luh-luh . . ."

"Milk?" asked Christabel, although it seemed unlikely.

"Glah-glah-umm-umm-mmm. Flaaay," said Bunty on a beseeching note. Her forehead glared with the effort. Christabel went to the kitchen and returned with a plastic beaker. She put it into Bunty's hand. Bunty ignored it and went on talking. The sounds that came were lilting and tormented. They held stubs of meaning, trailed ghosts. Christabel thought, She's trying to make words say things there aren't any words for. Bunty stared at Christabel's chin. The look in her eyes was both intense and inert, as if she were following an argument through invisible headphones. When Christabel took the beaker away, Bunty's fingers still made the shape of it on the table. There was puréed apple on her sleeve—she wiped it on her mouth. She poured out more words that no one could understand.

One afternoon, Christabel arrived at Waratah Lodge and encountered a tiny old man crossing the lobby. She was about to pass him when he put out his hand: it was copper-colored with a bluish undertone. His eyes gave the game away: they had kept the sheen of raw liver.

"How terrible!" cried Mr. Valente. "I see her—how terrible!" He couldn't keep from smiling. He made Christabel sit on one of the comfy chairs grouped next to a fire blanket and a framed photo of Princess Mary. He sat down, too, on the far side of a vase of synthetic anemones, his knees out wide. He had acquired a Padre Pio amulet and five grandchildren. Christabel was to examine a folder of photographs. "I bring them show her. But no good."

I bet you asked her questions, thought Christabel. I bet you said, "Do you remember?" and felt smug when she didn't. He was as transparent as the plastic pages he had dumped in her lap. "How terrible!" he cried again, and she understood that he was wild with joy. The idiot really believed that in picking God over Bunty he had made the right choice. He placed his hand on his jubilant heart and announced that he hoped to grow old with humility: "I thanking God for many blessings."

I see that all your grandchildren are fat, said Christabel silently, turning the pages of his album. They're as ugly as your wife and as stupid as you. On your way home, you will crash your car into a sewage works. Your descendants will fall out over your will—the quarrels will last longer than you have lived. A week after the funeral, no one will remember your face.

Her words vanished into the red-and-blue swagger of the anemones. Another senseless smile cracked his cheeks. His bald patch shone like an unlucky coin. Increasingly he saw himself this way, at one remove, like a man in a mirror. Events had slowed and lost their edges. But throughout the years he had retained a clear impression of the woman in front of him: a skinny, fast-moving creature. He wanted a glass of thick red wine. He wanted to make a phone call. The other one's laugh had always been the right shape. Not ten minutes earlier, he had knelt beside a sagging envelope of flesh, kissed the inside of her wrist, and put her finger in his mouth. Her face was a collapsed meringue. A long time ago, she had pulled him down beside a box of tiles he kept hidden under the counter. They were old, handmade tiles from Naples, individually fired, with red flowers and green leaves, and he had never been able to part with them. His mouth was full of gold. All the notes in his wallet faced the same way. He was frightened all the time.

In Bunty's room, everything seemed as usual. Bunty was in her chair, talking, the words all muddle and slur. The visiting hairdresser had dyed her hair that week. It was cut to within an inch of her shoulders for easy maintenance and looked like tarred twine.

Christabel kissed Bunty's cheek, laid her jacket on the bed, and looked around. She was checking for sinister traces of Mr. Valente:

holy medals, cakes that no one wanted to eat. The only flowers were the yellowing gardenias that she had stood in a glass on the weekend—he hadn't brought Bunty so much as a wilting 7-Eleven gerbera, the cheapskate. Christabel opened the bedside drawers to check if he had stolen anything. The middle one yielded a tartan slipper. "I wonder who this belongs to," she said, looking inside it for a name.

"Ger-ger-ger-ger . . ."

"I've brought new batteries for your radio."

Bunty went on and on. Her noises could sound angry or imperious but today were merely heartbreaking. Christabel opened the back of the radio. She was easing out the old batteries when Bunty cried, "Olly Faithful!" She beat her big fists on the arms of her chair.

Christabel clutched the radio. She asked, "Do you want to sing?" Then she saw what Bunty was staring at. In the dowdy tree outside the window sat a black-and-white bird. "Olly Faithful!" shouted Bunty. The magpie flew away, and Bunty threw herself about in her chair.

The phone call came while Christabel was getting out of bed the next morning. Sister Reena's voice turned quavery toward the end. She said, "Bunty always smelled of orange blossom." What a ridiculous thing to say—Bunty had never worn perfume! The entire conversation filled Christabel with something like rage. She was the one who suffered from chronic ailments: a wavering heartbeat, undiagnosable, stabbing pains in her eyes, an arthritic hip. Every year, she coughed through spring. Bunty once said, "That's a wolf's cough." After that Christabel heard it every time, the howl in her chest. It was understood, at least by Christabel, that she would go first. Even at Waratah Lodge, Bunty had remained fit and strong. Her blood pressure baffled every doctor she had ever seen. Just a few months earlier, "She's the type who goes on for years," Sister Reena had said, in the tone of one offering commiserations. So why talk now of a major cardiac event? Christabel went up the passage, then back to the kitchen, where she walked twice around the table. The incompetent blue saint offered her his book: it was all he had to give. She saw that she had forgotten to hang up the phone.

From Marrickville Station, Christabel set off on a familiar route. But when she reached the street that led to Waratah Lodge, she ignored it and walked on. Eventually, she came to a sports field; parkland and the river lay just beyond. There was also a toilet block: as soon as she spotted it, Christabel needed to go. There was paper! There was liquid soap! Like drinkable water from taps, clean public lavatories were one of the blessings of Australia. A metal bin stood near the door—Christabel needed that, too. She had read enough of George Meshaw's book to know that it concerned itself with the brutal and inadequate mechanism of the world. As if that were any kind of news! Why had she never told Bunty, You are everything: the lucky accident, the holy jacaranda, the luminous sauce? One morning, shortly before she went into Waratah Lodge, Bunty had sat up in bed saying, "I had such a round dream. It was full of hope." Christabel dropped George's novel into the bin and followed it with Pippa's. A lit fuse sparkled the length of her spine. She was a woman on a screen, renouncing love or claiming death with one stark, superb gesture. How wonderfully light her bag felt now!

She strolled past a playground where a tiny boy was climbing a slide. A woman and a baby were marveling at his earnest exertions. Christabel found herself wishing that she and Bunty had loved each other as Pippa believed: fully, giving love its whole importance. But what is not done is not done. She came to a bench and sat down. If her hair were long, she would have shaken it out. She scrunched her eyes at the sun bursting in the armpit of a tree.

One day, it must have been not long after Bunty stopped working, she had a big win on a horse. She said, "I've decided we should go to Romania."

"Romania!" Christabel thought of an objection at once. "We don't speak Romanian."

"We didn't speak Greek or Indonesian or Turkish either. Anyway, they speak French as well in Romania."

"But we don't."

"I do. The nuns taught me when I was a little girl. *L'oiseau*," said Bunty. "*La plume*."

And so they went. They visited fortresses and castles and monasteries, and a boat carried them down the Danube to a port. They caught trains. They looked at a modern pyramid, fronted by stiff trees, in which tyrants had lived—when they turned their backs on it, Christabel and Bunty were sure that someone was watching them from a window. They stayed in a converted palace, with seventeenth-century mosaics in their bathroom, and slept on straw mattresses in a dubious country inn. What was most astonishing of all was that the only clothes Bunty had brought with her were three dresses Christabel had never seen. There was a blue one, and a stripy pink cotton, and a sea-green gown with elbow-length sleeves—that one came out every evening. "It belonged to my mother," said Bunty. Openmouthed, Christabel saw that in Romania Bunty was as resplendent as a ship: her rich décolletage, her crown of jet hair. She had a waist. She wore a red velvet ribbon around her neck like an aristocrat who had survived a revolution.

Waiters looked through Christabel, dressed for sensible tourism, and led Bunty to the best table. They inclined their heads. They advised her to order river fish or smoky meatball soup, and everything that Bunty and Christabel ate on that holiday, even in the slab-built industrial town where a breakdown obliged them to linger, absolutely everything tasted delicious.

A month passed in a brilliant blur. Here and there a picture stood out: impassioned students with banners, and a mountain with a snowy spine, and a pack of stray dogs in a dusty park. What remained jewel-clear from start to finish was a day near the end of their stay. At breakfast, over pancakes filled with jam, Bunty said, "Let's go for a long walk in the country."

She had consulted a waiter and knew which bus to take and where to get off. The bus driver had a zip-up jacket and black hair combed in a style that Hitler had made unfashionable. He drove as if slicing through enemy lines. First factories, then fields fell beside the windows. All the way he watched Bunty and Christabel in his mirror, but wouldn't meet their eyes as they climbed off the bus.

Bunty walked a little way down a side road where flowers stood thick in the ditches, before turning off along a footpath that ran through tall grass. Christabel, who had fussed with keys and exchange rates and maps throughout the holiday, followed without question: the day belonged to Bunty. A tussocky ridge ran down the middle of the path between two wheel-worn ruts. There were faded poppies in the meadow, and scatterings of tiny blooms that seemed to be made of yellow wool, and cornflowers the color of Bunty's other dress—she was wearing the one striped in shades of pink.

The path headed for a wooded hill and began to climb in long, lazy loops. "We've come through the Flowery Meadow," said Bunty. "And now we're entering the Dark Wood." The trees were hornbeam and oaks and beeches, she said—in Romania, Bunty was bossy and knowledgeable, as unfamiliar and appealing as her clothes.

The path climbed gently on, compelling them. It gathered them into its purpose as if it would lead them to the end of the world. And while it carried them forward, it also seemed to lead back, into a dream landscape known from long ago. Every perspective ended in leaves. But once Christabel glanced down through branches and saw, far below, a sloping pasture folded like a secret into the side of the hill. It was late spring, and the lusty grass shone in the sunlight. She called to Bunty and pointed: "The Bright Field."

The morning wore on, and she could feel herself starting to flag; even Bunty seemed to have slowed. The path turned a last time, abandoned the forest, and led up into the sky. The sky was an extraordinary color: intense blue saturated with violet. "The Gentian Sky," declared Bunty. They came out onto a heath and found the grass clumped here and there with small flowers of the same exaggerated blue.

It had been cool in the woods, and they were glad of the sun. They sat down to rest, and Bunty produced cherries and pots of yogurt from a woven bag. She said, "The perfect meadow must be flowery. And set on the side of a hill."

Christabel spat out a cherry stone. "With trees along one side at least."

"Hedges are desirable."

"But a drystone wall will do."

Christabel must have dozed off. When she opened her eyes and sat up, Bunty was looking at the view. "*On springy heath, along the hill-top edge*," quoted Christabel. Grass stalks had woven a fleshy lattice into the backs of her arms.

"The Springy Heath is good," said Bunty, still labeling

everything like an illustration in a book. "And over there, I spy the Grim Castle."

The horizon was humpy with colored hills. In the middle distance, a line of poplars marked the course of a river that bisected a plain. Christabel saw a big boxy building on the far bank. "It's a factory," she said. "Look at the color of that water."

"It's a twentieth-century castle. Golden boys and girls are lured inside by tales of treasure, only to find themselves slaves of the Cruel Lord."

When they were on their way again, Bunty pounced. "*La plume!*" she said triumphantly, brandishing a large brown-and-white feather. Holding it like a visor, she looked up. "*L'oiseau!*" she called, and pointed to the dark scrap hovering on an updraft.

They followed the path downhill into squared-off little fields, yellow and green. Wind passed like a hand over a slope of grass. Something squealed in a hedge. Christabel looked over her shoulder, to the dark fur of the woods they had come through. Far away to the west, reapers working in a row, stooped or upright against the sky, were figures in a frieze. The path crossed a stream and joined a white gravel road. Presently, they saw roofs beyond the fields—the road was leading them to a village. A man cutting grass with a scythe didn't look up as they passed. The first house, painted blue, came into sight. A young woman in an embroidered shirt with a patterned scarf over her head was busy in the yard. "The Goose Girl," said Bunty quietly. "I'll ask for water and directions."

As if she had been expecting them, the girl smiled and swung open a wooden gate, saying, "Welcome!" They saw that she was wearing jeans, which robbed her of archaism: she was any modern girl with an angular face and too much mascara. She took them past flowering beans, and a hutch where wet-eyed rabbits waited to be killed or fed. There was a vine-wrapped arbor by the door, under which a table covered with an oilcloth had been placed. An old man sat there, his hands folded over a stick. The door, which stood open, made an emerald rectangle against the soapy-blue wall.

Beyond a curtain of plastic beads lay a dark room. The girl ushered them to a stiff sofa and went through to an inner chamber. Bunty and Christabel looked about, their eyes adjusting to the dimness. A magnificent shawl, with long, silky tassels, glimmered on one wall. On the table below it, a game of chess was in progress. Bunty crossed to the table and bent her head over the plastic pieces on the board. Her tongue clicked twice. "Holy moly," she murmured. "Poor old black. But you know, I think . . ." Her hand hovering in the gloom was a plump white spider. It dropped to close over a bishop.

"I didn't know you played chess," said Christabel.

Bunty was still looking at the board. "That's a little more interesting now," she said.

The girl returned, carrying a tray. She set sesame-flecked pastries before them and a jug of water. There was also a bottle of amber liquid, half full. Bunty accepted a glass of this and knocked it back, lifting her round chin. The girl told them that she was a teacher of English. "I used to work in a school near the sea. But last year, my grandmother died, and then I became ill. So now my grandfather and I look after each other." Until then, they hadn't noticed the bald skull under her flowery scarf.

Bunty wanted the bathroom, and the girl went with her to show her the way. Christabel looked about the room. In every corner, shadows coiled like snakes. A shelf displayed the plump golden figurine of a beckoning good-luck cat. Beside it were glass jars, one filled with long peppers and the others with pale, lumpy growths: mushrooms or mice. From the corner of her eye, Christabel saw something slink along the base of a wall—a rat! A small squawk escaped her. But it was a cat with mutilated ears, slipping out like smoke through the beads.

The room darkened: a figure with three legs didn't lift the bead curtain but barged through. The old man lowered himself onto an upright chair and nodded at Christabel. His hand shook as he poured out two glasses of the thick yellow drink and passed one to her; first it tasted of berries, and then it tasted of flowers, and then it tasted of fire. "To the buffalo!" said Christabel, raising her glass. Her host inclined his head.

His attention fell on the chessboard; he turned toward it, a careful swivel from the waist followed by a sideways shuffle of the feet. When his granddaughter returned with Bunty, he spoke to the girl.

"My grandfather would like to know who moved the bishop."

"That was me, I'm afraid," said Bunty. She put a whole pastry into her mouth and chewed.

The old man continued to stare at the board.

There was the no-sound of in-held breath.

The grandfather laughed once. His teeth were broken or missing—he looked as old people had looked when Christabel was a child.

"He says, 'Very nice! Very, very nice!'"

Bunty licked a crumb from the corner of her mouth. "Thank you," she said. "It might not save the day. But I think black's in with a chance now."

"He wants to know who taught you."

"My father. He played for his university. That was before the drink got him."

"He must have been a good teacher," said the girl.

"There were forfeits, you see, for every game I lost." Bunty said, "I haven't played since."

The old man moved a pawn. He sat back and smiled at Bunty. His face, brown, hairless, and faintly shiny, was a wrinkled egg.

Bunty craned to see what he had done. "Of course," she said. "Now that requires some thought." She pulled up a stool.

"My grandfather was a professor of mathematics," said the girl. "He played chess for Romania. He traveled to Moscow twice, and won against both Dementiev and Rusakov. The third time, he played Rashkovsky. The Russians fixed things and he lost."

"How can you fix a game of chess?" asked Christabel.

The girl tapped her glass. "By fixing the vodka the night before. Or maybe something in his food. He never went back." Her skin was so fine and pale that the liqueur seemed to stain her throat as it slid down. She said, "Later they fixed it so he lost his appointment at the university as well."

It was Christabel's turn to go out into the yard to the bathroom. And the less said about that the better! Afterward, there was cracked soap and a basin of water on a table outside the door. Shuddering inwardly, she dried her hands on a waffle-weave cloth. The croak of a saw reached across the fence. Someone coughed in the road. White primer had thinned the blue of the sky. For no reason Christabel was five years old, alone in the morning. Everything was about to begin.

Back inside the house, she heard, "He says you could be a great champion."

"It's a bit late for that," said Bunty, looking up from the board.

"I give him a game now and then. But it's so boring for him, even when he gives me a rook for free."

"Time to get going," said Bunty to Christabel.

The old man asked a question. "He wants to know your name," said the girl to Bunty.

"Bunty."

The professor spoke sharply. "He asks what you're really called, not this clown's name."

Bunty said, "My name is Alfrieda Maddalena Margaret Sedgwick."

The old man seized her hand in his trembling one and brought it to his lips. "*Chère madame*," he said.

The girl gave them directions. She stood at the gate and waved when they turned. Her cat crouched at the curve in the road and twitched a battle-scarred ear. A cool wind had sprung up—Christabel could feel it pawing her neck. "Where's the bus stop?" she asked.

"Didn't you hear what she said? We have to go up to the main road."

Christabel was sure that was wrong. "I heard her mention a bell tower." But Bunty had turned into a urine-scented alley between two houses, saying, "It's a shortcut."

The alley led to a field where only nettles grew. There were traces of a track, overgrown and oozing damp. The wind butted them in gusts. They labored through the sludge and razorish leaves, and Christabel was grateful for her jeans and sneakers. But Bunty's large pale legs scissored ahead, untouched.

On the far side of the field, Bunty plunged into a stand of firs. Here the wind was less savage, but the afternoon was cold and dark. All around them was a rattling, inhuman sound like the laughter of a doll. A jabby sort of bush offered luscious purple berries that they knew not to touch: "The Poison Tree," murmured Christabel. Next came a downward slope, treacherous with pine needles. At last they were in the open, and there, ahead of them, was the winding road.

They crossed a patch of waste ground, picking their way through rags and rusting cans. A brindle cow watched from one corner, munching on weeds. And whom should they find, on a low stone wall, but their bus driver! There was a priest, too, clad in authoritative black, and a boy with aquamarine eyes in an idiot face; all three sat in a row, smoking. The driver bent down and put out his cigarette on his boot, revealing three red lines across the back of his neck. His unshaven cheeks were raw beef on which a grayish fungus had taken hold. "Wait here," he told Bunty and Christabel, looking at them directly for the first time. His gaze was frank: it announced that he was unused to nonsense. He said, "The bus will be along at any minute."

"I don't believe a word of it," replied Bunty.

Close at hand, a bell began to peal. The priest and the boy sat up straight.

Bunty took Christabel's arm, and they rushed away up the road, toward the bell. It grew deafening as they rounded a corner and saw a clutch of people at the foot of a white tower. A woman in a heavy, belted cardigan was waving, and they crossed the road to join her—it seemed to take forever because a great weariness had seized their legs. All the time, a distant toy-town bus was growing larger, so they knew that they had come to the right place.

Christabel saw that the cairngorm had flown up from her bag and lodged in a tree on the far side of the park. She blinked and saw it turn into the sun, as round and orange as a sweet. Stretchy shadows were swaying on the grass, and the playground was deserted. It was time to go home, back to the silent, unhaunted house. One morning after another would make its entrance. She would light the oven, pull up the blind, and inspect the sky. Life is long! The phone rang: an Indian offered to fix her computer. Christabel didn't hang up but left the receiver dangling against the wall. Or else she said, “Shall we be friends? We could tell each other about our lives.” Winter came and was followed by spring. She coughed alone, doubled up and howling.

Small hearts ticked in the grass at her feet, in the lightless depths of the river. No one heard them, but they were there. The breeze snapped, and Christabel wanted her jacket but made no move to take it out of her bag. The park was filling up with people and dogs. Pombo and Raven. Sizzle. Trim. Not dogs’ names or clowns’, but the names of gentlemen. A gentleman could beat a child at a game and make her pay for it. Not that any of it mattered now: Bunty was gone, with her mysteries and her wasted gifts. Christabel stayed on, watching dogs of all shapes tumbling with one another or racing after balls. A gangly black-and-white mongrel abandoned the ruckus and turned to stare across the park. It was Bunty’s dog—Christabel was sure of it. He had come to lead her to Bunty. “Olly Faithful!” she called. He lowered his head and started moving toward her. Her arms rose, joyful and triumphant. And still he came.

ACKNOWLEDGMENTS

Thank you to Grove Atlantic for permission to quote from *Endgame* by Samuel Beckett.

Thank you to Pat Strachan, Jane Palfreyman, and Clare Drysdale, and their colleagues at Catapult and Allen & Unwin.

Thank you to Christina Thompson and her colleagues at *Harvard Review* for publishing an early version of "The Fictive Self."

For help with research, thank you to Yves Boscher, Justin Creedy-Smith, Tom Dundas, Martin Edmond, Mark Gillies, Zahia Hafs, and Walter Perera. Also to Janet and Roger Anderson, Kate and Stewart Sutherland, and especially Karen and Geoff Daniel.

Thank you to K. N. K. Wijayawardana, whose account of the 1977 anti-Tamil riots at Anuradhapura is published at www.island.lk/2003/08/27/midwee04.html.

Thank you to the English Department at the University of Sydney.

Thank you to Neel Mukherjee, who talked about the right books at the right time.

Thank you to Ivor Indyk, Mireille Juchau, and Fiona

McFarlane for reading the manuscript, and to Mireille and Fiona for much else besides.

A special thank-you to Sarah Lutyens: "*mast and sail and flag / And anchor never known to drag.*"

This book is for Chris Andrews, whom I can never thank enough.